ne,
y."

nn,
ork

"An enchanting novel. . . . Gaynor and Webb weave a wonderful tale of love and loss, graced with the scents of perfumes, magnificent vistas, and characters you will not soon forget. A delight for Francophiles, perfumistas, film buffs, and everyone who loves a good cry and a happy ending."

—M. J. Rose, *New York Times* bestselling author

"Webb and Gaynor's latest collaboration is a historical fiction home run. The duo brings to life a vivid, engaging heroine; a glorious Côte d'Azur setting; and the ultimate princess, Grace Kelly. *Meet Me in Monaco* is smart, romantic, and heartbreaking, and the tale captivates from the start."

—Michelle Gable, *New York Times* bestselling author of
A Paris Apartment

"*Meet Me in Monaco* offers a fabulous you-are-there glimpse into the lives of the rich and famous—and real. From Grace Kelly's royal 'wedding of the century' to the luxe lifestyles on the Riviera and in Paris and New York, this novel swept me away."

—Karen Harper, *New York T* ... ...thor of
It Girls

"A spellbinding historical romance. Set largely on the lush Côte d'Azur, *Meet Me in Monaco* is a tale of first, missed, and second chances—of relatable women and men trying to make good lives for themselves in spite of difficult circumstances. It is a fairy tale set in postwar Europe, with an enchanting, fascinating fairy godmother: Grace Kelly."

—Erika Robuck, nationally bestselling author of
Fallen Beauty and *Hemingway's Girl*

"A glorious, glamorous summer read! . . . The evocation of the 1956 wedding of the year is so sumptuous you feel you are there amongst the glitterati, sipping fine champagne and inhaling the scent of *Coeur de Princesse*."

—Gill Paul, bestselling author of
The Secret Wife

Last Christmas in Paris by Hazel Gaynor and Heather Webb

"Humor, love, tragedy, and hope make for a moving, uplifting read. A winner!"
—Kate Quinn,
New York Times bestselling author of *The Alice Network*

"For fans of *The Guernsey Literary and Potato Peel Pie Society* comes another terrific epistolary historical novel that is simply unputdownable. . . . It's a novel of war and loss, but it's also a story of friendship and love, and the connections of the heart made by solid strokes of pen on paper. Kudos to Ms. Gaynor and Ms. Webb for a seamless transition between characters, and for this remarkable novel that will undoubtedly go on my keeper shelf."

—Karen White, *New York Times* bestselling author of
The Night the Lights Went Out

"Gaynor's narrative seamlessly flows between the eras and the women, chronicling their longing, their pain, and their quiet triumphs. . . . Based on the real life of Grace Darling and two fierce storms, Gaynor's tale is both heartbreaking and captivating."

—*Historical Novel Society*

The Phantom's Apprentice by Heather Webb

"Webb combines music and magic seamlessly in *The Phantom's Apprentice*, weaving glittering new threads into the fabric of a classic story. Romantic, suspenseful, and inventive, this novel sweeps you along to its breathless conclusion."

—Greer Macallister, *USA Today* bestselling author
of *The Magician's Lie* and *Girl in Disguise*

"A performance worthy of the Paris Opera. . . . Christine's evolution from 'damsel in distress' to self-reliant woman is masterfully done, hooking the reader from the first page. Webb's work is immersive, well-crafted, and beautifully paced. A must-read!"

—Aimie K. Runyan, author of *Daughters of the Night Sky*

MEET ME IN MONACO

Also by Hazel Gaynor

The Lighthouse Keeper's Daughter
Last Christmas in Paris (with Heather Webb)
The Cottingley Secret
The Girl from The Savoy
Fall of Poppies (with Heather Webb and others)
A Memory of Violets
The Girl Who Came Home

Also by Heather Webb

Ribbons of Scarlet
Last Christmas in Paris (with Hazel Gaynor)
Fall of Poppies (with Hazel Gaynor and others)
The Phantom's Apprentice
Rodin's Lover
Becoming Josephine

MEET ME IN MONACO

A NOVEL OF GRACE KELLY'S ROYAL WEDDING

HAZEL GAYNOR

and HEATHER WEBB

WILLIAM MORROW
An Imprint of HarperCollinsPublishers

P.S.™ is a trademark of HarperCollins Publishers.

MEET ME IN MONACO. Copyright © 2019 by Hazel Gaynor and Heather Webb. All rights reserved. Printed in the United States of America. No part of this book may be used or reproduced in any manner whatsoever without written permission except in the case of brief quotations embodied in critical articles and reviews. For information, address HarperCollins Publishers, 195 Broadway, New York, NY 10007.

HarperCollins books may be purchased for educational, business, or sales promotional use. For information, please email the Special Markets Department at SPsales@harpercollins.com.

FIRST EDITION

Designed by Diahann Sturge
Part title one art © Natalya Levish / Shutterstock, Inc.
Part title two art © makar / Shutterstock, Inc.
Part title three art © vertigo illustration / Shutterstock, Inc.

Library of Congress Cataloging-in-Publication Data

Names: Gaynor, Hazel, author. | Webb, Heather, 1976 December 30- author.
Title: Meet me in Monaco : a novel / Hazel Gaynor and Heather Webb.
Description: First edition. | New York, NY : William Morrow, 2019.
Identifiers: LCCN 2018059053 | ISBN 9780062885364 (trade paperback) | ISBN 0062885367 (trade paperback) | ISBN 9780062913548 (hardcover) | ISBN 9780062911599 (large print) | ISBN 9780062885371 (ebook)
Subjects: | BISAC: FICTION / Contemporary Women. | FICTION / Biographical. | GSAFD: Love stories.
Classification: LCC PR6107.A974 M44 2019 | DDC 823/.92—dc23 LC record available at https://lccn.loc.gov/2018059053

ISBN 978-0-06-288536-4
ISBN 978-0-06-291354-8 (library edition)

19 20 21 22 23 LSC 10 9 8 7 6 5 4 3 2 1

For Grace

The idea of my life as a fairy tale is itself a fairy tale.
—Princess Grace of Monaco

Publicity shot of Grace Kelly during her time at MGM.

PART ONE

HEAD NOTES

*The initial impression of a perfume;
the notes that greet the nose immediately
and evaporate quickly.*

YES SHE CANNES!

Grace Kelly attends her first film festival.
Angeline West reports for the *Herald*.
May 1955

Following her recent controversial suspension from MGM Studios after refusing to make the picture *Tribute to a Bad Man*, Grace Kelly has had an interesting couple of months. But a surprise Oscar win for her role in *The Country Girl* returned her to the MGM studio executives' favor, and Miss Kelly was the undisputed Queen of Hollywood once more as she arrived in Cannes as part of a special American delegation for the eighth annual film festival.

Dressed in a demure two-piece suit, wearing her trademark white gloves, and carrying her favored Hermès handbag, Miss Kelly was first greeted by a swarm of international photographers and adoring fans in Nice as she alighted from the overnight train from Paris. Despite looking a little weary after her long journey, she smiled happily for the cameras and patiently signed autographs in the warm May sunshine.

In addition to a hectic schedule of formal galas and premieres at the festival, Miss Kelly said she hopes to manage a little sightseeing while on the stunning Côte d'Azur.

Stunning is the right word for Miss Kelly. Hollywood's brightest star already has Cannes, and this reporter, completely dazzled.

1

SOPHIE

Cannes
May 1955

Each scent holds a mystery, its own story. That was the first lesson Papa taught me. *"To be a parfumeur is to be a detective, Sophie,"* he'd say, bent in deep concentration over the mixing tube with a dropper of perfume oil. He would mix the solvent and sniff, mix and sniff, until he was satisfied. Only then would he soak a *mouillette,* a narrow strip of paper, and hand it to me. *"What do you see?"* he'd ask.

Because that was the real question: where the scent took me. I would inhale and be whisked away in an instant. A touch of jasmine hinted at carefree days in the sun. Woodsmoke conjured a cool autumn night and rich cassoulet for supper. Dry earth evoked our home in Grasse: a stone farmhouse surrounded by sunflower and lavender fields, windows standing open to wash the rooms with fresh air. I could almost taste the dust from the parched earth on my tongue as I fell into a memory of paper with smudged ink—the telegram announcing my father's death.

Papa's nature wasn't suited for war; part scientist, part artist, he was a gentle man who loved nothing more than the fragrant fields of Provence and the bounty they provided for his parfums. The day he left us to join the fight against the Nazis, I was a young girl just blossoming into womanhood and the lavender was in full bloom, painting the hillsides in shades of purple and blue. It was the last time I saw him, a silhouette against the sun-soaked horizon. That was the day Maman took over the finances of the family business, and the day I first understood that life did not always work out the way you wanted it to.

The death notification arrived the following spring, along with Papa's papers and personal effects. Dirt, blood, fear. The scent of a life so cruelly lost. Like all scents, it imprinted itself on my memory, and that was where I kept him now. A memory. An unanswered question of what might have been.

I sighed as I corked a small glass bottle and returned it to its place on the tray in my office. Nearly closing time, I stood and stretched, rolled my head from side to side to release a crick in my aching neck. I spent most of my time working on new scent combinations or overseeing the three perfumers who assisted me in my workshop in Grasse; they developed commercial scents to be sold to detergent companies, while I created fine parfums. That was my specialty: luxury fragrances. I blew out a tired breath. I wished I were in Grasse now.

During the tourist season, Papa had always insisted I accompany him to our little boutique overlooking the waterfront in Cannes. He wanted me to be the face of Duval one day, teaching me how important it was to mingle with our clients. Despite his humble background, he found it easy to make polite conversation with the wealthy tourists who came and went each year. I felt more at home among the hundreds of vials in our workshop, or rooting through the fields beneath the vast southern skies to track a new scent, but that shy child now found herself running the business. I played the part of confident socialite quite well, when necessary. I had to. I couldn't bear the thought of disappointing Papa.

I'd spent the last two weeks in Cannes at my apartment in the old medieval quarter of Le Suquet and the boutique. I'd remain in the city until the end of August, making occasional trips to the workshop in Grasse to check on things there. Mostly to check on Maman. A bitter taste flooded my mouth at the thought of her. I would have to visit her sooner or later. And I couldn't help but hope this time would be different, that I'd find her happy and healthy and not slumped over a half-empty bottle. I'd been hoping for the same thing for as long as I could remember.

"Natalie, could you check the shelves, please?" I called as I grabbed the keys and locked the door that separated the front of the shop from the office at the back. "It's nearly closing time." My feet ached from new shoes. My head ached from trying to conjure a new scent.

"We did well today," Natalie said. She brushed a long strand of lightly silvered hair behind her ear. "Thank goodness for wealthy movie stars. I can't believe I met Bernard Blier! He bought three bottles for the woman on his arm. She was exquisite."

I smiled at her enthusiasm. "So you said."

Natalie Buzay was beautiful, elegant, and warm. Everything my mother was not. Natalie took great pride in her work and the shop, and it showed in all that she did. I was grateful for her dependable presence; she'd known my father well and he'd entrusted the shop to her while he worked in Grasse the rest of the year. She was an excellent saleswoman, and enjoyed meeting the occasional Hollywood star and the affluent tourists that visited the shop. Though I enjoyed watching old movies with my elderly neighbor in Grasse, Madame Clouet, fame and wealth didn't impress me. My heroes worked at the great perfume houses: Guerlain, Fragonard, and Molinard.

"It's a shame you'd already left for lunch," Natalie remarked as she combed the rows of glass shelves, moving bottles a fraction to the left or right, wiping away invisible dust. Everything just so. "You always seem to miss the really big names."

"Yes, such a shame," I mumbled as I sifted through the register, pulling notes from the drawer and placing them into a zippered bank bag.

It had been a long week and I was ready to get home, sit on the balcony, and read a book over a glass of wine. I glanced at my wristwatch, hoping it would read six o'clock. I frowned. We had a quarter of an hour until closing.

As if on cue, the front door opened, bringing a fresh sea breeze rushing inside. My circle skirt billowed around my calves and a swathe of dark curls blew across my face. I grumbled under my breath, annoyed by the way the wind always twisted my hair into knots.

A tall, slim woman in pink Capri pants and a crisp white blouse closed the door behind her. Large dark sunglasses and a colorful headscarf concealed most of her face. "That's some breeze! It reminds me a little of California," she remarked, moving quickly to the far corner of the shop, away from the windows.

I noted the woman's elegance and soft American accent. Another tourist.

"Good afternoon, madame." Natalie jumped into action, switching easily into her heavily accented English. Working in a town that attracted so many tourists meant having a good grasp of the English language. Papa had been quite firm about this. "May I help you find something in particular?" she prompted. "We have a divine new perfume we've just developed. *Printemps*. Springtime. It's very popular with the Americans."

"I'll just take a look around first, thank you." The woman picked up a bottle, turned it over, and placed it back on the shelf without even smelling a sample. She picked up another and did the same before throwing an anxious look over her shoulder, toward the door.

I studied her from behind the counter. She hadn't removed her sunglasses, and her behavior was a little odd, as if she were hiding from someone. Her clothes were pristine. A Hermès handbag hung from her arm. A few strands of blond hair had escaped from the headscarf and fell around her temples. Upon closer inspection, she appeared to be breathing hard.

"Madame, can I help you?" I offered, stepping forward.

She flinched and turned. Giving me a shy smile, she approached the counter. A cloud of vanilla and lilac enveloped me. A sugary perfume with a heavy floral bouquet and vanilla base note. It didn't quite suit her.

Finally, she removed her sunglasses. "Yes, you *can* help me, actually. If you would be so kind."

My reply stuck in my throat. Eyes the color of the Mediterranean looked back at me as I stared at her creamy skin and strong, straight nose, her perfectly sculpted lips and cheekbones—I knew that elegant face. I'd seen it a dozen times on the covers of magazines. I'd seen it on the big screen. She was a favorite of Madame Clouet.

"Grace Kelly," I whispered.

Natalie stood dumbstruck, her feather duster poised in midair.

"Yes," Miss Kelly replied with a slight smile, casting another nervous glance over her shoulder. "I'm Grace." She held out a white-gloved hand. "Hello!"

I took her hand, thinking how American her greeting was, but I couldn't make my lips move to say anything in reply. The one Hollywood star I knew something about, the most beautiful and famous woman in the world, was standing in front of me. In my boutique.

"You were going to help me?" Grace prompted, sweetly.

I cleared my throat. "Yes, of course. How can I . . . what can I do for you, Mademoiselle Kelly?"

"Please, call me Grace."

I noted the sincerity in her voice, and despite my racing

pulse, managed a smile. "Of course. What can I do for you? Grace."

She leaned closer as if to divulge a secret. "I'm being followed by a photographer. He's terribly persistent. I thought I'd given him the slip, but he reappeared on the promenade. I ducked behind a palm tree and raced across the street, and, well, here I am. It sounds like a scene from a movie, doesn't it?" Relief and annoyance warred in her eyes. "I think I've lost him, but is there another exit from your store? Just in case? They can be terribly persistent. The British are the worst."

I nodded. "There's an exit through the back, but it's very close to the street. He might see you." She looked a little disappointed. "Perhaps if you wait in my office for a few minutes, he'll be on his way and you can duck out then," I suggested. "Will that do?"

"Oh yes. Thank you." She touched my hand. "Thank you so much. I only wanted to take a walk through this beautiful town, and along La Croisette. It's so fresh beside the water. I wanted to escape the madness of the festival for a few hours. I suppose I was silly to hope for such a thing."

There was something a little melancholy in her tone, a childlike vulnerability I didn't expect from someone in her position.

"Can we perhaps interest you in trying a new perfume, Mademoiselle Kelly?" Natalie offered, sliding behind the counter with her usual easy charm.

Though her tone was professional, I knew what she was up to, and shot her a warning look. She wanted to gossip with her friends about how she'd sold perfume to Grace Kelly, but now was not the time to play saleswoman.

"Perhaps another time, Natalie," I interjected. "Please, Grace, follow me."

I fished the keys from my handbag and flipped through them to find the right one. I tried to ignore my excitement and nerves, while the strong fragrance Grace wore irritated my nose. Vanilla was a bold scent, generic but comforting, reminding many of home. But it also covered deep insecurities. Papa used to say that those who wore a bold scent might have a large personality on the surface but often longed for approval.

"To be a parfumeur is to be a psychologist." That was the second lesson Papa taught me. He said that everyone had deeply hidden insecurities, and that many people wished to be something more than they were. Our job as *parfumeurs* was to uncover what that something more was and make it for them. Papa was extraordinarily good at guessing secrets, but I couldn't help wondering if he was wrong about vanilla. At least this time. I doubted the mighty Grace Kelly had any insecurities.

"Why don't you allow me, Sophie?" Natalie offered. "I'd be happy to show Miss Kelly to the cozy chaise in your office. I know you like to do a quick inventory of the shelves before you leave."

Though I'd have liked to spend more time with Miss Kelly, I couldn't very well argue with Natalie without looking foolish.

Grace held out her hand to me. *"Merci,* Sophie, is it?"

I nodded. "Sophie Duval."

Her eyes lit up in a smile. "Ah. Duval. You're the owner?"

"Yes."

"Well, thank you again, Sophie. I won't forget your kindness."

"I hope you might return to our shop under better circumstances, one day."

"I'd like that very much," she said, her blue eyes twinkling.

As Natalie escorted Miss Kelly to the office, the front door opened again. A very tall man peered inside. He lingered on the doorstep, half in and half out of the shop. He wore an old-fashioned Homburg hat and a shabby leather jacket, clearly underdressed for the Riviera. I noticed a camera hung from a strap against his chest. It had to be the photographer chasing Miss Kelly. I took an instant dislike to him.

"Pardon me, monsieur, we are just closing." I didn't bother to hide the irritation from my voice. "We open again tomorrow at nine."

In faltering French, he asked if Grace Kelly had come into the shop. His accent was terrible. His incorrect use of vocabulary was almost comical.

I pursed my lips. English. The worst kind of press hound. Miss Kelly herself had said so.

I sniffed, and replied in English. "I'm not in the habit of telling strangers whom I have and haven't sold perfumes to, monsieur. It's bad for business, and frankly, none of yours."

He regarded me a moment through golden-brown eyes and burst into laughter. "Well, aren't you perfectly French."

I felt heat rising to my face. How did Miss Kelly put up with such awful people pestering her all the time?

"You don't have to tell me what she bought," he pressed, casually picking up a couple of business cards from the counter. He glanced at them briefly before slipping them into his pocket. "I'd just like to know whether or not she came in here."

I raised a quizzical brow at him, incredulous he should try to jockey for information as if I were Miss Kelly's private secretary. "The name's Henderson, by the way," he added, extending a hand. "James. Jim to my friends."

Seeing my expression and realizing I wasn't going to shake his hand, or divulge any information, he took off his hat, and ran his hands through his hair, sending it sticking up every which way. I bit my lip to keep myself from laughing.

"Thing is, miss, I'm having a hell of a day and if I don't get a decent picture of her—of anyone important, really—I might not have a job to go home to and the cat will be terribly disappointed in me. Not that it's of any concern to you, but, well, that's how it is." He held his hands out in front of him. "Help out a useless English chap, would you?" He tilted his head to one side. "*Merci beaucoup?*"

I was suddenly very busy straightening the tissue paper and rolls of ribbon beneath the counter. "I believe the phrase you are looking for is *s'il vous plaît*. I'm afraid I can't help you, monsieur," I added. "If you are so incompetent at your job, I doubt a small perfume boutique can save you." I glanced up at him.

A wide grin split his face. "Quite right. I'm a ridiculous fool and should be on my way." He touched the brim of his hat in salutation and turned to go but when he reached the door, he hesitated. "Actually, before I go, can I ask what perfume it is you're wearing? It's really rather lovely."

I turned to meet his gaze. "And you are rude—"

A flash went off. I was blinded by the light, and my hand flew to my eyes. "What are you doing?"

He shrugged. "If I can't have a photograph of Grace Kelly, I might as well have one of a furious French girl." With that, he left, laughing as he closed the door behind him.

Furious French girl? How dare he! As I roughly turned the shop sign to *Fermé,* I watched him light a cigarette and saunter off down the street. The familiar aroma of leather and balsam lingered in the shop where he'd stood. Despite my bad humor, the scent provoked memories of happier times.

That was the third lesson Papa taught me. *"To be a parfumeur is to be a keeper of memories, Sophie. Every scent will remind you of something, or someone."*

It was only as I walked back to the office to assure Miss Kelly he'd gone that I realized who the English photographer reminded me of.

James Henderson reminded me of Papa.

2

JAMES

The scrum of press photographers was already ten deep outside the Palais des Festivals on La Croisette by the time I arrived. I was late, as usual. Lucky for me, so was Grace Kelly. I'd already missed one chance to photograph her and I really couldn't afford to bugger things up again—if, indeed, it *was* Grace Kelly I'd chased into the perfume shop yesterday. Thanks to Mademoiselle Duval I would never know for certain. I had to admire her, I suppose. If she'd really hidden a Hollywood star in the back of her poky little boutique she would have had quite the story to tell her friends over dinner. I wondered if she'd mentioned me at all.

I pulled one of her business cards from my jacket pocket. *Sophie Duval, Parfumeur. Cannes. Grasse.* Snooty, beautiful Sophie Duval. Infuriatingly French. And impossible to stop thinking about while the scent of her perfume lingered on the card. I returned it to my pocket and pushed my way through the mob, grateful for the gentle warmth of the afternoon sunshine after a morning of rain.

As I elbowed my way through the pack, I looked for Teddy Walsh. He'd promised to save me a space at the front as he always did. He was good to me that way. I might be late but I wasn't giving up a front-row view just because I'd overslept. A photo op like this—Cannes Film Festival, glamorous Hollywood stars—promised the opportunity to find something extra special through the lens and favors were being pulled in faster than the day's catch. We'd do pretty much anything for the best shot. Bribes. False promises. Tip-offs and spare film begged from here and borrowed from there. That's how it was in our line of work, and when a leading Hollywood actress was in town, the stakes rose even higher and our morals sank even lower.

I lifted my camera above my head and fired off a couple of speculative test shots of the crowd as I made my way forward. My eye was drawn to the contrast of the press pack's dark suits against the vivid blue sky. Colors and landscape were what really interested me. Celebrities, not so much. The fact was, I'd be much happier photographing the Riviera's cliffs and coves and terrifying switchback roads than I was photographing platinum blondes. But landscapes were for artists, and I was nothing but a hack, just a regular nine-to-five press photographer with bills to pay and an editor breathing down my neck. That was what kept me elbowing my way to the front, treading on toes. "Oi! Watch it, Henderson." "Get out of the way, Lanky." "Give a fella a chance, would you." I ignored their griping and insults. All I cared about, all any of us cared about, was the shot that would keep the boss happy and the paychecks rolling in. I'd had my last warning and Sanders was not the type to go back on his word. Cannes, or bust. That was the deal.

Pushing on into the crowd, I was surrounded by a wall of noise as flashbulbs were tested and film was loaded. Old friends greeted each other with a hearty slap on the back. The smell of tobacco clung to suit jackets and smoke wound from Gauloises cigarettes dangling from lips while busy hands fiddled with equipment. The familiar smell and the huddle of men sent me straight back to billets in Southampton as we waited to cross the Channel to the beaches of Normandy, but I pushed the memory away, like I always did, and moved on toward the front of the pack, the sickly sweet scent of cheap aftershave and brilliantine making my head throb.

Finally, I found Walsh. "Afternoon," I said, shoving in beside him, a barrage of complaints following from those behind. My height had never won me any friends.

"Jesus, Jim. You look bloody awful. What happened to you?"

I shrugged and grabbed Walsh's camera, peering into the back of the flash lamp. My face was peppered with day-old stubble and dark shadows lurked beneath my eyes. My shirt collar was creased. My leather jacket had seen better days. Teddy was right. I looked terrible. "Life happened to me, Teddy," I joked, handing his camera back to him. "You don't look too good yourself, I might add."

"It's this damned cough. It's keeping me awake at night."

"You should see someone about that. Or quit the smokes."

"Where've you been anyway?" Walsh mumbled, ignoring

me, a cigarette dangling from his bottom lip as he adjusted the shutter speed on his camera. "She'll be here any minute."

"Phone call to Emily. It's her birthday. She wanted to tell me about her new chemistry set. I couldn't exactly hang up on her."

Teddy offered a sympathetic slap on the shoulder and that was all there was to say about it.

We swapped lenses and checked settings for range and lighting, aperture and framing, the usual routines done almost without thinking. Just as well since I was a little groggy after too much cheap *vin rouge* last night. I didn't even like red wine but everything had felt better by the time I'd reached the end of the bottle. I could have done without the headache, but I didn't have time to think about it as a sleek, gunmetal-gray American sedan pulled up outside the venue.

Behind me, someone said, "This is it, boys! She's here." The car doors opened. The hunt was on. Flashbulbs went off like a ricochet of bullets. *Pop! Pop! Pop!* The cry went up all around me. *"Miss Kelly! Miss Kelly! Grace! This way! Over here! Give us a wave! How are you finding France?"* Like trained animals, we all responded to the clicking, clattering, clamoring madness of the moment, all for the tantalizing possibility that she might—just might—turn in our direction and give us the shot.

Apart from Marilyn, Grace Kelly was the Hollywood star everyone wanted to capture. We'd all imagined what it would be like to see our picture on the front page of the *Times*, or the *Washington Post*. We'd all written our Pulitzer acceptance speeches in our heads. One perfect shot from the hundreds we took. One image captured on film, and our reputations—our careers and futures—could change instantly. It was the ridiculous simplicity of it that kept us showing up time and time again, even when our puce-cheeked editors tossed our latest efforts into the bin in a rage, and threatened us with one more chance, or we were toast. While I didn't enjoy the thrill of the chase like I once had, I couldn't easily give it up, either. Like a stalker hunting its prey, I was on high alert: eyes wide, ears pricked, hands as steady as iron rods as I held my camera, took aim, and pressed the shutter.

Except, I didn't.

I froze.

As Grace Kelly stepped from the car, all I could do was stare. There was something about the way she moved—glided, almost—the way her smile lit up her face, the way she held her head at the perfect angle to catch the sunlight against her cheek. She was the epitome of femininity, gloriously photogenic, and I was captivated. I wanted to study her. Frame her. Light her. Get closer to her. And in my moment of hesitation, everyone else got the shot. By the time I'd gathered my wits and pressed the shutter, she'd turned to walk inside, and it was over.

Walsh whistled through his teeth. "She's something else, isn't she? Did you get a good one?"

I slung my camera strap over my shoulder, ran my hands through my hair, and lit a cigarette. "Didn't get a sodding thing."

Walsh laughed as he packed up beside me. "What? How? She was right there!"

I took a long drag on my cigarette and blew the smoke skyward. "Camera playing up again." Walsh rolled his eyes. He'd heard me blame my camera too many times recently. I tipped my head back, releasing the tension in my neck and shoulders, narrowing my eyes against the sunlight. "I could get used to these blue skies," I remarked. "They make England seem so bloody miserable."

"England *is* bloody miserable." Walsh stopped what he was doing and looked at me. "Is everything all right, Jim? *You* seem a bit bloody miserable to be honest. More than usual, I mean."

I sighed. "It's Emily, mostly. I feel like a rat for missing her birthday. Again. Apparently it's a big deal turning ten."

"I wouldn't worry about it too much. Girls need their mothers. It'll be all pretty dresses and tea parties. I'd say you're better off leaving them to it."

I smiled, but I couldn't agree. Emily wasn't like other little girls of ten. She preferred to read stories about scientists and explorers than to sip tea from china cups and play princesses. She needed a father. And I was doing a marvelous job of proving myself entirely inadequate for the role.

"And there's the small matter of my employment," I added, changing the subject. "Sanders will burst a blood vessel when I turn up with a few out-of-focus shots of the back of Kelly's head." I tossed my cigarette onto the ground, and shoved my hands in my pockets. "Don't suppose you fancy a quick drink?"

Walsh hesitated, torn between commitment to me and dedication to the job. "Sorry, pal. Can't. Have to get these back to the desk. I'll catch you later for dinner. And go easy on that wine. You're becoming far too French!" He placed a hand on my shoulder. "Don't beat yourself up about Emily. Children are far more forgiving than adults. You'll make it up to her."

I was grateful for the reassurance. Teddy Walsh was like a brother to me—always there to offer good advice, always looking on the bright side.

We'd seen things during the war that nobody should ever see, let alone young men away from home for the first time. Teddy was all optimism and silver linings. He lived each day for the sheer surprise of it and had a way of focusing on the present that I envied. Like looking through a good-quality lens, being around Teddy made things clearer, sharper. Even Marjorie (the former Mrs. Henderson) conceded that Teddy was good for me, and Marjorie didn't often dwell on the good in people.

Teddy was right, of course. Emily would forgive me. Even if I had been in London, taking her out for the afternoon would have become complicated. Marjorie would have made certain of that. And yet a familiar pang of guilt settled in the pit of my stomach. Was this life of chasing news stories and starlets around the world a symptom or a cause? Was I really a bad father, or was I simply afraid to try to be a good one? A few days ago, I'd woken up in my flat in Clapham, wondering if there was anything in the refrigerator for breakfast as I listened to the rain pelting the windows. This morning, I'd woken up in a beachfront hotel in Cannes, the sun glistening on the water as I breakfasted on an omelette and croissants. Life as a press photographer took me to some surprising places, but it was what it took me away from that appealed to me. It took me away from the lingering shadows of war. It took me away from the spectacular mess I'd made of my marriage. It was, after all, easier to focus my lens on something, or someone, other than myself. But my job also took me away from the one thing I really cared about. It took me away from my daughter.

As the press pack dispersed, I wandered along La Croisette, stopping at a *tabac* to buy a picture postcard. I took lunch alfresco at the Hôtel Barrière Le Majestic and wrote the post-card over a café crème. Emily enjoyed my weekly phone call home, but it was the postcards I sent that she looked forward to the most. She kept them in a treasure box under her bed, tied with a lemon-yellow ribbon.

I sat for a long time, people-watching, listening to the in-comprehensible babble of French conversation around me, wondering how it was that everyone here appeared to be so much happier and relaxed and in love than people did in Lon-don. People touched and kissed and caressed here, not caring who was watching. Maybe it was the weather, or the sea, or the cheap wine. Maybe it was that indefinable French *je ne sais quoi*. Whatever it was, it made my dour Englishness all the more apparent. I wondered if a person could change if they lived somewhere like this. Would Riviera life rub off on me?

While I wondered if I could improve myself by becoming more French—and tried not to think about how bad the rep-rimand from Sanders would be when I told him I'd missed the shot of Grace Kelly—I saw a familiar face across the street. Sophie Duval. She was standing outside a small arcade of de-signer boutiques beneath the hotel, struggling to stop her skirt from blowing up above her knees in the breeze. I pushed down the brim of my hat and watched her for a moment, amused by her annoyance. Or perhaps she was more upset than annoyed, I couldn't quite tell. Either way, I decided to go over and offer an apology for my rather abrupt manner in her shop. Perhaps I would pick up a bottle of Duval perfume for Emily as a belated birthday present.

Leaving a suitable amount of francs on the table, I grabbed

my camera, but I kicked the edge of my chair as I stood up and sent it toppling over. The clatter caught Miss Duval's attention. She looked over to the restaurant, spotted me instantly (I was difficult to miss), turned her back to me, and walked briskly away. I followed, threading through the tightly packed café tables as quickly as my gangling limbs would allow, but by the time I'd pushed past a couple who stopped inconveniently in front of me for a passionate kiss, she'd ducked down a narrow side street and disappeared into the shadows.

I wasn't giving up that easily. The only thing I had left to lose was my dignity, and what half-decent press photographer had that anyway? I broke into a jog, following the tantalizing scent of her perfume down the sleepy, shuttered streets.

3

SOPHIE

The sun peeked over the edge of the horizon, sending a glimmering path of gold across the water, its parting gift before retiring for the evening. I would have loved to sit for a while to watch the spectacle, but I was already late for dinner, and Lucien would be irritable.

I walked to Chez Benoît as quickly as I could manage in parley heels. It was never my intention to keep Lucien waiting, but I often got absorbed by my work, wrapped up in a world of fragrance and memories and dreams so that I completely lost track of time. Today, I had a particularly good reason for my delay. I smiled, remembering the flutter of excitement as I'd struck upon something special in my workshop, a seduction of the senses. Ambergris, rich with musk to act as a fixative, *note de tête* of dried cherry and violets, *note de coeur* of mimosa and oakmoss, the carefully balanced quantity of ingredients recorded in my *journal de fleurs,* the notebook where the formula for each Duval fragrance was held. It was Papa's before it passed on to me. He'd affectionately called it his book of flowers, and the name had stuck. Any *parfumeur* knew to keep their formulas a closely guarded secret. Science and magic, art and beauty, it was all there in a small vial that would one day become a beautiful glass bottle to be sold. My new fragrance needed more work, but I was close, *so close* to something exceptional.

I smiled again as I approached the door of the restaurant.

"Bonsoir, madame." The doorman nodded and held the door open for me. "Monsieur Marceau is waiting at your usual table."

"*Merci,* Jacques. I am late." I shrugged my coat from my shoulders as he took it from me.

"A woman as beautiful as you can never be late, madame."

I laughed at his easy charm and wound my way through the circular tables, each glowing with candlelight and covered in crisp white linens. Soft piano music mingled with laughter and drifted through the room. The delicious aroma from the kitchens hit me in waves: roast beef, wild garlic, the salty tang of fresh seafood. Lucien's favorite restaurant in Cannes had quickly become *our* favorite restaurant in Cannes. Though Chez Benoît was expensive, money was no object to the son of a millionaire real estate developer, although Lucien's easy way with money made me—the daughter of a humble artisan—feel uncomfortable at times.

He stood as I approached the table and made a point of checking his watch. "If you didn't look so radiant, I'd be angry with you." We exchanged kisses on each cheek. He pulled out my chair from the table before the waiter had the chance. "What took you so long?"

"I'm sorry." I sat, smoothing my floral skirt. "I came from Grasse." I couldn't wait to tell him about the progress I'd made that afternoon.

"I've been waiting nearly an hour." He tipped back the rest of his martini and held a finger in the air for the waiter. "We're ready for the first course, and we'll have a bottle of the Pommery."

"*Très bien.*" The waiter bowed deferentially before rushing from the dining room. They were used to Lucien's expensive tastes and demanding ways.

"I was considering joining another table," Lucien said with a hint of humor in his voice. "The Florents are by the front window."

I reached for his hand and squeezed it. "I will make it up to you."

"I like the sound of that." He winked as a smile spread across his face.

The sommelier arrived, uncorked the bottle, and poured a splash of the effervescent liquid into a crystal coupe. I sat back in my seat as Lucien went through the process of tasting before nodding his approval. The vintage was acceptable. Lucien had impeccable taste and wouldn't settle for less than perfect. I smiled at the sommelier as he poured two glasses and placed the bottle in a silver ice bucket beside the table.

"I've discovered something," I said, unable to suppress the excitement emerging again, like the ribbons of bubbles winding to the surface in my glass.

"Well, if this is why you were late, do go on."

"I'm in the process of developing a new fragrance. I think it could be a real breakthrough, Lucien. This may be it, the one I've been waiting for." I held out my champagne glass.

"That's wonderful. Congratulations." He clinked his glass against mine.

"Thank you. It's been so many years . . . if Papa . . . I wish . . ." I felt a lump form in my throat and swallowed hard. "If I could only talk to him about it. He would understand better than anyone."

"I know, *chérie*," Lucien said, lifting my hand to his lips. "I know."

I longed to tell Lucien more, to explain my ideas and my plans, but he humored my passionate musings only to a point. He was a true businessman, almost clinical in the execution of his work at times. He thought I let my emotions overtake my good sense too often. But our differences were what drew him to me in the first place, and the same was true for me. Opposites attract, after all. Recently, he had hinted at our relationship becoming more serious in the not-too-distant future, and he'd made it clear I would be busy maintaining his properties—the house in Cannes, the yacht, the Paris apartment—and playing hostess to his millionaire clientele. I would be expected to step back from the perfume business—at least to some degree—to make way for our family. I hadn't argued or worried. I knew he would change his mind in time. He knew how much Duval meant to me. Lucien often made offhand comments like this, but when it came down to it, he loved me and would support me, I was sure of it.

"Will you join me for a digestif after the party later?" he asked, changing the subject. "With the film festival in town, I can hardly manage the invitations. Grace Kelly is here with her boyfriend, or one of her leading men. It's hard to keep up with her."

"Oh?" For some reason I didn't tell him she'd visited the boutique. "I didn't know she had a boyfriend."

He leaned forward, lowering his voice conspiratorially. "She doesn't. Not officially. But she can't keep her eyes off Jean-Pierre Aumont. They're all over the newspapers. How convenient that they're here at the same time. Rumor has it he's the only reason she agreed to come to Cannes at all. Then there are the rumors she's already engaged to that fashion designer, Cassini." He leaned back in his velvet chair and laughed lightly. "Good for her, I say. Use your beauty to your full advantage."

Lucien enjoyed all the gossip and scandal that circulated during the film festival. He came alive as the boats packed the harbor and plenty of new, fascinating people filled the bars and hotels of Cannes and other nearby towns on the Côte d'Azur. Perhaps he enjoyed it a little too much. I was amazed at the energy he had, the endless hours he spent among the crowds, floating from one yacht party to the next. He acquired all the right invitations, managed to meet all the right people. Lucien Marceau charmed everyone he met. With his dark hair, aquiline nose, and expensive wardrobe, he always made an impression. Eyes followed him as he sauntered through a packed room dressed in Lacoste stripes and foulard, tied expertly at his neck, or attired in an elegant dinner jacket that complemented his build. It was no wonder he was so successful in business. It never bothered me that he sat firmly at the center of every party, while I receded quietly to a corner with a friend or two to talk more privately. When Lucien was happy, everything was easy. I only wished he would take a little more interest in the things that made me happy, too.

"I'm tired tonight, *chéri*," I said, laying down my fork. "You go on to the party without me."

He flashed one of his contagious smiles and kissed my hand. "Fine, but tomorrow night, *pas d'excuses*."

The waiter reappeared with a tray of fresh oysters. Lucien squeezed a wedge of lemon over the shellfish and we ate in silence until the potage of creamed asparagus soup arrived.

"What are you thinking about?" Lucien asked, tearing off a chunk of baguette and noticing my distraction. "You look like you're working out a plan for world domination."

I laughed. My thoughts had circled the meeting with Miss Kelly, then alighted on that irritating photographer, James Henderson. I pushed him quickly aside and returned to the thrill of my new discovery in the workshop. "I think this new fragrance could be the beginning of something really special. Perhaps I could launch a new line, like I've always wanted. I would need to speak to the accountant but—"

Lucien squeezed my hand. "*Mon amour,* you know you can't afford this. You already spent the money I gave you over a year ago. I know how much you enjoy your work, but this grand venture of yours would stretch your resources too thin. Think of the time it would take to make a name for yourself among the big perfume houses. You would be competing with the most famous names in Paris. Your parfums sell just fine here, in your shop in Cannes, and in Grasse." He dipped a bit of bread into his soup. "Besides, there's the problem of your maman to consider."

Maman. I sighed. She wouldn't go for my idea at all. In fact, she didn't care a wit for Duval. She cared only about her brandy and an "occasional" hand of vingt-et-un. Her habit had controlled our lives for as long as I could remember. Papa had argued and pleaded with her, and sometimes shouted until the panes on the windows shook. She would change her ways for a time and he would forgive her, but it never lasted. Somehow, he'd managed to keep us and the business afloat. I was now trying to do the same, but I hadn't yet created a fragrance that would catapult Duval to the next level. Lucien was right. We couldn't easily compete with the established reputations of the large perfume houses, even if we did have the funds. Yet I couldn't help feeling I was finally on the right path. All I needed was a new line featuring a star fragrance. I could give Maman her own allowance then and safeguard the rest of the finances. And I could continue to do what I loved most, whether or not she drowned herself in cheap wine.

"This could be it, Lucien. The one I've been searching for. I'll talk to Maman. I—"

"Let's not talk about expenditures tonight, *chérie*. I hate to see you upset. Financial strain, your maman, what-ifs." Lucien poured us each another glass of champagne, waving the sommelier away dismissively. "It will only spoil our evening." He checked his Rolex. "What little of it there is left."

My good humor dissolved as my dreams collapsed under the weight of hard reality. "Yes, you're right. Let's leave it."

He saw my disappointment and kissed my hand again. "We

will talk about this more, I promise. I want to hear all about it. But later. After you've had time to think about your new fragrance, scribble down your ideas. Perhaps devise a plan. How does that sound?"

I nodded, accepting his argument even as a stubborn part of me disagreed. I laid my knife and fork on the edge of my plate. Suddenly, I wasn't hungry anymore.

4

JAMES

Hollywood stars were elusive, but the Cannes sunset was impossible to miss. It was my favorite time of day, everything slowly mellowing to a soft rose-gold glow as the town shimmered. The light was too good to ignore, and I was glad to have an unused roll of film to catch it. I sought out interesting silhouettes and shadows and angles, focused on the way the water glistened like silk. It was where I felt happiest, framing the scene. Landscapes gave me all the time I needed to get the perfect composition. People, on the other hand, were unpredictable and erratic. Walsh kept telling me I had a good instinct for faces and should do more portraiture, but I didn't want to believe him. Scenery was my safe space. I understood it. People, I only ever got remarkably wrong.

As I walked along La Croisette, it was as if the whole town had exhaled. Everything relaxed in the fresh evening breeze, the palm trees rustling their leaves like hula girls shaking their grass skirts. As I strolled past the Duval boutique, I took one of the business cards from my pocket. The scent of Sophie's perfume was still captured on the slim piece of card. I brought it to my nose and breathed in. Sensual, but feminine. Perfectly French. It was surely no coincidence that I'd seen her again, and I couldn't stop thinking about the look in her eyes when I'd snapped her in the shop. Confused. Hurt. Vulnerable. Some people have a way of expressing themselves that the camera loves and enhances. I was no expert in portrait photography, but I sensed that Miss Duval had a face the camera loved, and I couldn't wait to get back to London to develop the image I'd taken of her. In the meantime, I had far more important things to think about. I had one day left in Cannes. One day to photograph a Hollywood icon or lose my job, and what chance would I ever have of making a proper home for Emily and me if that happened. Emily deserved the best, and I was determined to find a way of giving it to her. None of this was her fault, after all.

Back at the hotel I dialed Walsh's room. I hadn't seen him at dinner and it wasn't like Teddy Walsh to miss a meal. The phone rang several times before he picked up.

"Hello." His voice was sleepy, slightly slurred.

I pulled the receiver away from my ear as he coughed violently on the other end. "Walsh? It's Jim. Are you drunk?"

"I'm sick. Come up. I need to talk to you."

My old man used to say I was the luckiest kid he'd ever known. I'd get the best hand in the games of poker we played at Christmas. I'd find money in the street. I'd roll a six every time I needed one. The older I got, the more my luck seemed to run out, but that was about to change.

"I've been invited to a private press op tomorrow," Teddy explained as I poured him a glass of water and drew his curtains. "Pulled in a favor from a friend of a friend who works for *Paris Match*. Turns out the magazine's movie editor, Pierre Galante, has arranged a meeting between Grace Kelly and Prince Rainier at the royal palace in Monaco. It seems that Galante, his wife—Olivia de Havilland—and the editor in chief of *Paris Match*, cooked up the idea over dinner in the dining car on the train from Paris to Nice, and Kelly's people at MGM agreed to it. 'The Prince and the Queen of Hollywood.' I can already see the headlines."

I flopped onto the end of Walsh's bed. "Prince who? I've never heard of him."

"Neither had Miss Kelly by all accounts. Apparently she's not very keen on the idea. She believes her schedule is already far too tight. I suspect she'd prefer to stay in Cannes with that Aumont chap who seems to follow her everywhere, but it's all arranged. A small group of photographers have been invited to capture the meeting on camera. Good publicity for American-French relations, and all that."

I sat up and pushed my hair from my forehead. "And you're stuck in bed with the plague, so I get to take your place at the palace?"

"Exactly."

A broad smile spread across my face as I crawled over the bed and planted a kiss on his forehead. "I bloody love you, Teddy Walsh! Sanders will have no excuse to fire me now."

"Don't muck this up, Jim. It's a bit obscure but you know how popular Kelly is right now. This could turn into big news."

I promised I wouldn't muck it up. "Scout's honor. I'll get the shot."

He rolled his eyes and waved me away with a weary hand as another coughing fit left him gasping for breath.

"You sure you'll be all right?" I asked. I wasn't used to seeing him so listless. "You're not going to die or anything? I should probably warn the chambermaids if you are."

He attempted a smile. "Not planning to. I'd say I'll last the night anyway. Now get lost, will you? You're making me feel worse."

✳ ✳ ✳

The following morning, I got a lift to the palace with Walsh's contact from *Paris Match,* a diminutive fellow with fat fingers and limited English. We traveled in silence as his little Peugeot 203 struggled up the steep winding roads, gears crunching as he did his best to keep up with the American sedan MGM had provided to drive Miss Kelly to the palace. Pierre Galante was accompanying her, along with Olivia de Havilland.

"Hollywood stars pop up as often as champagne corks in this part of the country," I said, as much to myself as to my companion. He didn't reply. I was glad to see he kept his eyes firmly on the road. I rolled down the window and pulled back the seat, stretching out my legs as much as the cramped space would allow. I settled my gaze on the passing scenery and tried not to think about the sheer drop-off to our right. The sea was vivid blue far below the steep mountainsides. The scent of salt

and orange blossom mingled with the tobacco from my cigarette; the relaxed holiday feel of it all made me smile. Perhaps
everything was going to be okay after all, thanks to Walsh and
a dozen dodgy oysters, and Grace Kelly and a prince.

❊ ❊ ❊

At the palace, an aide explained, rather awkwardly, that His
Serene Highness was a little delayed. He offered to escort our
party on a tour of the palace while we waited.

Miss Kelly didn't seem too impressed and kept glancing
at her wristwatch, but she managed a polite smile as she was
introduced to the group of photographers and reporters. She
shook all our hands, one after the other.

"James Henderson, British press," I said when she reached
me. "Jim, to my friends."

She smiled warmly, said, "Hello, James," and moved quickly
on to the chap beside me who was sweating profusely. He
wiped his hand on his lapel before offering it to her. I was glad,
on her behalf, that she wore wrist-length white gloves.

"I'm told the prince won't be long, gentlemen," she said
brightly, when she'd been introduced to us all. "And I suppose
a prince is entitled to make an entrance! Perhaps we could use
the time to take some photographs inside?"

The consummate professional, she took control with ease
and charm. I'd expected her to be more aloof, hardened by
the Hollywood machine. But there was nothing aloof about
Miss Kelly. She was absolutely charming. Playful almost, as
bemused to find herself at a royal palace in Monaco as the rest
of us. Her soft American accent and girl-next-door look were

a far cry from the dazzling star we usually saw turned out in furs and diamonds. Her garish floral dress reminded me of the wallpaper in my mother's living room but it was no doubt the height of Paris fashion.

I followed the other reporters and photographers into the grand palatial rooms. Walsh had urged me not to draw attention to myself. "Look a little bored, if anything," he'd suggested. "You're good at that." I did my best, but it really wasn't easy in such ostentatious rooms and in the presence of such a striking woman.

If she was reluctant to be there, Miss Kelly didn't let it show for a minute. She posed when and where asked, her trademark smile illuminating every room we visited, making our job easy. We photographed her looking at marble busts and armory and portraits of the Grimaldi family. In each setting, she turned on the charm for the cameras. I was impressed, and more than a little amused, with her ability to look absolutely fascinated by so many inanimate objects. Maybe she was the perfect woman to stroke the prince's ego after all. I'd heard he could be difficult to engage in conversation at best, and about as interesting as a marble statue at worst.

After several posed photos in the library, I took a lovely shot of Miss Kelly walking along a long balcony, shafts of sunlight bursting between the ornate colonnades. She stopped for a moment, placing her hands on the stone balustrade as she gazed out over the courtyard below. She looked extraordinarily at home, as if she visited palaces all the time. I had to hand it to her. She was a fine actress indeed.

Eventually, it was announced that the prince had arrived

and we were all escorted to a grand sort of parlor, where he stood awkwardly beside a fireplace. He didn't strike me as being especially princely, or handsome even. He looked pretty ordinary in his dark suit. I wondered if Miss Kelly was thinking the same thing.

Our cameras clicked and whirred somewhat intrusively as the two were formally introduced. Miss Kelly removed the glove from her right hand and bobbed a little curtsey. The prince was horribly stiff, bending at the waist as he leaned forward to shake her hand. The poor man looked terrified, afraid to take another step toward her. He didn't even remove his dark sunglasses, which I thought was odd for a photo op and really rather rude to Miss Kelly, but she didn't bat an eyelid and looked for all the world as if she met princes in palaces every day.

"I'd get much closer to her if I were him," someone muttered behind me, which made me laugh and then cough. I apologized as everyone stared at me for interrupting the moment. I kept my head down after that, suddenly very intent on adjusting the levers and settings on my camera.

When one of the photographers suggested the light may be better outside, Pierre Galante—who appeared to have appointed himself in charge of proceedings—asked us all to step out into the gardens, where the two, again, posed stiffly beside a large formal hedge. Miss Kelly made polite conversation with the prince, putting him at ease. She was far more relaxed in front of the cameras, politely suggesting where they should stand to find the best light and angles. We followed a little way behind as Rainier gave Miss Kelly a tedious tour of the palace zoo.

"Poor girl. She looks bored stiff," I remarked.

"She didn't even want to be here," the chap beside me whispered as we followed behind at a discreet distance. "She tried to cancel several times. I think she'd rather be somewhere else with someone else." He winked.

I couldn't help feeling the same way as my thoughts turned back to Emily. I imagined her tugging on my sleeve, determined to ask her question. "Is he really a prince, Daddy? Shouldn't he be wearing a crown?"

Finally, we assembled at the foot of a sweeping marble staircase, preparing for the final shot before Miss Kelly and the prince descended the steps together, now chatting happily and looking far more relaxed.

As Miss Kelly prepared to leave and we packed up our equipment, a reporter asked if she'd enjoyed the meeting.

She hesitated for a moment before replying with a luminous smile. "He is a very charming man."

Diplomacy at its very best.

As everyone was saying their goodbyes, I noticed Galante patting his pockets, an unlit cigarette perched between his fingers.

"Here," I called, emptying the contents of my pockets onto an ornamental stone seat. I tossed a box of matches over to him, like I'd seen someone do in the movies once.

"*Merci*," he called, taking a light before throwing the box back to me.

Miss Kelly appeared at my shoulder as I began to return everything to my pockets.

"Excuse me. It's the strangest thing, but do I know you? I feel as though we've met."

I'd hoped she wouldn't recognize me. "I don't think so." I flashed one of my most charming smiles.

She frowned a little. "Perhaps I'm mistaking you for someone. My apologies."

"No apology needed. You wouldn't believe how often I get mixed up with Cary Grant."

At this, she laughed. "Can I ask what scent that is? It's quite lovely."

I realized she'd picked up the scent of the perfume on the business card, which I'd taken from my pocket to find the matches. "Ah, that would be this," I said, passing the card to her. "It's a small perfume boutique in Cannes. Near the harbor."

She placed the card to her nose, closed her eyes, and took in a breath. She smiled.

"Yes. I know it." She opened her eyes. "I've been trying to remember where it was. May I keep this?"

"Be my guest. I have another."

"Thank you. You've been very helpful, Mr. . . ."

"Henderson. James. My friends call me—"

"Jim. That's right. Well, thank you, Jim."

I watched for a moment as she stepped into the car, surrounded by her people. Dust flew up from the tires as the sleek vehicle drove away. Her job done, extravagant parties and French boyfriends waited for her back in Cannes. Miss Kelly had surprised me. Yes, she was every inch the Hollywood star, but she was more than that. She was warm and gracious. She had a sense of humor. She was also now in possession of Sophie Duval's business card. Perhaps she wanted to thank Sophie for offering a hiding place when I was giving her the chase. Whatever the reason, Miss Duval had clearly left an impression on Miss Kelly. Just as she had on me.

As the little French chap and his Peugeot took me back to Cannes, I reflected on how I'd arrived as a late addition to the film festival assignment, nothing much expected or asked of me other than to take one decent shot of Grace Kelly that we could use to satisfy the British public's fascination with her. Having spent the afternoon in the company of Grace and Rainier, I would leave Cannes with images only a handful of other photographers had. Surely, Sanders would get off my back now.

Buoyed by my eleventh-hour stroke of good fortune, I decided to take one last trip to the perfume shop, keen to leave Miss Duval with a better impression of me. If I could tell her I'd just given Grace Kelly her business card, perhaps she might even give me a smile.

Back at the hotel, I freshened up, chose a shirt that wasn't as creased as the others, topped everything off with my favorite Homburg hat, and made my way back to the boutique. What I was going to say when I got there, I wasn't quite sure. It wasn't in my nature to apologize, but perhaps I'd been a little presumptuous taking a photo of Miss Duval without asking her permission first. She clearly thought I was paparazzi crass. English paparazzi crass, at that. The very worst. And yet, for some inexplicable reason, I wanted to see her again before I returned to London.

Just before I reached the boutique, I stopped to check my reflection in the window of a nearby boulangerie. I adjusted my tie, checked my breath against the palm of my hand, and strolled casually toward the shop, only to discover a sign on the door saying *Fermé*.

I checked my watch. Closed for the day.

Deflated, I shoved my hands in my pockets and made my way back to the hotel. When it came to Sophie Duval, it seemed that luck most definitely wasn't on my side.

QUEEN OF HOLLYWOOD MEETS PRINCE OF MONACO

Grace Kelly in surprise visit to Prince's Palace.
Angeline West reports for the *Herald*.

This may be the first time Grace Kelly has attended the Cannes Film Festival but she is making it count. Yesterday she shook hands with His Serene Highness Prince Rainier III of Monaco in an unconventional meeting believed to have been arranged by *Paris Match* magazine and MGM Studios. Although this reporter didn't manage to secure an invitation to the exclusive *tête-à-tête* held at the Prince's Palace in Monaco-Ville, sources say the meeting was a rather rushed and unremarkable affair.

Miss Kelly made certain to be back in Cannes in time for the gala dinner held in her honor that evening. And her reaction to meeting the reclusive prince? "He is a very charming man."

A Prince Charming, indeed.

Having made quite an impact at her first Cannes festival, Miss Kelly is due to leave town early next week. It is understood she will spend time in Paris before returning to America to begin shooting her new picture, *The Swan,* in which she will play a princess alongside her leading man, Alec Guinness, who will play the part of a prince.

5

SOPHIE

After a steaming bowl of *moules frites* and a glass of rosé, I strolled back to the shop slowly to enjoy the sun on my face and the light breeze blowing off the water. It was a perfect day to luncheon outdoors, and it had refreshed me as much as I'd hoped it would. Maman had called several times over the course of the morning, but I'd avoided her. The familiar stab of guilt swept over me nevertheless, as it always did when I left Maman to her own devices. She needed someone to entertain her, pick out her clothes, clean up after her, and I was the only one to do it. But today I just couldn't face her.

"I'm back," I called out as I entered the shop. "You should have come with me, Natalie. It's a gorgeous day. I had lunch on the terrace at Maxime's."

Natalie shot me a look of warning and pointed to the office door. "Madame Duval is here to see you."

My heart sank, along with my good mood. Ignoring the phone calls hadn't worked after all.

Maman was slouched in my office chair, her hair mussed from the wind, or lack of combing. I suspected the latter. She wore lipstick the color of bubble gum that didn't suit her complexion. Her clothes were badly fitting and in need of being pressed. She was my opposite in every way: loud, sloppy, and eternally unsatisfied with her lot in life. Though she had always been a difficult woman, since Papa's death her flaws were amplified. I loved her on some level—she was my mother after all—but I didn't like her, and I had trouble understanding what Papa, such a gentle soul, had fallen in love with all those years ago. Dealing with her at all tied my stomach into knots.

"Why haven't you returned my calls?" she demanded between kisses to each of my cheeks. "I told you it was urgent."

A whiff of sunshine and jasmine wafted from her skin and I was transported back to the hillside in Grasse, in my white cotton dress and hat, happy amid my flower fields. At least Maman had the good sense to wear one of our parfums in public. It was an interesting choice of fragrance, though. I wondered who she wished she could be. In spite of my acute sensibility of people, my mother's true self evaded me. Pickled in brandy, she also evaded herself.

"Well?" She crossed her arms.

I sighed. It was always urgent with Maman. I should have taken her call. Now the rest of the day would be wasted. "What is it?"

"Michael Lever rang again. He's willing to double his offer."

My eyes widened. The fifty hectares of land we owned in

Grasse had captured the attention of several real estate developers in recent years but I'd been adamant about turning them away. Yet, this offer meant I would never have any debt again, as long as I kept Maman away from Monte Carlo's casinos. But where would our jasmine and cloves and tuberose grow then? To imagine the rows of brilliant lavender flattened by a plow took my breath away. I didn't care about the money, not when it meant destroying everything I loved and had worked for my entire life, and which Papa and my grandfather had worked for so tirelessly before me.

"*Non*," I said definitively. "It doesn't matter what the offer is, my answer is still no."

My mother's eyes tightened. "I am tired of watching you chase your tail, just to make ends meet. We are barely covering our expenses."

I clenched my jaw to hold back the comments that rose to my tongue. She could stop wasting our money on her late-night spending sprees for one, and two, she could work for a change. Oversee the factory so we could cut expenses, or perhaps she could help develop a new partnership with a detergent company, and I could strike that off my growing list of ideas to expand Duval. With the new fragrance I was developing and tourist season just beginning, I could use the help. But dear Maman worked best from her chaise longue with a glass in her hand, barking orders at a maid we couldn't afford.

"I'm on the verge of something breathtaking, Maman. I've just mastered a combination of—"

"You are just like your father," she cut in, waving a hand

dismissively. "Full of ideas and promises that do nothing but cost us more."

A flush of anger rushed to my cheeks. My father had been full of hope and longing and believed in our future, and I was just the same. We were dreamers, Papa and I, but we also worked hard and with passion—neither of which Maman could, or even tried to, understand. Her love of books and gardening, her interest in anything really, had withered away with her drinking, curling in on itself like the leaves on the sunflowers that grew in our garden.

And you are so full of spite, I wanted to say. Instead, I clenched my teeth, trying to tamp down my temper. She always brought out the worst in me.

The doorbell jingled. Natalie popped her head around the office door.

"I'll just pull this shut," she said, discreet as ever.

Maman's gaze flicked to Natalie, taking in her floral dress, the elegant sweep of silver hair brushing her shoulders. When Maman glanced at me again, her lips pinched as if she'd eaten something sour. She had never liked Natalie, but her dislike had only grown over the years.

Graciously, Natalie smiled back at Maman in her ever-charming way, as if she'd noticed nothing, and closed the office door for our privacy.

"I need a little more time, Maman," I said, trying to keep the pleading out of my voice. "I will prove to you this can work and then we won't have to sell. I'm really close."

She rolled her eyes. "You are wasting your time. You know

as well as I do that the market is shrinking. More and more parfum is made from synthetics now. Soon enough, our fields of flowers will be unharvested and left to rot, then nobody will pay the price we deserve."

I hated this topic of conversation, the possibility of the artisan side of the industry disappearing and with it, our craft and all the beauty it brought to the world. Each time my assistants broached the subject at the factory, I shut it down quickly. It crushed the joy I took in my work and destroyed a little piece of my soul. I couldn't imagine a world composed only of chemicals and plastics and manufactured food. Fake this, fake that. Didn't anyone care anymore about the true essence of nature and beauty, and a life well-lived? I couldn't imagine how Papa would feel about this new world in which we lived. In some ways I was glad he wasn't here to see it.

I rubbed my temples. "Maman—"

She held up her hand. "You have until the end of the year to develop this new fragrance, and the spring to launch it. I've already spoken to Lucien about it, and he agrees. If we don't see a solid increase in sales by next summer, we will meet with our lawyer *and* Monsieur Lever."

I smiled. "By next summer I will tell Michael Lever what to do with all of his British pounds."

How to handle Lucien was another matter entirely.

* * *

I breathed a sigh of relief as my mother left. I had just enough time to finish a few things before we closed, and I'd promised myself I wouldn't spend all evening working. For months I had mixed new scents and taken notes until midnight—until my temples ached and rosemary began to smell the same as gravel. My nose needed a rest. *I* needed a rest.

The telephone interrupted my thoughts.

Wiping my hands on a cloth, I reached for the receiver and cradled it on my shoulder. "Bonsoir, Duval."

"Bonsoir, may I speak to Miss Sophie Duval?" A soft American accent drifted through the line.

My heart skipped a beat. I knew that voice. "*Oui*, I am Sophie Duval. How can I help you?"

"Miss Duval, this is Grace Kelly. We met the other day when I took refuge in your shop. I hope you remember."

How could I forget? There was something about meeting one of the most famous women in the world that had a way of sticking with you. "Yes, Miss Kelly. Of course. It is lovely to hear from you again."

"I have your business card here in my hand and it has the most wonderful smell." She laughed lightly. "Of course it does, you're a perfumer." She cleared her throat as if she, too, was a little nervous.

I tried to remember when I had given her my business card. I couldn't recall. . . .

"I'm sorry," she said. "I don't know why I'm nervous. Sometimes I feel like a silly American in this town. The French women are all so effortlessly glamorous."

Her sincerity made me like her even more.

"I'm calling because my sister Lizanne is getting married

soon, and I would love to bring her a special gift," she continued. "One of your luxurious perfumes would be perfect, I think. Do you have a suggestion?"

I smiled as pride swelled in my heart. "I'm sure I can find something she would like, but I need to know a little about her."

Grace paused on the line for a moment as if thinking. "Well, Lizanne is very athletic. Loving and strong. And a little wild. She's the youngest so she always gets her way."

"Can you tell me a few of her favorite things? Her favorite holiday, her favorite clothing, her favorite memory, perhaps? Memories, dreams, and desires are entwined with scent. Since I cannot meet her, I need to grasp a little of who she is to make the best choice."

"I see, yes. Well, Lizanne has done some acting as well. She's pretty and confident. Funny. She loves her old wool sweaters and thick socks, and hiding under a blanket with a book. She never hides who she is, not for a minute. We all wish we could be more like her," she added quietly. "She is rather a favorite."

I wondered if I detected a twinge of sibling rivalry in her voice.

"I know just the thing," I said after a moment's pause. "When should I expect you?"

"I was hoping to . . . well, would you mind having it delivered to the Carlton hotel on Friday? I'll be here another few days before the festival ends and I leave for Paris, but I won't have time to stop into your boutique before then. My schedule is tight, with the film festival and the press."

I felt silly for assuming she would call to the shop to pick it up herself. Of course she wouldn't. She was Grace Kelly. "I will deliver it myself."

"Would you?" Grace was clearly delighted. "That would be wonderful. Why don't I meet you in the lobby around seven o'clock? Would that be convenient?"

"Perfect," I breathed, unable to contain my excitement. I would be meeting Grace again, and even better, she wanted one of my parfums!

"Terrific. I look forward to it."

"Grace, I'm sorry, just one more thing?"

"Yes?"

"Did someone give you my business card? I like to make a note of my referrals." I couldn't believe I had been so remiss as to not give her a card myself.

She laughed lightly. "You won't believe it, but you remember that awful press photographer who chased me into your shop? James Henderson is his name. He was at a photo op with me at the Prince's Palace in Monaco. I recognized him immediately, although he acted dumb and made out that we had never met. He turned out to be a nice enough fellow. He emptied his pockets to give someone a light and I recognized the fragrance from your boutique on the card he was carrying and, well, voilà, as you might say!"

I gripped the phone a little tighter. That photographer had given her my card? How had he found himself in the palace in Monaco? Hesitantly, I said, "He proved to be useful after all, then."

She laughed. "I suppose he did."

"Thank you, Grace. I will be at the hotel on Friday with the perfect fragrance for your sister."

I hung up the phone, buzzing with joy. I nearly skipped to the display shelves and studied the array of fragrances. Lizanne Kelly, based on Grace's description, was a tomboy, confident and friendly, but she probably didn't realize she wanted to be soft and feminine at times, even a touch exotic. I ran my hand over several bottles. *Nuit Douce*. That was the one. I gift-wrapped it in a dainty black box tied with silver ribbon and slipped it into my handbag.

Later, as I left the shop, I wondered why James Henderson had done me the kindness of passing my card along when I'd been so rude to him. *"To be a parfumeur is to believe in magic, Sophie. We must learn to trust our instincts, to accept that there isn't always a practical explanation, but to let things be."* I smiled at the memory of Papa's words, tugged a shawl around my shoulders against the cool evening air, and headed home as the horizon blazed with a glorious sunset.

6

JAMES

London

They say the man who is tired of London is tired of life, so I was relieved to find myself falling for her grand old charms as soon as I stepped off the plane. There was something comforting about the murky drizzle and the stuffy awkwardness with which friends and family greeted each other. For all that I'd enjoyed the easy alfresco atmosphere of Cannes, returning to dependable old London was like pulling on a favorite woolen cardigan, worn for comfort rather than style, the first thing you reach for when you take off your shirt and tie at the end of the working day. Yes, London was cold. Yes, the sky was grayer than an African elephant, but it was home. It was also the only place in the world where I could see my stubborn, curious, funny little girl.

Except I couldn't see her, not like any normal father could see his daughter. Even if I did have a box of special French bonbons for her, I couldn't see Emily without first having to navigate a tricky labyrinth of prior arrangements with her mother. Dealing with Marjorie was like dealing with a talking calendar: "Not today, James. We already have plans." "Sunday? Emily has Sunday school. You should know that by now." "I'm afraid Saturdays are inconvenient."

Our conversations followed a well-worn path. Even as I dialed the telephone number, I knew that my plans to see Emily that afternoon would be firmly dashed.

"You can't just show up on the doorstep and expect us to drop everything so you can spend time with her," Marjorie huffed. "You dash off on this whim and that whim. . . ."

"They're called assignments, Marge. It's my job to dash off. The news tends not to work around Emily's rigid schedule."

"Which is why you were an impossible husband and an unreliable father. Emily needs routine and stability, James. Not another 'Wish You Were Here' postcard from God knows where. Honestly, you're infuriating."

Marjorie Loftus (as she was, once again) was a barrister's daughter, which made it difficult to argue with her without feeling as if you were being cross-examined in the witness box. She'd said it so often, I expected the words *Honestly, you're infuriating* would be inscribed on her headstone when the time came. I had loved her once, albeit briefly. The hangover of war makes for peculiar decisions and actions. Ill-judged peacetime romances were inevitable, as were the resulting children. Of course I did the honorable thing and married her, although we both knew it would never last. It was almost a relief when she left me for the other chap. Horace. Harvey. Whatever he's called.

After a particularly terse conversation, it was eventually agreed that I could see Emily on Wednesday, after school. The bonbons and I would have to wait a little longer.

* * *

Monday morning arrived with blue skies and birdsong, as if London was mocking my silly affection for her comforting gray woolliness. I felt unusually jolly as I walked to Clapham Common station to begin my commute to Fleet Street. Sanders always got in early so I expected he would be waiting to deliver his verdict on the photographs I'd dropped through the office letterbox on my return from France. He wasn't one to mince his words, and the photographs weren't, after all, quite what he was expecting. Given the circumstances, I had no business being cheerful, but London put on an impressive performance that morning, like a vaudeville showgirl, all sequins and feathers and fluttering fans.

I stood on the right side of the escalator, content to let my thoughts stray back to Cannes while frantic city workers rushed past, determined to get to the office a minute or two quicker. It struck me that—fond as I was of dear old London—I hadn't seen enough of the Côte d'Azur or, more specifically, of Mademoiselle Duval. Like when a broken movie reel whirred to a halt halfway through the picture, I felt cheated, the story left tantalizingly suspended in a projection booth. I wanted to know how it ended.

I wrestled my way onto the Northern line train, northbound to Tottenham Court Road, avoiding eye contact with the pretty brunette who got off at Waterloo along with the man with the limp. I smoked two Pall Malls as I read other people's newspapers over their shoulders before changing to the Central line, eastbound, to Chancery Lane. My commute was one of the few predictable things in my life. I liked the little oddities of the routine. It was nice to switch off, let my feet take me where they needed to go instead of having to consult travel documents and maps and interpret incomprehensible road signs as I so often did when I was on a foreign assignment. Spat out of the Tube station as if I were a dazzled mole, I was propelled along the street in a tsunami of suits and bowler hats toward the office on Fleet Street. The familiar smells of tobacco and furniture polish made me smile, despite the knots in my stomach.

The office always felt smaller when I returned from an assignment, the staffers' and secretaries' lives having shrunk a little while mine had expanded in a fog of Gauloises cigarettes and petite dogs and irate perfumers. How could they bear to sit there, day in, day out? Where was their sense of adventure? An egg sandwich, rather than the usual meat paste, was change enough for some, but not for me. I grew restless if I sat still for too long, and with Teddy at the desk beside me, it was perhaps inevitable that his outlook on life had started to rub off on me. While I did my best to forget about the war, Teddy preferred to talk about it. "The fact that we came home in one piece is a lesson," he'd say, "that life should be absolutely and irreverently lived, not tolerated and—God forbid—secretly loathed." Teddy had a knack for saying just the right thing to prick at my conscience.

"Morning, Jim."

"Morning, Walsh." I threw my jacket over the back of my chair and sat down to check my calendar of appointments. It was empty. "What mood is he in?" I asked, leaning around the desk to see George "Bulldog" Sanders prowling around his office.

"A bad one," Walsh whispered, as Sanders opened his office door.

"Henderson!" he bellowed across the row of desks.

As I stood, I did a double take at Walsh, who still looked dreadful. It seemed the bad oysters had done a real number on him. He was noticeably thinner, dark circles ringed his eyes, and his hair had taken on a slightly greasy tinge. "You sure you should be here?" I asked. "You look bloody awful, and I mean that in the nicest way possible."

"Henderson, now!" Sanders shouted again, his face going slightly purple.

Walsh shrugged and wished me good luck.

I walked, as casually as I could, into Sanders's office. "Morning, boss."

"What the hell happened to you?" he barked as I sat down in the chair opposite his, the teak desk narrow enough that he felt unpleasantly close. Within punching distance, certainly.

"Boss?"

"In Cannes?" The thing with Sanders was that you could never be sure if his question needed an answer, or needed you to shut up and let him keep talking. I guessed correctly. This was the latter type. "First you spectacularly miss the Kelly money shot of her arriving at the festival," he continued, "and then you give me these?" He pushed the photographs of Grace Kelly and Prince Rainier toward me. I was quite proud of them, pleased to have caught some of the more honest moments of informality between the posed shots: Miss Kelly fixing her hair, the prince adjusting his tie. "Whose bloody stupid idea was this?"

"The movie editor at *Paris Match*," I explained. "A terribly French chap called Pierre Galante." My exaggerated French accent as I pronounced his name was a misjudged attempt at humor. Sanders glowered, clearly not in the mood for facetiousness. "His wife is Olivia de Havilland. The actre—"

"I know who she is."

"Of course you do. Anyway, apparently Galante and de Havilland set up the meeting between Kelly and the prince after meeting her on the train from Paris to Nice. The magazine wanted an angle for the film festival that would appeal in France, as well as abroad. America, more specifically. Make hay while the Hollywood sun was shining. That sort of thing."

Sanders rubbed the back of his hand across his lips after he drained a mug of coffee. "Who the hell is this Prince Raymond, anyway? I didn't know France had a prince."

"Rainier," I corrected, copying the pronunciation I'd heard in Monaco. *Ran-yey*. "He's the Prince of Monaco, actually. It's a principality. Like the Vatican City." I picked up one of the photographs. "He was awkward as hell. According to the chap I traveled to the palace with, he'd never met an American woman before. I don't think he had the faintest idea what to say to her."

I thought about the American nurses I'd met during the war. If I'd had any sense, I'd have asked one of them to marry me and I'd be going home to a hot dinner and hotter kisses instead of warmed-up leftovers and dodgy heating. But life had blown me in a different direction.

Sanders wasn't really listening. He flicked irritably through the photographs spread out across the desk. "Why is Kelly wearing her grandmother's curtains? She looks a fright. Her hair's a mess. Even I can tell that, and I'm a man."

I lit a cigarette, offering Sanders one as an olive branch. He declined. I already knew the conversation wasn't going to end well.

"The meeting with the prince was shoehorned into a tight schedule," I explained. "There was some problem with a power outage at her hotel that morning. She couldn't style her hair properly, or iron the dress she'd planned to wear. Something like that."

Sanders waved me on, bored of Miss Kelly's fashion dilemmas. "You seem to know an awful lot about her."

"I'm a good listener."

He laughed mockingly and stood up, his chair legs scraping against the floor, setting my teeth on edge. "You're paid to be a good photographer, Jim, not a good listener." He sighed and ran his hands through his hair. "And what about Kelly? Was she impressed by this prince?"

"I don't think she could have cared less about him to be honest, boss. I got the distinct impression she'd have preferred to be back in Cannes with that French actor she's friendly with. Aumont?"

"And, of course, you didn't get any photographs of her with him?"

I shook my head.

Sanders leaned forward, pressing his palms against the desk. The smell of stale sweat from a shirt evidently in need of a wash made my eyes water.

"Jesus, Jim. I wanted red carpets and diamonds, gossip and Hollywood glamour, not this stuffy formal claptrap with a prince nobody's ever heard of. They look like a pair of hostages let out on a day trip to the park." He shoved the photographs roughly back across the desk toward me. "I'm sorry, Jim. You're not a bad chap, or a bad photographer come to that, but I honestly don't know what's wrong with you lately. Whatever it is, it isn't helping me sell bloody newspapers!" He sighed and slumped into his chair. I knew what was coming. "I'll pay you to the end of the week."

I took a long drag on my cigarette. "So, that's it?"

He nodded. "That's it."

The phone rang. He made a shooing gesture as he picked up the receiver.

That was it, then. Even Grace Kelly and a prince couldn't save me this time.

I skulked back to my desk and flopped down into my chair.

"Well?" Walsh leaned back in his chair, pencil behind his ear, talent and ambition oozing out of his well-constructed genes.

I made a slicing gesture across my throat. "I'm done."

"Really?" He glanced toward Sanders's office. "What did he say?"

"That my photographs of Kelly and the prince looked like a hostage crisis."

I could tell Walsh wanted to laugh, but he was diplomatic enough to save it for the pub after.

"I'm sorry," he offered.

"So am I." Ten years brought to a screeching halt. Just like that.

"Maybe it's time for a change. Do more of that artistic scenery stuff you're always on about. Maybe he's done you a favor."

I appreciated the attempt to throw a silver lining around my cloud, but in all the years I'd known Sanders, the only favors he'd done were for himself.

The office was unusually quiet as I packed up the few things from my desk: a photograph of me and Walsh in uniform, a photograph of Emily as a baby, a battered copy of *Moby Dick* that I'd been reading for two years and wasn't even halfway through, an old flashbulb from my first press camera. It wasn't an awful lot to show for my time at the paper.

I left without sentiment. Without regret. I also left without my wallet, which made everything rather awkward when I returned for it a moment later and had to go through the goodbyes all over again. "It's *au revoir*, not goodbye," I said, repeating the words I'd used just a few minutes earlier. The secretaries smiled thinly from their row of desks. They were already clattering their typewriter keys before I'd closed the door behind me.

By rights, I should have gone straight to the Thames with bricks in my pockets, but I made my way home with a surprising sense of acceptance. As I rummaged in my pocket for change for the evening paper, my fingers found Sophie's business card.

Duval was printed in swirling black typeface on the front. I was about to toss it into the litter bin when the last remnant of the scent and the memory of the look in her eyes made me pause. I slipped the card back into my pocket. I wasn't tired of London, or of life. I was simply tired of being alone.

The sunset that evening was as pretty as the glass of rosé I'd abandoned in a Cannes restaurant to run after Grace Kelly, a chase that had led me to a small perfume boutique, and to an intriguing woman who had enchanted me even more than Hollywood's stars. And then I remembered. I still had a photograph of Miss Duval, waiting to be developed.

7

SOPHIE

Cannes

When Friday arrived, I paced in front of the mirror. The last few days I'd thought of little else beyond meeting Grace; what I should say, what I should wear. As evening fell, I walked to the Carlton hotel, forcing myself to be calm and appear relaxed, to be confident in my choice of perfume, and in myself. Once inside, I took in the elegant décor of marble and smooth wood paneling, the plush curtains and wonderfully fragrant floral arrangements. I searched the faces of the guests milling about, but Grace was nowhere to be seen. I stood by the reservation desk for ten minutes, but still, she didn't show. My mood deflated a little. Perhaps she'd forgotten. I'd give her another twenty minutes—she was a movie star, after all, and had places to be—and if she didn't show, I would leave the package for her at the desk.

As I glanced around the lobby, my gaze settled on the restaurant. Perhaps she'd meant I should find her there? I headed for the podium where the maître d' greeted me.

"Bonsoir, madame. Do you have a reservation?" He put a gloved finger on his registry.

"Not exactly." The man's lips pinched, but I continued. "I'm meeting someone here. Miss Grace Kelly. She's expecting me."

He squinted in suspicion until his eyebrows formed a straight line. "And your name is?"

"Sophie Duval. Miss Kelly asked me to drop off a wedding gift for her sister."

He made a scene of running his fingers over the list of names carefully documented in his reservation book, once, twice, and a third time, his forehead scrunched and lips pressed together. At last he said, "I am sorry, madame, but unless your name appears on this list, I cannot let you inside. You understand."

I felt my cheeks flush with embarrassment—and disappointment. I should leave the parfum at the front desk and get on with my evening. I pulled the beautiful package from my handbag.

"Sophie, is that you?" Grace appeared behind the maître d'. "It just occurred to me they might not let you inside since I didn't put your name on the list. Lucky, you've just arrived!" She extended a hand covered in a black silk opera glove that tapered to her elbow. "It's nice to see you again."

Grace looked stunning in a black Oleg Cassini dress, her hair styled into a perfect blond bob curled at the nape of her neck and around her chin. I was glad I'd worn one of my best dresses, though it wasn't nearly as elegant as hers. But then, who was ever as elegant as Grace Kelly?

I took her hand. "The pleasure is mine, Grace."

Her gaze dropped to the package in my hand. "Is that for me?"

"The gift for your sister. I hope she likes it."

"I'm sure she will. Even the packaging is beautiful!" She held up the box of *Nuit Douce,* running her fingertips over the satin ribbon. "Lizanne will love it. As for payment, I'll send a courier to your boutique tomorrow, if that's all right?"

"Of course." I beamed at the dazzling smile Grace offered me. She was pleased, and I, in turn, was thrilled. Though excitement fluttered in my belly, my nerves tingled with worry. What if she didn't care for the fragrance? Selecting a parfum for someone else could be presumptuous, in particular without meeting them. Who knew what truly lay in a person's heart? This was the key to unlocking the perfect scent, unearthing their secret selves. I pushed the doubt from my mind, scolding myself for second-guessing my instincts.

"Say, Sophie, would you join us for a drink?" Grace offered. "I'd very much like to thank you for hiding me in your boutique that day, and now this." She held up the box of parfum.

"Oh, you're very kind, but I really couldn't, I . . ."

She smiled encouragingly. "Oh, do join us. Please." She leaned forward and lowered her voice. "I'm bored of all the man talk, to be honest. I could use another girl to gossip with."

I hesitated. Mingling with Hollywood stars was far beyond my level of comfort, but mischief danced in Grace's blue eyes and I couldn't resist. "Well, in that case! *Oui,* I'd be delighted. Thank you!"

"It's all right, Charles," Grace said, giving the maître d' a look that could melt ice. "She's with me."

He grew flustered as he straightened his bow tie and stepped aside.

I followed Grace, trying not to stare at the way her dress swayed as she moved, and focused on the beautiful south-facing wall composed almost entirely of windows looking out at the bay.

As we approached Grace's table, I faltered. Several gentlemen dressed impeccably in light summer suits were laughing and talking and enjoying expensive-looking cocktails from the Carlton's renowned bar. It appeared I was interrupting a private gathering. Regretting my uncharacteristic impulsiveness, I stood awkwardly at the edge of the table, waiting for direction from Grace.

"Why don't you sit here, by me." Grace patted the seat next to her and I slid in beside her gratefully. "Everyone, this is Sophie Duval," she said, waving her hand at me with a flourish. "She's the one I told you about, who hid me from that pesky photographer. She owns a lovely little perfume boutique, and her creations are simply divine. She just personally delivered a package for my baby sister. I think I should thank her properly with champagne, don't you?"

"Here, here!" a gentleman said, taking a sip from his martini. "Get this lady a glass!"

The others smiled and nodded their agreement as a waiter set a champagne coupe before me.

Grace was gregarious and confident amid her peers, quite different from the soft-spoken woman I'd seen in my shop and talked with on the telephone.

After the champagne had been poured, she leaned in closer to me and said, in a conspiratorial whisper, "Lizanne would kill me if she heard me call her my baby sister in public, especially in front of a studio executive and Hitch." She laughed playfully and I was struck again by her charm.

"We won't tell your sister," I replied with a smile. And then I processed what she had said. "Hitch? As in Alfred Hitchcock?"

"The very same."

I scanned the faces of the four men at the table. And there he was, sloping nose, balding, plump and jolly, his cheeks stained pink from booze and laughter. I could hardly believe it. I was sitting among Hollywood royalty—and I couldn't be more out of place. I glanced down at my simple white linen dress tied at the waist with a light blue sash, my tasteful but simple heels.

Grace placed the box of parfum on the table "Mind if I try it out first? We won't tell Lizanne that, either!" She winked playfully.

"Please do," I said. "It's called *Nuit Douce*. The scent evokes the gentle caress of a warm Mediterranean night. Every ingredient is from the hills near my workshop in Grasse. In fact, it's one of my favorites." I felt the anxiety drain away and my limbs relax as I described the different varieties of flowers we grew and how we harvested them. This was my world, one in which I moved freely and with confidence.

She opened the monogrammed box and removed a small glass stopper from the bottle inside. A soft smile tugged at her lips as she inhaled the scent. Her eyes widened. She inhaled again, deeper this time. After a moment, she closed her eyes. "It's . . . I'm . . . it's perfect," she breathed. "There's something almost sparkly about it. I smell a hint of the sea. I'm on a yacht under the stars, tethered to a dock in the Mediterranean, the scent of roses on the breeze." Her eyes flew open. "Sophie, you have a gift."

My head spun with the praise. "You're very kind. I was raised among flowers and perfume. My papa taught me everything he knew."

"You all just have to smell this," Grace gushed, and passed the precious bottle around the table. "If you don't buy something from Duval for your wives and girlfriends before you leave Cannes, then I can't speak for your intelligence."

Everyone laughed, and passed the bottle around, remarking appropriately as they each smelled my parfum. I thought of how proud Papa would have been. He would have celebrated with a carafe of rosé on the terrace amid our fields, and then we would have talked about a million ways to use this opportunity to help promote our name, our reputation. Above all, he would have loved to know Grace. She was the epitome of everything he admired in a person: elegant, kind, effervescent even.

"I see empty glasses all around. How about another bottle of champagne?" A striking man who'd been introduced as Jean-Pierre, and couldn't take his eyes off Grace, motioned to a waiter.

"What a wonderful idea, darling," Grace said, her eyes glittering like jewels. "In fact, why don't you stay and eat with us, Sophie? There's no need to rush off, unless you have plans, of course?"

I didn't have plans. I rarely did, except when Lucien insisted I join him at some extravagant party or business dinner. It felt good to make a plan of my own for once. "That would be wonderful." I didn't hold back a grin this time.

As the waiter poured another glass of Dom Pérignon, a bubble of joy rose in my throat and I suppressed the urge to laugh. I rarely let down my guard, and never indulged in too much champagne, but tonight was special. I already knew it was a night I'd never forget.

When *Nuit Douce* reached Alfred Hitchcock, his brow arched in surprise. "You should wear this on set, Gracie. You're going to need it to seduce that prince. He could use a little aphrodisiac to get him going."

She leaned toward me to explain. "He means that my character falls for a prince in a film I'll be starring in later this fall. It's called *The Swan*. Dear Hitch isn't directing this one so he makes derisory comments about it at every opportunity. It's too bad, really. He's my favorite director by far." She winked at him. "Don't worry, Hitch darling. I'll bathe in the stuff and light the prince's fire."

Everyone laughed.

"Well, there's plenty more parfum, should you need it," I said, my tongue loosening beneath the champagne, the company, the wonderful praise for my work. I felt giddy to have a new friend in Grace. She had a natural and elegant way of making me feel welcome. I suspected she did that for anyone who spent time with her.

We feasted on rich bouillabaisse and crab beignets, and the fresh catch of the day served Provençale. To cap it off, they served my favorite pear and hazelnut *clafoutis* for dessert. By the time the sixth bottle of champagne was uncorked and poured, I felt so light-headed I could float away. I'd stopped caring how much my portion of the bill would be, and about the fact that my dress wasn't made by a designer, or that I was the only person at the table not associated with Hollywood in some way. They'd all been so kind and funny and full of vitality, I'd forgotten my usual reserve and laughed along with them.

"Grace, this has been a lovely evening," I said, clutching her hand. "Thank you for the invitation."

"I do hope you'll keep in touch," she said, smiling. "I have a feeling I'll want a lot more of your perfumes."

Another surge of joy flooded my chest. "I'd like that very much."

"In fact, let me give you the address of the studio." She rummaged in her handbag for a scrap of paper and a pen and hastily jotted down an address for MGM Studios in California.

The waiter brought the check and Hitch quickly scooped it up, peeled a wad of cash from his money clip, and handed the bill back to the waiter.

I pushed away my half-finished glass of champagne, too full to consume another drop. I was relieved to be spared my share of the cost. The meal must have been hundreds of francs.

Just then, I caught sight of a familiar form at a table near the windows at the back of the restaurant. I knew that dark, waving hair, the shape of those shoulders in a suit jacket. Lucien.

He'd told me he had dinner plans this evening, but he hadn't mentioned where, or with whom. I frowned as a beautiful platinum-blond woman laid her hand on his arm. A twinge of jealousy put a damper on the fine time I'd had. Should I approach the table? I didn't want to make a scene, and she could very well be another of his cousins. He had so many of them.

At that moment, Hitch threw his head back and belly-laughed at some remark or other, drawing the attention of several other patrons in the restaurant. Including Lucien. He turned to impart an imperious glare at the table of loud Americans when he spotted me.

I waved with my fingertips.

His eyes widened a fraction and then he put on his best nonchalant expression. It was one I'd seen a thousand times as he greeted millionaires and movie stars from all over the world. He wanted to look debonair and unfazed, as if he were just as important as they were. I suppose, in a way, he was. I watched as he excused himself from the table and made his way toward me.

"Sophie?" he said, faltering as he took in the group I was sitting with. "Bonsoir, everyone."

"Hello, dear. Everyone, this is Lucien Marceau." I smiled widely, drawing a look of surprise from the man who was supposed to know me better than anyone. Apparently I didn't smile often enough—or perhaps it was the way I'd slurred my words ever so slightly.

The table greeted Lucien, and he made polite conversation for a minute or two before reaching for my hand. "I see you've all had a fine evening, but I think I'd better escort the little lady home. I can tell she's had a better time than I have tonight." He smiled for the benefit of the others, but I heard the sarcasm in his voice.

They all laughed, and I flushed. Was I that drunk? I'd had fun for the first time in ages, and even among this table of famous names, not once had I felt silly or inferior. Until now. The euphoria I'd felt all night deflated. Cheeks burning, I took Lucien's hand and stood up, brushing the wrinkles from my skirt.

"Sophie was the epitome of charm and quite the conversationalist," Grace said, generously. "I do believe our party will be the lesser without her."

Lucien flashed Grace a smile, but I didn't miss the surprise in his eyes.

"Good night, everyone." I forced the words over my thick tongue and my sudden irritation. "I've had a lovely time. Thank you again."

Grace and I exchanged kisses and with another stab of regret at having to leave, I reached for my handbag.

Lucien gripped me by the elbow and steered me toward the door. "What are you doing?" he hissed. "Getting drunk in front of half of Hollywood! Are you trying to make Duval a laughingstock?"

"I just took your usual advice," I said, pulling from his grasp. "To enjoy myself and forget about my responsibilities for once. I suppose you meant I should only enjoy myself when you see it fitting. Well, maybe your exhausting parties just aren't all that *enjoyable*." Even as I said the words, I regretted them.

He stared at me for a moment, stunned, and then shepherded me through the hotel's main doors. "Clearly you need to sleep this off. Really, Sophie, I've never seen you this way. I don't know what's wrong with you."

He led me into the cool night air. "You should go back inside to your date. It would be rather rude of you to stick her with the bill."

"Is that was this is about? Don't be ridiculous. Barbara is the wife of one of my father's business acquaintances. He asked me to show her around town and take her to dinner, as a favor. I could introduce you to her if you like." His face softened. "You're beautiful when you're jealous, though. You know I love only you."

He reached for my face, but I dodged his hand, still smarting from the way he'd pulled me away from my lovely dinner. I knew he was trying to protect me from looking a fool and that I was being silly, prideful even, but something about his expression—and the way Barbara had laid her hand on his arm—made me dig my heels in. "I'll see myself home. Good night."

With that, I left a shocked Lucien outside the hotel and headed to my apartment.

I enjoyed the tranquility of the old town, preferring the historic Gothic architecture to Lucien's glitzy new buildings in other parts of town. As I walked up the steep cobbled streets, I replayed the conversations I'd had with Grace. Her reaction to the parfum couldn't have been any better. She'd said I had a gift.

A blanket of stars and the sound of the sea escorted me home that evening. By the time I turned the key in the apartment door, the first inklings of an idea for a new fragrance were already dancing on the edges of my mind.

ROMANCE ON THE RIVIERA!

Grace Kelly dazzles at premiere.
Angeline West reports for the *Herald*.

The undisputed darling of Cannes, Grace Kelly, has enjoyed the attention of the world's press, but she had eyes for only one person in the room. Jean-Pierre Aumont was spotted escorting Miss Kelly to a film premiere last night, happily holding her fur stole while she chatted to fellow guests, oozing glamour in a red satin dress, accessorized by a simple string of freshwater pearls and white *broderie anglaise* opera-length gloves.

Despite rumors that Miss Kelly is already involved with Russian fashion designer Oleg Cassini, who is said to have sent the actress a daily bouquet of red roses until she agreed to have dinner with him—and who claims to have created the "Grace Kelly look"—she certainly appears to have fallen for the Frenchman's charms beneath the starry Riviera skies. It is understood they will travel to Paris together when they leave Cannes.

Even Prince Rainier III of Monaco, one of the world's most eligible bachelors, doesn't appear to have been able to turn Miss Kelly's attention away from her Hollywood friends.

8

JAMES

London in the spring was a lovely place to be, even without the security of gainful employment to pay the bills. I'd put in a few calls to old friends, hoping someone might throw a bit of work my way to tide me over. The usual responses came down the line. "Terribly sorry, old chap." "What an awful stroke of bad luck." "I'm sure something will come up." But the fact remained that until something did come up, I was out of work and out of luck. I was, however, also at a deliciously loose end, with an unfinished roll of film and blue skies tempting me outside.

Quite done with chasing Hollywood starlets, I indulged my creative urge and set out for London's green spaces. I pottered around Hyde Park and Regent's Park, photographing the blossoms on the trees, the reflections of the clouds in ornamental lakes, the silhouette of landmarks against the sky. I'd been so focused on getting "the shot" lately, I'd forgotten what it felt like to stop and admire the beauty in everyday things. No need for couture gowns or an army of stylists. Mother Nature really knew how to put on a show. Like the new growth on the trees and the tender spring flowers pushing up from the ground, I felt a sense of renewal, of purpose. Perhaps Sanders *had* done me a favor. Perhaps now I would stop jumping from one assignment to another and think about what it was I actually wanted to do with my life. I was thirty-five. Life was hurtling past and I was in real danger of being left behind.

But a rainy morning two days after my brusque dismissal by Sanders saw me stuck indoors. To distract myself while I waited for Emily's school day to be over, I decided to tinker in my makeshift darkroom and develop some of my recent images, see if I was as good as I'd convinced myself I was.

I covered the small bathroom window with a tartan blanket and stuffed newspaper between gaps around the badly fitting doorframe. It wasn't perfect, but it was good enough, for now. I hoped to have my own studio, one day. There were, after all, some benefits to no longer being married to a woman who didn't see the point of *"all that faffing about with smelly chemicals and things."* Marjorie didn't see the point of photography, of art. She saw only time being wasted and walls being tastelessly decorated with amateurism. I'd often imagined myself set up in a loft apartment in Manhattan. Or perhaps a rustic farmhouse in Scotland, or a villa in the hills above Monaco would suit me well.

I prepared three trays of chemicals: developer, stop bath, and fixer. Working in the dark, I followed the various steps in the process, taking the film from the camera, carefully rolling it and placing it into the first tray, judging the developing time of around seven minutes, agitating the chemical every thirty seconds. I lifted the film from tray to tray, everything done by feel and instinct until I knew it was ready, and hung it on the line above the bath to dry.

There was something about the alchemy of photography that I especially loved: the magic of watching an image appear beneath the dim light had fascinated me as a child as I'd stood beside my father, quietly transfixed by the process. It was my old man who first sparked my love of photography. We'd never really got along the way some boys do with their fathers, all chummy and the best of friends. My old man was more like a stranger who'd moved into our home and wasn't entirely sure what he was doing there. Cameras and photography were our one connection. The only thing that pointed to us being related at all.

Focusing back on the process at hand, I cut the negative of Sophie from the contact sheet. A minute in the developer, a quick dip in the stop bath, and two minutes in the fixer. With each stage she became clearer until she'd fully emerged on the page, and what I saw made me pause.

It was really rather good.

Very good.

Striking, in fact.

The light was perfect, the black-and-white film adding a sense of drama to a moment that was, in reality, nothing more than a shot taken on a whim, as much to annoy her as to amuse me. The instinct to take her photograph had turned out to be a good one. Sophie was beautiful, but not in the usual way. I studied the photograph for several minutes. She wasn't beautiful because she was perfect. She was beautiful because she wasn't. There was anger in those dark eyes, yes, but there was so much more. Confusion. Hurt. Doubt. Passion. She was a collage of emotions and textures, light and dark.

Maybe Walsh was right after all (he usually was). Maybe I *did* have a talent for portraiture. The longer I looked at the picture, the more I wanted to get to know the woman on the page, photograph her again. But how? I'd only met her once—and not in the most positive of circumstances. I settled on sending her a copy of the photograph by way of apology for my rudeness. What was the worst that could happen? She'd toss it into the wastepaper basket in a temper, and I'd forget all about her.

After I'd made several copies of the image, I enlarged one, scribbled the date on the back, and wrote a short letter with my address and phone number, ever hopeful. Taking a leaf straight out of the Teddy Walsh Guide to Living, I walked straight to the post office before I changed my mind.

From the post office, I took the Tube to Parsons Green, arriving a few minutes late for my carefully scheduled appointment with my daughter. I hoped Emily would forgive me for missing her birthday when she saw the box of French bonbons, tied with a cheery yellow ribbon. It was her favorite color and I'd asked for it especially, although it would no doubt only be the contents of the box that would interest her. Much to Marjorie's consternation, and my extreme delight, Emily wasn't a girl for fussy frills and decoration. She would prefer to clamber up a tree and tear holes in her stockings than tie ribbons in her dolly's hair.

She was sitting on the gate, poking a worm with a stick. As soon as she saw me turn the corner at the end of the street, she jumped down and ran toward me, squealing with excitement. "Daddy! Daddy! You're back!"

I broke into a jog, an enormous smile on my lips, everything else forgotten, irrelevant, unimportant.

The box of bonbons tumbled to the ground as she launched herself into my arms.

The yellow ribbon trailed in a puddle of rainwater.

Neither of us cared.

I was the only surprise Emily ever wanted, and she was the greatest gift of all.

9

SOPHIE

My time with Grace and her friends had lit a fire inside me that burned even two weeks later. I spent every waking moment working on ideas for a new line of fragrances, Hollywood inspired. Grace Kelly inspired. I would develop not just one, but three new fragrances: one for everyday, perhaps one for evening, and one—my most exciting new fragrance—for special occasions. This would be Duval's crowning glory. A fragrance to rival any other. I'd launch my new line with beautiful packaging. The only problem was how. I hadn't the slightest idea how I would afford it. With my debts, it would be difficult to find the money I'd need to do it properly.

I bent over my desk in the office, shuttering the doubt, evading the unwanted words of reason from Lucien, and the angry retorts from Maman. I needed peace to work, space to breathe. For now, I'd concentrate on developing the fragrances, and figure out production costs later. I closed my eyes and envisioned Grace's enigmatic beauty, her confidence and humble charm. And there was something else about her, something that couldn't be easily explained. Like sunlight or shooting stars, or the shimmer of light on the sea, always shifting and changing, tantalizingly elusive. All mixed with a deeply vulnerable quality I'd seen as she ducked into my office to hide.

My eyes flew open. I took the *journal de fleurs* from the desk drawer, a gold mine of carefully noted formulas of Papa's parfums, along with years of my own notes, all documented in one precious book. The edges of the journal were frayed and soon the paper would separate from its binding. It had always brought me good luck and I couldn't imagine working without it. Even more precious than the formulas themselves, the book contained pages and pages of dear Papa's handwriting and sketches, hastily scribbled notes and eureka moments underlined three times. The verbena, vanilla, and ginger combination he used for *Délice,* the first parfum he'd made for younger women; and then there was *Ravissant,* composed of violet, oakmoss, and cinnamon, the parfum he'd made for Natalie that became one of our bestselling fragrances.

I ran my hand over the pages tenderly, as if I were soothing Papa's own hand to reassure him it was all still here. Much as I hadn't been ready to navigate life without him, I wasn't ready to lay the journal to rest. And yet that was what I knew I must do. Soon every last page would be covered in ink and I would retire it and store it in a prominent place on my bookshelves. I had already transcribed most of the formulas and stored them in my permanent files. One day I'd find something worthy of replacing Papa's old book, but for the young adolescent who'd watched her dear papa depart for war, the journal was the last thing connecting me to him, and I couldn't bear to break the bonds.

Snatching up a pen, I quickly scribbled down my ideas for the everyday scent. It had to be as enchanting as the woman who would wear it, with a hint of sparkle. Lime and jasmine. I'd call it *Lumière d'Étoiles*. Starlight. Perhaps it should be an eau de toilette, a fragrance that made its wearer feel special each day, not just an expensive parfum reserved for special occasions. Yes, that was it! I could hardly wait until tomorrow to get back to my workshop in Grasse to work on Starlight. When I perfected it, I would package a sample, and send it to MGM Studios as a gift for Grace. If she liked it, she might share it again with her friends. My mind reeled with excitement. Maybe meeting Grace Kelly was the touch of serendipity I'd needed.

A short knock came at the office door before it opened.

"The post is here," Natalie said, laying a large envelope on the desk. "It's postmarked from London."

"Who do I know in London?" I hoped it wasn't more tedious correspondence from Michael Lever's solicitor. I tore open the flap and pulled out a large sheet of glossy paper. A handwritten note said: *Sophie Duval. Cannes. May 1955*. I turned the sheet over and gasped at the image on the other side.

Of me.

My lips were parted as if I were about to say something. Thick, dark waves fell to my shoulders and a stray curl lay softly across my forehead. My skin glowed in the black-and-white film, my lips appeared lush, sensual. Rows of perfume bottles gleamed behind me as if they held beams of light. But it was my eyes that were the focus of the image. Dark pools of anger and curiosity. It was a version of myself I'd never seen before, one I didn't even know existed. I put my hand to my mouth, my eyes wandering over every shape and play of light.

"Let me see," Natalie said, moving to my side to peer over my shoulder. "Goodness, Sophie, it's beautiful. Whoever took it?"

"That press photographer. Remember the tall Englishman who chased Grace into the shop?" I remembered the scent of leather and balsam that lingered after he'd gone, the casual way he'd lit a cigarette, his maddeningly playful smile.

"Oh yes. Him. He was quite attractive, wasn't he, in a very English sort of way."

I knew Natalie was looking for a reaction, so I ignored her remark. "He turned his camera on me just before he left. He was so rude."

"Well, he is certainly talented. It's a stunning shot of you. Is there a note?"

I turned the envelope upside down and shook it. A single sheet of writing paper tumbled onto the desk, along with another photograph. I unfolded the page.

Dear Mademoiselle Duval,

It seems Grace Kelly isn't the only one who takes a great photograph. In fact, I think I prefer this image of you to any I took of her. I thought you might like to have it. If not, throw it in the bin. I'll be only slightly offended.

Also, since my editor didn't care for the shots I took of Miss Kelly and her prince (and now I find myself without a job as a result), I thought you might like to have one. It isn't every day one gets to hide a Hollywood star in their shop, is it? Of course I knew she was there. I just didn't want to press you any further.

I also wanted to ask your advice on a suitable perfume for a special lady in my life. Something light and subtle, yet feminine. Nothing too mature. I can't stand those old-lady perfumes. You know, those overpowering flowery smells that give you a five-day headache.

My address is below. There's no need for you to reply, but perhaps there's also no need for you not to.

James Henderson (Jim)

I laughed. Why should I recommend a perfume for his girlfriend or wife or whoever she was? So presumptuous. The photograph of Grace Kelly and Prince Rainier was similar to those I'd seen in the *Paris Match* article about their meeting, but James had captured something else. Something more intimate. There was a particular look in Grace's eye. A look I recognized from when I'd first met Lucien and fallen for his charms.

Natalie put her hands on her hips. "Well? Are you going to write back to him? This Jim?"

I paused a long minute. "It's James. And don't be silly, Natalie. He's an opportunist, that's all."

I scrunched the note into a ball and tossed it into the waste-paper basket.

Natalie turned to leave the office. "I hope you're not going to throw that beautiful photograph away."

I fussed with some papers on the desk, grateful when the doorbell jingled and Natalie left to attend to the customer.

I looked at my photograph again and plucked the note out of the basket. *My address is below. There's no need for you to reply, but perhaps there's also no need for you not to.* I gave in to the smile that brimmed at my lips.

10

JAMES

Despite Sanders's disregard for them, I was pleased with my photographs of Grace Kelly and Prince Rainier. Admittedly, they weren't the typical Hollywood glamour shots one would expect from the Cannes Film Festival, but I liked them more because of that. They were different. Fresh. Honest, in a way that so many other images of movie stars weren't.

Everyone had seen the diamonds-and-fur, red-carpet-ready Grace Kelly. But how many had seen her as a young woman, a little out of place, without the benefit of hairstylists and dressers? The more I studied the images, the more I found Grace's girl-next-door vulnerability utterly charming. Besides, there was something about the way she and Rainier had walked and talked and laughed—perhaps even flirted a little. My images captured some of their more relaxed interactions: the unintentional brush of a hand, the obvious delight in their demeanor, the easy way they'd said goodbye as if it wasn't a goodbye at all but very definitely an *au revoir*. I liked the sentiment: *until we meet again*. In some ways, it echoed my own thoughts about France. Although I'd returned to London, my short trip to Cannes nagged, like a loose thread pulling me back to the Côte d'Azur.

When a postcard from France arrived, the pull became even greater. The clunk of the letterbox woke me from a pleasant afternoon nap in a sunny patch on the sofa. There were, it transpired, some benefits to being without gainful employment.

Grasse, France

Mr. Henderson,

Thank you for the photographs. You and Grace Kelly are both full of surprises, it seems. Thank you, also, for passing my business card to her. She has taken an interest in my parfums, and I am very grateful.

I'm afraid I wasn't at my most welcoming that day in the boutique. If you find yourself in Cannes again, please do call by so I may thank you in person. As for recommending a fragrance, if your wife/girlfriend/mother could let me know what scents she enjoys, I will be better informed to help her.

Sophie Duval

"Wife/girlfriend?" I snorted. Of course she'd jumped to that conclusion. I intentionally hadn't mentioned that the perfume was for my daughter.

Instinctively, I pressed the postcard to my nose. It was scented with her perfume. I closed my eyes, instantly transported back to the small shop, the glass shelves and mirrors, rows and rows of Alice in Wonderland–style bottles. And there, in front of me, Sophie. Eyes like cherries soaked in a fine brandy. Questions and hope etched across her face.

"She wrote back, Winston!" This, to the cat, whom Marjorie had been perfectly happy to leave with me since Harvey (Harry?) was allergic to felines. Winston stretched languorously in the windowsill, unimpressed by my news. Winston wasn't impressed by many things, other than the saucer of cream the lady at number 13 left out for him on Fridays. Lucky for him. "She actually wrote back!"

I was surprised by my reaction, by how pleased I was to know Sophie had thought about me. Not only had she written, she'd invited me to visit. I was also delighted to have played a part in leading Miss Kelly back to her. It felt like a decent thing to have done, albeit unintentionally. I knew some good had to come out of my assignment in Cannes. The place was far too lovely for it all to have ended in my being fired and Teddy struck down with food poisoning.

And as much as Sophie's words caught my attention, so did the image on the front of the postcard. A glorious Technicolor vista of sun-drenched flower fields—purple lavender, bright yellow sunflowers, and something impossibly pink—converging on a central image of a medieval church spire, across which the words GRASSE, CITÉ DES PARFUMS, CÔTE D'AZUR, FRANCE were printed. Scenery. Color. Vibrancy. History. Everything I'd always wanted to photograph.

"Winston! That's it!" I slapped my hand onto the sofa cushion, sending the cat scrambling from the windowsill.

For all the picture postcards I'd bought and sent to Emily over the years, it had never occurred to me that somebody had photographed the images on the front. Seascapes and mountains, rolling fields and rugged cliffs, ancient fishing villages and grand palaces. "That's it! That's bloody it!" I sat up straight and ran my hands through my hair, turned the postcard over and rotated it onto its side, peering at the minuscule print along the left margin: the address of a photography studio in Cannes.

Carte Postale. "Les fleurs de Grasse."
M. Roux. Real-Photo. Cie des Arts.
15 rue Meynadier, Cannes.

I washed and shaved, suddenly eager to spruce myself up and do something with my life.

Winston regarded me with slant-eyed suspicion for the rest of the day, as if he already knew what I was thinking.

❉ ❉ ❉

I posted my letter of enquiry to Monsieur Roux at the photography studio in Cannes the next day. *Freelance photographer looking for work for the summer. Available to start immediately. Samples of work enclosed. Speaks fluent French. . . .*

I regretted the last part as soon as I dropped the envelope into the letterbox, but it was too late to get it back. I could learn French. Eventually.

The reply arrived two weeks later. Teddy kindly translated it for me over a beer beside the Thames. It was the least he could do since he'd encouraged me in my plan to write to the studio.

He still hadn't shaken his cough and despite his insistence that he was perfectly well, I wasn't convinced. The cheekbones he'd had when we were new recruits in the British army had returned at an alarming rate, but whenever I mentioned his health he told me to stop fussing.

"You'll make someone a wonderful wife one day," he said, with his trademark sarcasm. "Or maybe there's a new career for you in nursing. Jim Nightingale. Has rather a nice ring to it, don't you think?"

I told him to stop mucking about and tell me what the letter said.

"It says something along the lines of *Come to the studio at your earliest convenience. I would like to meet you and see more of your work.*" He put the letter down and picked up his pint. "Will you go?"

My silence was the only answer needed. I was already thinking about how I would tell Emily.

* * *

Of course, she wanted to know why I had to go back to France so soon. I'd always encouraged her to ask *why*, telling her it was the most important question of all, much to the irritation of her mother, who had no patience for her daughter's endless questioning. Ironic really, for a barrister's daughter.

"I just need to, Em, that's all. Grown-ups need to go away sometimes. For work. And to think."

"Why can't you think in Clapham?"

Damn it, she was good. "Because it rains too much in Clapham, darling, and the light isn't very good for taking photographs. I need more sunshine to take nice images for the postcards. More flowers."

"Do they have lots of flowers in France?"

"Oh yes. They grow in enormous fields in a place called Grasse. It's terribly pretty. I know a lady there who turns the petals into perfume."

Emily was amused by the notion of flowers growing in a place called Grasse, and fascinated by the idea of making perfume. "Does the lady use microscopes and a laboratory? Can I go with you? It sounds very nice there."

There was such innocence in her nut-brown eyes. Such unconditional love written all over her freckled cheeks. I sighed and pulled her into the nook of my arm. I'd overdone it on the flowers.

"You know I'd love to take you with me, darling, but you have school. Besides, it's actually quite boring taking photographs of fields and things. And the French food can be very funny. They eat frogs' legs, you know." At this she quailed. "And escargot," I added, knowing what would come next.

"What's escargot?"

I leaned my lips to her ear. "Snails."

At this she squealed and all thoughts of coming with me were, thankfully, forgotten. I couldn't bring myself to tell her that if everything went well, I could be gone for the whole summer. Or longer.

As she swung her legs beneath the bench and threw stale bread to the Regent's Park ducks, it struck me how life could be so wonderfully simple and yet so complicated at the same time.

I had been a very ordinary child, and an unremarkable schoolboy. A wife, a couple of children, and a steady job was all I'd ever imagined for my future until war came thundering toward me with the Nazis' bombs. They didn't just blow up our cities and reduce our homes to rubble. They shattered our hopes and relationships and futures. I could still hear the barrage of machine-gun fire raining down on us on the beaches at Normandy, could still taste the salt on my tongue and feel the gritty crunch of sand against my teeth as I lay facedown in the dunes and accepted my fate. Teddy was right. When you've stared death in the face and come out the other side, life takes on a different meaning. It becomes a privilege, not a right. It makes one rather more aware of the need to make it matter in some way.

"I'll write, darling," I said breezily, as if a few scribbled lines on a postcard were a perfectly acceptable substitute for being there. "And I'll telephone." Emily brightened a little at this. Our phone calls had become something we both looked forward to. "I could always talk to Mummy and Thing about letting you visit, once I'm settled," I added, and instantly regretted it.

"His name's Humphrey." She giggled.

"I know. But Thing suits him better, doesn't it?"

"Could I really visit?"

Why I'd even suggested the idea I didn't know. It would be a logistical nightmare and I could only imagine the consternation it would cause Marjorie if I so much as mentioned it. And yet, would it really be so difficult? Emily was growing up. She had my sense of wanderlust, an urge to see more of the world than Clapham High Street and Piccadilly Circus.

"Perhaps," I conceded. "We'll see. And in the meantime I'll send lots of postcards to tell you where I am and what I'm doing." And whom with, I added quietly to myself.

She liked this idea, especially the postcards because she and her best friend, Winnie Matthews, had started to collect stamps, and with Winnie's daddy secure in his job at the Tate & Lyle factory at Limehouse and definitely not the type to go off to think and look at flower fields, Emily would easily have the most stamps by the end of the year.

I ruffled her hair. "See. Not so bad, is it?"

She didn't answer, only brushed crumbs from her skirt and asked if it was time for tea.

We ate sticky buns, made paper airplanes from our napkins, and conjured up silly names for the customers in the tea rooms. It was a game we liked to play. Ignatius Popplewell drew the biggest laugh from Emily, although I liked the Sergeant Rufus Buzby she bestowed upon a pompous-looking fellow with a splat of mustard on his tie. Tea with Emily was one of life's perfect simplicities. Knowing that it would be the last for a while, I treasured that particular afternoon more than most.

Back at the flat, Emily entertained the cat with an old shoelace while we waited for Horatio to pick her up. As well as stealing my wife and being allergic to cats, he was a terrible timekeeper.

When he eventually arrived, he tooted the car horn from the street. He didn't want to interact with me any more than I wanted to interact with him.

"This is for you, Daddy," Emily announced as she grabbed her school satchel and hat, placing her hands furtively behind her back. "Close your eyes and hold out your hands."

I did as instructed. My fingers closed around a sheet of paper. "Whatever can it be?" I said. "Is it a chocolate cake?" Emily giggled. "A teddy bear? I've got it—it's a hairbrush."

"Daddy! You're being silly! Open your eyes!"

The page was filled with brightly colored flowers and a huge yellow sun. My heart filled with bottomless joy—and sorrow—at the sight of it.

"It's wonderful, darling. Are you sure you didn't have any help?" I winked.

"Now you have lots of flowers and sunshine. So you can stay in Clapham."

I could hardly breathe as I wrapped my arms around her and kissed the top of her head.

"Bye-bye, Daddy," she called as she stuck her head out of the car window, her pale little arm waving madly.

"Bye, darling girl," I whispered, as I waved back.

I watched and waved until the car turned the corner and then I stepped back inside, closed the door, and turned the latch, simultaneously locking Emily safely away into the very special place she occupied in my heart.

Later that evening, as a light London drizzle speckled the windows, I pulled the old steamer trunk out from beneath the iron bedstead and finished packing. Whether destiny or distraction, France had asked me a question and I would only find the answer by going back.

11

JAMES

Cannes
June

The journey to France was as journeys are: tedious. A no-man's-land between the past and the future. A twilight world of poor sleep and forced interactions with other people and a perpetual state of mild anxiety about modes of transport arriving on time: the boat to Calais, the train to Paris, the train to Cannes. It was one of life's great conundrums that for someone who traveled so badly, travel was such a necessary part of my job. Or had been. And hopefully might be again.

The French countryside slipped invisibly past under cover of darkness like an SOE agent, while I tortured myself with *Moby-Dick,* relieved to finally turn the last page and bid farewell to Ishmael and his white whale. I left the book in the gentlemen's conveniences, hoping to never see it again, and was pleased to discover, in return, an abandoned copy of *To Catch a Thief* in the dining car. It was a decent read, vastly improved by the absence of revengeful whales. Its French Riviera setting was the perfect distraction for the remaining miles to my destination.

Cannes, when I eventually arrived, was just as I remembered, if much quieter without the glitz and glamour of the film festival. Like a tired host at the end of a party, the town had gladly kicked off its shoes and poured itself a drink. It was a much nicer place without the Hollywood circus, and I soon relaxed beneath its spacious warmth.

After checking in to a petite pension in the old town run by the equally petite and rather elderly Madame Bisset, who sang opera to wake up her guests, I made my way through the narrow streets to the address of the photography studio on rue Meynadier. I wasn't entirely sure what I was going to say when I got there, but I'd learned that spontaneity was the best way to approach many situations in life. The sun was already high in the sky and the heat prickled at the back of my neck. I fanned my face with my hat and dabbed at my brow with my handkerchief.

When I eventually found the premises, I was greeted with a sign declaring it to be *Fermé*. This was becoming something of a habit. I checked my watch. One o'clock. Damned French with their leisurely lunches. It was a wonder anyone ever bought or sold anything.

Deflated, overheated, and resolving to return later, I followed my nose to Sophie's shop. I'd intended to wait until tomorrow to visit, hoping to announce my appointment as a postcard photographer at Real-Photo, but there was little point in delaying since I found myself at a loose end. I quickly checked my reflection in a tobacconist's window, adjusted my hat, straightened my collar, and added a Gallic shrug for good measure. "Come along then, James," I said to the crumpled-looking chap staring back at me. "Get on with it. And do try not to be a complete donkey's ass this time."

A bell jangled above the boutique door as I pushed it open. The scent of her fragrance hit me instantly.

Miss Duval wasn't at the counter, or anywhere to be seen. I casually inspected a row of gleaming glass bottles.

"Bonjour?" I called out, my French accent as ridiculous as ever. "Hello!" I felt like a fool. Perhaps I should leave it until tomorrow after all.

I was about to turn and make a hasty retreat when movement from a door behind the counter made me wait a moment longer. She was here. Should I be charming, or confident? Apologetic, or play the hapless buffoon? Which James Henderson would be required to elicit a favorable response?

As it transpired, I needn't have worried. It wasn't Sophie who appeared through the door, but an elegant, more mature lady with incredible cheekbones and lips as red as ripe strawberries. She carried that particular air of effortless continental panache that the Englishwomen I knew would never pull off.

She looked a little surprised to see me and rattled something off in French. Only when she'd finished did I politely explain that *je ne parle pas français.*

"Sophie? Miss Duval?" I added, with questioning hands. "*Je m'appelle* James Henderson. From *Londres*. London?" I really wished I'd paid more attention to my French master at school.

"She wrote to me," I explained, pulling her postcard from my breast pocket as evidence.

At this, a smile of recognition. "Ah! Monsieur Henderson. *Très bien*." The woman held out a pale, neatly manicured hand, and switched effortlessly into perfect English. "I'm Natalie. Sophie's assistant. She is taking lunch. But you must wait. She will be pleased to see you, monsieur."

"Really?"

Natalie chuckled lightly, leaving me no less certain whether she was being sincere or sarcastic. "Come, come," she said, as she wrapped both her hands around mine as if we were the oldest of friends. "You must wait in the office. You like pastis, *non*?"

Evidently it didn't matter whether I liked pastis or not because Natalie poured me a generous glass regardless, insisting I sit in the chair beside the desk and make myself comfortable.

The office was small and neat, like Natalie. Vials of colored liquids stood in a locked cabinet. Reams of bright ribbon and tissue paper in all imaginable shades reminded me of a favorite sweetshop at the end of the road when I was a young boy. Official-looking paperwork was neatly stacked in a tray on the desk. A signed photograph of Grace Kelly stood in a silver frame beside a powder-blue Remington typewriter. I couldn't help peering at the photo. Miss Kelly was the epitome of Hollywood elegance in a shimmering silk dress, elbow-length opera gloves, and pearl earrings. The image was everything Sanders had wanted from me, and that I'd spectacularly failed to provide. Beside it was the photograph I'd taken of Kelly and Rainier in the palace gardens. She'd kept it, then. But I didn't see the photograph I'd taken of Sophie.

"Taken when she won her Academy Award," Natalie explained, noticing my interest in the photograph of Grace Kelly. "*Très, très belle.*" She picked up the image I'd taken. "You do not care so much for the Hollywood glamour, *non?*"

I shrugged. "I prefer to photograph people as they really are. Honest. Undecorated. My real passion is landscapes, actually."

"Huh. Then you are in the right place. We have the most beautiful scenery." She studied the photograph of Grace and Rainier a moment longer. "They like each other, I think," she remarked as she replaced it on the desk.

"How can you tell?"

"Oh, I can tell. Woman's instinct." A playful smile crossed her lips.

I took a hesitant sip of the pastis. "Will she be long at lunch?" I asked, wincing at the sharp tang of aniseed. "And do you mind if I smoke while I wait?"

Natalie assured me that Sophie would be no more than ten minutes but yes, she did mind if I smoked. "Tobacco is not the friend of parfum, or *les poumons.*" She pointed to her upper back and took a deep breath before acting a terrible cough.

"Ah, lungs," I translated.

"*Oui.* Lungs. You should not do it."

She said this with such certainty and a dismissive wag of her finger that I almost agreed there and then to never smoke again. I slipped the packet of cigarettes into my pocket and while Natalie returned to the shop to attend to a customer, I sat like a schoolboy waiting to see the headmaster—or, in this case, headmistress—and wasn't entirely sure why I'd come at all.

12

SOPHIE

The beautiful June weather brought plenty of sunshine and a warm, fragrant breeze. The roses and mimosas were in full bloom, while the smell of the sea changed from briny and metallic to a rich mélange of seaweed and sunbaked sand as the waves lapped at the shore. Yet even with the good weather I was distracted, and during lunch with Lucien at Café Madeleine, I had trouble banishing my terrible mood.

I glared at the stack of papers Maman had sent on to me from Michael Lever. She'd insisted I at least consider the proposal from the real estate developer, the shark after my land in Grasse, and though I would never admit it to her, I *had* pored over the initial sketches of his development ideas and suffered through the sample advertising campaign and preliminary sales materials. We could pay our debts and make a sizable profit should we sell, but Lever would make a fortune with his housing development and hotels. Lever was arrogant and came from new money—and I had the feeling it wasn't of the most honest variety. In fact, he reeked of something not quite right. I would no sooner sell my family's legacy, now over one hundred years old, to a dishonest man, and an Englishman at that, than I would chop off my right arm.

I signaled to the waiter for a vodka martini. My nerves were fraying rapidly.

"You're having a drink?" Lucien asked, as he laid down his fork and knife across his plate. "But you're finished with your meal. It seems your Hollywood friends have rubbed off on you."

I didn't bother to dignify his comment with so much as a look. He knew I was very prudent with alcohol, and that I'd had good reason to be with Maman's incessant drinking.

"I need to spend some more time studying this proposal," I said. "And I don't have anything pressing to work on this afternoon anyway. You go on. I know you have a meeting."

He covered my hand with his and squeezed gently. "All right, but Sophie, it really is a tremendous offer. You should seriously consider it."

I scowled. "I know you like the idea of selling, but it's not that simple, Lucien."

With his thumb, he traced my bottom lip. "You're adorable when you pout."

I bristled. I wished he wouldn't do that: treat me like a child.

He reached for the bill, paid it swiftly, and said, "Would you like me to walk you back to the boutique?"

I shook my head. "I'm going to read through this last section one more time. Go. I don't want to hold you up."

He moved around the table to kiss me on the forehead. "I'll

leave you to it. See you tomorrow." I watched him pull on his hat and stride to the door, the eyes of the other female diners following him.

After another sweep through the proposal, I was sick to my stomach at the sight of it. I left the martini untouched, packed up my things, and headed back to the shop.

I walked along the avenue, relishing the sunlight on my face, trying to push away thoughts of Michael Lever for now.

Natalie was waiting for me in the shop doorway. She grabbed my hand as I entered. "At last. I thought you'd never come back. There's someone waiting for you, in your office."

"Oh?" I was surprised at her enthusiasm. "Who? Anyone special?"

"You'll see for yourself." She smiled and brushed a curl behind my ear.

"Why all of the secrecy?" I walked around the counter and through the office door—and stopped.

A man sat in the chair beside my desk, studying the rows of parfum vials I kept in a cabinet. His Homburg hat gave him away. He turned and looked up, and I met a pair of caramel-colored eyes that were imprinted on my memory.

James Henderson.

"Mademoiselle Duval," he said brightly, an enormous smile on his lips as he stood up and walked around the desk, knocking over the framed photograph of Grace Kelly in the process and fumbling a little to right it. "Bonjour!"

I stared at him, mouth agape, unable to conceal my shock. "Monsieur Henderson!" I shook his hand quickly and pulled mine away. "I . . . what a surprise. What brings you to Cannes?"

"You invited me here. Remember? And I had a devil of a journey. France becomes endless when you're on a train traveling across it."

Had I invited him? I was certain I'd merely told him he was welcome to stop by, should he ever be in Cannes again.

He laughed at my stunned expression. "I've surprised you, I see. You really aren't good at hiding your feelings, Miss Duval."

He made a move to step around me just as I moved in the same direction. We bumped into each other, my face landing squarely in the middle of his chest. The scent of balsam and leather hit me and—instinctively—I inhaled deeply. But something more clung to his clothing and his skin, something warm and earthy. Something all his own.

"Oopsy-daisy!" He beamed, his hand against my shoulder. "I'm sorry."

My head filled with a rush of ideas about what I'd pair with his scent. Something light to accentuate his earthiness, or perhaps a lively head note like grass. Yes. *Yes.* When I realized I hadn't moved out of his way, I felt my face go hot and rushed around the corner of the desk.

"I wanted to thank you for the lovely photograph you sent," I said, changing the subject to detract from the awkward moment. "You are very talented, Mr. Henderson."

"James. Please. Call me James."

"Very well. James."

He smiled again. "You make it sound so exotic with your accent. *Schames!*"

One eyebrow arched, I said defensively, "Your accent is the one that is *exotique* here."

He grinned. "I suppose that's true." He leaned casually against the wall. "I'm glad Grace Kelly was in touch. I hope you don't mind that I gave her your business card. It must be quite awful to find yourself in demand by the crème de la crème of Hollywood. Exhausting, I should imagine."

He really was disarmingly charming.

I laughed softly. "You were kind to refer my boutique. If I can repay you—"

"I think I have an idea how that might be done," he said, standing a bit straighter. "I find myself in France on something of a wing and a prayer. I was inspired by the postcard you sent, actually."

"Inspired?"

"Yes. When your postcard arrived, it struck me that somebody takes the images on the front of all these picture postcards people send to one another. Long story short, there's a photography studio a few streets away that specializes in postcard scenery. I sent a letter of enquiry to the owner, a Monsieur Roux. Since he's short-staffed, here I am, hoping to be hired for the summer! I called by a while ago, but they were *Fermé,* as is so often the case in France."

I ignored the jibe. "I know the shop, yes." I frowned. "And I'm sorry you were fired from the newspaper. That's a shame."

He shrugged. "It was time. The boss didn't appreciate my style."

"And you wish to live in France for the summer?" I stared at him in awe. How easily he could pick up his life in a snap and move on to the next thing without looking back. I could no more leave my home than I could give up making my parfums.

I was wedded to my land and my *parfumerie*, tending to it and cherishing it with every fiber of my being. But this man had clouds for feet, never touching the ground, at least not for long.

He nodded. "I was wondering, and please say no if I am overstepping the mark, if you might be able to help me when I meet Monsieur Roux. My French is bloody hopeless. If you could make an introduction, explain who I am, I'd be ever so grateful. And then I promise I'll leave you alone and never trouble you again. Unless you want me to. In which case, perhaps we could go for a drink on the waterfront. Or not. Either way. And I'm rambling, so I'll stop."

I busied myself with some paperwork on my desk, trying to hide the smile that tugged at my lips. "I have several appointments this afternoon, but I'd be happy to make a telephone call on your behalf. I can spare Natalie for a while. She can assist you if he is able to meet you. If you'll wait just a moment."

"Really? Would you? That's very kind." He sank back into the chair, his eyes never leaving mine.

I cleared my throat and picked up the telephone, trying to focus on the numbers. Something about him made me forget everything else. When I looked up again, he winked and I blushed, wishing my emotions didn't show so clearly on my face. A hazard of being a Scorpio; a passionate soul. As Monsieur Roux answered the phone, I already knew this wasn't the last I'd be seeing of this persistent English photographer.

13

JAMES

Luck, it would seem, was on my side once again. Not only did Miss Duval make a phone call to Monsieur Roux to explain who I was, she also arranged for Natalie to accompany me as translator.

"No time like the present," Sophie said when she'd hung up the phone. "He will see you at three o'clock."

I was so struck by her—mesmerized by the musicality of her accent, like a carousel with its dips and falls; the intensity in her eyes; the way she tucked her hair subconsciously behind her ear—I forgot to reply. In my mind I was framing her, picking the best angle and lighting, wondering which lens and filters to use.

"James?" she prompted.

"Gosh. Sorry. Miles away. Three o'clock? Terrific. *Très terrifique! Merci.* I believe I very much owe you a drink."

Finally, she relaxed a little and allowed herself to smile. "I believe you very much do!"

It was agreed that I would meet Natalie outside the studio in an hour, so I thanked Sophie again and took a stroll along the promenade, enjoying the heat of the sun on my back. As three o'clock approached, I made my way to Monsieur Roux's studio.

"*Vite! Vite!*" Natalie scolded when she saw me ambling along the cobbled street. "*Merde!* You are late."

I apologized, kissed her cheeks in the French way, and gladly let her take charge as we entered the studio. After Natalie had spoken to a rather disinterested-looking woman at a small desk, she explained that Monsieur Roux was also running a little late. I liked the chap immediately.

We sat together on a battered sofa that sagged dreadfully in the middle and almost consumed us among its faux-velvet cushions.

"Could I see them?" Natalie asked, indicating the manila envelope on my lap that constituted my portfolio.

"My photographs?"

"*Oui.*"

Natalie flicked through the images, admiring the scenic shots I'd taken in Cannes, the winding switchback roads snaking along the cliff tops, and the close-up shots of the bougain-villea I'd taken at the palace in Monaco. It was strange to think I'd taken them only a matter of weeks ago, and how much had changed since. Here I was, in a photography studio in France with the promise of a drink with Miss Duval to look forward to, and if the next few minutes went smoothly, maybe a new job doing something I actually enjoyed.

"You are very good with the landscape. The flowers. You see their personality."

"Thank you. You have a good eye, Natalie."

"I was a student of art before I became a student of parfum. I see you are also a student of little people," she added, as a photograph of Emily tumbled onto her lap. "She is a delight."

"My daughter," I explained, taking the photograph and slipping it into my jacket pocket. "Emily."

Natalie looked at me, a sparkle in her light-gray eyes. She carried that rare beauty of experience and maturity.

"She is here with you?" she asked. "With her maman?"

I winced at the potential simplicity of it all. How much easier everything would be if that were the case.

"Regrettably, no. My daughter is in London." I wished she wasn't so far away. She would love France. "But she is also in here," I added, placing my hand to my chest.

Nodding, Natalie patted my knee. "She will wait for you. Children are very, how do you say . . ." She stared up at the crumbling plasterwork on the ceiling as she fished around for the right word.

"Patient? Understanding? Forgiving?" I offered.

She shook her head at each of my guesses before clicking her fingers in victory. "*Loyal.* That is the word. Children are very loyal. They do not easily fall out of love with us."

I hoped she was right.

"You liked to photograph Miss Kelly," she continued, as she reached the shots I'd taken at the palace. She tapped the images with a neatly manicured fingernail. "They are unique pictures. This is not her usual style of dress for a start." I smiled as I remembered how derisory Sanders had been about the floral dress, making jibes about his grandmother's curtains. "I think Rainier likes her," Natalie continued. "See? The way he looks at her in every photograph, even when she is looking elsewhere. He is a little bit in love with her, perhaps."

"He was in awe of her, that's for sure."

"It is love. I am certain." She passed the photographs back to me, a knowing smile blooming in her cheeks.

"Can you always tell? When someone is in love."

"Oh yes. It is very easy when you know the signs." She leaned closer to me. "You like Sophie a little?"

"Well. Gosh, I . . ."

"Monsieur Henderson?" A stout fellow limped toward us, rescuing me from the need to reply.

"Yes. *Oui.* Bonjour," I mumbled, pulling myself up and assisting Natalie to extricate herself from the sofa before offering my hand to him. "James Henderson. Jim. Jolly nice to meet you."

As we shook hands, Natalie chattered away in French, introducing me and, from the little French I understood, exchanging pleasantries about the weather and possibly about somebody's son.

Monsieur Roux seemed satisfied. "You are a little *fou,* monsieur?" He chuckled. "Crazy? I like it!"

He directed us to follow him through to a bright office with canary-yellow walls and a collection of potted plants arranged on one side of a dilapidated desk. A clock ticked the wrong time on the wall. A very small dog snoozed in a very large chair beneath a shuttered window.

"Cigarette?" Monsieur Roux asked, pushing a packet across the desk toward me.

I took one gladly, sacrificing my lungs for the benefit of a shared vice and ignoring the pointed stare Natalie offered beside me. If I'd learned anything from my years working for Sanders, it was that a pint in the pub or a ten-minute discussion about cricket over a cigarette was as important as any boardroom meeting. Monsieur Roux nodded his approval as I lit the cigarette and held it between my thumb and index finger in that particular French way.

The interview, if that's what it was, was efficient. It was conducted almost entirely in a language I couldn't understand, but my photographs elicited a series of approving nods and *very beautifuls* ("*très belles*"). After Natalie had explained that I was keen to find work in France for the summer while something more permanent came up in England, I found myself shaking Monsieur Roux's hand and agreeing to start on Monday. My first appointments would be to photograph the old town of Villefranche-sur-Mer and the flower fields in Grasse. Later in the summer, I would capture the jasmine festival there. I agreed enthusiastically to everything, my mind whirling with possibilities.

"Natalie, I don't have a car," I whispered as Monsieur Roux stepped out of the office for a moment to fetch some paperwork for me to sign.

"Then you have luck, Monsieur. I have an old Vespa scooter rusting in the garage," she replied with a wink. "I used to fly around the Riviera on it. They're great fun."

I imagined Teddy laughing at my good fortune.

Back at the boutique, as I thanked Natalie, she took my hand in hers.

"You never answered my question," she said.

"Which question?"

Her eyes flickered with amusement as she placed a hand on my arm. "I asked if you like Sophie. *Oui,* or *non*?"

I could see Sophie through the window behind Natalie, chatting easily to a customer, her hands animated, passion in her eyes. She came alive when she spoke about her creations, sparkled like the sun on the water in the harbor.

"*Oui,* Natalie," I whispered. "*Très oui.*"

Laughing at my dreadful French, Natalie disappeared into the shop, the familiar scent of Sophie's perfume escaping before she closed the door.

I stood for a moment, breathing in the scent, before I turned and walked toward the water, a grin as broad as the Seine on my lips, a sense of renewal and possibility washing over me like a mist of fine cologne.

14

SOPHIE

July

Summer on the Côte d'Azur was like a bee sting, a sudden injection of action and adrenaline, and I found myself longing for the calmer days of autumn and winter, the seasons when I could disappear into my workshop in Grasse without being missed. For now though, I would have to find a balance. This was our busiest season. I needed every customer I could get.

I arrived at the shop early to make a head start on the day. It wasn't often the post gave me a reason to be excited, but today was different. Usually, there were overdue bills to pay and complicated letters about land registry, and title deeds from Lucien's solicitor to pore over. But an airmail letter sent from California set my blood racing. I sliced through the top of the envelope and unfolded the thin piece of paper inside.

Dear Miss Duval,

I'm writing on behalf of Miss Grace Kelly, who has asked me to inform you that her sister, Lizanne, adored the perfume you selected for her. So much, in fact, that Miss Kelly would like to request another bottle be sent as soon as possible, for her mother. A check is enclosed to cover the expense.

You may send it to Miss Kelly, c/o MGM Studios at the above address. She sends her best wishes and wanted to express her sincere thanks once again for your kindness to her in Cannes.

Yours sincerely,
Morgan Hudgins
Publicist to Miss Kelly, MGM Studios

I read the letter again, running my fingers over the address. MGM Studios. Hollywood! Maman would never believe it and Natalie would burst! *I* couldn't believe it. Grace wanted more of my parfums! This was the perfect opportunity to send her a sample of *Lumière d'Étoiles*. Goose bumps traveled over my arms and up my neck as I smiled at the perfect serendipity of it all.

Starlight, the everyday fragrance in my new line, had come quickly and easily, like a gift, but the special-occasion parfum was missing something to really elevate it. I'd affectionately called it *Maison*—Home—until I came to know it and understand it, to memorize its head, heart, and base notes, to feel at one with it like the rhythm of my breathing. *Maison* would be my star fragrance, the most luxurious, the cornerstone of the new line, and hopefully of Duval.

As I'd tested *Maison* over the past months, trying out slight variations in proportions to get the formula right, I'd grown frustrated with my lack of inspiration. Only pedestrian scents and ideas came to me. The fragrance had to be sensational and unique, and so did its launch. As much as I hated to admit it, Maman was right. Synthetics were encroaching upon the industry, and fewer people were willing to pay for authentic parfum, making it more and more expensive to produce. I felt the familiar rise of panic in my chest and reached for my journal. If I was to make any more progress, I needed to spend more time at my workshop in Grasse. Not just a few days snatched here and there, but long continuous weeks.

As I closed the office door, one of James's photographs caught my eye. Since his arrival, he'd stopped into the shop often to solicit an opinion from Natalie and me on a photograph he had taken, or to tell us how irritating the French found a tall Englishman traipsing around the Côte d'Azur with his camera. Nevertheless, he had impressed Monsieur Roux with his work and had already made himself quite indispensable. Several of his images had been put into print, and, of course, he hadn't been able to resist writing a note on the first postcard bearing his photographer's credit and delivering it through the letter-box. It still sat on my desk.

Much as James had impressed Monsieur Roux, he'd also left an impression on me. After meeting for a drink to celebrate his being hired, we'd met on other occasions for no particular reason at all, other than that we enjoyed each other's company. James made me laugh, and laughing wasn't something I'd done easily since Papa's death. My good humor bloomed in response to being around James. Even Lucien had noticed it. I didn't tell him what, or who, was the cause.

"You're here early this morning," Natalie commented, interrupting my thoughts as she breezed into the office, and placed a freshly baked *pain aux raisins* on the desk. She looked at me quizzically and folded her arms across a sea-green blouse. "What is it? What's happened?"

"What do you mean?" I asked, innocently.

"That smile on your face. You can't hide things from me. You should know that by now."

"Oh, Natalie! You won't believe it. Look!" I thrust the letter into her hands and perched on the edge of the desk as she read it.

"*Non!*" She gasped. "This is wonderful." When she finished reading, she hugged me with all the love and support of a mother, and we clung to each other for a moment, absorbing the goodness that infused the room.

We chatted over coffee, dreaming up scenarios of Hollywood stars wearing Duval. Our name on everyone's lips. Our fragrances on everyone's skin. A dream for any perfume house.

Later, when we'd both calmed down a little, the conversation turned to my missing ingredient for *Maison* and my desire to spend more time in Grasse.

"Talking of which, are you going to take James up on his offer?" Natalie asked.

"To meet him in Grasse today, you mean?"

She nodded. "You know very well that's what I mean."

"Well, I need to go anyway, so I suppose so," I said casually, blushing at the thought of scheduling my day around him.

"If you want to catch the early bus, it's leaving in twenty minutes. You'd better go." Natalie kissed my cheek. "I'll see you Monday. And congratulations again. It's wonderful news. Grace Kelly! It was so clever of me to suggest we hide her in the office, wasn't it?"

I pressed my nose to the glass as the bus rumbled past a sunflower farm, the flowers' bright yellow faces crowned with green tendrils reaching for the sun. The lavender fields bloomed a vibrant royal purple and would soon be harvested, the jasmine to follow. In pockets of forest scattered throughout the craggy landscape, thickets of wild strawberries grew in the shade. Their happy red faded as the bus climbed the winding road to Grasse. I touched a divot in the windowpane with my finger. Reds, purples, yellows, and greens, and the aqua sea of the coast. The landscape was saturated with color. Beautiful Provence and the Côte d'Azur. My home. I couldn't imagine living anywhere else.

Once settled into the house (and relieved to discover Maman wasn't home), I took my bicycle from the barn and dropped a bouquet of fresh flowers and a few other items into the basket. In my good mood I rang the little bell tied with checkered red-and-white ribbon. Before heading to the factory where I'd arranged to meet James, I had time to check in on my favorite neighbors. I'd been negligent with the busy tourist season in Cannes, and I missed them. My first stop would be the boulangerie and then on to Madame Clouet, a war widow in her sixties who'd never been blessed with children of her own. She'd known me since I was a child and I enjoyed spending time with her, gossiping like hens about the happenings in town and our mutual love of the cinema. Once a month, I escorted her to Cannes to see the latest film. She was never happier than when we huddled into our seats, her hand in mine, the steady whirr of the projector in the background. I smiled as I turned from the gravel path. I'd told Madame Clouet about meeting Grace Kelly, but she didn't believe me. I could hardly believe it myself.

Inside the boulangerie, the aroma of warm bread permeated the air. A large man with red cheeks and an apron tied tightly around his bulging middle bustled behind the counter, selling his delicious creations to loyal customers.

"Bonjour, Monsieur Renault," I said, when it was my turn. "I see you've neglected your poor vase again." I slid the assortment of fresh flowers I'd brought into the vase near the cash register. "Now your shop will look as pretty as it smells."

He smiled. "You haven't been around much, Sophie. Old Jacques mentioned you yesterday. He's waiting to finish that game of chess."

Dear Jacques. My other elderly friend. Monsieur Jacques had family in Paris, but he lived alone in Grasse, and though he didn't seem to mind most of the time, he was always happy to see me. He would be next on my list. The truth was, as much as I pretended these dear old friends relied on me, it was really the other way around. They kept me up-to-date on all the latest goings-on in town and since they had all known Papa well, they also loved to reminisce about the good old days. They were a connection to my past. They were part of the nutritious Grasse earth I was firmly rooted to.

"What will it be today, Sophie? Your favorite *tarte au citron*?" Monsieur Renault asked cheerily.

I chose a slice of asparagus quiche for lunch later, a baguette with olives for Jacques, and a boule of rustic bread dotted with raisins and nuts, Madame Clouet's favorite.

After coffee with Madame Clouet and a short visit with Jacques, I cycled up the hillside to the factory on the outskirts of town. I could hardly wait to check in on my employees, and afterward, spend time tucked away inside my workshop with *Maison*. As for James, it would be . . . well, I wasn't sure what it would be like to show him around the beating heart of Duval. It felt a little like exposing my heart to him: my secrets and desires.

I made my way to the entrance of the factory to find James already there, a striking figure leaning casually against the doorframe, his hat shading his face, shirtsleeves rolled to his elbows, and a camera slung around his neck. He always looked as if he were about to embark on a safari. I wondered if he ever wore a suit and tie, but I couldn't imagine him without that hat glued to his head. Nevertheless, I suspected he would look handsome in formal wear. Surprised by the turn of my thoughts, I fanned my face against the heat gathering in my cheeks and that of the sultry afternoon.

James made an exaggerated gesture of checking his wristwatch when he saw me. "I was on time for once," he said, grinning. "And I believe you're five minutes late."

"I wasn't sure if you would remember our appointment," I replied, ignoring his attempt to tease me.

"I thought it was more of a casual arrangement than an appointment as such, but, yes. I remembered. And here I am!"

I hid a smile as I fished in my basket for the key and unlocked the door, placing one hand on my wide-brimmed sun hat as a hot wind kicked up and threatened to blow it away. The sun was fierce, and I'd dressed in preparation to spend at least part of my day outside checking on the workers in the fields. There was so much to do every time I came to Grasse, but I loved it—the labor, the processing, the creating.

"Are you ready for a tour, monsieur?" I asked.

"*Mais oui oui,*" he said.

I laughed. "You really shouldn't try to speak French. You do it very badly."

"And you shouldn't be so serious," he replied, wiggling his eyebrows.

I rolled my eyes in mock irritation but a smile touched my lips. My gaze shifted to the camera around his neck. "I'd prefer if you didn't take photographs inside, but you can walk the grounds after and take any that you like in the flower fields."

He frowned briefly and then said, lightly, "What are you making in there, top secret weapons?"

"Of a sort," I said, leading him inside. "A *parfumeur*'s formulas can take years to perfect. They are what make each parfum special, valuable. Should they become common knowledge, they would lose that unique something that makes them a work of art, and for which our customers will pay good money."

"Of course. Everything has a price. I suppose only the wealthiest can afford to smell the best."

"Something like that," I conceded. If only he knew what a

tightrope I was walking between financial ruin and potentially life-changing success. "*Bon*. Here is the lobby."

I stood back to admire the chandelier, the silk curtains at the windows, and the tiles that fanned across the entrance in a charming but traditional checkered black-and-white pattern. Bouquets of orchids and lilies stood in sconces and vases around the room. A luxurious settee stood against the far wall, overlooking the view of the rambling streets and the fields and valleys beyond. Maman had always accused Papa of being too extravagant in his choices, but he wanted only the best for Duval, and I admired him for that.

"We're here in the center of town to entice tourists to tour the factory, and of course buy our parfums and soaps. We have eight rooms in total—office, workshop, storage room, gift shop, and the rooms where the machinery is hard at work, of course." I waved at my receptionist who answered the telephone. "We're on the smaller side, compared to the likes of Fragonard and Molinard, but we have all the space we need. For now."

James raised an inquisitive brow. "For now? Are you planning to expand?"

"One never knows what the future holds." I smiled at his expression. He was clearly impressed by what he'd seen already. I was surprised by how much it mattered to me. "And this is Juliette, my receptionist and all-around problem solver."

"Bonjour, Mademoiselle Duval. Monsieur," Juliette said, her eyes alighting on the tall stranger beside me.

"Any messages?" I asked, ignoring her interest in James.

"Yes. Michael Lever called. Again. And an Eduard Beaumont of Beaumont Parfums, and two real estate agents from Paris." Her pencil-thin eyebrows arched in suspicion. I hadn't told the staff about the proposed buyout. I didn't want to worry them, but I knew how they talked among themselves. They weren't being disloyal, they were just concerned for their futures. As was I.

Irritated, I snatched the list of messages from Juliette's hand. Maman had clearly continued to talk to agents without consulting me. With all of them crowding me and interrupting my thoughts, I'd never develop my star fragrance in time.

"Are you all right?" James asked, noticing my reaction. "You look a little pale."

"Thank you for the compliment," I said, dryly. "It's just my mother, and—" I clamped my mouth closed, not ready to spill all the family troubles in the middle of the factory lobby, especially not to someone who didn't understand the first thing about my family or the legacy I was trying so desperately to protect. "*Rien du tout.* This way."

Swallowing the lump of emotion in my throat, I ushered James through a set of double doors into the factory itself. We passed the extraction room, where glass shelves were lined with flowers pressed in grease to retrieve their essential oils. Across the room on the far wall, animal fats were heated for the same purpose. I explained that after extraction, the parfum oils would be blended and distilled. I pointed to our giant copper vats fitted with all manner of tubing and pressure gauges.

"One fragrance can have hundreds of ingredients, which is why it's so important to document the formulas carefully." I slipped my hand inside my shoulder bag to verify my journal was there, a habit. When my fingers met its soft leather cover, I withdrew my hand, satisfied.

"It's fascinating," James said, carefully studying each piece of equipment and machinery. "I had no idea there were so many processes involved, or that it was all so exact."

"It is a science as well as an art. A bit like your photography, I think."

As I talked about the various growing seasons and answered James's questions about the way we harvested the blooms, the swell of frustration and panic began to ebb away. I would finish the new parfum, make it the most ethereal, dynamic, and evocative scent I'd ever developed, and save all this, save Duval. I'd already made progress with it, and the new line was well on its way with *Lumière d'Étoiles*. I would find the money to fund it all, even if I had to beg for it. I'd figure out what to do with Maman from there.

"Do you ever work on this floor?" James asked, staring intently at the assistants as they supervised the machinery.

"Not often, no. I spend most of my time in my workshop or in the office."

He stood next to me as we watched for a moment, and I was acutely aware of his presence. There was something about James that I couldn't put my finger on. There was an energy about him, an air of untapped potential, like a volcano about to erupt with something wildly brilliant. Yet while he glowed with a natural confidence, I sensed he was also unsettled beneath, as if he were searching for something to repair a deep wound. The combination of strength and fragility was alluring, and a formula began to spring to mind: bergamot for its clean sharp scent, amber for its almost animalistic sensibility—and moss for the grassiness I'd thought of before. A Duval fragrance for men.

Quickly, I dug through my bag for my journal and flipped to a clean page. At the top I wrote his initials, *JH,* and jotted down five ingredients as well as a few character traits to describe him. Satisfied, I snapped the book closed and slipped it back into my bag.

James watched me closely. He stood only inches away, curiosity shining in his eyes.

"What are you writing there?"

My breath hitched at his nearness. "I had a flash of inspiration. For a gentlemen's cologne."

"And I suppose you can't share it." He tapped the side of his nose conspiratorially.

"*Pas de chance.*" I smiled.

He raised his hands in mock surrender. "Fair enough. I suppose your perfumes are like an undeveloped photograph. Everything is there in the frame, but only in the final processes of mixing and developing does the image come to life and you finally see what it was you'd tried to capture when you looked down the lens. We are alchemists, Miss Duval. Magicians!"

I laughed at his enthusiasm. He sounded liked Papa. "That is true."

At the next workstation, I gestured to a woman moving slowly through a mound of fresh soaps. "These tables are where the perfumes and soaps are packaged before being put on display in our store or shipped to other parts of the country, and the world. We don't have a strong international presence yet, but we have some products placed in London and Amsterdam, and many in Belgium."

"It looks as if it's color-coded, or grouped into some sort of system." He leaned forward, his face almost flush against the glass.

"You have a good eye." I cringed at the stupidity of my comment. Of course he had a good eye! He was a photographer. "We divide them by the year they're created and place them in our gift shop according to seasonality, or by themes."

"You have quite an operation here." He looked at me then, his expression serious. "And you run all this?"

Under his earnest gaze, I shifted subconsciously from one foot to the other. "I do now, yes. It's a lot some days. My father ran things before me." My voice softened. "He died during the war."

James tensed, before nodding his understanding. "I'm sorry to hear it. Too many good men were lost. I carry my own scars of war." I studied his face. It was smooth and without blemish or imperfection. "Not all scars are physical," he added.

Not knowing what to say—or why I opened up to James so easily—I changed the subject.

"So, yes. All our production and packaging is done by hand."

"The old-fashioned way."

"The only way," I said firmly. "We must maintain our reputation for fine quality and luxury."

He laughed. "You clearly know what you like."

I met his eye. "Of course I do." His light brown eyes warmed to amber, and I realized what he thought I'd meant. "Most women know what they want, although that is often a surprise to the men in their lives." I wasn't usually so bold or outspoken. Judging by the look on James's face, I could tell I'd surprised both of us.

He cleared his throat. "It seems to be the French way. It's a commendable quality. Really, I admire what you're doing here, Sophie. You should be very proud of yourself."

I was so touched I didn't know what to say. Nobody had admired me or told me to be proud of my work for a very long time. I picked up my pace as we walked on.

I could feel James's demeanor shift as we walked. He became quieter, more serious.

"Have dinner with me sometime, Sophie?"

"Dinner?"

"Strictly business."

"Business?" What was wrong with me? I acted like a school-girl around him, blushing and bumbling, lost for words. "What sort of business?"

"There's something I'd like to discuss with you. About the perfumery."

My shoulders dropped a fraction and I flicked my dark curls over my shoulder to appear nonchalant. Part of me was disappointed that it was strictly business, and I knew I shouldn't be. What would Lucien say if he heard I'd been dining with another man? Yet I remembered his business dinner with the blonde at the Carlton hotel the night I'd met Grace there. He was entertaining her while she was in town. I would only be doing the same.

"*Très bien,*" I said. "Dinner it is. I will check my schedule."

His smile could have lit a thousand candles. "And I will check mine."

WHEN THEY MEET IN MONTE CARLO, HOLD TIGHT TO YOUR SEAT!

Grace Kelly at New York premiere of
To Catch a Thief.
Angeline West reports for the *Herald*.

After the recent premieres of Alfred Hitchcock's latest picture in L.A. and Philadelphia, the stars were out in force again at the Paramount Theater for the New York City premiere of *To Catch a Thief*. The stars of the movie, Cary Grant (coaxed out of retirement by Hitch to play the part of cat burglar John Robie) and Hitch's favorite leading lady, Grace Kelly (perfectly cast in the role of Francie), braved a rain-soaked night in New York to greet assembled guests, who were glad to be transported to the movie's setting of the sun-drenched French Riviera.

Miss Kelly dazzled in a full-length gown designed by Edith Head of MGM Studios. Head designed all the costumes in *To Catch a Thief,* and in Miss Kelly's previous picture, *Rear Window*. She also designed the stunning teal gown Miss Kelly wore to accept her Oscar for Best Actress at the twenty-seventh Academy Awards earlier this year.

It is said that during the filming of *To Catch a Thief* on the French Riviera last year, Miss Kelly took an interest in the gardens of the Prince's Palace in Monaco, which she had seen from the coastal roads above the small principality. In a curious turn of events,

Miss Kelly was invited to visit the palace by His Serene Highness Prince Rainier III of Monaco while she attended the Cannes Film Festival in May of this year. In a memorable scene in the movie, Kelly's and Grant's characters stop for a picnic lunch along one of the twisting roads synonymous with the Riviera. Roads that left this reporter, quite frankly, terrified!

Miss Kelly and Cary Grant are pictured reading the *Philadelphia Bulletin,* where the front-page headline reads "City Sees World Premiere of Grace Kelly Movie." Perhaps Bob Hope wasn't too far from the truth when he joked, at the opening of the Academy Awards, that there should be a special award for bravery for the producer who didn't cast Grace Kelly in their picture.

She is, indeed, in great demand—a star shining ever brighter. It makes one wonder what the future might hold for this quiet Philadelphia girl turned America's darling.

15

SOPHIE

Grasse
August

The business dinner with James was eventually arranged for a Friday evening in early August. I'd suggested we eat at the house. Keep it casual. Maman wouldn't be at home on a Friday night, but would be at the casino in Monte Carlo, where they served plenty of free booze to a frequent customer. Though it might be reckless to invite a new friend to the house—a male friend at that—I hardly cared. With Lucien out of town for a while, I was at my own disposal for once.

It was a perfect night, more perfect than it had a right to be. I eyed James across the table, my wineglass pressed to my lips, wondering what Maman would think of this charming Englishman. He was so different from Lucien in every way.

Over a digestif, James outlined his business proposition, holding nothing back.

"I don't mean to be rude, Sophie, but your boutique in Cannes looks more like a pharmacy than a place connected to flowers and fields. It is all a bit . . . sterile." At this I raised an eyebrow. "I see empty space on the walls where a lavender field might hang, or a bland mirrored window where a collage of rose petals and gardenia could add so much color. You can tell me to mind my own business, but I really think you should evoke the essence of each perfume with images of the flowers that made it. Bring out this glorious landscape you love so much. Isn't that what your fragrances are really about? The essence of Grasse, the power and beauty of nature."

He went on to talk about the unused space on the back of my business cards and making brochures to illustrate the ingredients. "Like a recipe book for perfume."

I soon found myself becoming convinced that he was right.

"You are very persuasive," I remarked, reflecting on how interested James was in the business, and how quickly he had understood my passion for the landscape and the traditions around which my papa had so carefully built Duval. We sat on the terrace beneath the plane trees surrounded by endless fields of jasmine. Bees hummed in the background, and as night settled over the land, James remarked on the occasional flicker of light from a few lingering fireflies.

"You've come at the right time of year," I said, stretching my arms over my head in a lazy gesture. "Soon the fireflies will be gone again. It's too dry for them. I'm a little surprised there are any here now."

He poured another glass of rosé for each of us. "They should go to England. They wouldn't find it too dry there."

I smiled. "Does it rain all the time?"

"A lot of the time, yes. You've never been?"

I shook my head. "I'd like to see Buckingham Palace, walk the Mall."

He laughed. "You are a royalist, then? Fascinated by queens and princesses?"

I took a sip of wine. "You should not assume so many things. I am fascinated by history and tradition. It is what I was raised on." I leaned back in my chair. "And of course, the little girl within once imagined herself as a princess. Don't all little girls?"

He hesitated before raising his glass toward mine. "And now you are the Queen of Perfume. To your continued success, Miss Duval. To true artists, everywhere."

I clinked my glass against his, took a sip, and stared out at the surrounding fields, the colors shifting from green and white to shades of blue and silver as the sun sank ever lower in the sky.

"It is the care and attention to detail, and the devotion when things go wrong, that separate a true artist from a hobbyist," I remarked, my tongue loosening with the warm glow of wine in my veins.

James didn't reply. He ran his finger around the edge of his glass, making it sing.

"Now *you* are quiet, James. It is unlike you."

"I have reason to be quiet sometimes. As much as anyone does."

I wondered what, or who, it was that occupied his thoughts in his quiet moments.

He continued, "The light here is amazing. I'm taking the best photographs of my life. I never imagined living anywhere other than London, but there's something enchanting about Provence. It casts a spell."

I smiled, delighted more than I should be by his words. "You already think you would like to make Provence your home? You fall in love very quickly, James."

My words were an invitation, which he accepted.

"Perhaps I do," he whispered, lifting my hand from the table and pressing it to his lips.

I should have pulled away, but I didn't. When he stood and walked around the table and pulled me to my feet, I should have resisted, but I didn't. And when I saw the desire in his eyes, I didn't waver, but leaned toward him.

He cupped my face in his hands and pressed his lips to mine.

I yielded to their warmth and soft insistence. I yielded to him, this charming man I had known only weeks, yet felt I'd known always. And for a perfect blissful moment, I stood beneath a blanket of stars, enveloped by the scent of jasmine and by his arms, and I became a candle flame dancing in a breeze, suddenly alive. Carefree and happy.

So happy that I didn't hear Maman return. So happy that I didn't hear the *click-clack* of her heels against the terra-cotta tiles as she walked out onto the terrace. So happy that even when I heard her shriek my name, when I heard the shock and anger in her voice, I didn't even care.

It was only later, when the shouting and the explanations had been blown away across the fields on the night's warm breeze, that I was able to reflect on what had happened. And when I did, I didn't regret it for a moment.

Whoever she was, this new Sophie who corresponded with Hollywood stars and laughed and flirted with handsome Englishmen and opened herself up to the moment, I liked her much more than the Sophie who went home early, succumbed to her mother's demands, and ordered whatever her boyfriend was having.

I liked this Sophie far, far more.

16

JAMES

The last time I was seen off the premises by someone's mother, I was a spotty seventeen-year-old fueled by a cocktail of hormones and cheap whiskey. I didn't remember the girl's name, but I did recall the smack of her mother's handbag against my backside as she swatted me away like an unwelcome horsefly. Once again, I found myself on the receiving end of an irate mother's handbag, and Sophie's mother had much better aim than the other girl's.

I apologized to everyone, grabbed my hat, ducked out of the garden gate, and, thigh smarting, ran to the front of the house where I'd parked Natalie's old Vespa. As I fumbled for the keys, I heard the two women shouting, hurling accusations at each other in French. The only word I could clearly make out was *Lucien,* whoever he was. The dead papa, perhaps. I didn't fancy hanging around to find out.

The night was one of those perfect Riviera evenings: moonlit and balmy, fragrant and full of possibility. I gripped the handlebars of the Vespa, hoping the soft breeze would cool my passion and my mood as I followed the winding cliff-top roads, a little terrified and yet exhilarated by the hairpin bends and snaking switchbacks and the sheer drop to my left. Natalie was right. The scooter *was* fun. But even with the distraction of the road, I couldn't push Sophie from my mind. I could still taste the wine and her lipstick against my mouth.

"Damn it, Sophie." I peered out at the blackening landscape in frustration. "You are bloody delicious."

I tried to lose myself in the sound of the wind in my ears. It didn't help. Perhaps it was for the best that we'd been interrupted. Sophie was right. I fell in love too quickly. Provence and Mademoiselle Duval had seduced me, clouding my thoughts and coloring my judgment. To have feelings for Sophie made no sense whatsoever. We were too different, for a start. She was serious and focused and cultured, her feet planted firmly in the French soil of her family's heritage. I was none of those things. Flippant and easily distracted were Marjorie's favored accusations. I hadn't mentioned Emily—even when I'd had the perfect opportunity—or Marjorie and Thing, or any of the complications waiting for me in England. How could I possibly have a relationship with Sophie when she knew nothing about me? For all that I pretended I'd left my life in England behind for the summer, I hadn't. It was all still there, like a country house whose rooms were covered in dust sheets for the season, waiting for the maids to pull back the curtains and ready the place for the family's return. When I thought of Emily's puzzled frown and her cheeks painted with freckles, I wondered what I was doing here at all.

As I followed the lights along the coast, the road dropped steadily down toward Cannes and the miles fell away behind me. The moon rose above the horizon, like a pearl suspended on an invisible necklace. I would need to have a cold shower to wash Miss Duval away. And tomorrow I would try to forget our kiss, about her, even if the sting of her mother's handbag still smarted against my thigh.

But the night wasn't done with me yet.

As I pulled up outside the pension, I saw Madame Bisset waiting at the door. It was late, and she was usually early to bed.

"Bonsoir, madame," I said. "It's a beautiful evening."

She passed me an envelope. "Telegram, monsieur. From *Londres*. I hope it is not *mauvaises nouvelles*. Bad news."

I thanked her and went straight to my room, where I read the message in private.

```
JIM. BAD NEWS, I'M AFRAID. SEEMS I SURVIVED
THE NAZIS ONLY FOR THE BLOODY CANCER TO GET ME.
THEY'VE GIVEN ME SIX WEEKS. SIX BLOODY WEEKS.
IT WOULD BE GOOD TO SEE AN OLD FRIEND. PERHAPS
WE COULD OPEN THAT BOTTLE OF WHISKEY YOU'RE
SAVING FOR A SPECIAL OCCASION. I'M AT ST. THOMAS'S.
TEDDY.
```

Madame Bisset took my passport from the safe. My decision was immediate. I would travel back to London that night. Six weeks felt like six minutes and every one of them I spent in France was time not spent with Teddy.

Heart in my throat, hand shaking, I sat at the writing desk and composed a letter to Monsieur Roux at the photography studio. I explained my sudden departure, offered my sincere apologies and asked for his understanding. What else could I do? Madame Bisset assured me she would deliver it personally the next day.

From Cannes to Paris and on to Calais, I traveled without pause and took the first boat to Dover. As France slipped away behind a light sea mist, I tried to understand how Teddy could possibly be dying. Selfishly, I thought about him not being there to offer advice or set me straight. To think about his wife and children was simply too awful. Wiping a tear from my eye, I folded my handkerchief and pushed it into my pocket, folding Sophie away, too, for another time: her searching eyes, the softness of her lips, our perfect day together, all stored among the creases and folds. For now, all that mattered was going home.

17

SOPHIE

Despite the horrible fight with Maman, I languished in bed the next morning with a smile upon my lips, enveloped in a daydream. A daydream with plenty of James in it.

That kiss.

How could I think of anything else? The vision of him silhouetted in moonlight, his face bent over mine, set my pulse racing each time I replayed it in my mind. But a few moments after the memory came, guilt washed over me. I'd kissed another man. I pulled the coverlet up to my nose and squeezed my eyes closed against the golden glow of the sun-drenched room. How had I allowed myself to spend an entire day and an evening with James? Business indeed. Lucien would be furious with me, and then proceed to have James blackballed all over town, if he ever found out.

I needed to put Monsieur Henderson from my mind.

I rose from bed and dressed in lightweight linen culottes and shirt, donned my sun hat, and plucked a basket from the stack in the barn. Maman was in bed, sleeping off a brandy hangover without doubt, and I wasn't about to disturb her. I needed a walk in the fresh morning air, out among my fields before the workers arrived. This way I could clear my head and take in the world before I had to face my responsibilities.

I slipped out of the house and stalked across our narrow lawn, picked my way over a stony ledge and through the fields to the tea roses beyond. I smelled the roses before I saw them, their fragrance elegant and distinct—like that of rain and sugar mixed with a deep floral essence all their own. This was my favorite time in the fields amid the blooms. In late July or early August, when the roses had already reached their peak weeks before, and were now in decline. It was as if the blooms held their deepest, most intoxicating perfume until the end. A last gift, a final breath before the life cycle would begin all over again.

I thought again of last night as the sun poured over the fields and the back of my neck dampened in the climbing heat. The conversation with James had been rich, and our feast— tomatoes and basil, cheese and wine, the olive-studded *fougasse* and the *pain de campagne*—although simple was exquisite. I stopped in the middle of a row plucked almost entirely clean of blooms, an idea springing from the memory. Of course! The yeast in the cheese and the wine and the bread. That's what *Maison* was missing! The warm essence of yeast! Excitement zipping through my veins, I rushed back to the house to take down some notes, a bounce in my step, my basket swinging on my arm, humming the whole way.

After breakfast I headed to my workshop, the whole day ahead before I had to return to Cannes. Something akin to happiness flowed through me until I remembered Maman's admonishments and threats. She wouldn't dare tell Lucien about the dinner and the kiss, would she? As much as she adored Lucien, she wouldn't want to endanger my relationship with him. Besides, it was none of her business. I should be the one to tell him if necessary, and I wasn't sure that it was. James must have lots of women friends, as charming and talented as he was. He would quickly lose interest in a *parfumeuse* who worked too many hours and liked the quiet of her fields of tea roses. Not to mention a *parfumeuse* with a boyfriend whom she loved. I did love Lucien, didn't I?

The hours slipped by as I attempted many different formulas for *Maison*. The addition of a yeast scent definitely worked, but I didn't have the percentage of the ingredient correct yet. There was something else missing. Something I couldn't put my finger on. I took out my journal and thumbed to the page where I'd begun writing ideas for the new fragrance. I stared at the components I'd listed already, and found the exact percentages of each element in the formula. I shook my head. I knew the fragrance needed another element to balance its headiness, but I wasn't sure what that could be. Flipping through the first section of the journal, I took in Papa's familiar handwriting, which he had so meticulously crafted to make his formulas clear. My eyes blurred as I ran a finger down the page, and a memory of the first time he'd shown me how to invite inspiration bloomed in my mind.

"You must let the idea come to you," he'd said, tugging my hand as he led me through an open-air market.

"Will it just pop into my head?" I'd asked, eyeing the stalls of brightly colored fruits and vegetables, wondering when we'd find the man who sold the sweets.

"Not exactly, no. You have to go out into the world, away from your desk and your home, open your senses. Smell, listen, touch. Take in all sorts of experiences. You're a scientist, Sophie, collecting data. You must absorb it all, into your brain and also into your soul." He picked up a strawberry and waved it under my nose. "Something magical happens when you open yourself to the sights and smells around you. You create a memory. Now, every time you smell a strawberry, you will think of this moment and how it made you feel. That is the magic you will mix into your parfums, *ma chérie.*"

He kissed my head and we filled our basket with leeks and mushrooms, fresh herbs, and a fat tub of olives. We arrived home earlier than expected. Papa remarked on the green Peugeot in the drive. Our neighbor's car. We trundled up the path and slipped inside to find Maman in the arms of Antoine Neville. They were both as drunk as sailors.

My parents fought all night as I hid in my room, trying not to hear the horrible things Maman said to Papa. That she'd never wanted children, never loved him, felt trapped by his factory and lands and his foolhardy dreams that he would one day become as famous as Fragonard. She mocked him. Taunted him cruelly. The next morning, she apologized profusely to both of us, kissing my head and telling me she loved me very much. Yet she drank again that night and the raging began anew.

Papa was right. I'd made a memory that day at the market. I hadn't eaten a strawberry since.

I sighed as the memory faded, and picked up my dropper for a new test, just as the office door swung open.

I started in surprise. "Lucien! You scared me half to death. I nearly lost my dropper."

"Hello to you, too, *mon amour*." Lucien planted a kiss on my forehead. "Your mother called, said you needed some assistance today, but you were too embarrassed to ask so I am here to rescue you."

So this was the game she was going to play—send in the boyfriend she all but worshiped to scare away the dreaded Englishman. Shifting in my seat, I opted for some version of the truth.

"Yes, I need help in the storeroom with packaging. I had to let another worker go last week."

"That's all?" He shrugged. "Your mother made it sound like the house would burn down if I didn't come immediately."

"Oh? You know how she can be dramatic." My voice cracked. I focused my gaze on the vial in front of me.

Lucien didn't appear to notice the inflection in my voice. "How much longer are you working today? I have tickets for the ballet in Monte Carlo. I thought we'd get some dinner first, maybe do a little shopping. I'd like a new pair of sunglasses."

Shopping and spending the night on the town was the last thing I wanted to do. I was deep inside my head, lost in a world of creation. To be interrupted during a crucial time like this could derail me for days. Lucien would never understand, especially after having traveled to allegedly help me out with something I was "too embarrassed" to ask about myself.

I covered my irritation with a smile. "Why don't you start on the packages and I'll join you in just a few minutes? I'll clean up here first and then we can talk about plans for tonight."

Ignoring me, he scooped me in his arms. "I've missed you the last few weeks. I think you like your little perfumery more than you like me."

Even as I began to deny it, I realized he might have struck upon an uncomfortable truth, or at least a version of it. Though it wasn't as if I could choose between my business and my feelings for him. It was an absurd—and unfair—comparison. I pressed my lips to his to avoid the need to reply.

He leaned into the kiss, moaning a little as he pulled me closer. I was struck by how different his scent was from James's. His was a warm, earthy scent. Lucien smelled sharp, cool, and clean. I flinched at the way he dipped into me hungrily, as if he wanted to take something from me. James had been gentle, coaxing and teasing, inviting my affection rather than seizing it.

I pulled away, a ripple of guilt running through me. Why was I comparing my boyfriend, a man I loved, to a man I'd only met a couple of months ago—and shouldn't have kissed in the first place? "Goodness, you're like a starved man!"

He peered at me through heavy lids. "I am. Starved for you."

I had to force myself not to roll my eyes. "How many times has that line worked for you?"

He laughed. "More than you know."

I pushed him playfully. "I'd rather not know."

"Let's go. I insist you put down your toys and have some fun tonight."

Toys? I brushed off the slight, not bothering to explain that creating scents in my workshop *was* fun. And inspiring and satisfying—and very hard work. Nor did I contest his choice of entertainment for the evening. Instead, I left my work and went with him, not because I wanted to, but because my head told me it was the right thing to do. Even as I stepped into Lucien's car, my thoughts were elsewhere. Whether or not I cared to admit the truth to myself, it lingered in the air around us.

Like a perfume evaporating against the skin, the head notes were the first to go, leaving the heart notes to linger next. As we wound down the twisting roads toward Monaco, all I could think about was the scent of jasmine that had laced the air as James pressed his lips against mine.

18

SOPHIE

Cannes
August

I returned to Cannes Monday morning, distracted and more reluctant than ever to leave Grasse. The events of the weekend—first James, and then Lucien—had left me confused and frustrated. At the office, I flicked casually through the newspaper and magazine clippings Natalie had left for me in an attempt to broaden my knowledge of celebrities in case any more stopped by the boutique to seek refuge. I was delighted to come across photographs of Grace Kelly on set in Cannes while filming *To Catch a Thief*, directed by her dear Hitch. I regarded her smile, remembering how kind she was, how often we'd laughed together that night at the Carlton hotel. I felt as if we'd started a friendship of sorts, and I was truly lucky to know her. I hadn't heard from her again after sending the samples of Starlight and hoped I hadn't been too presumptuous.

And there was someone else I was hoping to hear from, too. It had been nearly three days already without a word from James. Perhaps Maman had scared him away for good with her staggering and shouting. I flushed in shame. What did it matter anyway? I was with Lucien.

"Lunch today, at Maxime's?" Natalie said, dropping a stack of receipts on my desk.

"I'm not hungry. You go on without me."

She searched my face as I shifted in my seat. "You look perturbed, *chérie*. Any word from James?"

I shook my head.

Natalie often looked at me in a way that made me feel exposed, as if she could see through all my layers and barriers to the very center of my heart, the way a mother should see her daughter. I wanted to lay my head in her lap, tell her everything. My confusion and excitement. My guilt. But I didn't need to voice any of those things. She knew already.

She laid her hand atop mine. "*Bien*. Why don't you go to Roux's studio? He might know something."

I looked into her knowing eyes. Why didn't I? I was a modern woman, after all, and didn't need to wait on a man. Besides, James was a friend, and I was growing concerned about his silence.

"Good idea," I said, rising from the desk. "I will."

It didn't take long for the mystery to be solved.

Monsieur Roux clucked his tongue against the roof of his mouth as he explained that James had rushed back to England after learning that a close friend was terminally ill. "He is gone, madame." He shrugged. "It's too bad. He took *les photos magnifiques.*"

My heart sank as I thanked him for his time and swiftly ducked out of the studio. James had gone. Left for London, without so much as a goodbye. I was disappointed—hurt that he hadn't thought to leave a letter for me as he had for Monsieur Roux—but I understood. His loyalty to his friend didn't surprise me. It sounded exactly like the sort of thing James would do.

Eyes smarting, pride stinging, heart crumbling, I took the long way back to the shop.

Determined to throw my disappointment into my work, I tossed my bag onto the desk and sliced through an envelope at the top of a stack of letters. Expecting more bills, I paused as I read the words on the paper inside. I perched on the edge of the desk as I read it.

MGM Studios
Hollywood, CA 90067

My dearest Sophie,

I wanted to thank you so very much for the beautiful packages that were waiting for me at the studio.

My mother is thrilled with her own bottle of Nuit Douce, *but—my word! Your Starlight is divine. Truly, it is unlike anything I've ever worn before. You mentioned that it was a sample, but I hope you are making it by the gallon. You have a gift, dear Sophie. You must treasure it.*

I haven't forgotten your lesson at dinner that night at the Carlton, that all perfumes have head, heart, and base notes, each evaporating in their own time until only the longest lasting remain. Starlight is all heart, surely!

After my trip to your beautiful country earlier in the year, I have reason to think your lesson in perfumes might also be true of romance. That what we notice first in a person soon settles into something more lingering, until our heart is truly captured.

Now, I must sign off before I say too much. A woman must retain some of her secrets after all!

Fondly,
Grace

Once again, Miss Kelly had arrived just when I needed her. As surely as if she stood beside me, she'd spoken my own thoughts. My eyes strayed to the photograph James had taken of me that day in the boutique. My heart strayed to the kiss we had shared only a few days ago.

The decision was made quickly.

I wrote a short letter, offering my sympathies and wishing his friend a peaceful final few weeks, sealed it, and put it with the other correspondence for Natalie to take to the post later. On second thought, I placed it in my handbag to take to the post office myself.

A woman must retain some of her secrets after all.

PART TWO

HEART NOTES

The main body or heart of the parfum;
scents that emerge in the middle
of the dispersion process.

I fell in love with him without giving a thought to anything else.
—GRACE KELLY

TO CATCH A PRINCE

Hollywood's queen to become a princess!
Angeline West reports for the *Herald*.

After a fateful first meeting in Monaco last May, His
Serene Highness Prince Rainier III of Monaco has found
a bride, and Grace Kelly has found her prince.

The future princess announced her surprise engagement at the Kelly family home in East Falls, Philadelphia. Miss Kelly, age twenty-six, wore a shirtdress by
Branell of New York and showed off the dazzling Cartier
engagement ring, featuring a 10.47-carat emerald-cut
diamond flanked by twin baguettes.

It is understood the couple struck up a courtship
after corresponding with each other these past months.
When he arrived in America shortly before Christmas,
speculation was rife that the Monegasque prince had
come to find a wife, although he strenuously denied it.
When asked by a reporter what sort of wife he would
like if he *were* looking for one, his reply was "I don't
know. The best."

He has certainly found that in the stunning Grace
Kelly.

The happy couple made their first public appearance at a special ball held in their honor to celebrate their engagement at the Waldorf-Astoria in New
York. The evening was themed "Imperial Ball—A Night
in Monte Carlo." The couple looked happy and relaxed
in each other's company, and despite the prying lenses

of the world's media, and the undoubted nerves felt by any young woman newly engaged, Miss Kelly maintained her usual air of calm. She will now begin filming her new picture, *High Society* (based on the play *The Philadelphia Story*). Miss Kelly will star alongside Frank Sinatra and Bing Crosby. The prince will accompany her to Hollywood for a short while before returning to Monaco.

It is not yet clear where the couple will be married, or what impact the role of princess will have on Miss Kelly's acting career. The talk in Tinseltown is that Kelly is looking for a way out of her contract with MGM. In the meantime, the Hollywood Foreign Press Association Awards—the Golden Globes—will be held in L.A. next month, where Miss Kelly is tipped to win the special Henrietta Award for World Film Favorite—Female.

Miss Kelly's father, Jack Kelly, a former Olympic gold medalist and building mogul, said he was very happy for his daughter and that the union has his blessing.

19

JAMES

London
January 1956

Poor Teddy didn't even get the six weeks he'd been promised. In the end, it was a mercy he went sooner.

I cried like a child that last evening, telling him he was the brother I'd never had. I reminisced about all he'd taught me: how to fix my rifle when it jammed, how to place a roll of film into a camera and develop the negatives, how to go after what I wanted in life rather than waiting around for things to happen. Skills that had saved my life both on and off the battlefield. I don't remember how long I sat with him before the nurse asked me to step outside. I couldn't even look at his wife.

I didn't leave the house for weeks, and only then to attend the funeral. After that, nothing seemed to matter anymore.

Not the flower fields of Grasse, or the job I'd begun to enjoy in Cannes. Not Sophie Duval who had enchanted me for a few perfect weeks in France. Even Emily became a responsibility I didn't want while I processed my grief. Life fell away like old paint peeling from a wall. I was hollowed out, as lost as it is possible for a person to be, and I didn't have the faintest idea how to find myself.

London was especially cold over the winter, as if it, too, felt as numb and empty as I did. People mostly grumbled, as they do. Too hot in the summer. Too cold in the winter. I had no reason to complain, grateful for the snow and the thick fogs that rolled in from the Thames and gave me an excuse to stay indoors. I was glad to hibernate, to turn my back on the world.

Teddy had been gone for nearly five months. I kept expecting him to turn up with tickets for a match, kept looking for him in the faces I saw on the street on the rare occasions I popped out. But of course, he wasn't there.

Lost in my thoughts, I ignored the doorbell at first. Only on the fifth persistent and prolonged ring did I eventually haul myself up from the sofa, if only to stop the ear-splitting noise.

The last person I expected to see was Sanders. I don't know who was more surprised: me, to see my former boss standing on my doorstep, or him, to see me in my pajamas in the middle of the afternoon.

"You look like hell," he said, stepping inside without waiting to be invited, and stamping snow off his shoes. "You've thirty minutes to get dressed."

Sanders always acted as if you were in the middle of a conversation, even when you hadn't spoken to him for over six months.

"And a happy new year to you, too," I muttered.

I took the milk bottle off the doorstep. It was frozen solid from being outside all morning. The blue tits and robins had seen away most of the cream, the foil lid peppered with punctures from their beaks. Closing the front door, I followed Sanders into the kitchen. He'd already made himself at home and put the kettle on.

"Christ, Jim," he bellowed, despite the fact that I was practically standing beside him. My kitchen was on the small side. "You look like you've been burgled."

I winced as I noticed how much of a mess the place was in.

"Would it be too much trouble to ask what you are doing here?" I asked.

Sanders blew his nose into a grubby-looking handkerchief and tossed a copy of the morning paper onto the kitchen table, where it landed among a collection of unwashed teacups and whiskey tumblers.

"That," he said, pointing to the front page. "*That's* what I'm doing here."

I picked up the paper and read the headline. It declared, in large bold type, that Grace Kelly was engaged to His Serene Highness Prince Rainier III of Monaco.

"Well, would you look at that! It's your Prince Raymond," I scoffed. "So, the actress becomes a princess." I dropped the paper back onto the table and went to take a cigarette from my pocket before remembering I'd given them up. "Good for her."

"Good for him, more like."

"Well, yes. I suppose. She is rather beautiful, isn't she?" I sat down and studied the engagement photographs more closely. They'd been taken at the Kelly family home in Philadelphia. "Couldn't they have found a bigger sofa for them all to sit on? Her father looks like he's about to fall off the end." Sanders blew on his hands, ignoring my remarks. "Anyway, what does all this have to do with me getting dressed? Is it tradition that everyone must dress in morning suits when a royal engagement is announced?"

Sanders spooned tea leaves from the caddy into a cracked teapot.

"Help yourself, by the way," I added, my sarcasm lost on him.

"I hate to say it, Jim, but because of this bloody engagement, I need you back. Well, I need your photographs, more specifically, but you as well. If you're feeling up to it?"

I laughed. "Would that be the photographs that look like a hostage crisis?"

He didn't even have the decency to look embarrassed or apologetic. "Yes. Those. With this engagement, your photographs of Kelly and Rainier at the palace turn out to be very useful." He put the teapot down. "We ran the one I kept, but I could really use the others. Please tell me you didn't throw them in the Thames."

I let out a long sigh, playing out the moment for all it was worth. "Yes, I still have them. So, does this mean I'm hired again?"

Sanders poured two cups of tea, spilling at least another cup's worth onto the table in the process. "Listen, Jim. I'll be straight with you. I know you've been struggling since Walsh . . ." Even Sanders couldn't bring himself to say it. "Well, I know you two were good friends, and it's a bloody awful situation, but I need someone on this Kelly/Rainier story because the world has gone crazy for them. Since you already met them, sort of, and have nothing better to do, I'd like you to follow the story from here. There's no wedding date set yet, but speculation suggests spring in Monaco. You look like you could do with some sun on your face. You can start back this afternoon. Your desk has already been cleared."

I nearly choked on my tea. "This afternoon?"

"The Hollywood press are in a tailspin," Sanders continued. "They're saying it's the biggest story to hit town since Marilyn left Joe. Even the writers at MGM couldn't make this stuff up. I need you on it."

I could hear Teddy laughing at my turn of fortune.

For the first time in many months, I felt a spark of enthusiasm. Everything had been dulled by Teddy's death: my appetite, my love of photography. I'd even stopped thinking about Sophie for a while until Emily had found the photograph I'd taken of her in the boutique and wanted to know who the pretty lady was. My reaction to seeing Sophie's face had surprised me. I'd found myself telling Emily all about the workshop in Grasse, remembering far more than I'd expected to. Emily was mesmerized. To learn that you could work with flowers and make perfume and live somewhere where the sun shone most of the year was a revelation to her young mind. I could already see the wanderlust in her eyes. She wasn't so different from me after all, even if she preferred chemistry sets to photographs.

In the end, I talked about Sophie so much that Emily insisted on sending her a Christmas card. I enclosed a short note to offer an olive branch after my abrupt departure from France, and for my disregard for the sympathetic letter Sophie had written to me shortly after. Although I'd tried to forget about her, Sophie was a memory I couldn't erase, a negative not fully developed. While the passion I'd once felt for her amid the heat of the Riviera and a bottle of rosé had been doused by a British winter and the creeping chill of grief, my feelings persisted nevertheless.

"So?" Sanders prompted, bringing me back into the moment as he poured more tea. "How about it?"

I raised a suspicious eyebrow. "What's the catch?"

"No catch. For the love of God, Jim, you're better than . . . this." He swept his arm in a wide circle of dismay, taking in the pile of dishes in the sink, the empty glasses on the table, the general state of my appearance. "You were one of my best photographers. You just couldn't follow directions. Bloody infuriating, actually."

Neither of us spoke for a moment, the only sound coming from the passing cars on the street and Winston's plaintive meow at the back door.

"You're wrong, actually. I *am* one of your best photographers." I stood up and shook his hand. "Give me an hour to smarten myself up, and I'm all yours."

My life was beginning to feel like the Circle line Tube train: the end was also the beginning. For Teddy, if not for myself, I had to step aboard, mind the gap, and see where it would take me next.

20

SOPHIE

Cannes
February

Winter on the Côte d'Azur had brought the mistral winds tearing over the Alps from Siberia and sweeping across the southern coast. Fierce and bitter cold, the winds ravaged the barren flower fields and dormant olive trees. Sometimes the blustery weather only lasted a few days, sometimes well over a week. On those days, I hid in my workshop and later by the fire in the house, listening to the gusts howl against the eaves as I lost myself in a good book.

Christmas had brought its own surprise in a letter from James and a card from his daughter. A daughter he'd never mentioned. Men, too, had their secrets to keep, it seemed. It struck me how James was not unlike the mistral winds, coming into my life like a tornado, tousling everything about until it was upside down, and then sweeping away like it had never been. I missed his company, the laughter, the connection we'd formed the instant he'd chased Grace Kelly into the shop. We'd exchanged a few short letters since, but I sensed there was more left unsaid than was ever written on the page.

Occupied by my new fragrances, the winter passed quickly— far faster than I would have liked. I luxuriated in my slow season, the time I could spend in my workshop, trying new scent combinations, exploring new possibilities, and making plans for the spring and summer ahead. This year's high season would be busier than ever. After the new line launched, I would need to visit department stores to convince them to carry it, send samples to everyone I knew. Perhaps I'd even ask Lucien to host a party to celebrate its arrival on the market, although a stubborn part of me wanted to do this alone, without any help or favors. With the tip of my pencil eraser, I stabbed the adding machine buttons to tabulate the costs for the hundredth time. I frowned, resting my chin on my hand, and my thoughts turned to doomsday. The day I'd have to sign Michael Lever's paperwork. No matter which way I looked at things, it seemed all but inevitable now.

The postman interrupted my thoughts as he dropped three letters on my desk. "Bonjour, Mademoiselle Duval. I hope you're having a fine day."

"What do we have today? More bills?"

"I wouldn't know, because I don't read other people's mail, but it looks as if something has come all the way from California." He winked.

"California!" I said, eagerly reaching for the envelope. This was starting to become a regular occurrence.

I tore open the envelope.

Morgan Hudgins
MGM Studios
Hollywood, CA 90067

Dear Miss Duval,

I am writing on behalf of Miss Grace Kelly since she is currently very busy filming her next picture, High Society. *As you undoubtedly also know, she is to wed His Serene Highness Prince Rainier III of Monaco.*

We are in the throes of coordinating the many details of the ceremony and celebrations that will take place in Monaco in April. Miss Kelly has commissioned cosmetics from Max Factor for the occasion and would also like to commission a new fragrance for her wedding day. I am delighted to inform you that she would like Duval to develop this very special fragrance for her consideration.

We hope you are amenable to this proposition. If you agree, please send a telegram to confirm, as well as several samples. As you can imagine, there are many other perfume houses that would like to have this opportunity, should you decline or not be able to meet the tight deadlines. Should your fragrance be chosen, we will require exclusivity until the wedding, after which time Miss Kelly is happy for the scent to be produced more widely.

Miss Kelly expressly asked me to send her regards and looks forward to seeing you in Monaco soon.

Sincerely,
Morgan Hudgins
Publicist to Miss Kelly, MGM Studios

A commission for Grace's wedding! I shouted in joy, hugged the paper to my chest, and then promptly burst into tears of relief. This was precisely what I was looking for, something that could really boost our name and bolster sales. It could save Duval! Dear Grace. She didn't know how much this meant to me. She was giving me a real chance—just in time—and I knew the perfect fragrance. *Maison,* my special luxury fragrance, not yet officially named. Only now I knew precisely what it should be called: *Coeur de Princesse.* Heart of a princess.

A thousand details raced through my mind and I began to pace. I needed to test the formula that had been aging these past months. Like a fine wine it needed to settle to find a harmony among all the elements. I didn't have much time to adjust it, with the wedding coming in April. I needed to work on the gentlemen's cologne as well. Perhaps it could be a companion scent for the prince? My mind raced with ideas.

"Natalie!" I grabbed my handbag and rushed into the shop, pressing the letter into her hands. "You won't believe it! I've a wedding parfum to make! For a princess! Look!"

Natalie looked at me, then quickly read the letter. She laughed and threw her arms around me. "Oh, Sophie! This is incredible!"

"Isn't it? It's . . . it's . . ." Unable to speak, I laughed, beside myself with joy. "I'll call you later from the factory." I kissed her cheek and stepped out into the chilly afternoon, the breeze swirling around me, tossing my thoughts this way and that, infected with my excitement and enthusiasm.

Later that evening, after hours in the workshop, I pulled on my favorite pair of wool socks and an old robe, and poured myself a small glass of pastis. It had been a successful day, in all. The cologne was coming along, and the closer I came to working out the formula, the more I thought about James. Still, it wasn't ready to be presented as part of the new line. *Coeur de Princesse,* on the other hand, was perfect and on schedule. I'd be ready to ship a sample to Grace by next week. I prayed she would like it. If she chose another's fragrance, all would be lost. I gripped my glass and stared at the fire in the hearth. But that wasn't going to happen.

I fished my journal out of my handbag and flipped it open on my lap. Dipping my head into the middle of the pages, I inhaled deeply. Dusty decaying paper and worn leather met my nose. I thumbed through Papa's early notes. I could see his dark eyes, dancing with excitement—could almost hear his laugh as he took my hand and led me inside the boutique for the very first time.

"We'll put shelves on this wall to display our bottles," he'd said, gesturing with his long, thin hands. A gentleman's hands. "And here, we'll have a stack of beautiful gift boxes and gift bags with our insignia on them."

"Where will you work, Papa?" I'd asked.

He pulled me around the counter and showed me the office.

Tapping the leather-bound journal on his desk, he said, "I will make my magic here, during the tourist season. I'll need an assistant. Do you think you can help, when you're older?"

It was all I'd ever wanted, to spend time with Papa, to learn his secrets. "Yes! I want to learn everything."

He'd chuckled, ruffled my hair, and scooped me onto his knee, the scent of his aftershave enveloping me like a cloud.

As I stared into the fire, I was struck by the memory of Papa's aftershave, laced with cinnamon and the scent of polished mahogany. Inspired, I reached for my pen and added to my notes. When I was satisfied I'd captured the memory, I whispered, "Thank you, Papa."

The cologne, my final fragrance in the new line of three, would be called *Mémoire,* in honor of my father, and for another man who had passed through my life too quickly—but had left his imprint *pour toujours.* Forever.

THE PRINCESS BRIDE

Angeline West reports for the *Herald*.

Wedding fever continues to grip the world's press as we sail ever closer to the day when Grace Kelly will marry His Serene Highness Prince Rainier III of Monaco. And *sailing* is the right word because Miss Kelly is to travel toward her husband—and her new life as a princess—by boat from New York.

Filming of *High Society* with Bing Crosby and Frank Sinatra having recently wrapped, Miss Kelly has been staying at her eleven-room Fifth Avenue apartment overlooking Central Park in New York, where she is making final preparations for her big day and adding to her already impressive wedding trousseau. Her beloved pet poodle, Oliver, is never far from her side and, it is believed, will make the long ocean crossing with her, along with the wedding party and many items of luggage.

Already known affectionately as "Her Grace" in close circles in Hollywood, Miss Kelly will take the official title of Her Serene Highness Princess Grace of Monaco when she marries the thirty-two-year-old prince and "the world's most eligible bachelor" in a Catholic wedding ceremony at Saint Nicholas Cathedral on April 19. Not bad for the daughter of a one-time bricklayer! The formal ceremony will be preceded by a civil ceremony at the royal palace on April 18, which, rumors suggest, will be repeated to allow MGM's cameras to capture the

entire spectacle for a mini-documentary to be titled
The Wedding in Monaco. When she is officially married,
Miss Kelly will become sovereign of a principality
measuring just eight square miles, and will reside in
the royal palace overlooking Monte Carlo.

In an interview shortly after announcing their engagement, Prince Rainier confirmed that his future wife
would "have enough to do as a princess" and would not
continue her acting career. He added that he has discussed this with Miss Kelly and that she is in agreement. The prince has also banned the showing of any of
Miss Kelly's movies during the period of the wedding
ceremonies.

Details about the wedding, and the much-anticipated
dress, are still scarce, although the London Festival
Ballet announced that it has been engaged for six per-
formances during the wedding celebrations. Monaco of-
ficials have also announced that two American football
teams have been invited to play in the Stade Louis II
in the principality on April 17, the day before the
first of the official wedding ceremonies.

In a strange twist of fate, the start of the ninth
Cannes Film Festival will be delayed from April 10
to April 28 because of the royal wedding on April 18
and 19. Miss Kelly and Prince Rainier first met during the film festival last year. Proof, perhaps, that
there really is such a thing as love at first sight.
Some observers, nevertheless, prefer to speculate on

rumors that the marriage is one of political arrangement rather than of true love. I guess only time will
tell if this is, indeed, a marriage of convenience, or
a union built on the foundations of good old-fashioned
love.

This hopeless romantic knows which story she prefers.

21

SOPHIE

Grasse
March

While I was preoccupied at my desk, the landscape around the Côte d'Azur warmed to early spring. Greenery graced the cherry and almond trees, shoots of lettuce poked out of the earth, the first eager green buds of flowers appeared in the fields, and the town began preparing for the busy season ahead. Instinctively, I could feel it coming, too, like the fluttering of butterfly wings in the back of my mind.

I ordered my fields to be tilled for poppies, roses, and jasmine, leaving the duties entirely in the hands of the farmer we had depended upon since I was a little girl. I'd been too consumed to oversee much this year, running to every bank I could think of in Cannes, Nice, and even Marseilles. Nobody would lend me the money I needed to produce and launch the new line of fragrances. To my great embarrassment, Duval had too much debt and a history of defaulting on payments. The deeper I dug into the business accounts, the more I realized the size of the problem. Maman's management of the books before I was old enough—and her taste for fine brandy—had brought us to the brink of financial ruin.

Frustrated and distraught, I walked through my factory, staring at the beautiful operation Papa had built and which I had tended so lovingly. The copper vats, the soap grinder, the wall of beautiful bottles. What would become of it all? What would become of me? Parfum was all I knew.

I tried to distract myself by following news about the royal wedding. I'd never read so many newspapers or magazines. Everyone wanted to follow Grace's journey. Columns and front pages were dedicated to her latest appearances in New York, where she was making final preparations for the wedding, and for her new life as a princess in Monaco. Speculation was rife among the gossip columnists about whether this was a marriage of love or convenience. I chose to believe in the former. And in quiet moments at night when the chaos and clutter of the day was hushed beneath Provence's calm skies, I allowed myself to dream that Grace would choose my fragrance, and my fortunes would turn around.

As I wound my way through the factory to the lobby, I settled on going for a walk in town to clear my head. Perhaps I'd pay my neighbor Madame Clouet a visit, too. She loved to talk about the royal wedding as much as I did. She wasn't easily able to get out of the house by herself, so I saved the newspaper clippings with all the latest details and speculation for her. As I walked across the tiled floor, the phone rang at the front desk.

Juliette answered in her usual cheerful tone. "Duval. Yes, I speak English. Mademoiselle Duval is just here. One moment, please."

"*C'est qui?*" I mouthed, not in the mood to make polite conversation.

"Mr. Morgan Hudgins of MGM Studios," she whispered, covering the mouthpiece. "From California."

My heart leapt into my throat, and I accepted the receiver. "Hello, this is Sophie Duval." Though I could hear someone, static crackled in the receiver, masking the voice at the other end. "Hello? Can you hear me? This is Sophie Duval."

The line stabilized and a male voice spoke clearly. "Miss Duval, this is Morgan Hudgins, Miss Kelly's publicist at MGM. In the essence of saving time, we thought it best I call instead of waiting for the mail. We received your fragrance sample and Miss Kelly loves it. 'It's absolutely divine,' to quote the lady herself. I'm very pleased to tell you that she has chosen to wear it on her wedding day."

A surge of relief and joy shot through me. I wanted to jump up and down—to cry! Instead, I forced my voice to remain calm. "Oh, how wonderful! This is terrific news. Thank you so much."

The gentleman gave me the shipping details as well as the quantity of the fragrance they would need. He explained that the dress designer planned to sew satin pouches soaked in *Coeur de Princesse* and attach them to the inside of Miss Kelly's wedding gown. He mentioned the dress would also be packed in tissue paper scented with the parfum for its long journey from New York to Monaco. My mind raced as he spoke. I jotted down notes, my hand shaking.

"Miss Kelly would also like to extend an invitation for yourself and a guest to join her in Monaco for one of the celebratory events during the week before the wedding, as well as the formal ceremony. An invitation will be sent in the mail. Could you confirm your guest's name, please, Miss Duval?"

I hesitated, thinking how much Natalie would love to attend, but Lucien would be outraged should I not afford him the opportunity to mingle at the world's most prestigious party.

I gripped the receiver tightly. "Lucien Marceau. He will be my guest."

As I hung up the phone, I squealed, rushing around the desk to embrace Juliette. This was exactly what I needed, such happy, happy news!

Taken aback by my uncharacteristic display of emotion, Juliette laughed. "I suppose you have good news."

"Oh, it's amazing news!"

I filled her in on the details before racing to my office to call Natalie. She cheered on the other end of the line and promised to meet me for dinner at Le Lys in town to celebrate.

But there was someone else I couldn't wait to tell—I had to write to James. It didn't matter how many months had passed since I'd seen him. He would understand how much this meant, and he would wish me well. After all, it was James who'd chased Miss Kelly into my boutique. It was James who had given her my business card. It was James who had set off this entire chain of events. Reaching for pen and stationery, I hastily scratched out a letter.

Dear James,

Thank you for your recent letter, and the photograph of Buckingham Palace. I am determined to visit London to see it for myself one day!

*I've received some wonderful news just this afternoon, and since you were a big part of why this has come to be, I wanted to share it with you. Grace Kelly has chosen one of my new fragrances—*Coeur de Princesse—*as her wedding day parfum! I'm over the moon! Who knew that day you chased her into my boutique would lead to this? It could mean very good things for Duval. Very good things indeed.*

Are you following the wedding talk in the papers? There's great excitement building in Monaco. I wonder where they're going to find room to accommodate the world's press. It seems everyone loves a fairy-tale romance!

Warmly,
Sophie

As an afterthought, I added a postscript.

P.S. I've enclosed a sample of a new gentlemen's cologne I've been working on. Mémoire. *It's still in the development stages, but it has notes of tobacco and tea, among other "top secret" ingredients. In it, I hope to have captured some of your quintessential English charm.*

I spritzed the letter with the cologne, addressed it to his London home, and put it in the pile of mail to be sent. It wasn't until after a lovely dinner with Natalie and a chilly but exuberant walk in the moonlight later that night that I realized I'd told Natalie—and James—my big news, but I hadn't yet called Lucien. In fact, I hadn't thought much about Lucien at all these past weeks. Like the clouds that scattered across the moon, I sensed that we were drifting apart. How I felt about that, I wasn't entirely sure.

22

JAMES

New York
April

After chewing me up over a long London winter, life spat me out in Manhattan in the spring. It was my first time in the Big Apple. The chaos of Times Square with its bright neon signs, the dizzying skyscrapers, and the blossoming trees in Central Park were all a tonic. It was the jolt I needed. A change of scenery. An injection of the good old American Dream.

I'd been dispatched to America as soon as the news hit the wires that Grace Kelly would sail to her wedding in Monaco aboard the S.S. *Constitution* from New York.

"There'll be a press conference before she departs," Sanders had barked, slapping a ticket for my flight to New York onto the desk. "And you'll be there for the buildup and departure. You fly in two days."

He'd been much easier on me since my return to the paper, sending me on assignments closer to home, letting me find my way slowly back. Whether intentional or not, it was appreciated all the same, but Sanders was no fool, and he wasn't going to let me coast along forever.

"One question, boss?" I said as I slipped the ticket into my jacket pocket. "If I get some decent shots, can I stop chasing princesses around the world and do something a bit more . . . meaningful?"

He laughed. "If you get some decent shots you can do whatever you like. If your pictures sell enough papers they might pay for us *all* to go around the world."

I'd followed the story of Grace Kelly and Rainier closely since the engagement announcement. It was impossible not to see the photographs of the couple covering the front pages: at the engagement ball held in their honor at the Waldorf-Astoria in New York, less formal shots of Miss Kelly in the days following the surprise engagement, images of the Kelly family at their impressive two-story colonial home on Henry Avenue in East Falls, and more relaxed pictures of the happy couple on the set of *High Society* in Hollywood.

More than just a passing voyeur, I felt in some way connected to them. I'd been there right at the start, seen their first hesitant handshake, observed their first awkward interactions. Theirs was apparently a romance forged through letters exchanged over the year since that first meeting, and I, more than most, understood something of that first spark of connection between two total strangers. I'd felt it with Sophie and, as she had pointed out in her latest letter, if it wasn't for me chasing Grace Kelly into her shop, we would never have met, and neither would Sophie have ended up making a bespoke perfume for the most famous woman in the world. Funny how something formed from such questionable morals could have such a happy ending. The three of us had apparently become as entwined as a tangled spool of thread and I couldn't help wondering where the thread would lead if I followed it.

Unlike Prince Rainier, however, I didn't have a royal crest on my personalized writing paper, or a father to influence my romantic ties. Nor did I have a Catholic priest at my disposal to help woo my woman and win her family's approval on my behalf. (It was widely rumored that Jack Kelly had brokered his daughter's union with Rainier through Rainier's priest, Father Tucker.) I was just a hack with a reputation for being late. Not quite the credentials to easily win a girl's heart. And yet my heart was precisely where Sophie lingered, all the same.

I walked down Broadway, stopping at a street vendor for a hot dog with sauerkraut and a weak cup of coffee before I headed toward Fifth Avenue to Grace's apartment building. She came and went a lot in these final days of preparation and didn't always have her entourage with her. Jack Kelly, and a pain-in-the-ass publicist from MGM Studios, kept tight control over Grace's public appearances, keen to prevent anyone apart from Howell Conant (her official photographer) from getting too close. At public engagements she was rushed from car to door without stopping to wave and smile to the cameras. Carefully selected wide-brimmed hats, large sunglasses, and lavish headscarves all added to the press pack's frustrations. It was impossible to tell it was really her beneath the accessories.

I was determined to get a clear shot of her, even if no one else could. She knew my face, if only a little, and that surely had to give me some advantage. My fortunes had taken a turn for the better and I was going to cash in while my lucky spell lasted. As much as I needed Sanders to trust me, I needed to trust myself. New York, with its can-do attitude, was a good place to start.

It was a murky day, and light rain was beginning to fall. Not even a dozen other hacks were waiting outside the apartment block at 988 when I arrived. A couple of them packed up a few minutes later as the rain threatened to spoil their equipment and further dampen the already frustrated mood. I was beginning to lose patience myself when she appeared from out of nowhere, carrying a bunch of long-stem red roses. No hat, no gloves, no headscarf. She was right there in front of me, in all her natural beauty. As the wind blew off the East River and sent her blond hair dancing in light curls about her face, she laughed, tucked her hair behind her ear, and looked right at me. The huge Cartier diamond engagement ring Rainier had had created especially for her could not have been any clearer.

"Good luck on the big day, Miss Kelly," I said as I focused through the lens and fired off a couple of shots. I was so close to her I didn't need to shout to get her attention like I usually did. "You'll be a beautiful bride. And you'll smell great, too!"

"Thank you," she said, clearly surprised by my remark. For a moment she looked as if she wanted to say more, but her attention was caught by the few other photographers calling for her to turn their way, and by several passersby who'd stopped to admire her and wish her good luck. "You're all very kind," she added before rushing inside the apartment building, gone as quickly as she'd appeared.

As much as the photographers were running out of patience with the lack of easy access to Miss Kelly, feature writers were also running out of superlatives to describe her beauty. Movie premieres. Lavish balls. Shopping trips. Walking her dogs. Wherever Miss Kelly went, so did the media, describing every detail of her clothing, carefully name-checking every designer. When Miss Kelly herself wasn't available for comment, the designers grabbed the column inches themselves.

It was a kind of madness. Like nothing I'd ever experienced. I'd only been in New York three days and already I felt like a piece of driftwood, blown from here to there on the tide, following Miss Kelly, shouting for her to look this way or that way. Tempers were unraveling faster than a snagged stocking, and as the day of the S.S. *Constitution*'s departure grew closer, I longed to send the blushing bride-to-be on her way and get home to Emily and my paycheck.

Teddy's death had made me take stock, and made me value how precious life is. I'd been a much better father to Emily since coming out of my fog of grief, and while part of me was ready to return to Monsieur Roux and the warm summer winds of the Riviera, not to mention the prospect of another perfect evening with Sophie—preferably without the addition of her mother's handbag—I couldn't leave Emily indefinitely. I hated to be away from her at all.

After another frustrating day hanging around outside

Miss Kelly's apartment, where she barely stopped to say hello, let alone answer the reporters' questions, I returned to my hotel and started to pack for my flight home, glad that my part in this particular fairy tale was done. At least I had some good shots of her to appease Sanders.

"Good afternoon. Your key, sir?"

The acne-riddled young man at the front desk irritated me with his unnecessary formality. We'd followed the same routine every evening. Would I like my room key? Had I had a good day? Was there anything else he could help sir with?

I smiled through a grimace. "Yes, please. Thank you."

"And there was a telegram for you." He rummaged in the little pigeonholes behind the desk, then placed a cream envelope on the marble desktop. "Will there be anything else I can help sir with?"

I muttered no and added a tardy thank you as I wandered toward the elevators, where an eager bellboy with epaulets and a peaked cap pressed buttons for me that I was perfectly capable of pressing myself. I opened the telegram.

ONE-WAY TICKET BOOKED FOR S.S. *CONSTITUTION*, NEW YORK TO MONACO.

    DEPART NOON, 4 APRIL.

    SANDERS.

I whistled through my teeth. How the hell had Sanders managed to pull this off?

"Is everything all right, sir?"

I glanced at the bellboy as the elevator door opened. "Do you know something, young man? I'm about to sail to Monaco with Grace Kelly, so, yes, I think everything is perfectly all right!"

I rushed to my room, tossed my hat and jacket onto the bed, and poured a neat whiskey from the drinks tray. The last thing I wanted was to extend my time away from Emily, but it would only be for another couple of weeks and this was an extraordinary turn of events. Not only did I get to travel with Miss Kelly to her so-called wedding of the century, but I would be sailing right back toward Sophie. It was fate, surely?

For weeks, the papers had been full of details about the ship that would take Grace Kelly and her wedding party to Monaco. I'd photographed the vessel in Manhattan, framing shots of its impressive outline against the skyline. Not once had I imagined stepping aboard, but that's precisely what I was going to do. Once again, Sanders—or perhaps it was Miss Kelly—had set my life on a different course.

I sent a telegram to Marjorie to explain my extended absence, and mailed an envelope full of souvenirs to Emily, along with a note promising to call as soon as I arrived in Monaco. I also sent an impulsive, whiskey-fueled telegram to Sophie.

NEW YORK. 3 APRIL 1956

DEAR SOPHIE. CONGRATULATIONS ON YOUR COMMISSION! WONDERFUL NEWS! I FIND MYSELF EAGER TO CELEBRATE WITH YOU IN PERSON. WHAT DO YOU SAY? I'M SAILING WITH MISS KELLY ON THE *CONSTITUTION*. MEET ME IN MONACO WHEN WE ARRIVE ON THE 12TH? I'LL BE AT

RAMPOLDI IN MONTE CARLO AT 7 P.M. I REMEMBER YOU
TOLD ME YOU'VE ALWAYS WANTED TO GO THERE. JIM. X

I added the kiss as an afterthought and spent too long imagining it was real. Those sensual lips of hers pressed hungrily against mine. The warmth of her breath against my cheek. I'd never known a woman less and thought about her more. However much I tried to deny it, Sophie had settled against my skin like one of her fine perfumes and no amount of scrubbing or distance could lift her from me. If ever I needed the wise counsel of Teddy Walsh, it was now. I imagined what he would say. *Stop thinking about falling in love and get on with it, Jim. Life's too short for what-ifs and maybes.* I didn't like to put words in a dead man's mouth, but he was right. I had no right to expect Sophie to meet me in Monaco, but I sent the telegram anyway. She would either be there or not. Until then, I had to forget about her and focus my thoughts and my lens on the young American woman who was about to make the most important journey of her life.

As I packed my case I wondered how Miss Kelly felt on the eve of her departure, knowing the next day she would say goodbye not only to her home, but possibly to her glittering acting career as well. Many thought the engagement had happened too quickly. Many thought the marriage wouldn't last.

But who was to say that love at first sight wasn't real, or that a romance built on passion and words couldn't bloom into something lasting.

Who was to say what constituted real love at all?

23

SOPHIE

Cannes

Though receiving Grace's commission created a whirl-wind of excitement, the reality of my financial issues still plagued me and I felt as if I were perched on a seesaw. After a rushed breakfast of espresso, sliced ham, and a croissant, I made my way to the boutique. I was at a stalemate and it was time to make some serious decisions about money.

I sighed heavily as I peered out at the aquamarine sea. Only two real options remained: sell my land, or ask Lucien to loan me more money. He could afford it, that was for certain, but each time I thought of how much he had already given me, the prospect of asking him for more left my stomach in knots. There was also the fact that we'd seen a lot less of each other recently since we were both so busy. While he was pleased to learn that Grace Kelly had chosen my fragrance for her wedding day perfume, his reaction—surprise that she had chosen Duval rather than a bigger name—had left me a little deflated. The fact was, I didn't miss Lucien as much as I should and it was that, perhaps more than anything else, that made me reluctant to ask him for help.

"You have a telegram," Natalie said, smiling, as I closed the shop door behind me. "Your James again?"

"He's not *my* James," I replied, mildly exasperated, but inside, I tingled with happiness.

I glanced at the New York address. Why was he in New York? "And?" Natalie prompted.

I read the telegram quickly.

"He's covering Grace's wedding for his paper! He's aboard the ocean liner with her, headed for Monaco." I slipped the telegram into my pocket, trying to hide my delight. "He wants to meet me in Monaco when they arrive."

Natalie watched me intently. I'd told her about the kiss with James, and how we'd exchanged letters since. She knew I had feelings for him, despite my relationship with Lucien. I was glad of her understanding and discretion. I wasn't certain what I wanted to do about it yet—if anything. When I said nothing, she asked the question on my mind.

"And? Will you meet him?"

"I—"

At that moment, the phone rang.

I jumped at the sudden intrusion and laughed, reaching for the receiver. "Bonjour. Duval."

A voice I recognized changed my mood instantly—the

creditor at the Banque Nationale de Paris à Marseilles. As he explained Duval's precarious financial situation, the levity James's telegram had brought to my morning slipped away, despair filling its place. They wanted to liquidate my assets. Nausea rolled over me as I replaced the receiver in disbelief.

"What was all that about?" Natalie asked, eyes wide. "Is everything all right, Sophie?"

"They're going to collect on my bills." I dropped my head in my hands. "I'm out of time, Natalie. I'm going to have to sell the land."

I glanced at the photograph of Grace smiling at Prince Rainier and imagined her wedding gown scented with *Coeur de Princesse*. In a matter of weeks, a future princess would be wearing *my* parfum. Was it really too late?

* * *

I went to Grasse, back to the place that grounded me, the place I always felt safe.

I walked up the short path toward the two-story home I'd grown up in, its stucco facade cracked in places but the red tiled roof still holding fast. Fields hugged our property as far as the horizon, our closest neighbor some kilometers away. We were somewhat isolated on the outskirts of town, something I'd always loved about our home: a sense of space, of privacy.

But now I would have to let it go. I'd have to give it all away, as if it were nothing but another of Lucien's properties to sell in a meaningless exchange of francs and signed documents and empty handshakes.

I sat wearily on the steps leading to the front door as alternating waves of despair and anger washed over me. I should have been more aggressive about my creations long ago. I should have cut corners on the packaging to save monies there. I should have commuted to and from Grasse daily rather than paying for the apartment in Cannes all these years. At least now it was paid for in its entirety.

The property in Cannes . . .

I looked up and wiped the tears from my face as an idea struck me. The real estate in Cannes must be worth a fortune now that it had become such a hot spot, especially with the film festival running the last ten years. If I sold the apartment and the boutique, I might save the factory and the fields, my home. Yet if I closed the shop, I'd lose a lot of revenue and direct-to-customer sales. How would I reach customers to sell the Duval name? And Natalie. What would I tell her? Duval was as much her home, her career, as mine. She'd worked for us for twenty-five years. She had exquisite taste, inspired me when I was stuck without ideas or direction, carefully guided me when I wasn't sure. She was more of a mother to me than my own had ever been. I couldn't just turn her away, but it seemed like the only possible answer.

And there was something else. Papa would hate to see Natalie hurt in any way. Although it had never been spoken about, I knew their relationship had developed beyond a friendship. I'd seen them together, locked in a passionate embrace in the office. I'd carried the secret all these years, noticing how they'd hummed like happy bees around each other, understanding Natalie's deep distress when he didn't return from war. I was glad that Papa had found real happiness with a woman he loved, and I admired him for doing his best to keep up appearances at home for the sake of the woman he had married. Maman's love affair with her brandy destroyed everything meaningful in her life. I understood why Papa had sought refuge in a woman who shared his passions, a woman who helped his dreams grow rather than trampling all over them. I understood him, and I forgave him.

I stood and went inside.

Predictably, Maman was passed out on the chaise longue, a half-empty bottle of cognac and a glass lying on its side on the end table next to her. I sighed, wishing it could all be different, but I had forgiven her over and over, and still she never changed. If she couldn't help herself, how could I possibly help her?

I reached for the glass and bottle, cleaned the table, put things away. It was important to me, the process of tidying up, putting things straight. It's what I did, what I'd always done.

After I'd helped Maman into bed, there was only one thing left to do.

Drawing in a weary breath, I made the call to the bank to beg them for more time. Soon I would be known as the creator of the princess's perfume. Suddenly, my entire future hinged on the young woman sailing across the Atlantic.

24

JAMES

S.S. *Constitution*

A lingering fog and a murky gray drizzle settled over Manhattan's Pier 84 as members of the press gathered by the hundreds in the Pool Café room on the sundeck of the *Constitution*. At last, we had an official press conference with the bride-to-be before our departure at noon.

It wasn't the romantic setting I'd imagined, more like a bare-knuckle fight with television crews, photographers, and reporters jostling for position, suffocating beneath the smell of tobacco and hair pomade. I already felt nauseous after a late night in the hotel bar, and the prospect of being at sea for over a week wasn't helping. The mob pushed forward in an unstoppable wave as Miss Kelly appeared. Officers from the New York

Police Department pushed the crowds back to make way for her, like Moses parting the sea.

The noise was like nothing I'd ever heard, everyone shouting for her to turn in their direction and arguing with each other when someone got in the way. At least three fistfights broke out directly beside me as frustrations spilled over into scuffles and punches. The potential earnings from these photographs of Miss Kelly's final days as a single woman were huge. The stakes had never been higher, and if someone blocked your view, now was not the time for a polite shrug.

I used my height and my elbows to their full advantage, protecting my spot like a pioneer staking a new claim on a plot of land. For nearly an hour, Miss Kelly—perfectly calm and poised—patiently waved and smiled as she answered idiotic questions from reporters. Questions and answers were batted back and forth until I was sure the poor woman must have been dizzy.

"We will honeymoon in the Mediterranean on the prince's yacht. The only guests will be my poodle, Oliver, and the prince's two dogs."

"Yes, of course I love him! Very much."

"No, I haven't had time to think about the future of my acting career. I'm far too excited about the wedding."

"I have a secret little wedding gift for the prince in my luggage."

"Yes. We hope to have a large family, and yes, I will become a Monegasque after the marriage but my American citizenship will remain."

"No, I won't wear a crown. The occasional tiara, perhaps."

On and on the barrage went.

"Miss Kelly," I shouted when I got the chance, waving so she might see me. "Do you believe in love at first sight?"

She turned to me, surprised by the question. A smile lit up her face as she answered. "Why, yes. I do. I absolutely do."

"Save the *I do*s for the wedding, Miss Kelly," someone shouted from behind me and we all laughed.

For a woman who'd always been notoriously reserved, very private, and reluctant to engage with the press unlike so many of her publicity-hungry contemporaries, Miss Kelly was surprisingly gregarious. She looked like any young bride-to-be: excited, a little nervous, and radiant, and yet although she was surrounded by her family and friends and the dozen or so members of a handpicked press entourage, I couldn't help thinking that she looked incredibly lonely as the wall of cameras was pointed at her. No wonder she kept her little black poodle tucked under her arm.

I took some shots from various angles and managed to creep around to an upper deck to capture the media circus from Miss Kelly's point of view. It was the first time I'd ever been on her side, looking out. It wasn't a view I especially liked.

"Makes you wonder how we sleep at night, doesn't it?"

I turned to see that the voice to my left had come from an intense-looking woman at my shoulder. She was scribbling her observations onto a lined notebook:

Classically simple camel coat worn over a beige tweed skirt. Peter Pan–collared shirt. Button-down cardigan.

White scarf. Gray fur carried over the arm. Timeless ele-
gance. Miss Kelly's trademark style. Cream coat and pillbox
hat for departure. The press is getting restless.

"Huh. You must write for the fashion pages," I remarked. "I
hardly ever notice what she's wearing. For me it's all about light
and angles. The look in her eye. That smile on those painted
lips."

The woman held out her hand. "Angeline West. Senior fashion
editor for the *Herald* and self-confessed Grace Kelly obsessive."
She shook my hand firmly. "I doubt you've heard of the paper;
we're small, based in Philadelphia. I doubt you've heard of me,
for that matter." She laughed. "But that's all about to change."

"James Henderson," I replied. "Photographer. Working for
anyone who'll pay a decent fee. So you're about to get a promotion?"

"That's the plan. I've been following Grace's story for a year.
Since Cannes. I'm writing a feature about the Grace Kelly look."
She sighed as she lowered her voice. "It's really nothing new. The
classic American college-girl look. A little safe and predictable
if you ask me, but who am I to doubt the fashion choices of a
future princess? I guess we've just never had anyone to showcase
the look so well until now." She paused for a breath as she con-
sulted her page of notes. "I'm sorry. I tend to get a little carried
away when it comes to Grace Kelly. I'm besotted with her."

I laughed at her enthusiasm. "Who isn't?"

She smiled. "And we're here, Mr. Henderson. Right among
it. Almost within touching distance of her. We're watching history, Jim. Can I call you Jim?"

"You just did." I politely declined as she offered me a cigarette. "Don't touch the things. Not anymore."

"Good for you," she muttered as I offered her a match. "You still keep a light handy though, just in case?"

"Habit," I explained. "Always carry a box of matches. It's surprising how often it gets me an introduction, or a date." Angeline rolled her eyes. "Sorry. That came out wrong. I wasn't suggesting . . ." She waved my explanation away. "So, what does a fashion editor do?" I asked. "Is there much to talk about? Besides the wedding dress, of course. Even *I* know that's a big deal."

"Much to talk about? Have you been living under a rock? She's a fashion editor's dream!" She tucked her notebook inside a tan handbag hanging on her arm. "And here's a delicious bit of gossip for you. The wedding shoes—made by New York designer David Evins—were specifically requested with low heels, apparently. So His Serene Petite Highness won't be dwarfed by his wife at the altar! Details on the wedding dress are rarer than hen's teeth. Helen Rose will create something stunning, I'm sure of it."

"Helen Rose?"

"Really? Where have you been? Miss Kelly's wardrobe designer at MGM Studios. She's making the dress. She's down there, look. In the yellow coat. Or maybe I should say, cantaloupe coat."

"As in the melon?"

"Yes. It's the same color as the bridesmaids' dresses. And that older lady beside her. That's Virginia Darcy, Miss Kelly's hairstylist. Also from MGM. She's doing Miss Kelly's hair on the big day. Caused all sorts of noses to be put out of joint when she got the job. I hope she doesn't do anything too fussy. A neat chignon would be perfect, don't you think?"

"I feel sorry for the dog," I said, keen to change the subject from outfits and hairstyles.

"Ha! He was a gift from Cary Grant after they filmed *To Catch a Thief*. He's called Oliver. I wouldn't be at all surprised if he dines on caviar and champagne for breakfast. Grace quite loves him—possibly more than she loves her husband-to-be. He's being kept in an air-conditioned kennel above Miss Kelly's suite."

"Poor Rainer. That's a little mean."

Angeline batted my arm playfully. "Concentrate, Jim. I'm giving you the who's who. That officious-looking guy to Kelly's left? That's someone you definitely need to know. Her publicist from the studio. Hudgins. Sent to safeguard the dress, as well as assist the bride-to-be with press relations. He spent last night with the dress in his room at the Plaza, according to my sources. Refused to let it out of his sight. It's packed in tissue paper scented with the perfume she'll wear on the big day. We're all trying to find out who made the fragrance."

At this, she firmly had my attention. "Really? Why?"

"Because whoever created that perfume is about to become a household name. I only hope they aren't one of those tiny artisan places capable of producing one bottle of fragrance a year. Everyone will want to smell like Miss Kelly. You wait and see."

I imagined how pleased Sophie would be to know that people were talking about her. "Actually, I have some gossip for you, Miss West."

"Oh? And please, call me Angeline. I'm not at typing school now."

"I know who made the wedding perfume."

"What? How?" She grabbed her notebook and pen from her bag. "Is it Krigler? We all assume it is."

I shook my head. "It isn't Krigler. It's Duval."

"Who?"

"Duval. Based in Grasse in Provence. The creator is Sophie Duval, the owner."

Angeline scribbled furiously. "Never heard of her. She your date or something?"

I laughed. "Unfortunately not."

"Well, this is quite the scoop, Jim. Can you tell me more?"

"I can, but not just now. We seem to be getting ready to depart."

As the pier became a hive of activity, and anyone not sailing was ushered off the ship, I accompanied Angeline back to the press conference area.

"So, what's your plan, Jim?" she asked as we walked. "How are you going to get *your* scoop?"

I placed the cap over my lens, laughing at the concept of a plan. "When it comes to Hollywood celebrities I've learned that it's best to toss any and all plans firmly aside. My only plan for the duration of the journey is to not get seasick. If I can arrive in Monaco in one piece and take some decent photographs of the wedding, I'll be a happy man."

Angeline shrugged. "You surprise me. I heard there were four hundred or so reporters and photographers whose applications to travel with Miss Kelly were turned down. You've got to make opportunities like this count. Infiltrate a private party. Talk to the bridesmaids. Get to know the MGM guys. Make a nuisance of yourself. We are on a boat, after all. There are only so many places they can hide her away." A mischievous smile spread across her face as she powdered her nose. "I'm not known for being the friendliest person at the paper," she said, "but friends never won anyone a Pulitzer." She snapped the compact shut. "Martinis in the cocktail lounge at five if you're interested. Toast the bride-to-be and a successful voyage and all that."

Without waiting for an answer, she turned and walked away.

Miss West was a delightful surprise. Smart, confident, and with more than a whiff of danger about her, she was one of those ruthlessly ambitious American women I'd heard about but never met. She was, quite frankly, terrifying, but I suspected she might also be a very useful ally.

As the liner slipped its moorings and began to move away, the crowds of well-wishers lining the pier threw colored streamers and called out, "Good luck, Grace." She smiled warmly in return and waved one of her iconic white gloves. There was a poignancy to the moment, all of us aware that she was waving goodbye to far more than her adoring fans, and I couldn't help feeling that this brave young woman from Philadelphia would need far more luck than most new brides.

Shrouded in a fog, we steamed down the Hudson, the skyline of Manhattan instantly obscured from our view, Lady Liberty bidding us *bon voyage*. The weather reflected the somber mood that fell over the ship. Not the atmosphere of celebration I'd expected, but one of uncertainty. I wondered what thoughts occupied Miss Kelly's mind as she disappeared to her private suite, no doubt glad the razzmatazz was over, for now. All any of us traveling with her could do now was blindly follow her into the Atlantic fog and hope that brighter weather was waiting on the other side of the ocean.

My own thoughts turned to Sophie. Was she thinking of me at that moment? Would she be at Rampoldi as I'd suggested?

I smiled as I turned away from the railing and made my way below deck. Sometimes the greatest thrill of all is the anticipation, and at that moment, everything was possible.

HERE COMES THE BRIDE!

Grace Kelly leaves New York for Monaco.
Angeline West reports for the *Herald*.

Today at just past noon, Grace Kelly bid a regal *au revoir* to her beloved America as the S.S. *Constitution* began her journey toward Monaco. Miss Kelly is accompanied by her family and an impressive array of wedding guests, including friends and business associates from the world of entertainment. And let's not forget her precious pooch, the French poodle Oliver, who was held by Miss Kelly as she patiently answered questions from the world's media, who had gathered to see her off.

At one stage before the departure, the pushing and shoving among the two hundred reporters and newsreel and television cameramen, who had gathered for a press conference, became aggressive, with Miss Kelly's press secretary threatening to end the conference unless the mob would "back up and give this lady some air." The blond actress handled the frantic melee with her usual calm dignity (she isn't known as the "ice queen" for nothing) and said she was very flattered by the attention but "wished people would be more considerate of each other."

During the final stages of the press conference, the twenty-six-year-old appeared to become a little misty-eyed and admitted that she was sad to leave her home but "like any girl" was "excited at the prospect of being married."

It is reported that Miss Kelly's luggage includes some twenty hatboxes and an impressive array of outfits for the week of pre-wedding galas befitting a princess, not to mention the trousseau for her Riviera honeymoon following the nuptials. The outfits are said to be in Miss Kelly's favored shades of beige and blue, with a few evening gowns of yellow, pink, and cream. In addition, Miss Kelly is also understood to have packed nine outfits from *High Society*, which were gifted to her from Metro-Goldwyn-Mayer Studios. But of course the wedding gown is the most hotly discussed item of luggage aboard the S.S. *Constitution*. The design of the gown is a closely guarded secret, although we do know that it is packed with tissue paper scented with a perfume made especially for Miss Kelly's wedding day. And the perfume house behind the special fragrance? Duval, of Grasse, France. You may not be familiar with the name, or that of the perfume's creator—Sophie Duval— but I expect Mademoiselle Duval will soon find herself in high demand.

As the ship departed, Miss Kelly waved to well-wishers from the railing, with her parents at her side. She was later spotted taking a rare moment alone, and this reporter wonders what thoughts might have crossed the young bride's mind as she watched America—her home—disappear behind a blanket of fog. One can only hope that the future awaiting her on the other side of the Atlantic will be a bright one.

The *Constitution*, with 858 passengers on board, is destined for Algeciras and will call at Genoa and Naples, as well as making a special stop at the principality of Monaco on April 12, where the ship will be met by the royal yacht belonging to His Serene Highness.

A real-life fairy tale if ever there was one.

25

SOPHIE

Cannes

After I'd made the dreaded call to the bank, time moved swiftly. When I explained the commission for the wedding perfume, they agreed to give me until the end of the month. Nevertheless, they pulled out the estimates they'd conducted last fall and set up a series of meetings. I'd never forgotten the way the property inspectors had marched first into the boutique in Cannes and then into my factory and home in Grasse, clipboards in hand, weighing Duval's worth. They'd invaded my home and scurried among the rows of naked rosebushes like black ants crawling over a picnic while I'd tried to maintain my composure. It had been merely a precaution I'd taken back then, gathering official estimates of the property value as a last resort if I didn't find a way to save Duval. Now, it appeared I would need them after all.

As I leafed through the paperwork again, my mind boggled at how much the estate was worth in its entirety. Now I understood the large sum Michael Lever had offered for my fragrant fields. But he couldn't have them. I'd made my decision, hard as it was—I would first sell the boutique and the apartment in Cannes. The money from the sale would stave off the creditors for a while, at least long enough to see what impact the wedding commission would have and to launch my new line of fragrances. The only thing left to decide was when to tell Natalie. I couldn't seem to find the words to tell her that her time with Duval, after so many years, would soon come to an end.

I tucked my handbag under my arm and walked along the wharf to Lucien's boat, my heart lodged in my throat. I'd need his help with the sale—and I could use a shoulder to lean on—so when he'd invited me for a quiet lunch, I didn't hesitate. Perhaps we'd even go for a sail and I could clear my head amid the waves. With my emotions so confused, I felt drawn to the things and the people I knew best. Habit and familiarity were important with so much of what was normal for me under threat. Offers for the boutique had been coming in all morning, and though that was a good thing, it also made everything very real. Things were changing, and quickly.

"Lucien? *C'est moi.*"

He emerged from the deckhouse in a sweater threaded with the softest hint of purple and a pair of dove-gray pants, handsome as always. The moment his eyes alighted on mine, I burst into tears.

"Oh, Sophie." He held out his arms, gathering me close to him.

I fell into his clean scent, searching for the comfort I so desperately needed. For a moment, in spite of my sorrow, all seemed as it should be. Me, wrapped in Lucien's arms on a cool, early spring day.

I filled him in on the latest as I pulled off my flats and tossed them to the floor. "I need a martini strong enough to peel paint off the walls. Oh, and I've been working on some bottle designs for *Coeur de Princesse*. Take a look." I fished the *journal de fleurs* from my bag.

Lucien chuckled, kissed my forehead, and stalked over to the bar, ignoring the journal and my designs. His chinos were taut across his derriere and had I been in better spirits, I might have commented on them. Instead, I stared on glumly.

He poured a splash of this and that into his cocktail shaker, and shook the mixture brusquely, the ice clattering inside it with a metallic ring. "Once you've paid off some of the debt, you'll feel better," he coaxed. "You'll see. And then we can talk about what to do next."

"I'm so glad Papa can't see all this. He would be so upset."

Lucien handed me the drink. "He would never want this sort of stress placed on your shoulders. He'd want you to be safe and have stability, and I'm certain he would do the same thing—sell the properties and retire in style."

I downed the martini. "No, he wouldn't retire. Creating parfums isn't like banking, Lucien. You don't just stop and play tennis instead. It's part of your soul, part of the very fibers that make up who you are. Fragrances and their individual scents are like words, a way to express myself. Without them, I have nothing to say."

"That just isn't true," he said, setting a tray of cold meats, cheeses, and bread on the table in the galley kitchen. "There's much more to you than your father's work."

"But it's not just *his* work," I said, my head suddenly woozy. I hadn't eaten for hours and the alcohol hit my system hard. "It's mine now." I set the martini glass down. "This isn't about what my father left behind, though that is a part of it, too. It's about everything I've added since he died. It's about *my* art, not just his. I don't know how to make you see—"

"Let's change the subject, shall we?" Lucien slid into a chair next to me. "Talk about something more cheery?" He kissed my nose as if to punctuate the conversation and begin again. "My father just closed another big deal. He's buying a house in Tuscany to celebrate. I think that's worth a toast, don't you? Perhaps we might take it over one day. Live there together." He held up his glass to toast mine, and took a sip. "Of course we'd have to make things more official first."

"Are you asking me to marry you?" I asked, rattled by the way he'd dropped it so casually into the conversation.

He kissed the palm of my hand. "Give me more credit than that. I'd make a proposal far more memorable."

My head swam at the prospect of marrying Lucien, of marrying anyone, and I quickly changed the subject back to the topic plaguing me. "You can afford to buy them all out. The bank, my debts. I could . . . I could repay you. In the future, after my new line becomes a sensation." I no longer had time to be prideful.

I needed help. "Grace's wedding will help spread my name and bring in many more sales."

He frowned. "Perhaps, perhaps not. And it isn't about your repaying me. It was never about that. The fact is, Duval isn't a good business investment unless you can sustain the market changes, and you, *mon amour,* cannot. You have a fairly well-known name, but that isn't enough. You need the kind of buying power and reputation that you haven't achieved. Chanel, Molinard, Givenchy. You will never be able to compete with them. Even if I pay off your debts, or buy the property outright, it won't be long before you'll be running on a deficit again. We both know that, *chérie.* Besides, Marceau is still technically my father's business, not mine. And he would never agree to saving a little *parfumerie.*"

His words stung, and I just couldn't sustain any more pain at the moment. I stood and pulled on my coat.

"This is why you can't possibly understand. It's never *your* money. You don't create anything on your own, not from here." I pointed to my heart. "Where is your passion, Lucien? What is there to you, after all? A man who has charm and nice clothes, and only his father's yachts to prove his worth." I balked inwardly at my ability to be so hurtful, even if, deep down, I believed what I'd said was at least partially true.

He looked as if I'd slapped him. A moment passed before he spoke in a low steady voice.

"I'm going to ignore that because you're upset, but I think it's time you went home. Get some rest. I'll check on you tomorrow."

"Don't bother," I seethed. "I have work to do."

"Stop this nonsense, Sophie. You know I want nothing but your happiness."

And what did my happiness look like to him, exactly? Having a family and acting as a dutiful little wife in some sprawling estate in Tuscany? Letting him decide what makes good business sense and what doesn't, even if it meant destroying part of who I am? Bolting for the door, I didn't bother to close it behind me.

I ambled along the beach, the crisp wind whipping around me, drying my tears on my cheeks. The heart notes lingered beyond the head notes, it was true, but even they didn't last the longest. Eventually they evaporated too, leaving only the most grounding, fundamental base notes behind. I knew what grounded me—my *parfumerie.*

As I threw pebbles into the sea, I pictured the *Constitution* sailing over the horizon, Grace Kelly's wedding dress on board, infused with my parfum. And James, whose funny letters and words of support had helped to keep me afloat these last difficult months, when others were only intent on helping me drown.

I inhaled a deep breath of salty air, turned toward La Croisette, and forged ahead against the wind.

* * *

I awoke the next morning with a fuzzy head and puffy eyes. As the events of the day before flooded back, I groaned. It wasn't Lucien's fault my business was in trouble. I knew perfectly well that mixing financial matters with my relationship would most likely create problems, and it had already. It was a terrible idea. But his snide comments—and that hint at marriage! I cringed as I slipped from bed and slowly readied for the day before heading to the shop.

Today, I needed to settle on the bottle design for *Coeur de Princesse* and order another batch of business cards. With nearly a week in Monaco, I would have ample time to share my card and the Duval name. I didn't relish the prospect of all that salesmanship and the exhaustion that inevitably followed when I had to focus on promotion instead of hiding in my workshop, but I pushed any negative thoughts aside. In less than a week I'd be in Monaco, at the heart of the wedding festivities, and my parfum would drift down the aisle with the princess. In less than a week, James would be in Monaco, too. My heart somersaulted as I thought of his telegram. *Meet me in Monaco when we arrive on the 12th? I'll be at Rampoldi in Monte Carlo at 7 P.M. I remember you told me you've always wanted to go there. Jim. x*

I sighed absentmindedly as I entered the boutique. I shouldn't think about James so often—but I couldn't help myself. I *liked* him. I liked him very much. In fact, I liked him enough that I'd already decided I would meet him at Rampoldi to say hello. What harm could it do? And yet Lucien would be with me in Monaco. My stomach clenched at the thought of the two of them in the same place.

"Why the big sigh, *chérie*?" Natalie asked, following me into the office, arms filled with flowers to put in the vase on my desk. When I didn't reply, she put the flowers down and tilted my chin to meet her eye. "Well?"

I felt my walls come tumbling down. "I can't stop thinking about James." I sank into my chair. "There. Now you know."

A smile bloomed on her face. "He's a lovely man, Sophie. Talented, clever, and beneath his somewhat tough exterior, I think he's quite a tenderhearted fellow."

I nodded and looked down at my hands. "But what about Lucien? I feel so guilty."

"First of all, you aren't engaged or married to Lucien, so you are a free woman. You've only kissed James. Once. That's no reason to berate yourself, but if you think you have feelings for him, it might be time to make some decisions."

"What in the world will I tell Lucien? He's to be my date to Grace's wedding events."

"*Rien,*" she said, crossing her arms. "You tell him nothing until you're sure of how you feel."

I chewed my lip. "What I feel is that Lucien doesn't believe in me. When I broached the subject of another loan, he said his father would never agree to such a poor business venture. We argued yesterday. I'm still furious." I looked up at Natalie, preparing myself to tell her about selling the properties in Cannes, but the words fell away as she clasped my hands across the desk.

"You must follow your heart. If you are uncertain about Lucien, don't ignore those feelings simply because they frighten you. You will live to regret it."

Perhaps I already had regrets. I recalled the two years I'd spent with Lucien, how we often seemed to want different things, but how I'd relished our differences, as had he, at least initially. Then I remembered how James had looked at me just before we kissed. With adoration and tenderness. I'd never seen Lucien look at me that way. If I had regrets, it was that I'd so often blamed myself for being lacking in some way, unable to inspire true devotion from Lucien, for never quite pleasing him.

I picked at a piece of lint on my blouse. "Natalie. Can I ask . . . you and Papa?"

"I loved him very much," she said quietly.

"And he loved you?"

She nodded, her eyes full of memories. "Sophie, I know your mother . . . I'm sorry that . . ."

I shook my head. "Never be sorry for loving him the way he deserved to be loved. He and Maman should have never married. Even after his death, she didn't value him or all that he gave to her. Me included."

"She loves you in her way," Natalie said, brushing the stray lock of hair out of my eyes. "She's just trying to fix a spiritual problem with a bandage. It can't be done, and until she sees that, she will remain as she is. Embittered, alone."

"And drunk."

Natalie pulled me into her arms. "We must grasp happiness with both hands, hold tight, and armor ourselves with it against the world." She kissed my forehead. "Do not think too much. Follow your instincts. They will guide you."

Though I felt some relief sharing my feelings with Natalie, I felt like a trapeze artist, navigating a thin line between success and failure, happiness and heartache.

Sighing, I reached for my handbag. "I suppose we should get to work. Tell me what you think of these bottle designs."

I peeked inside my bag for my journal, where I'd sketched

ideas for various designs—and paused. It wasn't there. Frowning, I rummaged inside the bag again. Where had I put it? I set down my handbag and searched all the logical places it might be in the office.

"Natalie? Have you seen my journal?"

"No," she called from the counter.

"I was sure I'd brought it with me. I'm going to the apartment, see if it's there." My voice was steady, but a hint of worry trickled through my veins.

At the apartment, I checked the kitchen counters and my writing desk. When the journal didn't turn up, I dug deeper, beneath the bed and in the cabinets, behind cushions, even beside the bathtub. Perhaps I hadn't looked thoroughly enough at the boutique. Panic mounting, I hurried back to the shop and searched every corner, every drawer, again. Each minute that ticked by, my anxiety rose a notch higher and my hands began to tremble. All our precious formulas! Papa's careful notes. Where was it? Where had I seen it last?

I grabbed my keys and headed to Lucien's yacht, retracing my steps from yesterday in my mind. I'd taken my journal with me to lunch. Perhaps it had fallen out there and slipped under the leather sofa in the cabin. I broke into a run along La Croisette, ignoring the way my feet smarted in my heels, feeling only the beat of my heart thundering in my ears. The formula for *Coeur de Princesse* was in the journal. I couldn't let anyone else get their hands on that. It was my secret, my future. I ran faster. By the time I reached Lucien's boat, the back of my dress was damp with perspiration and my heart thrashed against my ribs.

I stepped over the rope and onto the boat, and without pause knocked insistently on the cabin door. No one answered. My breathing quickened as I knocked again, louder. Still, no one came. *Dieu,* where the hell was he when I needed him? This time, I banged loudly, calling Lucien's name. Fumbling with my keys, I found the spare he had given me and, willing my hands to stop shaking, unlocked the door.

The scent of leather and cool metal washed over me, a trace of Lucien's cologne. I frantically checked all of the countertops and cabinets. Crouching on my knees, I searched beneath the sofa and chairs, pulling the place apart in my panic. I remembered taking the journal from my handbag to show Lucien the bottle designs, but I couldn't remember what I'd done with it after that. Had he picked it up? After our quarrel I'd walked on the promenade, and then gone straight home to my apartment. I felt a rock lodge in my stomach. The journal definitely wasn't here, so where was it?

Deflated and helpless, I headed back to the boutique. I prayed that it would show up somewhere because the alternative was too awful to contemplate: not only would I have lost the complex formula for *Coeur de Princesse* and all my other new fragrances, but I would also have lost part of Duval's history, and the last piece of Papa.

26

JAMES

With the American coastline soon far behind us, the gray Atlantic was all I could see in every direction. I wasn't the greatest fan of the water (due, in part, to a rather unhealthy obsession with the fate of R.M.S. *Titanic*), so I was glad when we were called to our muster stations for the obligatory lifeboat drill.

Eddie O'Reilly, a grouchy Irish-American chap who looked like he'd seen the bottom of far too many tumblers of single malt, walked with me from the cabin we'd been allocated. He'd already found great amusement in my failed attempts to arrange my limbs so that they might fit into the small bunk bed.

"Put a hundred press photographers anywhere and there'll be trouble," he remarked as we made our away along the endless corridors and stairwells. "Squeeze them all onto a boat sailing across the Atlantic and there's no telling what might happen." He whistled dramatically through his teeth.

"What do you mean?" I asked, ducking to avoid bumping my head on a low door.

"I mean that if Jack Kelly doesn't arrange regular press ops with young Grace, all hell might break loose. We all want a story, and—as yet—they're not giving us one."

When we arrived at the designated muster station I was surprised to see the Kelly party also assembled, having assumed they would be excused from such things. It was chilly on deck and everyone was keen to get back inside as quickly as possible.

"At least it gives us a chance to get a few more shots of her," I muttered, rubbing my hands to keep them warm as I adjusted my camera settings.

Eddie wasn't impressed. "Who wants to see the world's most beautiful woman trussed up like a Christmas turkey in an ugly life vest?"

He had a point. Even the mighty Grace Kelly in her trademark sunglasses and headscarf couldn't pull off bright orange nylon. I wasted half a roll of film anyway in the hope that Sanders would prefer to have something rather than nothing.

As the formalities reached their conclusion and we were permitted to take a few shots, Miss Kelly's poodle became startled by the flashbulbs and our shouts for Grace to look this way and that way. He scrambled from her arms and made a dash for it along the deck. She squealed and chased after him. While everyone else stood around to watch the drama unfold, I set off in pursuit, rugby tackling the dog to the ground with an impressive swan dive.

Miss Kelly was very grateful to have him safely back in her arms.

"Thank you so much," she gasped as the dog licked her face, setting her off into a fit of the giggles. "He's such a very dear pet. Aren't you, Oliver darling? Yes, you are!" She turned her attention back to me. "Thank you. I couldn't bear to think of anything happening to him."

"You're welcome," I said, adjusting my hat and straightening my jacket. "Haven't made a tackle like that for years. I'm quite pleased to discover I still can, to be honest."

"You were very gallant. And very fast!" She smiled at me in a way that made me realize how lucky Prince Rainier was. Imagine waking up to that smile every morning. That face. Those eyes. It took all my self-control not to point the camera at her and capture her beauty up close. "Oh, and you've torn your trousers. I hope you're not hurt?"

I patted myself down. "Nothing broken. Sacrificed a pair of oxfords, but rather that than sacrifice your happiness, Miss Kelly." I had no idea I was capable of such fawning insincerity.

"I guess we all have to make sacrifices sometimes."

Her smile faded as she said this, as if her thoughts had taken her far away from the deck of the *Constitution* and she were somewhere else entirely.

"I guess we do," I replied.

She studied me, a slight smile at her lips. It was a look that drew you right into the depths of those ice-blue eyes. "I know you, don't I? Didn't we meet in Monaco? At the palace? We did!"

Given the dozens of reporters on the boat, not to mention

the hundreds she'd encountered recently, I was surprised she remembered me—and relieved she hadn't remembered me for chasing her in Cannes, or if she had, was gracious enough not to mention it.

I held out a hand. "That's right. James Henderson. Jim to my friends. Henderson to my adversaries."

She shook my hand surprisingly firmly. "Of which I am quite sure there can't be many."

"You'd be surprised!"

She laughed brightly. "So you were there when I first met Rainier, and now you're here sailing with me toward our wedding! Do you remember that dreadful taffeta dress?" She shook her head and looked a little embarrassed. "There was a power outage at the Carlton that morning and . . . anyway, I don't suppose it matters now. I guess he must love me very much if I didn't put him off with my appearance that day."

"Love is blind, Miss Kelly. And anyway, you looked perfectly lovely. As always." That laugh again. Like pure crystal.

"And you gave me the business card, didn't you? For the perfumery. Duval."

I smiled. "Yes. Sophie is a friend of mine."

At Sophie's name she brightened. "She's your friend? But that's marvelous! The fragrance she developed for me is exquisite. She called it *Coeur de Princesse*. Heart of a princess. It's simply perfect!"

I pictured Sophie's face in my mind, imagined her bent over her little vials and mixing bottles in her workshop in Grasse, intense concentration on her face as she peered through her spectacles. I could almost smell the vanilla and musk and orange blossoms and the delicate scent of tea roses that lingered in her hair, as if they bloomed there.

"I'm afraid we haven't seen each other for quite a while now," I explained, not wishing to overemphasize my friendship, which, let's be honest, was hanging by the most fragile of threads. "Rather difficult circumstances. Long story. I'm hoping to meet her in Monaco, actually."

Miss Kelly thought for a moment. "Really? Well, that's wonderful. What cabin are you staying in, Jim?"

"156. Not quite steerage but I wouldn't fancy my chances if we encountered an iceberg."

At this she smiled. "Then let's hope we don't. You can expect a package to be delivered to you. I would be very grateful if you would pass it on to Sophie when you see her. A little thank-you. I'd hoped to meet her myself, but I'm not sure I'll have time once we arrive. Things have become a little hectic."

"Consider it done."

As she walked away, she turned to glance over her shoulder, and damn it if the light wasn't perfect as a smile to outshine the moon danced on those strawberry-red lips.

"Join us for a pre-dinner drink, would you, Jim?" she added. "First-class deck. Seven thirty. A thank-you from Oliver and I."

She didn't wait for a reply. I suppose when you're about to become a princess you don't need to.

27

SOPHIE

Grasse

After forty-eight hours of searching everywhere and checking with some potential buyers who had stopped into the boutique on the day it had disappeared, I still couldn't find the journal. I'd even asked Lucien if he'd picked it up by mistake, but he hadn't seen it. It had simply vanished into thin air. Grief hit me in waves as I felt as if I'd lost Papa all over again. All his precious notes, gone. Although I'd thankfully transcribed most of the formulas to my permanent files, it was the essence of Papa, captured between the faded pages, that could never be replaced.

I wanted to hide at the cinema with Madame Clouet and lose myself in make-believe to escape my thoughts, but instead I headed to the house to check on Maman. As I opened the door, the final notes of "L'Homme et L'Enfant" by the Constantines drifted from the record player in the living room.

"I'm home," I called out, dropping my keys on the table.

"Where have you been?" she snapped, giving me a sharp look as I joined her in the living room. "I haven't heard from you in days."

"You know it's the start of the busy season," I explained. "I come as often as I can."

As often as I can stand to, I added silently.

I walked into the adjacent kitchen and, leaning inside the refrigerator, rooted around until I found cheese and cold chicken. I snatched a hunk of bread from the counter, and carried the plate of food to the table in the dining room.

"Have you eaten?" I asked, watching her as she slid into the chair opposite me. I never knew what to say to her. Sometimes, it was like living with a stranger, and not one I especially liked.

She waved a hand through the air dismissively. "I'm not hungry."

She never was. All she hungered for was another drink.

"You're quiet. What's happened?" she asked, looking at me from the corner of her eye.

"Nothing," I mumbled through a mouthful of baguette. I avoided the topic of the lost journal, reluctant to share the news with her. In my head I could already hear her well-worn rant about responsibility, and it would infuriate me to sit through a lecture from a woman who had never been responsible about anything in her life.

"This new fragrance line is only going to put us deeper into debt, you know," she said, spilling some of her brandy as she leaned forward. "And yet you won't consider accepting an enormous sum to sell the land so we can live comfortably."

I weighed whether or not it was worth talking to her about it.

"I'm trying to save the business, Maman. Our livelihood. Papa's legacy. But you always do that, don't you? *'This won't work'* and *'You need to move on'* and *'This is a waste of time.'* Negative at every turn. You've always rejected my ideas."

Rejected me, I thought. From the very beginning. The food turned to sawdust in my mouth. Why had everything become so difficult, gone so horribly wrong?

Maman rose from her chair. "Rejected your ideas? *You've* rejected me! You and your father both!" She ran through a list of her favorite curse words, then began with the usual barrage of insults against Papa, making little sense. Her face flamed red and she shook her fist at me.

"You're drunk. Go to bed, Maman."

"I don't say things I don't mean."

My eyes shuttered briefly. "Please, I don't want to do this. Go to bed."

"If you weren't so incompetent, the journal with the new formulas wouldn't be missing," she slurred.

My eyes narrowed. "What? How did you know the journal is lost?"

She stumbled a little. "Well . . . Lucien rang this morning. He said you were upset about it."

Maman was a terrible liar, always had been. I watched her stagger to the kitchen before asking why Lucien had called. "What did he say exactly?"

"He . . . he wanted to speak to you. Wondered if you were here since he couldn't get hold of you at the shop." Her voice caught, betraying her. "We talked about your future together if you must know. He really loves you, Sophie."

I ground my teeth in frustration. "I'd appreciate if the two of you didn't discuss my future when I'm not around." I pushed up from the table and put my plate in the sink.

"I like Lucien," Maman pressed. "He doesn't talk down to me the way you do."

He hadn't suffered her drunkenness for all these years, either.

"You've given me plenty of reasons to talk to you like that," I shot back.

"Sometimes I don't know what Lucien sees in you, Sophie. A man like him could do better."

Stunned by her words, I stared at her, speechless, then grabbed my handbag and left, slamming the door behind me.

Tired of always being treated like a child, I summoned Lucien to my apartment in Cannes, insisting he cancel whatever business luncheon he had planned because we needed to talk.

"First of all, I would prefer that you didn't tell Maman my business," I fumed as I set an espresso and a café crème on the dining table. "If I'd wanted to tell her about the journal, I would have."

He pressed my hands between his. "I'm sorry. I thought you'd have already told her. I wasn't thinking."

"No, you weren't. And I also wish you wouldn't discuss *our* future with her. You've hardly even discussed it with me." The telephone rang and I set down my coffee. "That had better not be her. I really don't want to talk to her again."

I picked up the receiver to discover it wasn't Maman, but a reporter from *Paris Match*. I was surprised to learn that word had got out about my commission to make the wedding parfum for Grace. Though wary he might turn the interview into one of those wretched gossip columns, and uncomfortable with him having called me at home, I agreed to give a brief interview. Duval needed all the publicity it could get, and I needed a bright point to cling to. *Coeur de Princesse* would give Duval the attention it desperately needed, and that would help launch the new line.

After I'd answered all the reporter's questions, I hung up the phone and glanced at Lucien, who sat quietly at the table, his blue eyes trained on me. It hadn't escaped my notice that he'd listened to every word.

"What was that about?" he asked.

I shifted my gaze from his, focusing on the window that looked over the marina.

"A reporter with *Paris Match* wants to feature Duval in the magazine. Isn't that great news." I smiled, and cradled my coffee cup in my hands.

Lucien cocked one eyebrow at me. "Do you think it's wise to speak to reporters with your plan to close the boutique? It's a little like false advertising, isn't it? Besides which, parading your name through the gossip magazines will only scare away potential buyers. It doesn't make sense, Sophie."

I slammed down my coffee, spilling half of it onto the table.

"You know what doesn't make sense? The fact that you don't understand how important this is to me. The fact that you cannot grasp how hard I'm willing to fight for everything I've worked for. You're a businessman yourself. Why don't you see this is the same—working hard to protect your livelihood, possibly even expand it?"

"Because it isn't the same," he replied sternly. "As a man, I'm expected to work hard. It's my responsibility to secure our livelihood, our future. You don't have those responsibilities. You don't need to work at all. I honestly don't know why you're not jumping at Lever's offer. It's quite obvious running Duval has put far too much stress on you."

I seethed at his second allusion to marriage. His timing was terrible, as ever, and I doubted his actual intentions. Lucien enjoyed the attention he often received as one of the Côte d'Azur's most eligible bachelors. Perhaps we were just too different after all, hurtling along like trains whose paths cross briefly before speeding rapidly away in opposite directions.

I fixed him with an icy glare. "After two years together, you don't know me at all, do you?"

Leaving a confused Lucien to fend for himself, I went to the bedroom, closed the door, and lay on the bed, staring numbly at the ceiling. My heart sank again at the thought of someone thumbing through the journal, dismissing the notes so dear to me, turning to the page where I'd written my ideas for the head, heart, and base notes of Grace's perfume. Grace Kelly! I'd written, underlining the words three times. Princess Grace of Monaco! And underneath, one other word.

James.

✳ ✳ ✳

There was one final thing I had to do before I traveled to Monaco for the wedding celebrations. I had to tell Natalie about selling the properties in Cannes. I couldn't put it off any longer.

When I arrived at the boutique, my stomach sank.

Natalie was already at the counter, preparing everything for the day ahead. She looked pretty in the half light of early morning.

"Bonjour," she said as I opened the door.

Her cheerful smile was the first thing I saw most days. Even when I spent the night with Lucien, he'd usually left for the office long before I was awake.

I paused for a moment in the doorway. The scent of the boutique hit me as if I was smelling it for the first time: juniper and vanilla, a trace of verbena. It touched my heart. I felt my resolve waver beneath the sense of familiarity and nostalgia this place provoked.

Having been held back so long, the words rushed from my lips. "I have something to tell you, Natalie. And I'm—I'm sorry. This is the most difficult thing I've ever had to do."

Without a word, she held out her arms for an embrace. I fell into them, let her hold me against her for a long while. When we parted, I saw tears in her eyes.

"I was waiting for you to tell me, my dear girl."

I wept without control. "I have to sell the boutique. And the apartment."

"I know. It isn't your fault," she said softly. "You've done everything you could."

"What would Papa say? I've lost his journal and almost destroyed his legacy. The factory may be next." Tears barreled down my cheeks.

"*Mon amour.*" Natalie wrapped me in her arms. "You have always lived under your father's shadow. But you don't need to. You're a very talented *parfumeur*, Sophie. In fact, I think you're

even better than your father ever was. He knew this." She
brushed a tear from my cheek. "He told me so, many times."

"He did?"

She nodded. "This is why he pushed you so hard. Taught
you everything he knew. You must build your own legacy, now,
chérie. See this as a good thing. You've never really liked the
noise and bustle of Cannes, have you?" She smiled, knowing
she was right. "Perhaps you should travel to new places, have
new experiences to pour into your parfums. I have faith in your
abilities, just as your papa always did. And now your famous
friend Grace Kelly does, too." She pressed her hands to my face.
"So should you."

She was right. "Thank you, Natalie. For everything."

We stood in silence for a moment before she continued.

"Now, don't worry about me. I've saved carefully over the
years. I can retire, or perhaps work in another little shop along
the harbor. Whatever I desire. This is a good thing for me, too.
We will have our lunches and walks along La Croisette. And
should you need me at the factory, or if you open another shop,
I'll be beside you every step of the way."

"*Je t'aime,*" I said, meaning the words of love with all my heart.

"I know," she said, gently wiping my face with a handkerchief before she kissed each cheek. "Now, you must enjoy the
wedding! And after, when it's over, we'll go through the boutique and the apartment together. Move your things to Grasse.
How does that sound?"

I embraced her fiercely. "I don't know what I'd do without you."

"I hope you never have to find out!"

28

JAMES

I didn't tell anyone about the drinks invitation from Grace, but of course the other chaps wanted to know why I was smartening myself up with a suit jacket and tie. Or trying to. It wasn't easy with the rocking, rolling motion of the ship. My stomach was in a continual state of turmoil and the remaining days of sailing ahead already felt like months.

"Meeting that American journalist again, are you?" Eddie asked with a hearty dig to my ribs. "Be careful. She's got a reputation. She'd eat you for breakfast."

I laughed, happy to let him think whatever he wanted, as long as he didn't find out where I was really going. Nobody liked the popular kid who snuck his way into the inner circle without inviting anyone else to join him, and I didn't fancy spending the rest of the voyage being teacher's pet.

Much as it pained me to do so, I left my camera in the cabin.

I felt I'd gained Miss Kelly's trust. The last thing I wanted to do was blow it when I was getting close to her.

Ignoring the churning in my stomach, I breezed my way confidently onto the first-class deck and took two martinis from a passing waiter trussed up like a penguin. I downed one immediately and handed the empty glass back to him before making a beeline for Miss Kelly with the other drink gripped firmly in hand. I couldn't help wondering what Marjorie and Thing would make of it all, and what Emily would think about the elegant ladies. She'd no doubt take more interest in the engine room and corner the poor captain with endless questions about the construction of the ship.

But mostly, I let myself imagine what Sophie would say if she were here, her arm looped gently through mine as we made an entrance together, dressed to the nines. She would lean her head softly toward mine and whisper something witty.

My daydreaming came to an abrupt end as Miss Kelly arrived at the soiree. She positively shimmered in a peacock-blue cocktail dress. I thought briefly of Angeline West and how frantically she would be scribbling down every detail of Miss Kelly's outfit: calf length, satin, fitted to perfection.

I waited a while as she was swept up among the guests, choosing my moment to emerge from behind the large potted palm where I'd been attempting to remain inconspicuous.

"Miss Kelly. You look radiant."

"Jim. You made it." She offered a gloved hand in greeting before turning to Jack Kelly, who stood with a group of important-looking men beside us. "Daddy, this is the Weimaraner breeder I was telling you about."

She stared at me pointedly. I tried to hide my surprise and

horror as I shook Jack Kelly's hand. I didn't know the first thing about dogs, let alone breeding them. I didn't even know much about cats, despite owning one.

"Good to meet another hound man," he barked. "I'm not fond of those miniature dogs. Poodles and the like."

"Daddy!" Grace batted his hand playfully. "Oliver will hear you!"

Grace winked at me and excused herself for a moment, leaving me with her father. He was an imposing man, and not overly welcoming. I played to his ego by asking him about his Olympic success, which softened him a little. The martinis helped bolster my confidence and, much to my surprise, I was almost convincing when it came to matters of dog breeding.

The evening passed quickly as I was introduced to various friends and members of the wedding party: an eclectic mix of Hollywood darlings, old school friends of Grace's, influential business colleagues of Jack Kelly's, nervous aunts, and shy second cousins. I decided it was best to depart before I outstayed my welcome or blew my cover and was glad when Miss Kelly approached me to say she was ducking out herself.

"I don't know about you, Jim, but I find these social events exhausting. I'm escaping to my suite to read a good book in peace." She took a small velvet box and a sealed envelope from her evening bag. "I thought it might be simpler to give this to you in person, rather than have it sent to your cabin. It's only something small, but I hope Sophie will like it. I'd be ever so grateful if you could pass it to her when you meet?"

"Of course." I took the items and tucked them into my jacket pocket. "She'll be delighted."

She would be more than delighted. That smile I'd seen the night we kissed on the terrace would fill her lips, and her eyes would dance with excitement. I imagined her again at my side. What would she wear to a cocktail party with Grace Kelly? Deep blue, perhaps, to bring out the black in her hair. I closed one eye, framing her in my mind, pressing an imaginary shutter to capture her.

"Jim? James?"

I opened my eye.

Miss Kelly was smiling at me, her head tilted to one side. "I think you are daydreaming about Mademoiselle Duval?"

I coughed awkwardly and in reply muttered something about Weimaraners making wonderful pets. She wasn't fooled.

"I don't blame you," she added. "Such beauty and talent. I hope she finds true happiness, as I have." She blushed a little at the confession. "I'm afraid I've had a little too much champagne. If you'll excuse me."

I watched her leave, finished my martini, and slipped quietly away without drawing attention to myself.

I didn't have a photograph of Grace Kelly, but I had something to bring a smile to Sophie's lips. And that was worth more than a hundred photographs of a future princess.

A large boat, it turned out, could hide a princess-in-waiting extremely well. Or rather, her father and the hired henchmen from MGM Studios could hide her well. After my first twenty-four hours with her, it was almost as if Miss Kelly had disappeared entirely.

There were no details given about her schedule for the duration of the journey, nor any mention of additional press conferences. She and her dog were hidden away in her luxury apartments, while we were bunked up four to a cabin, jostling for space to stow our luggage and our limbs and feeling in turns seasick and restless. Mostly, we were bored.

"That sodding MGM chap makes me want to punch his perfectly tanned smug little face," I grumbled as I lay on my bunk, hands behind my head, my feet hanging off the end of the bed.

"At least we're not holed up in the ship's hospital," Eddie quipped. "I heard that's where Kelly's private press party are sleeping."

"I doubt that includes Howell Conant. I presume he's sleeping in the ship's penthouse," I replied.

Conant alone had exclusive access to Kelly's every move. As a result, he wasn't much liked by the rest of us.

"We'll just have to take our chances when we get them." Eddie sighed as he clambered onto the bunk above me, causing the mattress to dip alarmingly. "It's a ship, for Christ's sake. She can't get *that* far away from us."

But, evidently, she could.

An unsettled mood fell over the *Constitution* after that first day. Reporters and photographers lurked like snipers, hiding in corners and snooping around, obsessed with getting a shot of Miss Kelly, or a bit of gossip to fill the column inches. Impatient editors concocted sensationalist headlines about an unhappy bride-to-be, hidden away in the bowels of the ship as she sailed helplessly toward her new life under the control of a miserable prince. We heard of regular passengers being bumped

from their first-class cabins and reassigned to cabin class to accommodate the Kelly party. An especially disgruntled couple
from Long Island, celebrating their ruby wedding anniversary,
provided some excellent copy for the reporters, who exaggerated the couple's ire where necessary. "The Wedding of the
Century Has Ruined Our Honeymoon!" and similar headlines
were sent down the wires, knowing they would hit the newsstands long before we arrived in Monaco.

A frustrated press photographer can easily make friends with
a bored table waiter with a taste for half-decent whiskey. I soon
learned of secret passages that could give me access to a sneaky
shot of Kelly's black-tie dinners with the captain. We all knew
Jack Kelly was footing the bill for this bizarre wedding cruise.
Having been spared the cost of the wedding itself (the prince
and MGM were handling all that), he'd made no secret of the
fact that he was covering the cost of the entire wedding party's
passage to Monaco, and all they could eat and drink along the
way. But photo opportunities were few and far between.

After dinner, Miss Kelly preferred to politely escape to the
relative privacy of low-key gatherings with her close friends
and family, where she kicked off her shoes, put on her reading
glasses, and played late-night games of charades in the Tattoo
Room, deep in the ship's bowels and far away from our prying
lenses. Who could blame her for wishing to hang on, just a
little longer, to that girl next door with whom we'd all fallen
a little bit in love.

Like warring enemies hunkered down in our trenches, the
press pack and the Kelly entourage tolerated each other as the ship
pressed on, and a prince, and all of Monaco, awaited our arrival.

29

SOPHIE

Cap-d'Ail to Monaco

Although in many ways I wanted time to slow down, I felt buoyed by the prospect of the wedding, of seeing Grace again—and James. So I was glad when the day arrived for me to leave Cannes and make my way to Monaco. Cannes had become a noose around my neck. My future lay elsewhere.

I packed two cases of clothes for the various events I would attend leading up to the wedding and on the big day itself. One contained evening wear and pumps; another held an array of cardigans, chinos, and scarves. A third, smaller case was filled with precious samples of *Coeur de Princesse, Lumière d'Étoiles,* and *Mémoire,* each presented in a black gossamer bag tied with gold ribbon. I'd debated whether or not I should bring hand-made soaps from the factory, too, since they were so popular, and finally decided on several packages of rosemary, orange blossom, and lilac to dazzle the magazine editors.

The last outfit I packed, for the evening gala I would attend with Lucien at the opera house, was a royal blue chiffon ball gown with A-line skirts and white gloves. I wrapped it carefully in tissue paper and placed it on top of the other outfits, beside a lace tea length dress. I wanted to look my best. Not for Lucien, but for Grace and for Duval.

Despite our argument, I'd decided to make amends with Lucien for appearances' sake. But we both knew something had shifted between us. Something irrevocable. The ground beneath my feet felt unsteady, as if I were walking barefoot over a pebbled beach. I already knew what I was going to do about Lucien, but that was a matter for after the wedding celebrations. For now, I would focus on enjoying my time in Monaco and promoting Duval.

As I snapped my case closed, the reunion with James at Rampoldi flitted through my mind. Natalie had assured me the restaurant was easy to find, near the casino square. I closed my eyes, remembering his scent, his laugh, the way he listened to me so intently. My mind traveled over every detail of our time together, like a well-worn road. If only I could bottle it up like a fine fragrance, release all the warm memories with a simple dab to the skin. So many months had passed since I'd seen James, and though I was anxious about how things might be between us, I knew that meeting him was exactly what I was supposed to do.

I hopped in a taxi with my travel cases and began the journey to Cap-d'Ail, a town in eastern France near the Monaco border. A friend had agreed to let me stay in her summer home for the week to be near the festivities without having to pay a hefty hotel bill. It would have been impossible to find rooms in Monaco anyway, given the number of people and press flooding into the country from all over the world. Recent reports in the newspapers had said to expect thousands of journalists and photographers and well-wishers, and to prepare for a frenzy when Miss Kelly arrived. I'd agreed to accompany Lucien to a party on his yacht in the harbor to celebrate the occasion. How I would manage to get back onshore and away to meet James, I didn't yet know.

When the taxi pulled into the driveway at the apartment in Cap-d'Ail, I quickly unloaded my things, tied a silk scarf over my head, slipped on my sunglasses, and jumped back into the car to head on to Monaco for an interview with a Monegasque journalist.

I arrived half an hour early and decided to peruse the news-stand at a *tabac* near the meeting place. Thumbing through the many newspapers and magazines, I selected three that featured articles about Grace and Prince Rainier, and a copy of *Paris Match*. I skipped ahead to a feature on the wedding by Marc Milan, the reporter who had interviewed me the morning Lucien was at the apartment with me in Cannes. It was a lovely three-page spread detailing the upcoming list of events in Monaco for the wedding: several dinner parties, some intimate and others by invitation only; an opera gala, an event at the sporting club, and the civil ceremony and the formal church ceremony and reception. According to the article, Grace could hardly wait to join her new family in Monaco and had no regrets about leaving Hollywood behind, contrary to the reporting I'd seen in other articles about her regret over ending her acting career. It was refreshing to see this side of the story, to believe that the heart could conquer all. I devoured details about the dress designer, the banquets, and the flowers, and then I saw the name Duval. Heart in my mouth, I read on.

Duval has a strong legacy in Grasse and Cannes as a premier *parfumerie* and boutique. It was established by Victor Duval, the son of a local farmer. Duval was killed by the Nazis during WWII, tortured, it is believed, for his part in the Resistance. The business is currently run by Duval's daughter, sophisticated *parfumeuse* Sophie Duval. Though Duval's fragrances are unique—and clearly fit for a princess—Jeanne Duval recently confirmed that despite her daughter's best efforts, the struggling *parfumerie* may soon be forced to close its doors. It seems that the wedding of the century came just at the right time. Monaco's princess may have unwittingly rescued this small family business from closure.

My hand flew to my mouth. The reporter had included almost nothing I'd told him on the phone. Nothing about the new line, about our long history, or how I derived my inspiration. Nothing about how I found Grace to be a lovely woman and muse. I'd purposefully avoided prying questions about Papa and the business, but the reporter had clearly found Maman more willing to talk, and now he'd shared my greatest humiliation with all of France. Furious with them both, I balled up the magazine and tossed it into the litter bin.

Pride smarting, I stormed into the brasserie to meet the next journalist, determined to set the record straight.

30

JAMES

As our voyage continued, relations between Miss Kelly's team and the press didn't improve. Long tedious hours were spent waiting for the next possible sighting of her, which often turned out to be nothing but rumors and idle gossip. I was determined not to be beaten by some hotshot Hollywood publicist.

Thanks to an especially helpful cabin boy called Ralph, who, I discovered, had a taste for Camel cigarettes and no money to buy any, I was shown a spot on the first-class deck from where I could see into Grace's private cabin. She liked to read the papers over breakfast, Ralph told me, but I would have to be quick because her people checked the windows all the time and two other photographers had already been reported to the captain and threatened with having their cameras confiscated.

"They can't do that. Can they?" I asked.

"They can do whatever they like, mister. This is the captain's ship, and we're in international waters so it's his rules until we reach Monaco."

I tossed him a full packet of Camels and told him to scoot before anyone saw us.

It was far from the job I'd imagined when I'd strolled into Sanders's office as a cocky twenty-five-year-old. I'd had no experience at all, but I did have a manila folder full of images I'd taken during the war and enough misplaced confidence to believe I could do the job as well as the next man. I hadn't imagined it would lead to the indignity of sneaking about in grubby stairwells, spying on young women while they had breakfast. Where was the art in that? Where was the sense of accomplishment? The pride? This royal wedding was rapidly making a paparazzi hack out of me. I felt as dirty as one of Angeline West's martinis. (Having met her for the suggested five o'clock cocktail on our first evening at sea, I now knew this was her preferred beverage. I also knew she could hold her liquor better than most men.) Despite any artistic notions I might have once harbored, here I was among it all, and a hundred other hacks would swap places with me in a heartbeat. I had to get the job done. Prove myself worthy of Sanders's second chance. Prove myself worthy of anything.

I raised my eyes to heaven. "I know it doesn't look good, Teddy, but Christ, even you would struggle to get a decent shot in these conditions."

Thankfully, the early morning light was perfect, just bright enough, but without the glare of midday. I hunkered down behind a lifeboat, watching as Miss Kelly stood with her back to me, arms folded, talking to someone in the room. I was so close I could see the neat sweep of her hair tied up in a pony-tail, and the bracelets on her wrist as she reached over her shoulder to scratch an itch at the back of her neck. Maybe she could sense me.

For half an hour I waited, my thighs cramping, until she finally picked up the newspaper and settled in a seat beside the window, but my angle was off and I knew I would have to change position to get any sort of shot. It was worth the risk. I stood up, raised my camera, and was about to press the shutter when my clumsy feet kicked a fire bucket over and Miss Kel-ly's silly dog started a terrific barking, giving me away. She promptly raised the newspaper to hide her face and the shot was ruined. Whether she knew I was there or not, I would never know. I liked to think that she did.

✳ ✳ ✳

Rumors went around the press pack that afternoon that some of the photographers were taking too many liberties and that Jack Kelly had made a formal complaint. Hudgins, the MGM publicist, called an emergency meeting in a too-hot room be-low deck, where tempers frayed and voices were raised.

"Miss Kelly is to soon become a princess and must preserve her dignity," Hudgins pressed. "Being spied upon at all hours of the day is distressing for her and, quite frankly, gentlemen, not acceptable."

"But you won't give us any access to her," someone com-plained. "She's about to become the world's most famous woman. You've got to give us something here. Work with us, for crying out loud."

"Even a daily photo op would be better than nothing," someone else called from the back of the room.

A voice at my shoulder whispered, "It was you, James, wasn't it?"

I turned to see Angeline West and raised my hands in faux surrender.

She tutted and smiled. "Good for you. Someone needed to bully them into submission."

Hudgins prattled on for an age until he brought the meeting to a close with a rather unexpected announcement.

"For the remainder of the voyage, there will be a scheduled daily photo op where you will have access to Miss Kelly for a short while and can take all the photographs you like. For the rest of the time, we ask that you respect her privacy. Can I take your word on that?"

We all mumbled our assent, knowing that not one of us would abide by it if an opportunity presented itself to get a great shot and make a name for ourselves.

"It's a simple as this," Hudgins added. "If you can't play ball, I will have to arrange for you to leave the boat."

"Will we walk the plank?" someone called from the back of the room, at which we all burst out laughing. I thought Hudgins was going to explode.

Between the still-too-infrequent and overly stage-managed photo ops, which included such delights as Miss Kelly having a fun game of shuffleboard with her nephews, I amused myself by lunching with Miss West and wondering about my rendezvous with Sophie. I'd tried to put her out of my mind, but her name came up unexpectedly over a Waldorf salad when I asked Angeline if she was having any luck getting details about the wedding dress.

"Not really. Everyone is being disappointingly loyal and very tight lipped. I've heard snippets about the dresses Kelly has worn for formal dinners on the ship, and some of the gowns she's packed among her trousseau. Apart from that, her fashion choices—if you can call them that—appear to be a variation of slacks and sweaters for dog walking and deck games. It's just all so . . . beige."

"Beige?"

"Yes. So dull, when I think of what she could be wearing. All the American designers whose names she could be showcasing to the world." She shook her head in frustration and took a long drag of her cigarette. "There are only so many ways one can describe beige slacks and sweaters. Gloves: white. Stockings: seamless. Bag: Hermès. Yawn. We're all under pressure to report something exciting, and she's giving us very little to go on. I've taken to describing the attire of her bridesmaids and her mother. It isn't exactly the cutting edge of American fashion."

I empathized with her frustration.

"I did at least manage to get my hands on a sample of the wedding perfume, made by the woman who *isn't* your date!" She flashed a rare grin. "What do you think?"

She leaned forward, tilting her neck so that I could inhale the scent against her skin. I closed my eyes, the better to focus on the fragrance, to concentrate on its creator. It reminded me of a starlit terrace, a lingering kiss beneath the stars, passionate eyes beneath furious brows.

"It's rather nice, isn't it?" I pulled away and opened my eyes.

"Nice? It's exquisite. Quite unlike anything I've smelled before. *Coeur de Princesse*. Heart of a princess. Nobody knows anything about the creator," Angeline pressed. "Everyone's dying to know who my source was on revealing the royal perfumer. Do you think you could set up an interview for me with Miss Duval when we get to Monaco?" She scribbled the name of her hotel on a page of her notebook, tore it off, and gave it to me. "This is where she'll find me."

I finished chewing a piece of lettuce and took a long sip of my martini. "I don't see why not. Unless she isn't where I'm hoping she'll be when we arrive. Then it could prove tricky."

Angeline raised her glass to toast her appreciation, and my good luck. "*Bonne chance,* monsieur. I hope she's worth it."

Angeline—or maybe it was the martinis—had a way of making me open up like a shucked oyster. By the end of our lunch, there wasn't much she didn't know about my life. Marjorie and Thing, Emily, Sanders. Teddy. But most of the conversation revolved around Sophie.

"You tell a fascinating tale," Angeline remarked as we settled the bill and made our way to the final press conference. "I find myself quite invested in you and this Sophie Duval. A proper pair of star-crossed lovers."

"I wouldn't go that far. We had one kiss, for which I received a smack on the behind from her mother's handbag. The rest has all been said in letters."

"Which is precisely how Grace fell in love with her prince." She studied me through narrowed eyes. "My advice to you, Mr. Henderson, is to tell the woman exactly how you feel. Sure, you've already been around the block a few times, and you may not have a palace to offer her, but you're terribly endearing and not bad to look at. She'd be a fool to turn you down."

She was right, of course. I had nothing to lose by telling Sophie everything. As the *Constitution* steamed across the Atlantic, and Monaco drew ever closer, I realized there was an awful lot I wanted to say. Not just to my traveling companion, but to Sophie.

As the press conference commenced, I studied Miss Kelly through my camera. She'd taken a chance on a man she hardly knew, given up everything for love and true happiness. I had nothing but admiration for her. As her eyes found my lens, it was as if she was looking beyond the camera and straight into my soul; as if her fate was connected to mine. I pressed the shutter. She blinked at the flash, smiled, thanked us all, and melted away with her people around her.

As I stood alone on the deck a little later, enjoying the solitude and the breeze, I finally understood why I was on this ship, making this journey. Grace Patricia Kelly had led me to Sophie once. Now she was leading me back to her.

31

SOPHIE

Monaco

The day of Grace's arrival in Monaco dawned cool, but the weather didn't dampen my mood. I could hardly wait to join the thousands of onlookers who would soon greet their princess. Like in a fairy tale, her prince would be waiting for her, too. Moving across the globe to be with the man you loved was impossibly romantic, and I was grateful to be part of such a special moment.

Glancing at the clock, I threw a few things into my handbag. With the *Constitution* set to show at ten o'clock, I didn't have much time. I was to meet Lucien at Cap-d'Ail marina at eight thirty, from where we would sail the short distance to Monaco and secure a good vantage point from his yacht well in advance. I was dreading the next few hours, having to play the happy couple when we were anything but, having to mingle with Lucien's awful business acquaintances. But it would be worth it for what would follow. My nerves tingled at the thought of seeing Grace again, of the reception I would attend tomorrow evening among royalty—from Monaco and from Hollywood. But I was mostly looking forward to my appointment with James. My mind kept returning to how it would be to see him again. Everything else felt like a distraction, hors d'oeuvres before the main course.

Before leaving the apartment, I stepped out onto the balcony overlooking the marina and beyond to the vast Mediterranean. I wondered what was happening aboard the *Constitution* now. Was Grace anxious about the response she would receive from the people of Monaco? Was she nervous about marrying her love with the world watching? Marriage wasn't something I'd ever been keen to rush into, despite it being expected of me and all young women. Surely we needed a man to support us? But I didn't. Papa had taught me to think and *do* for myself, and life had taught me to survive on my own wits.

I leaned against the railing. The usually stunning view was veiled in a light April mist, and a brisk breeze whipped over the water, blowing my curls across my face. Shivering, I stepped inside and closed the door, pulled on my white wool coat, and walked the short distance to the marina, glad that the apartment porter would transport my many items of luggage.

I spotted *La Mathilde* instantly, and heard the music coming from it shortly after. Lucien had named the yacht after his mother, a touching gesture on one hand and a dig at his father on the other. His father had named his own boat *L'Adele,* after his mistress. I didn't understand the way the Marceau family conducted themselves, but it wasn't terribly uncommon to have a mistress when one was as wealthy as a Marceau. Perhaps Mathilde had her own lover, too. She never seemed to care that her husband was off spending money on some other woman, and good for her. I thought of dear Natalie, and how happy she'd made Papa. Sometimes relationships didn't belong within the confines of normal expectations. The heart was chaotic and passionate and had many needs. There were many different kinds of love, after all.

"Land ho!" Lucien shouted as he spotted me, jumping down from the boat onto the dock, his dark hair waving in the breeze. "Climb aboard and let's set sail. The bay is starting to get crowded already."

I gave him my hand. In seconds, a waiter had given me a glass of champagne and I was circulating among some of Lucien's acquaintances I vaguely recognized. Everyone wore cashmere and silk and smiles on their faces. Jazz poured from a record player.

As we cruised out into the bay and tracked the rugged coastline, I found a quiet spot on the deck and focused my attention on the passing scenery. Soon, Monaco and the Prince's Palace came into view, set into the rocky hill of Monaco-Ville. The Grimaldi family had ruled from the famed pink structure since the thirteenth century. Parts of the building still looked like an ancient medieval fortress, while other areas displayed a variety of architecture representing the era in which they'd been added over the centuries. So much history there, and now a former bricklayer's daughter would call it her home.

Shading my eyes from the sun, I looked out at the water where hundreds of boats had begun to gather around Port Hercules. Overhead, prop planes and helicopters swished across the sky, while crowds of well-wishers were just visible as tiny dots along the harbor in the distance. A welcome fleet by sea, by air, and by land. Energy crackled in the air as everyone waited in the natural amphitheater of rocky cliffs that hugged Monaco's harbors.

As I watched the spectacle unfold, two thoughts turned over and over in my mind: How should I tell Lucien it was over between us, and if things went well with James, what in the world would I do when it was time for him to leave—again?

I peered out at the blue sea, searching for answers among the depths, but my thoughts were interrupted as Prince Rainier's impressive royal yacht, *Deo Juvante II,* sailed gracefully into view. An eruption of cheering broke out from the gathered flotilla, followed by a rousing rendition of the "Hymne Monégasque," the national anthem of Monaco. Fifteen minutes later, we caught our first view of the S.S. *Constitution* on the horizon. The massive transatlantic liner would drop anchor in the bay to transfer its precious cargo to the prince's yacht.

They were here, at last. Grace—and James—were here! I smiled broadly, heart fluttering in my chest.

More cheers rippled through the crowds, and a multitude of American songs played, one after another, from the gathered brass bands, their jaunty melodies a fitting accompaniment to the occasion. When the *Constitution* finally came to a stop, the crew dropped anchor and the boat listed gently as the wedding party appeared at the railings to wave.

A hush fell over the crowd.

A door opened and Grace Kelly stepped onto the deck, all elegance in a navy blue coat and a wide-brimmed white hat. From above, a plane released red and white carnations that floated like confetti on the breeze. Grace smiled and waved.

The crowds roared their approval. I cupped my mouth with my hands and shouted, "*Bienvenue,* Grace!" An out-of-character gesture, I laughed at my sudden lightness of spirit. Perhaps love really could conquer all, and it was only a matter of finding the right person to live out your dreams with you. I waved gaily until my arms ached, even though she could not see me.

A little black dog tucked against her chest, she walked along the gangway now secured to the prince's yacht. Once she was safely on board, Prince Rainier took his future bride's hand and turned to wave at his people. The crowd cheered again with joy, and I couldn't help but join the revelry. Several minutes later, the royal yacht made its way to shore and I lost sight of it from our vantage point. Soon, they would disembark and the festivities would begin.

Soon, James would be waiting for me.

I gulped down my glass of champagne like a woman dying of thirst and glanced over at Lucien. I had to get off this damned boat.

"When are we docking?" I asked.

He reached for an amuse-bouche from a passing waiter's tray. "Oh, sometime after lunch, assuming we can get through the boat traffic, but the party will go on all day. We'll have a lot of guests coming and going. Why do you ask?"

"I have some things I need to take care of in Monaco-Ville. A meeting with another reporter."

"More reporters? I wish you wouldn't, Sophie. They don't have your best interests at heart, you know."

I thought about the piece I'd read in *Paris Match*. Perhaps he was right, but I refused to admit it, especially when I had other plans.

"It's the last one. Nobody will be interested in writing or reading about anyone other than Grace Kelly now that she's here."

He sighed and relented. "I suppose I can't very well keep you hostage, can I?" He laughed, but there was a tiredness about him. About us. "Before you go, say hello to Michael Lever, would you? He asked about you. He's there, at the bar."

Michael Lever's face was flushed from too much champagne. He was talking to that awful woman, Barbara Andrews. Lucien had invited her, too, of course. I hesitated. I had nothing to talk about with these people, nothing in common. But Michael Lever had spotted me. He waved and bared one of his strained smiles as he headed toward me.

"Miss Duval, what a pleasure to see you again." My skin crawled as he planted a wet kiss on both my cheeks. "And on this day of all days. That was quite a show, wasn't it?"

"Indeed," I said, tight lipped. "I can't begin to imagine the emotions Grace must be experiencing. A new home. A new husband. A whole new chapter in her life."

As I spoke, I thought how wonderful it sounded.

"Something old. Something new," Lever added. "We can't always hold onto the past, can we? Sometimes we have to let go. Move on?" He leaned forward until his mouth was uncomfortably close to my ear. "I heard you decided to sell the property in Cannes. I always knew you were a clever girl, Sophie. My offer for your property in Grasse is generous. I know you'll do the right thing."

He raised his glass in a toast. I ignored him and placed my glass on a table.

"If you'll excuse me, I must be going. Enjoy the party." I turned on my heel, fuming with annoyance. I couldn't suffer Lucien's shallow, conceited crowd another minute.

"Sophie!" Lucien caught my arm and whirled me around as he pulled me roughly to one side, just out of earshot of the other guests. "Whatever is wrong with you? You were horribly rude to Michael just then."

"Why is he even here, Lucien? Today, of all days?" I demanded. "You know I don't exactly enjoy his company."

"He has made you an incredibly generous offer. And he's been nothing but professional and aboveboard with you."

"He has also been relentless, and doesn't understand the word 'no.'"

He sighed, clearly irritated. "Is this still about your father? You're still stewing on that lost scrapbook of his, aren't you? For God's sake. It's time you let go of the past, Sophie. Move on with your life." He didn't bother to hide the exasperation from his voice but softened as a business acquaintance passed us. He kissed my head, like a father would a child. "Go then. Take care of those last wretched interviews. I'll see you at the party tomorrow. And please be in a more receptive mood."

Furious at the condescension in his tone, I pushed through

the crowd, desperate to get away, to get some air on the deck. But I knew I couldn't as easily escape the unavoidable reality of what I would have to let go of when the wedding was over: my beautiful apartment, the boutique, Natalie.

As we approached the harbor and docked, I threw a last look at Lucien and walked the gangway.

A WELCOME FIT FOR A PRINCESS

Grace Kelly arrives in Monaco
amid much celebration.
Angeline West reports for the *Herald*.

After an eight-day journey, the liner S.S. *Constitution*
arrived in Monaco today, delivering its precious cargo
of a young bride-to-be, who wept at the warm welcome
she received from her Monegasque subjects.

At precisely 10:10 A.M., a gangway was lowered from
the *Constitution* to the royal yacht, *Deo Juvante II*.
Closely followed by her bridesmaids and clutching her
beloved pet poodle to her chest, Miss Kelly—dressed
in a navy sheath dress and a blue faille coat lined in
white, and sporting a wide-brimmed white organdy and
Swiss lace hat—walked slowly from one vessel, and from
one life, to another. As His Serene Highness Prince
Rainier III took his bride's arm, the private plane of
shipping magnate Aristotle Onassis flew overhead and
showered Port Hercules with a cascade of red and white
carnations. The *Constitution* blew its horn, as did the
hundreds of yachts and other smaller vessels crammed
into the bay. The noise was amplified by the natural
backdrop of the cliffs and the thousands of spectators
lining the bluffs. This reporter has never heard, or
witnessed, anything quite like it.

Miss Kelly, her family, and wedding guests will reside at the palace until the ceremonies. It is believed
the Kelly and Grimaldi families will have a luncheon

together later today, which could prove to be a little awkward as Prince Rainier's parents, Prince Pierre de Polignac and Princess Charlotte, are divorced and it is rumored there is bad blood between them. Oh, to be a fly on that grand palatial wall!

In an unexpected turn of events, Prince Rainier recently agreed to allow American camera crews and news photographers to film and photograph the cathedral wedding ceremony. He had previously been firmly against the media intrusion, fearing the event would be "vulgarized by the wrong kind of commercials."

The coming days will see the couple host a dizzying number of galas and dinners as the clock ticks down to the wedding of the century. Hold on to your hats, ladies and gentlemen! I think we are in for quite a ride!

32

JAMES

Monaco

Monaco looked different as we approached by water. A wall of golden-hued cliffs covered with plane trees and shrubs soared up in a horseshoe curve, dotted with terra-cotta-tiled houses and impressive Art Deco villas. I pointed my lens at the cascades of houses and grand hotels, all packed tightly together and seeming to tumble down the rocky hillside toward the harbor. It was a little tired looking, like a woman whose beauty had faded with age. It was chilly, too, the sun temporarily hidden behind clouds that dotted a moody sky. It was far from the sun-drenched, cobalt-blue Riviera welcome I'd anticipated. I stood at the portside railing as the *Constitution* slowed and finally dropped anchor in the bay. We'd arrived, at last.

"Is that it?" Angeline West stood beside me, disappointment laced through her words. "I was expecting more Beverly Hills than Compton. It all looks as if it could do with a lick of paint."

"Welcome to Monaco." I laughed. "Bet you're glad *you're* not marrying the prince!" I wondered what was going through Miss Kelly's head as she looked out at her new home. But perhaps a future as a princess made up for Monaco's tired appearance.

"The poor woman," Angeline said, voicing my thoughts. "I bet she wants to turn around and go straight back to Philadelphia. Is the palace as disheveled as the rest of the place?"

"Not quite. It isn't Chateau Marmont, either, from what I remember."

Our great vessel was soon surrounded by a flotilla of speedboats and yachts as desperate photographers tried to get the first shots of Grace Kelly. I'd been so caught up in the growing feelings of resentment among the press on board the liner that I hadn't stopped to fully appreciate how lucky I was to have traveled on the same ship as her. We'd had conversations, exchanged more than just pleasantries, and it struck me, as I observed the developing chaos around me, how lucky I was. I would always have those eight days with Miss Kelly. I would always have this story to tell, to Emily and to any grandchildren she might bless me with one day.

"You know, Angeline, it's not a bad life really, is it?" I remarked. "Sailing into Monaco with a future princess."

She laughed. "I've had worse days, I suppose."

A great cheer went up from around the harbor as Grace

Kelly emerged, an enormous hat and sunglasses all but concealing her face.

I snorted. "Well whoever chose that outfit definitely didn't want her face splashed all over the papers tomorrow. It'll be impossible to get a decent shot with that sombrero covering her face."

"Good lighting for the official photographer, though," Angeline pointed out.

She was right. Almost as big as a photographer's lighting umbrella, the hat would cast perfect light onto Miss Kelly's face for close-up shots, and protect her from any unflattering shadows.

"Helpful for Howell Conant. Not much use to the rest of us."

We watched as Miss Kelly boarded the tender that transported her across the water to the prince's yacht, and then we watched as she walked across the gangplank between the two boats, her little dog still clutched in her arms. That shot, I got.

"And there she goes. Stepping from one life as an actress to another life as a princess," Angeline remarked as she scribbled notes about the outfit. "She's either incredibly brave, or incredibly foolish. I guess only time will tell us which."

Her words applied to my own turmoil. Was it brave to have asked Sophie to meet me, or foolish?

Finally, the happy couple were reunited with a remarkably unromantic handshake. Not the steamy embrace all the photographers' lenses and reporters' pens were hoping for. Just a handshake, hampered by Miss Kelly's insistence on clinging to that damned dog.

The prince's yacht transported them across the bay to the

harbor, escorted by Monaco's police and countless pleasure craft. Unable to see them clearly anymore, we only knew they'd disembarked thanks to the honking of horns and the cannon fire saluting their arrival.

"That's it, then," I muttered. "Show's over, folks."

As we awaited the tender that would transport us to the harbor, I turned my lens on the scene around me, my focus settling on the building that I recognized as the casino and opera house.

Angeline shoved me lightly with her shoulder and held out her hand. "Great to meet you, Jim. You helped eight days feel like eight hours." She smiled. "Hey. You promise you won't forget about the interview with Miss Duval?"

I patted my jacket pocket where I'd placed the piece of paper with the name of Angeline's hotel. "I won't forget. Scout's honor."

"Go get her, James. She'll show. She'll be there, waiting for you. If not, you can always call me!"

At this we both laughed, and she made her way below deck to prepare to disembark.

I lingered a moment longer. I hoped Angeline was right. Although I didn't understand why I felt so strongly about someone I knew so little, I hoped, more than anything, that Sophie would be waiting for me at Rampoldi. I imagined her sitting at a table on the terrace, her hair tumbling around her shoulders, onyx curls against a simple cream dress, her slender legs crossed, the toe of her shoe tapping impatiently against the table leg. I saw her look up, and as our eyes met, I stopped walking and just smiled, because she was there and she was so beautiful. So very . . . Sophie.

33

SOPHIE

M y pulse thundered in my ears as I weaved through the crowds of locals and tourists who packed the narrow harborside streets, lingering to soak up the atmosphere long after the official motorcade had passed. Reporters and photographers jostled for space, while musicians jammed every corner. People partied on the decks of their yachts in the marina, and on every balcony and veranda of the hotels and wealthy apartments. Monaco, though small, had given is future princess an enormous welcome.

But despite the carnival atmosphere, I couldn't shake my bad mood. I felt suffocated by Michael Lever's aggressive business tactics, and swamped by Lucien's overbearing power and influence. I was restless and unsure of myself, doubting my decision to meet James, doubting the appeal of my new fragrances, doubting the future success of Duval. The missing journal still unsettled me deeply. Its disappearance had left part of me exposed, uprooted. So much had happened lately I hardly knew who I was or what I wanted anymore.

The winding streets of Monte Carlo took me this way and that. I ambled to the casino square, sat for a while in the gardens, walked some more, all the while trying to find a way back to myself until, eventually, it was time.

When I reached Rampoldi, evening had already begun to fall, the sun already low on the horizon. The wash of the sea mingled with the sound of laughter. The scent of lilacs perfumed the air around me. There was something enchanting about nightfall in my little corner of the world, especially as the cool air coated my skin and all the fragrances filled my senses. I took a calming breath and exhaled, pushing away thoughts of Lucien and his wretched friends, and of the missing journal. I wanted to enjoy the wedding festivities, and James's company, not be anxious and morose. I took a seat at a table outdoors on the terrace. A waiter walked from table to table, lighting candles and freshening the vases of cut roses, red and white for the special occasion.

But I didn't touch my aperitif when it arrived and my leg bounced impatiently beneath the table. As the minutes ticked by, I wondered if James would come after all.

I glanced at my watch. He was ten minutes late, then twenty, then almost an hour. Maybe he'd been caught up in the crowds, or had mixed up the meeting time? Perhaps he'd decided he didn't want to see me after all. The whole arrangement now felt impossibly foolish, meeting a man I didn't know all that well, and yet here I was, putting my trust in him, letting my heart play games with me. Until I'd met James, I'd been too often ruled by my head when it came to my relationships, by what made sense. Now I felt entirely different. The heart was what mattered.

As I waited, I wrestled with my conscience. I should tell James about Lucien, but it didn't feel like a good place to start, and might ruin any chance of something developing between the two of us. I sipped my martini, wishing I smoked so that I could do something to pass the time. Instead, I reached for the one thing that always soothed me. I took out a pad of paper to take some notes. *"To be a parfumeur is to be a keeper of memories, Sophie. Every scent will remind you of something, or someone."* Papa had always told me that a good *parfumeur* captures every emotion, not just love, but also loss and regret and sorrow. *"Every feeling has a scent. Every experience can teach us something."* What scent would represent disillusionment and regret, broken promises? I scribbled and sketched: autumn rain and stone, chrysanthemums withering on the vine, a blown-out candle flame, the dying embers of a fire. If James wasn't going to meet me after all, I'd at least capture my emotions in a new fragrance.

Just as I was about to ask for my bill and leave, I heard a faint whistle drift toward me. A familiar hat appeared to dance above the crowd as its owner moved closer. A pair of broad shoulders came into view, a camera strap slung over one side. My eyes found his familiar tousled sandy-brown hair, a crooked nose that had been broken at war. He was more handsome than I remembered—taller. My heart raced as he strode toward me, all smiles. He paused as our eyes met, and in that moment it was as if my life had begun all over again.

In another few easy strides, there he was, leaning into me. He bent down as if he might scoop me off my feet, but instead, he took my hand gently in his and brought it to his lips.

"Sophie Mademoiselle Duval. *Enchanté!* What a sight you are."

We both laughed as he mixed up his words.

"Hello, James." Breathless, I brushed his cheeks with a kiss. I caught the scent of his cologne as my gaze flickered to his kind, amber eyes, like a fine armagnac. "You wore it. The cologne."

He grinned. "Of course. *Mémoire.* I've never worn cologne in my life and yet you managed to make something I like. I've had more compliments than you can imagine."

"I've imagined a lot of things." I said the words before I could stop them. I blushed in response.

His eyes darkened and his lips curved into a smile. "Have you indeed?"

My pulse raced from his nearness. "Would you like to sit down? We should order dinner. You must be hungry."

"Dinner sounds delightful," he said, taking my other hand and holding them both against his chest. "But first, there's something I must do."

He leaned closer and his lips found mine, taking my breath away. I melted into him, into his soft but insistent kiss, his hand cupping my face, and I forgot everything as the world around us dissolved. Nothing mattered but the sensation of his lips against mine. Only now did I allow myself to admit how much I'd longed for this moment.

When he pulled away, he rested his forehead against mine, his breath tickling my cheek. "My apologies. I thought we should finish what we started in Grasse."

I laughed softly as he took the seat opposite mine. "No apology needed." I touched my fingertip to my lips.

"Jolly good. Then, shall we eat something, darling? *Fromage de snails? Moules à la marina. Bonbons avec frites?*"

I laughed again, pushing his arm playfully, but secretly I tingled with pleasure at the word of endearment. "I see your French hasn't improved."

"Sadly not." He put down his menu and stared at me as he took my hand in his. "But the same cannot be said for you. Were you always this beautiful?"

* * *

Two hours later, we'd covered every detail of the voyage from New York and the week of press conferences and parties to come. We'd feasted on escargots, sea bass with fennel, and a cheese and fruit plate, accompanied by a lovely Bordeaux. My head was light from the wine, and I was aglow with happiness. How easy it was to be myself with James. There was no pretense, no wishing I were somewhere else, no sense of feeling trapped or misunderstood. The true Sophie Duval emerged, and I wasn't afraid to share her with this wonderful man.

"Oh, I have something for you." He reached into the inside pocket of his jacket and pulled out a small black velvet box and an envelope. "Grace asked me to give you this."

"Grace?"

He nodded. "You have quite the fan, I believe."

I smiled, thrilled Grace would send me a gift and personal note. I slid my knife beneath the flap of the envelope and pulled out a simple cream-colored card with gold script that said "Thank You" on the cover. Inside, it read:

My dearest Sophie,

I hope you will accept this small gift. A reminder of how we met and a memento to thank you for the exquisite perfume you made for my wedding day.

You're a true talent, Sophie, and I wish you all the success in the world with your business. I do hope we will see each other, even if briefly, in the coming week. There are many events ahead, and I've ensured that you and a guest will be invited to the opera gala and the cathedral wedding.

Coeur de Princesse will be my something new. I'm a hopeless traditionalist and terribly superstitious, but every bride needs a little luck, wouldn't you say?

Sincerely yours,
Grace

I tore into her package, eager to see the gift. Inside the box, nestled against more velvet, was a brooch in the design of forget-me-nots. I gasped.

"Oh, how thoughtful and lovely."

I showed James the dainty piece of jewelry before fastening it to my dress. I could hardly wait to see Grace again, even if only from afar, but I hoped I could thank her properly in person for all she'd done for me and Duval.

"You'll be attending some of the events no doubt, Mademoi-selle Royal Perfumer, and I expect you will need a date? I might be able to make myself available."

I felt my smile freeze. How could I tell him that I'd been listed with Lucien on the invitations?

"But you'll be too busy capturing all the galas and dinners with your camera," I said, grasping at an excuse. "Isn't that the point of you being here?"

He put up his hands. "You make a very good point. Then again, you know what they say about all work and no play." He winked and poured us each another glass of wine. As we ate, he asked me about the business. "Booming, I imagine. Every-one will want to smell like a Duval princess."

My mood darkened a little. I put down my knife and fork. "Not quite booming. Things have been difficult recently. And I lost something really important to me. You remember my journal?"

He thought for a moment, and said, with a wink, "That tatty old book you write all your perfume recipes in?"

How did he manage to say things like that and make me smile, when Lucien only made me bristle?

"Yes. *That* 'tatty old book.'"

"I'm sorry. I know it was very special to you."

"Actually, I'd prefer not to discuss it just now, if that's all right. I don't want to spoil the evening."

"Another time, then," he said, bringing my hand to his lips. "There will be another time, I hope? Tomorrow, for instance?"

As he motioned to the waiter for the bill, I stalled. I didn't know what to say.

He noticed my silence. "Ah. I'm sorry. I've made you uncomfortable."

"You haven't. It's just . . ."

"You don't need to explain. Come on. Let's go for a walk. It's a lovely evening and I'm relieved to be back on dry land again."

Though glad to extend the evening a bit longer, I didn't know if I should. Lucien's face flitted behind my eyes and guilt settled over me. I studied James's face, the gold eyes and crooked nose, the line of his jaw. His lips.

"*Oui*," I said at last. "A walk sounds perfect."

We pulled on our jackets and sauntered past the Monte Carlo casino, through the lush tropical garden, and finally to a lookout point over the bay. Boats filled the harbor and lights glittered on the gently lapping water. Red and white flags and pennants fluttered in the breeze above our heads.

As a light rain began to fall, James took my hand and drew me against him. Without a word, we found each other in the darkness. I didn't—couldn't—resist. As the kiss deepened, the world floated away, and all my worries with it.

MONACO RAIN HERALDS A NEW REIGN

Bad weather hampers wedding festivities.
Angeline West reports for the *Herald*.

The weather gods must not have heard that a significant wedding is to take place in Monaco this week, for the rain hasn't let up since Miss Kelly's arrival. Nevertheless, the show must go on and the disappointing weather can do nothing to dampen the spirits of those of us eagerly awaiting the wedding of the century.

Although the poor weather has ruined floral displays and dispersed the local Monegasques and some ten thousand visiting well-wishers, there is still an air of celebration in Monaco. While everyone awaits the wedding ceremonies, there is plenty to keep the bride busy with a hectic schedule of gala dinners and late-night parties at Monte Carlo's many iconic locations, including the casino and the International Sporting Club. Crowds of photographers wait for hours in the rain to get a photograph of Miss Kelly and her many famous friends from the world of stage and screen, and they are usually left disappointed as the guests hurry from venue to waiting limousine, shielded by large umbrellas.

Miss Kelly's latest choice of evening gown was a flaring bouffant lime green, worn with an elegant brown mink stole. When it comes to matters of style, even the rain can't douse this princess's natural flair.

34

JAMES

woke up in a buoyant mood after my evening with Sophie. Everything about being with her felt right. She was intriguing, and I couldn't wait to discover more. I took a cold shower, playing the night over and over in my mind. The scent of her perfume on her neck as I'd kissed her skin, the way she'd brushed my ear with her lips and avoided my questions, preferring to talk about my life in England than focus on her family and the business. Something was clearly bothering her, something far more than a missing journal, but she'd said it could wait. For now.

I'd told her all about Emily, shown her the many photographs I kept in my wallet. I'd even explained about Marjorie and Thing, doing what I always do and making a joke to lighten the reality of the situation. The truth was, I envied their holiday together in the Highlands. I envied the memories they

were making with Emily. I'd often imagined retiring to a remote cottage beside a loch or a ruined castle, surrounded by
pine trees and heather. There was something liberating about
the open spaces and the soaring mountains. The scenery in
Scotland wasn't unlike the Riviera in some parts. I hoped I
hadn't talked about Emily too much, but having done so, she
was on my mind and I was delighted when the hotel reception
put a long distance call through to my room.

"Daddy! It's me. Emily. I'm in Scotland!"

I sank onto the bedcovers, so pleased to hear her exuberant
little voice. "Darling! Oh, it's so good to hear you. Are you having fun? Did you find Nessie?"

My heart melted as she started to talk, telling me all about
the lochs and castles she'd visited. For a few moments, nothing
else mattered. My world shrank to the sound of my precious
little girl and I kicked off my shoes, lay back on the bed, and
smiled as she chattered on.

"We're going on a long drive up to the mountains tomorrow. Mummy says we might stop for a picnic if the weather
improves."

I knew those exhilarating mountain roads, how they twisted
and turned and made one's stomach lurch. I knew the urge to
pull the car over at every corner to take in the view, afraid it
would be obscured by mist on the way home.

I told her to have a terrific time, and to take lots of photographs. "I'll be home in a few more days, darling. Once the
wedding is over."

I hung up the receiver, wishing life could always be as simple as it was for a ten-year-old, and I resolved to make sure

Emily's life was always full of mythical monsters and picnics and mountain drives. She was my lost journal, a part of me I couldn't bear to be without.

After I'd showered and dressed and checked over my camera, I set off for the local school building that Rainier had arranged to be converted into a makeshift press center. It was very quickly apparent that neither the prince nor his people were in any way experienced in the needs of the world's media. Despite the rows of shiny new typewriters and a dozen private phone booths, it was cramped and stuffy and already carried the stench of stale sweat and tobacco. Besides, what was the use of all the fancy new equipment when we had nothing to report and none of the principal players in the performance willing to be photographed?

We harangued and hustled, pressing the MGM stalwarts for information: When will we get a chance to see the couple again? Were any official photo ops scheduled? Would Miss Kelly remain in hiding until the civil ceremony? Was it true that she was suffering from exhaustion? Complaints from the press assembled in Monaco came thick and fast as the rumbles of dissent that had followed Miss Kelly from the first chaotic press conference in New York grew louder beneath Monaco's moody skies. It was five days until the civil wedding ceremony, which would be held in the throne room at the palace. Six days until the main event, the so-called W-Day, at Saint Nicholas Cathedral. Nearly a week for hundreds of restless reporters and photographers to hunt for scraps of information or any scandal that would send ripples around the world and readers flocking to the newsstands. In the meantime, opinion pieces and rumor filled the void, the gossip columnists going into overdrive in their attempts to sustain public demand for news about Miss Kelly and her prince. Was it true that Rainier had picked Marilyn as the first choice for his American bride? Had Father Tucker, his priest, really favored the angelic Miss Kelly? Speculation and scandal were the only tools at the editors' disposal.

Even the hectic schedule of receptions, galas, dinners, ballets, and celebratory fetes didn't help our cause, since the press corps was not usually permitted access to these private functions, reserved for the couple's closest family and friends.

Photographers hid around corners and jostled for position on narrow pavements outside Monaco's finest buildings while the wedding party feasted on lobster and caviar inside. News of thousands of dollars' worth of jewelry being stolen from the hotel bedroom of one of the bridesmaids gave us something interesting to report on at least. It was ugly, bad-tempered work and, once again, I found myself longing to return to landscapes and seascapes, fields of flowers, rustic Provençal churches, and winding cobbled streets. I found my thoughts turning to how I might make a life for myself in France, and how I could ever convince Marjorie to let Emily be part of that.

In the long hours between formal events, the press pack gravitated to Monaco's bars and casinos, trading complaints and cigarettes and tip-offs over expensive French beer. We were as restless and petulant as the brooding Monegasque skies.

"You get anything decent yet?" Eddie O'Reilly asked as he

pulled up a chair outside a street-front café and ordered us both another beer.

"Nothing. The sooner this wedding happens, the better." I stretched my arms above my head. "I'm sick to death of Grace bloody Kelly."

He laughed. "Someone special waiting for you back home, is there?"

"Yes, as it happens. My daughter."

As the waiter placed our beers on the table, a fight broke out beside us. Someone stumbled backward, knocking everything over and sending O'Reilly and his camera sprawling to the ground.

"You bloody idiot. This is ruined," he shouted, staggering to his feet and squaring up to the chap who'd fallen into us. He just smiled, spread-eagled on the ground.

I tossed a ten-franc note onto the table. "Let's get out of here. I'm not sure it's Miss Kelly's kind of place anyway."

We were forced to mob the cars transporting Kelly and Rainier to and from their many appointments, firing off speculative shots, flashbulbs popping like gunfire as the chauffeurs furiously tooted their horns and a security detail attempted to hold us back to let the vehicles through. Far from being happy for them, we began to resent Miss Kelly and her prince.

I was glad to have more to occupy my mind than the forthcoming nuptials. Emily and Sophie jockeyed for my attention as I waited outside one grand building or another. Emily was never far from my mind, constantly tugging at my conscience, while Sophie intrigued me more each time we met, pulling at my heart. And there was my conundrum: How could I combine my responsibilities as a father with my feelings for Sophie?

As Monaco prepared for its grand wedding, Sophie and I found privacy wherever we could, requesting a table at the back of restaurants where low lighting and cigarette smoke offered a sort of barrier between us and the city gone mad with wedding anticipation. We held hands as we talked, brushed our legs against each other as we dined. We kissed between courses and danced long into the night, lost in the seductive rhythm of the music and the pleasure of our closeness. But things only ever went so far. I had the feeling Sophie was holding back. For what, or whom, I wasn't sure, but I didn't want to push her. There was a delicacy to her that deserved my respect.

"You dance well, James," she whispered, her breath warm against my neck. "For an Englishman."

"And you smell delicious," I replied, as I closed my eyes and ran my hands along her spine. "For a Frenchwoman."

We laughed as much as we talked, danced as much as we could, parting reluctantly when the day's appointments called us away from each other. And all the time there was a sadness in Sophie's eyes that I couldn't shake from her.

"I wish you would tell me what's on your mind," I said as I helped her into her coat. I couldn't hold my tongue any longer. "I can tell there's something."

"You are far too inquisitive." She smiled. "A true newspaperman. Always looking for a story where there isn't one."

"But my hunches are always right." I held her hands as she stood in front of me. "I told you before. These ears of mine? Great for listening. A problem shared and all that."

She stretched onto her tiptoes and planted a kiss on my lips. "You are sweet to worry, but you mustn't. I can look after myself."

But I did worry. The truth was, Sophie was the first good thing to happen to me in a very long time, and I wasn't prepared to let her slip away. Where things might lead between us, who could possibly know? One thing was certain: she would never leave her beloved flower fields and her business, or her friends and neighbors in Grasse, nor would I want her to.

Maybe that's what was troubling her. Maybe, like me, she was counting down the days to the wedding not because she couldn't wait to celebrate Grace Kelly's union with her prince, but because that very union would signal our separation. I would return to England, and what then?

NO CAMERAS ALLOWED AT CIVIL CEREMONY

Prince puts his foot down with the press.
Angeline West reports for the *Herald*.

As a result of the strained relationships between the prince and press, cameramen will not be permitted inside the palace throne room for the civil wedding ceremony on April 18. The prince will permit only three official photographers to record the event.

It is understood that the continued harassment of the prince and Miss Kelly by the press prompted the prince's announcement. The couple were harangued once again on their return from a luncheon with the prince's sister, Antoinette, at her villa in the nearby hilltop village of Eze. Press had earlier been refused access to the family luncheon. It is reported that a group of photographers formed a roadblock of sorts to prevent the couple's car from passing. One photographer is said to have lain in the road in front of the vehicle. With the ongoing poor weather, and the stresses caused by this friction between the prince and the press, it is a testament to Miss Kelly that she still manages to smile on the rare occasions the photographers manage to capture her. The couple are reported to be in a very happy mood as the clock counts down to their weddings!

Commenting on the matter of the press relations with his future son-in-law, Jack Kelly remarked, "I guess the prince is going to have to learn to roll with the punches."

In other bad news, opportunist thieves have struck three times during the wedding festivities in Monaco, making off with loot valued at $150,000. In the latest theft, $95,000 worth of paintings were stolen from the apartment of a Russian physician. Earlier this week, jewels valued at $55,000 were stolen from wedding guests staying at the Hôtel de Paris, one of whom is a bridesmaid to Miss Kelly.

Not even a royal wedding runs smoothly, it seems. Let's hope all the wrinkles are well and truly ironed out by the big day, and that the only things being stolen then are the kisses of a happy couple.

35

SOPHIE

I floated through the following days, hopping between the quiet solitude of the apartment in beautiful Cap-d'Ail and the thrum of Monaco's bars and restaurants, my feet never touching the ground. Wedding fever had taken hold of me with all its romance and promises of forever. Or perhaps it was just James who left me feeling that way. Spending time with him, I felt seen and heard. Understood. Even amid Monaco's crowded spaces, I felt like the only person in the room, the only person he wanted to be with. Well, almost. One thing was certain—he adored his little girl, and I only liked him all the more for it.

My newfound happiness consumed me, but despite the lingering kisses and those warm tawny eyes that pushed most other things from my mind, there were still a few very real, very difficult things I needed to do. I was glad, in the end, to have told Natalie I was selling the boutique in Cannes. The thought of letting it go was almost a relief. I felt freer. Closing the door on that chapter would give me more time in my work-shop in Grasse, where I loved to be more than anywhere, and sales could be handled from the smaller shop at the factory. The only negative would be living with Maman, but that might be something to reconsider as well. I hoped to find a small apart-ment in Grasse when—if—finances allowed.

I sat on the balcony in Cap-d'Ail, savoring the view of the distant mountains above the coastline, grateful for the break in the weather. Specks of gold, white, and orange showed how many people had made their homes here on the rocky cliffs. It amazed me how the buildings didn't tumble downhill and fall into the sea. Sometimes I felt as if I were tumbling from a great height, too, giving up so much and yet gaining so much at the same time.

The whine of a scooter cut through my thoughts. I stood up and leaned forward on the iron railing as I watched the driver pull into a parking space below. My heart somersaulted as James emerged from the shadows and waved up to me.

"I thought we might go for a spin. What do you say?"

I laughed, told him to give me a moment, grabbed my scarf and sunglasses, and rushed downstairs. I greeted him with a kiss on each cheek, anxious not to be seen by anyone, but his lips found mine and I couldn't resist. I looked at him, at his adorable smile and crooked nose, the light stubble on his chin. I wanted to cradle his face in my hands, cover every inch of it with kisses. Tell him what he meant to me.

"Are you all right?" he asked, wrapping his arm around my shoulder.

I exhaled a breath I didn't know I was holding. "I am now. Where are we going?"

"Who cares! Let's just follow the road."

I laughed and climbed onto the scooter behind him.

We buzzed away from the town and headed to a little bistro in Saint-Antoine. We indulged in a wonderful lunch of creamy vegetable soup and braised beef to ward off the chill that lingered in the spring air. After our meal we strolled, hand in hand, along the beautiful wild beach, beside the rocks and crashing waves, happy and surprised by what had bloomed so naturally between us.

"I don't know how you've done it, Sophie, but you've managed to make me want to stay in one place for the first time in my life. Plant my feet in the ground."

"Like a weed?" I teased, eliciting one of his contagious laughs.

The hours slipped by, but we couldn't seem to break away from each other.

"Care for another ride?" he asked, rubbing my hands between his. "We could watch the sunset."

"You're a romantic, monsieur." I sighed with happy fatigue. "That's a fine idea."

We twisted along the looping clifftop roads until the rosy light of sunset illuminated the hills. When we parked, we climbed onto a nearby ledge and watched the light shift from brilliant gold to soft lavender.

"Wait here." James jumped to his feet, rummaged through the small basket on the front of the scooter, and returned with a sheepish grin on his face.

He plopped down on the ground beside me. "I have something for you. It made me think of you immediately and well . . ." He cleared his throat as if nervous. "I hope you like it."

He laid a beautiful journal bound in light gray leather in my hands. Its soft cover was embossed with flowers and in curling script beneath, the letters *SD*. I ran my hand over the leather, feeling its grooves and indentations. Opening the journal, I turned several of the luxurious, violet-scented pages. Inside he'd written an inscription:

To the future of Duval. And to us.
—James

"It's a new journal, for your perfumes," he explained. "I know it can't replace your father's, but I hoped it would at least—"

I covered his mouth with mine in a fervent kiss, my heart soaring into the early evening sky. I felt him smile against my lips and I pulled away for air, a lump of emotion rising in my throat. I swallowed back tears of gratitude and happiness.

"It's perfect. This is all so perfect." I waved my hand around me at the breathtaking scenery. "*You* are perfect."

He locked his eyes with mine. "I believe you can save your perfumery, expand it even, in time. I know you can. I thought this might be a good place to start."

"It is. It's a very good place to start."

We sat in silence for some time, my head upon his shoulder.

"Imagine if you hadn't chased Grace Kelly that day," I said. "If I hadn't sheltered her from you, you wicked photographer." I smiled, but my tone grew serious. "We would have never met." I looked into his eyes, losing myself in their golden depths. "I would never have known you."

"So you're saying it's a good thing I'm a persistent bugger after all?"

I laughed and slapped him playfully on the arm.

He caught my hand in his, cupped the back of my neck, and pulled my face gently to his until our noses touched. His rich, intricate scent enveloped me.

Throat hoarse, he said, "Come with me, Sophie. Back to the hotel?"

Though I knew things might go further, and that I was still in a relationship with Lucien—even though I'd already left it in my heart—I could think of nothing but being with James.

Within the hour, we were back at his hotel in Monaco. I perched on the chaise as James poured us both a drink, but we didn't touch a drop. As our gazes locked, a rush of heat spread over my skin. Gently, James pulled me into his arms. We folded into each other, losing ourselves in a passionate kiss until we were gasping for air. His hands tangled in my hair, then slid over my shoulders and down my back. I leaned into him, exploring the contours of his chest. My fingertips traced a ridge of raised skin beneath the fabric of his shirt.

"A scar," he rasped. "From the war." He pulled his shirt over his head and showed me the row of buckled flesh across his rib cage.

I put my lips to it, following it softly until it stopped. I moved to his shoulder, his neck, planting kisses along the way, spurred on by the rumble of pleasure in his throat. When I found his mouth again, he took me hungrily.

When at last he reached for the zipper of my dress, he stopped. "May I?" he asked.

Full of desire, I nodded. "Please."

He grinned and moved carefully then, slowly. As my dress and underthings slipped down my body to the floor, he paused. "You're so beautiful, Sophie. Did anyone ever tell you that?" His fingers trailed across my stomach and caressed my curves.

I shivered at his touch. And the only word, the only thought in my mind, released from my lips as a sigh.

He lifted me into his arms and carried me to the bed. As he laid me down, he covered me with kisses, leaving a pathway of fire in his wake. When his body enveloped mine, he tucked his face against my neck.

"Sophie," he whispered. "This is absolute madness, but I'm in love with you."

Something inside me broke free as I tucked his words inside my heart like precious jewels in a velvet box. Yet I couldn't bring myself to say the same. Not until I'd faced Lucien and set things right.

I replied with kisses, words no longer necessary as we found each other in the dark.

36

JAMES

Sophie Lauren Duval was perfection. I'd sensed—hoped—there was more waiting beyond that first tentative kiss on her mother's terrace, but just how much more I could never have imagined.

We made love before breakfast, and after, too hungry for each other to let fresh croissants and good coffee distract us for long. There was a recklessness to our desire, a passion fueled by the atmosphere of expectation and romance that crackled across the city like a lightning storm. But there was more to it than succumbing to our obvious mutual attraction and physical urges. We talked all morning, asked questions about each other's family and friends. We relished the gentle process of discovering each other, piece by piece, like archeologists carefully chipping away at layers of rock and sand. It was clear to both of us that some far deeper connection than a purely physical one had blossomed between us since that first impromptu meeting in Sophie's boutique. Despite the complications of circumstance and distance that had transpired to keep us apart, something had stubbornly thrived.

Through words exchanged in a few simple letters in the year since, our connection had grown roots. The gentle process of writing, the time it had taken for our words to reach each other and be returned, had infused our feelings, rather than dampened them. Ours wasn't a romance built on stolen kisses and discarded clothes. It was a romance built on patience and a curious sense of destiny. Like the lingering scent of perfume or an image coming slowly into focus in the darkroom, we'd each clung to the faintest fragments of the other. It made no sense whatsoever, and yet it made the most sense of all.

"Are you always this impetuous, Miss Duval?" I asked as we lay in each other's arms, oblivious to the madness of the wedding preparations taking place beyond the window: banners and flags being hoisted, floral arrangements being displayed in the Monegasque colors, the streets never cleaner, the shop windows decorated in tribute to their prince and his bride.

Sophie propped herself up onto her elbows. "Honestly?"

"Honestly."

"Never. I'm far too sensible to do anything this erratic."

"Or erotic?" I winked, enjoying the flush of color on her neck, the fullness of her lips as they curved into a smile. "You're a terrible woman, leading me astray. A poor lost foreigner who can hardly speak the local language. You should be ashamed of yourself, mademoiselle."

She laughed in that slightly husky, impossibly attractive way of hers. "James. Stop."

"Never! You're far too delicious."

I pulled her into my arms and held her in a way I'd never held anyone. So this was what it felt like to be in love. Not just to love someone, but to be *in* love with them, hopelessly and recklessly. What I'd felt for Marjorie had been more akin to duty or obligation. An idea of love. With Sophie it was different. It was pure and unfiltered. Extraordinary. We made love a third time, slowly and sensually, savoring every delicious part of each other until we were both satisfied and exhausted.

"Dinner tonight?" I asked as I helped her zip up her dress, planting more kisses on the back of her neck as she held up her hair and stepped into her shoes. "Or are you busy dining with royalty?" I teased. She wobbled a little in her heels and I held her arm to support her. For all her business acumen and tough exterior, there was a fragility to Sophie, a vulnerability she didn't often expose. I sensed she could be easily hurt, and I was sure I wouldn't be the one to do it.

She turned around and placed a tender kiss on my nose. "If you promise to try the escargot, then yes. Dinner would be lovely."

"For you, mademoiselle, I would eat a garden *full* of snails."

She laughed but I noticed a slight frown fall across her face. I noticed these little details about her: the small mole beneath her left ear, the shape of her eyes, the way she looked away when I told her how beautiful she was. Like shadows, I also noticed the shifts in her mood, too.

"Are you sure about this?" I asked. "I know it's all happened in a rush." I tucked a curl behind her ear. "You seem so worried."

She looked into my eyes. "Yes, James. I'm sure. There are just a few things I need to straighten out. With work." She picked up her handbag and placed her hand lightly against my cheek. "I'll see you later."

I called to her as she walked down the hotel corridor. "Don't forget to call Angeline West. She was really keen to talk to you. I promised, with scout's honor."

She smiled and blew me a kiss before stepping into the elevator, leaving the scent of her perfume and a love-struck fool in her wake.

I lay on the crumpled bedsheets for a while, a light breeze blowing through the open balcony doors as I replayed the events of last night in my mind. It was almost too good to be true—*she* was almost too good to be true. I wondered what the catch was, because lucky though I had been recently, I couldn't believe fate had brought such a wonderful woman my way. I wanted to tell someone about her, or rather, I wanted to tell Teddy about her. I could hear the surprise in his voice. "*You?* Jim Henderson? In love? I never thought I'd see the day!"

He'd promised he would be my best man when the time came, just as I'd been his. He was the only one to ask me if I was sure about marrying Marjorie. "You don't have to do this, Jim," he'd said. But I did, because Marjorie was expecting our baby and I was at least decent enough to do the honorable thing.

I didn't regret it. Not for one moment. Because despite the mess Marjorie and I had made of things, we had Emily to show for our struggles, and she was worth a thousand hesitant *I dos* in a cold English church.

FIT FOR A PRINCESS. WEDDING DRESS
DETAILS AND ROYAL PERFUMER REVEALED

Grace Kelly dress will dazzle.
Angeline West reports for the *Herald*.

Sketches were released today of the two wedding dresses designed for Grace Kelly by Helen Rose of MGM Studios. For the civil wedding ceremony in the palace throne room, the princess will wear a stunning dress of hand-run *Alençon* lace (sometimes called the Queen of Lace) in a shade of blush tan, layered over rose silk taffeta. The separate jacket has a small collar, and ties at the neck with silk thread.

The much-anticipated formal wedding gown for the Catholic ceremony at Saint Nicholas Cathedral is absolutely exquisite. It is described as "regal style designed along Renaissance lines." Ivory in color, the gown and veil are comprised of twenty-five yards of matte satin *peau de soie*, twenty-five yards of silk taffeta, one hundred yards of silk net, and three hundred yards of French Val lace. Thousands of pearls decorate the veil and the bell-style dress has three petticoats of crepe and taffeta. No wonder an ocean liner was required to transport it here!

The French couturiers can hardly contain their ire. Many had hoped that Miss Kelly would chose a French designer for the gown, but who can blame her for putting her trust in the woman who has dressed her on set for many years. It is understood that after the wedding, the dress will be displayed at the Philadelphia Museum of Art.

It was also recently revealed that the mystery woman behind the perfume created especially for Princess Grace's wedding was local "nose" and perfumer Sophie Duval. In a recent interview, Mademoiselle Duval explained how she and Miss Kelly had become acquainted last year while the movie star was in Cannes for the film festival. "A British photographer chased her into my boutique," she explained, laughing at the memory. "We struck up something of a friendship after that."

Usually a favorite of German perfume house Krigler and having been courted by renowned French perfume house Lancôme—who also offered to create a fragrance especially for the wedding—Miss Kelly surprised everyone by selecting the relatively unknown Duval as the one to create her wedding day scent.

"The family business goes back many years and at least two generations," Miss Duval explained. "I am very proud to have the Duval name associated with a princess, and extremely grateful to Grace for putting her trust in me."

Coeur de Princesse is created from jasmine, one of the four signature flowers of Grasse (along with tuberose, lavender, and violet), where Duval is based. The exact recipe remains a special and closely guarded secret, but no doubt the six hundred guests who will gather in Monaco's Saint Nicholas Cathedral will remember the scent for many years to come. The wedding dress itself is lined with silk pockets soaked with the perfume.

Miss Duval commented that she was honored to have received an invitation to the cathedral wedding but would not disclose whether there would be a special someone on her arm for the service.

The 375 acres of the small principality of Monaco are now filled to bursting. Monaco could well be the most densely populated country in the world at this moment.

Following the continuing tensions between the world's press and the prince, a more joyous mood has returned to Monaco, along with a much-welcomed spell of sunshine. Last night's fireworks display lit up the whole of Monaco-Ville, and British and American ships in the harbor fired their salvos as they entered the port.

Ladies and gentlemen, please take your seats. We are almost ready for the performance to begin!

37

JAMES

After days of seething animosity between the prince and the press, a last-ditch attempt was made by Hudgins and his MGM bullies to restore some sort of cordiality. It was announced that fifty photographers would be permitted to attend the wedding rehearsal, and of the nearly two thousand journalists in Monaco, two dozen would be permitted into Saint Nicholas Cathedral to attend the wedding ceremony.

I was nothing short of dumbfounded when a message was delivered to my room to inform me that I was one of the privileged few.

F.A.O. James Henderson. London Daily.

Enclosed press pass to wedding rehearsal today. Be there at 10:30 A.M. sharp. Also enclosed, press pass to main event.

You can thank Miss Kelly. She recognized your name on the list and insisted you be included.

Hudgins

I made myself presentable for the wedding rehearsal photo op, pondering my reflection as I straightened my tie. A few more days and I would leave all this behind. Part of me was ready to go home, to see Emily, but part of me also wanted to stay here with Sophie. Life had become exceptionally complicated. As I checked over my camera, I wondered how I would ever manage to work this one out.

As I made my way to the cathedral, I passed expensive yachts moored in the harbor and sleek sports cars parked outside opulent hotels. I wound my way up to Monaco-Ville, through rows of golden stucco buildings framed by palms and exotic flowers, while fragrant roses and honeysuckle perfumed the air of the narrow streets. Monaco was pleasant, especially in the sunshine, but it was the vast fields of Grasse and the medieval hilltop towns that really spoke to me.

The impressive Saint Nicholas Cathedral stood on an elevated position overlooking the Port de Fontvieille. The building's white columns and tiers. I searched out interesting angles, drawn to the architecture of the building and the way the light filtered through the leaves of the palms that stood at the bottom of the steps.

As I stepped inside the enormous doors, the light and warmth of the morning sun was sucked away, the hushed gloom of the interior lending a sobriety to the occasion. Even Miss Kelly's nieces and nephews responded to the shift in atmosphere, their endless chatter and fidgeting on pause as they were instructed on the roles they were each to play on W-Day.

"It feels more like a funeral than a wedding." I turned to the voice at my left. Angeline, poised with her notebook and pen. "The poor woman looks exhausted," she whispered. "No wonder she always wears sunglasses. I bet there are bags the size of Macy's largest beneath those shades."

Miss Kelly, dressed in a beige suit with one of those dreadful turban-style hats and short white gloves, took charge of the rehearsal, directing everyone with the confidence and skill of a woman who'd spent many years on set. The prince lurked in the background, chatting to his minions.

"Still, it's the first time I've seen her look relaxed since she arrived here," Angeline continued.

"This is her world, isn't it?" I agreed. "It's what she knows: rehearsing, directing, going over everything again and again."

Angeline detected the weariness in my voice and patted my arm encouragingly. "Only two more days, Jim. We're nearly there, and then we can all get back to reality."

I took plenty of photographs, pleased to get some decent shots of Miss Kelly, at last.

"Oh, and by the way," Angeline said, moving a little closer. "Thank you for your help in setting up the interview with Miss Duval. She's a delight. So clever, yet so humble about her talents as a nose. *Le nez*. Funny sort of a job title when you think about it! And *oh là là*. What a beauty. I hope you're making, how should I say it . . . progress?" She winked suggestively.

I winked back.

As the rehearsals came to an end, a cry went up from the photographers for Miss Kelly to remove her sunglasses.

"Give us that famous smile, Grace! One last smile as a single woman!"

She glanced at Rainier for his approval and then at Hudgins, who nodded, before she removed her glasses and turned her famous smile on us all. For once, I was ready.

"Thank you for your patience, gentlemen," she said. "I know it has been a little difficult. Now, if you'll excuse me, I have rather a big day to prepare for."

To calls of "Good luck, Grace," the wedding party dispersed into their waiting cars and we filed out of the great cathedral doors after them.

"Will you be at the civil ceremony tomorrow?" Angeline asked as we walked down the cathedral steps together.

"No, but I did get a pass to the main event and I'll be jostling for position outside the opera house at the gala tomorrow evening. You?"

"Well, aren't you the lucky one. I'm hoping to find my way into the garden party after the civil ceremony tomorrow. These Monegasques had better give me something decent to write about. The style has been so disappointing." She shook my hand at the bottom of the steps. "Well, I have to run. Good luck, with everything. Remember, you only get one shot!"

I knew what she meant, but I heard something else in her

words, and she was right. I already knew I was serious about Sophie, keen to see where things might lead beyond a romantic week of parties and royal weddings. But first, I needed to get to the bottom of whatever it was she was hiding from me. Sophie was a gift, but I sensed there were more layers to unwrap before I found exactly what I was looking for.

STARLET BECOMES PRINCESS IN CIVIL CEREMONY

Princess Grace receives royal titles.
Angeline West reports for the *Herald*.

Romance was in the air at the Grimaldi palace this morning as His Serene Highness Prince Rainier III and Grace Kelly said *"oui"* and were officially married in the sixteenth-century palace throne room in front of a party of close family, friends, and dignitaries numbering around one hundred in total.

The formalities took just forty minutes, during which time the couple maintained a serious expression and appeared fidgety and nervous. Her Serene Highness's 140 official titles were read aloud. She is now twice a princess, four times a duchess, nine times a baroness, eight times a countess, and 111 times a lady. After the ceremony (which was repeated to allow MGM's cameramen to record the formalities for their special documentary, *The Wedding in Monaco*), thousands of Monegasque citizens poured past the Carabiniers du Prince in their white dress uniforms and helmets with plumes, and through the palace gates into the formal gardens to congratulate their monarch and officially welcome their new princess. Dressed in their Sunday best, the crowd drank champagne and the atmosphere was jubilant. Red roses and white lilies, the flowers of Monaco, adorned every lapel.

When the prince and princess appeared on the balcony

to greet their guests, hundreds of flashbulbs went off and a roar erupted.

The couple will be married again tomorrow, in front of six hundred guests, in a formal Catholic ceremony at Saint Nicholas Cathedral. The celebrations will continue tonight at the most lavish of all the festivities, the opera gala, an event described by those in the know as "the biggest thing since *Ben-Hur* or the winning of the West."

38

SOPHIE

The day of the civil wedding ceremony passed in a flurry of news bulletins, playing out on the radio and television as I tried to distract myself at the apartment at Cap-d'Ail. There was a palpable sense of relief that everything had gone smoothly. Next would come the evening celebration at the opera house, the event that Lucien and I had been invited to. Tomorrow would be the grand occasion of the formal cathedral wedding, and then it would be time for me to stop living in the past and face my future.

I glanced at the clock. It was time to get ready. I took my dress from the wardrobe, styled my hair and made up my face, and finally fastened the clasp on my necklace and bracelet and thought of Princess Grace going through the same rituals. After a full week of lavish events, she must be exhausted. As I thought about the prospect of spending the evening with Lucien, I was exhausted, too.

At six thirty, he pulled up to the apartment in his silver Mercedes. My stomach clenched. I'd avoided his calls and hadn't spoken to him or seen him since Grace's arrival in Monaco. He'd been too busy entertaining to hardly notice. It was all wrong, being between two men, and I wanted it to end.

Lucien kissed my cheek as I slid into the front seat of the car and checked my makeup one last time in my compact mirror. I noticed the light purple skin beneath my eyes, evidence of a long, luxurious night of lovemaking. I'd barely slept a wink in the hours since James had left. I loved him. Although guilt and fear had stifled my ability to tell him. I smiled into the compact mirror as I pictured him standing over the bed, camera in hand. He'd photographed me in a silk dressing gown, my hair mussed. He'd told me I was the most beautiful woman he'd ever seen. I'd laughed and launched a pillow at him, knocking him off balance.

I glanced at Lucien's perfect profile. No crooked nose there. No scars of war. I'd once loved the idea of loving a man like Lucien, but there was no fooling myself anymore. It wouldn't be easy to pretend I was happy to be by his side tonight, but I owed him that much, at least. Later, when the gala was over, I would tell him I wanted to end our relationship. With a sigh, I snapped the compact shut and adjusted the neckline of my gown.

"Why the sigh? Aren't you looking forward to tonight?" Lucien glanced at my gown as he started the engine. "You look nice, though I was hoping you'd wear the red dress. It's more becoming."

I stared at him, speechless, surprised I hadn't noticed before how often he "suggested" I might do something better, look better, feel better, everything always on his terms. How each time we argued, our words and accusations didn't seem to stick to him the way they stuck to me, like it didn't matter what I'd said, or that I'd said anything at all.

"Should I change?"

The muscle along his jaw clenched. "Of course not." He wore a smile that looked strained. "Forget I ever said it. Let's not spoil the evening, *chérie*." He gripped my knee possessively, then returned his hand to the wheel to navigate the winding roads. "I'd like tonight to be special."

I straightened the long folds of my royal blue gown, glad to have changed my mind at the last moment and packed it instead of the red. Lucien was right about one thing. We shouldn't spoil the evening. I didn't want to make a scene or ruin the special occasion. Grace had been far too kind to invite us.

Lucien brought my hand to his lips, and I tensed as the smell of alcohol tinged the air.

"Can you slow down?" I said. "You've been drinking."

"Don't worry. It was only one scotch."

I bit my lip as we twisted around each bend. As we wound around the roads and approached the circular drive of the sporting club, dozens of cars and pedestrians filled the street and we thankfully slowed from the thickening traffic. Clouds threatened and any moment the sky would open—not the greatest weather while dressed in gowns and heels. I peered out of the window at the sea. Though it was evening, the water-front glowed from the light cast by the casino, luxury hotels, and beautiful lanterns that lit the streets. And something else.

The flutter of flashbulbs.

The press swarmed the casino and the square in front of us. James had mentioned he'd be here tonight, keeping his boss happy with plenty of photographs. My heart skipped a beat as I pictured him among the crowd of photographers, elbowing his way to the front. I only hoped he'd be too busy to notice me on the arm of another man. Another man I was desperate to escape. I willed the rain to fall, to give me an excuse to rush inside.

An incredible racket filled the air. The throngs of onlookers gathered outside the building, many shouting, some screaming in delight, others gossiping over the beautiful people in ball gowns streaming toward the entrance.

"Shall we slip in around a back entrance?" I suggested. "It's all a bit chaotic out here."

But Lucien wouldn't hear of such a thing. This was his moment to be seen mingling with royalty. "Don't be silly. The chaos is part of the thrill, Sophie."

I wished I were squirreled away in my apartment in Cannes or in Grasse. I didn't like the chaos, didn't need the thrill. I could only imagine the pressure Grace—Princess Grace—must feel, not to mention the fatigue. So many people always wanting to see you, to be near you. I shuddered at the thought of my private life forced to center stage for public scrutiny. I admired her courage and her stamina.

"Here we are, *mon amour*," Lucien said, pulling the car to a stop and tossing his keys to the valet.

I stepped from the car, heart pounding. The cool night air, pregnant with impending rain, washed over me. I pulled my shawl around my bare shoulders, stomach aflutter. There were so many people! I glanced at the entrance, where a line of *carabiniers* stood in powdered wigs and livery.

I kept my head down as Lucien's hand cradled my elbow, and I felt myself being led toward the door. He paused in front of a roped area at the foot of the stairs, behind which hundreds of press photographers and onlookers gathered. Salty air billowed around us, sweeping my rich blue skirts around my ankles.

"Monsieur Marceau!" a photographer shouted. "Who's the pretty lady on your arm tonight?"

Another whistled loudly to gain Lucien's attention. "We heard your welcome party for Grace was a smash. Will you be attending the wedding?"

Lucien ignored their questions and waved. Dozens of flash-bulbs went off.

I bristled at the way he enjoyed the attention. He was a wealthy and handsome socialite, and hardly a month went by when there wasn't some mention of Lucien or Marceau Senior in the papers. I thought of the irony of my dislike for the press and their photographers, while one of their own had captured my heart.

Lucien tugged my arm, moving me closer to him.

"What is it?" I asked, pulling away slightly, desperately trying to keep my face away from the crowd. The first fat rain-drops began to fall, patterning my gown. It wasn't going to be a light rain, but a real soaker, just as it had been off and on all week. "Let's go inside. It's starting to rain."

But Lucien ignored my plea and kissed my cheek in a gallant gesture. "Sophie, I have something to say first, right here, on this very romantic day of love and commitment." He pulled a velvet box from inside his jacket. "I'd like to take our love a step further. It's time, wouldn't you say? Marry me?"

My heart raced. Bulbs flashed around us, the night driven away by the insistent display of light.

No. No, Lucien. Not here, not now. All I wanted was to go inside, away from the press.

"Lucien," I hissed. "Don't. Not here . . ." I tried to nudge him toward the door but to no avail.

He resisted and leaned into me. "I know it's a little ostentatious, but my fiancée will have only the best." He opened the velvet box, turning it at several angles. More flashes from the cameras went off as he displayed a large princess-cut diamond ring, more for the cameramen's pleasure than mine.

Somewhere in the background, I heard a voice say, *"Regardez!* Love is in the air in Monaco. A proposal. How romantic!"

"Kiss her! Let's see a kiss, monsieur!"

"Did she say yes?"

In seconds, many more cameras turned on us. Lucien gave them his best smile, wrapped his free arm around me and dipped me, giving me a long and ardent kiss.

A wave of nausea washed over me as I considered the spectacle he was making. He'd planned this, here, in front of the press. Anything he could do to upstage royalty.

I pushed him away and straightened. "What are you doing?" I hissed through a false smile for the cameras that surely looked like a grimace.

He laughed, took my hand, and pushed the diamond into place. Too stunned to protest, I stood as wooden as a statue, trying to find the words that screamed through my mind.

This is wrong! All wrong!

In that moment, the sky tore open and rain bulleted down.

Lucien tucked my hand into the crook of his arm. My mouth dry, I allowed myself to be rushed toward the door. As Lucien stepped inside, I glanced over my shoulder at the spectacle, everyone—except the press—ducking out of the rain. Yet my eyes rested on only one person in the melee, as if drawn to him like a magnet. A pair of broad shoulders and a familiar hat, water dripping from its brim.

As he looked up from behind his camera lens, James's beautiful, haunted eyes locked on mine.

"Darling, come along," Lucien nagged, tugging insistently on my arm. "We've given the cameramen more than enough."

Sick to my stomach and stunned by the turn of events, I followed him limply inside, James's stricken look burning behind my eyes.

39

SOPHIE

As everyone took their seats for the performance, a wave of nausea washed over me. I covered my mouth with my hand, the diamond ring flashing brilliantly beneath the light, a cruel reminder of who Lucien expected me to be. I pulled away from him, in need of air.

"What is it now?" he asked, his tone one of annoyance. "You don't like the ring? I can have the stone replaced with something else if you prefer—"

"My stomach is upset." I closed my eyes briefly, trying to push the thought of James's expression from my mind, and to gain control of my rising panic.

Lucien drew his mouth into a tight line. "I must say, I'd hoped for a more enthusiastic reaction, Sophie. I thought you'd be happy with the ring. With the publicity for Duval."

I shook my head. How could he misunderstand me so

completely? I swallowed my retort. We'd already made a spectacle of ourselves. "We'll talk about it later."

"You haven't been yourself lately," he said. "Maybe we'll get away. Take a trip to Rome, or Greece." He kissed my forehead and led me through the elaborate entrance of the building and to our seats.

I trained my eyes on the elegant sweep of curtains framing the stage. The sounds of the orchestra tuning their instruments mingled with the rumble of voices as everyone settled in preparation for the start of the performance. But before the lights dimmed, I stood to go to the ladies' room. I couldn't sit here, pretending, another minute.

"Where are you going?" Lucien whispered, his eyes full of surprise.

"To the ladies' room."

"Very well. But hurry or you'll miss something," he said, brusquely.

Such a gentleman, I thought.

I ducked inside an empty stall, locking the door behind me as tears of frustration and anger threatened. I bit back a sob and pressed my forehead against the door. What was I to do now? How would I ever make James see that Lucien's proposal meant nothing? I should have told James sooner. I should have ended things with Lucien sooner. I'd ruined everything.

I froze as I heard the door open. A cloud of glorious parfum filled the air. A fragrance I knew so well I could dictate the list of scents that composed the fragrance: berries, musk, jasmine. Grace's parfum, *Coeur de Princesse*.

I brushed my tears away and gathered my wits, preparing to

thank Grace for her invitations, but a clatter of footsteps and several new voices made me hesitate. I held my breath as they giggled and chattered like schoolgirls. I peeked through the crack in the door. Her bridesmaids.

"Oh, Gracie, everything has been so beautiful and elegant," one woman said. "But you must be exhausted."

"I am," Grace said, reapplying her lipstick. "There are so many people to meet and to thank, but I mustn't complain. It's hard to believe, sometimes, that this is all for little ol' me."

Another woman bopped Grace playfully with her hips and they laughed as they stumbled sideways a few feet. "Little ol' you indeed! Hollywood star. Princess of Monaco! It's dreamy, really, Gracie. An absolute dream. Anyway, in a few days you'll be on your honeymoon, away from us all."

"You're right. Really, I can't wait for the honeymoon. Being alone on the yacht will be heaven. You know, we're going to escape to the hills later in Rainier's car. He said he wants to watch the sunrise and show me how perfect everything looks in the morning light. 'I will show you your principality,' he said! But don't tell anyone! We want it to be a secret. The wretched press will ruin everything if word gets out."

The bridesmaids chatted about flowers and wedding guests, while I got the uneasy feeling of being a spy. And yet, for that moment, when I felt like a sandcastle being washed away by the tide, I was glad to be part of their happy world. It was a gift in a moment of despair.

"I'll be out shortly," Grace said, as the others returned to the performance. "I just need a moment."

I stood quietly, watching as Grace closed her eyes and inhaled a deep breath, as if trying to regain her calm, find her center. Her elegant white ball gown swept to the floor behind her, the hundreds of sequins and pearls on her skirts glittering in the light. Across her middle, she wore the royal red-and-white sash, around her neck an exquisite diamond necklace, and atop her head sat a dazzling tiara. She really was a princess.

Slowly, I opened the stall door. "Hello, Grace . . . Your Highness."

She turned from the mirror, surprise on her face. "Sophie! Goodness. You gave me a fright!" She stepped forward and took my hand in hers. "Have you been in there this whole time?"

I looked down to hide my shame. "I . . . *oui,* I have. I needed to collect myself a moment and then you all rushed in and began talking and I didn't want to interrupt. I'm terribly sorry. I didn't mean to intrude."

She smiled. "Think nothing of it. We all need a gossip in the bathroom with our girlfriends, don't we—especially on a day like this!" She sighed a little. Shadows lingered beneath her eyes. "I'm so pleased to see you, even if for a quick moment. I'm not able to spend enough time with anyone I'd like to this week. That's why I had to steal a moment with my bridesmaids." She tilted her head to one side. "Is everything all right? You look a little upset." As she said this, her fingertips found the rock on my finger. She pulled back and held out my hand. "Gosh! What a beauty. It seems I'm not the only one celebrating."

I couldn't find the words but stared numbly at the ring. "It's not . . . I didn't . . ."

Noticing my expression, Grace squeezed my hand gently. "I don't wish to pry but let me say one thing. We only get one chance at true love. Till death do us part will hopefully be a very long time—too long to be with the wrong person. Men often think they're the ones to make all the decisions, but I think that women can do anything they decide to do. Follow your heart, Sophie."

I felt a smile tug at my lips. "Thank you. I will remember that."

She leaned closer to me. "Can you smell it?"

"*Coeur de Princesse*. Of course! I would know it anywhere. I can't tell you how pleased I am that you like it."

"I adore it!" She smiled brightly. "Everyone does."

Gratitude rushed in, as my angst and regret ebbed a little. "Thank you, Grace. Thank you for choosing my fragrance. And thank you for your kind invitations. You've been so generous and gracious. If you only knew how important this was for my *parfumerie*—"

"Anything for a friend." Her eyes gleamed as brightly as the thousands of sequins that sparkled on her dress. I was dazzled by her. "I hope that's all right to say? Friend? I will need new ones as I settle on the Côte d'Azur. I don't know a soul here apart from Rainier, and feel a little like a fish out of water. It would mean a lot to me to keep in touch. Perhaps we could meet for a gossip in the bathroom every now and again!"

I stared at her, surprised she would admit her insecurities to me. She seemed born to be a princess. Bold, beautiful, talented, and yet I remembered the strong vanilla parfum she'd worn the day I first met her. A fragrance that masked insecurities and suggested the wearer longed for approval. In creating *Coeur de Princesse*, I had done precisely what Papa had taught me to do: created a fragrance that complemented her, elevated her, reflected who she was meant to be. And I was proud.

I returned her smile. "I'd like that very much. Now, I imagine they're missing you in there?"

"I suppose they are." She gave me a kiss on each cheek. "I hope you enjoy the evening. And remember what I said."

I nodded, and as she turned to the door, I took one last look at the stunning woman who had so bravely left everything she knew to follow her heart. I wondered if I would be able to give up so much for the man I loved. I didn't yet know. The one thing I knew for certain was that I couldn't wear Lucien's ring another moment.

As I walked back to my seat, a sense of courage and assuredness thrummed in my veins. I removed the ring from my finger.

When I reached Lucien, I remained standing. He glared at me. "What are you doing? Sit down. The show is beginning."

"I know how much you like to draw attention to yourself, so here." I dropped the ring in his lap. "I never liked flashy things, as you well know. And I don't like your friends. They aren't nice to me. I don't like your world, Lucien, I don't belong there. My answer is no. I won't marry you. Perhaps the reporters can add that to their headlines."

Too flabbergasted to speak, he let his mouth fall open as I turned on my heel and walked away, head held high, trying desperately to bite back my tears and retain my poise.

Only when I was through the foyer did I lift up my skirts and run out into the rain. I had to find James. I had to explain everything to him before it was too late. Maybe it already was.

I barged through the press corps, my gown instantly soaked

by the downpour and sticking to my skin, but he was nowhere to be seen. In a wild panic I asked if anyone had seen him.

"James Henderson? British? Very tall? He was here a while ago."

But all I got in reply were disinterested shrugs.

"He's most likely done the sensible thing, miss, and gone home for the night. I suggest you do the same."

But I couldn't give up that easily. I made my way to his hotel. If he wasn't there, I would leave him a note. Tell him everything. It was, after all, how we'd first fallen in love: through our words. I could only hope I would find the right ones to make him understand.

LOVE IS IN THE AIR IN MONACO

Local property tycoon proposes at the opera house.
Angeline West reports for the *Herald*.

Single ladies across the Côte d'Azur are as gloomy as
the Monaco skies tonight, as local businessman Lucien
Marceau took the opportunity to propose to his girlfriend of two years on the steps of the opera house
in front of hundreds of photographers. Sophie Duval,
the local perfumer who was selected to make the perfume
for the princess's wedding, looked rather shocked. The
couple dashed inside as the heavens opened and were not
available for comment after the event.

Guests arrived in the pouring rain, resplendent in
jewels and ball gowns at an event to celebrate the
civil wedding of the prince and princess. Designs from
Balmain and Dior drew gasps of admiration from the
gathered onlookers but the person they really wanted
to see was their new princess, who chose a Lanvin
gown for the occasion—a glittering high-waisted dress
of ivory silk organdy, embellished with thousands of
sequins, pearls, and rhinestones—designed by Antonio
Castillo for the Parisian couture house. She also wore
a dazzling tiara and a diamond necklace. But perhaps
the most significant part of the outfit was the red-and-
white ribbon of the Monegasque Order of Saint Charles,
given to her by the prince earlier in the day. It was
this sash that made the former actress look every inch
the regal princess.

40

JAMES

"Monsieur? Same again?"

I stared at the barman, glassy-eyed as I swayed on my stool, silently loathing him and all French men with their seductive accents and sex appeal.

I slapped my wallet down onto the bar. "Sure. Keep 'em coming," I slurred, waving my empty glass around in front of me. "Isn't that what they say in the movies?" I felt like I was living in one, my actions and decisions directed by someone else.

"You are a photographer, *non*?" he said, gesturing toward my camera. "Chasing the princess?"

I nodded. I barely knew what, or who, I was chasing anymore.

He wiped the marble bar with crisp, precise movements while a pianist played something annoyingly cheerful in the background. Everything about the Hôtel de Paris was crisp and precise. Even through the fog of drink I was sober enough to realize I would have been better off finding a seedy bar to drown my sorrows, but Monte Carlo didn't have such a thing, and the smartest hotel in town was the first place I'd come upon after leaving the opera house.

The last few hours were a blur.

Kelly and Rainier had arrived shortly after Sophie's little performance, but they'd rushed from their car without so much as a glance at the photographers, receiving our thanks in a barrage of boos and bad feeling. I'd stood numbly outside the opera house with the other members of the press, all of us soaked to the skin thanks to an almighty downpour. We hunkered down, hoping to get a better shot of the new princess when the event was over. I couldn't think of anywhere else to go. Standing outside in the rain was a fitting place to be since the only person I wanted to be with was inside on another man's arm. At least she'd had the decency to look guilty as she'd glanced over her shoulder.

Cold and angry, I'd unleashed some of my frustration on Hudgins, telling him exactly what I thought of Their Serene Highnesses and their miserable wedding.

Hudgins only laughed in that brash Hollywood manner of his. "What's eating you now, Henderson? You usually have something to complain about. Monte Carlo too damp for you, is it? Or perhaps the beer is too cold for you. You won't find a pint of warm ale here!"

"*This* is eating me!" I shouted, gesturing to the assembled mob. Someone had told me the press now outnumbered the Monegasque army eight to one. I could well believe it. "No wonder we're causing trouble. Held back like sheep, or cattle at a rodeo, or whatever you do over there on your ranches. There are a thousand press people in Monaco right now, in a space no bigger than a square mile, all of us trying to photograph people we never bloody see. It's a farce. If they even took a minute to stop and smile as they came and went, we'd at least have something to show for our day's work."

Hudgins patted me patronizingly on the shoulder. "You're a hack, Jim. You don't deserve the smile of a prince and his princess."

It wasn't just the press situation I was angry with. I was hurt and confused. Hudgins was the unfortunate recipient of it all.

In the end, we booed as Kelly and Rainier left the venue. She kept her head down against the rain. Rainier kept his back to us as his people shielded them both behind well-placed umbrellas. The mood was as dreadful as the weather.

"Go home, Grace," someone beside me shouted.

I was propelled forward as tempers frayed until the inevitable punches were thrown and a policeman threw someone's camera to the ground, smashing it. I couldn't say I especially blamed the chap for turning on his assailant and delivering a bite to the policeman's arm.

"Animals! Dogs!" the policeman shouted as the offending man was dragged off into a car and bustled roughly inside.

I watched it all, my camera hanging limply at my side, rain spilling in ribbons from the rim of my hat. I was drenched and miserable. The wedding of the century looked like it was heading toward being the greatest washout of all time.

I didn't wait for Sophie in the end, although part of me wanted to see her squirm when I confronted her. What was the point? She was with him now. *Lucien.* I'd heard them call his name. The same Lucien Sophie's mother had made reference to right after smacking me with her handbag. Lucien was what Sophie had been hiding from me all this time.

"A bad night, *non*?" the barman offered as he polished a glass, raising it to the light now and then to check for rogue fingerprints.

"*Oui,*" I sighed. "The worst. *Très terrible. Merde. Bleh bleh bleh.*"

I stared into the bottom of the tumbler and rolled the ice around like a gambler about to take his last chance at the roulette table. Where would my fortunes land? Clearly not with Sophie. No matter how many times I replayed the scene, I couldn't get it straight in my head. It didn't make any sense. We'd made love as we watched the sunrise over Monaco. We'd stood, wrapped in each other's arms, at the top of the long winding road to the ancient hilltop village of La Turbie. The scent of her perfume was still on my pillow. And now she was engaged to another man. *Monsieur Marceau,* they'd called out. Clearly he was somebody here. And me? Very much a nobody. How could I possibly compete?

"What do you know about a Monsieur Marceau?" I asked, waving my empty glass at the barman. "Handsome bugger. Tanned to kingdom come. Looks like he eats gold bullion for breakfast."

Louis, as his nametag informed me he was called, smiled wryly.

"Aha. Monsieur Marceau is your problem." He leaned forward across the bar, keeping his voice low. "He has many enemies but he also has money and friends in the palace." He raised his hands in that what-are-you-going-to-do-about-it Gallic shrug they all did so well over here. "What has he done to you? A bad business deal?"

"He's stolen my girl, that's what."

My girl. It was the first time I'd really thought of Sophie as mine. Not in the way that I wanted her to be my possession like Miss Kelly had become the property of the Monegasque crown, but my girl in the sense of being my friend, my lover, my . . . everything.

My shoulders slumped as my anger subsided into resignation. Had she been stringing me along all this time? But why? Maybe it had all been an act. Maybe Miss Kelly wasn't the only talented actress in town. *"Oh, James. Touch me there again, James. You do make me laugh, James."* And I'd stood there, snapping away with the rest of them like Pavlov's salivating dog as Monsieur Marceau made a mockery of me without even knowing I existed. A very public society engagement was just the sort of story the newspaper editors were crying out for. Romance. Drama. Sophie and Lucien had provided it all.

Louis placed the whiskey in front of me. *"Salut,* monsieur. She is probably not worth your sorrow. Most of them aren't."

"Salut," I replied, raising the glass to him. "I thought she was worth everything."

I downed the whiskey, savoring the warmth as it slipped down my throat. The muzzy sensation in my head was all I could feel. Everything else was numb. I left too much money on the bar, threw one arm into my jacket sleeve, and staggered outside, knocking over a stupid plant on the way, apologizing to it profusely as I wrestled it back onto its Grecian plinth.

The rain had eventually stopped, but a cool breeze settled over Monaco. I swayed and hiccupped my way toward the port. The buildings and street lamps were all festooned in Monaco's colors of red and white, ready for the big day, although it had rained so much the colors were running into each other. Each lamppost was topped with a gilded crown and banners embroidered with an entwined *R* and *G*. Everywhere I walked there was a party. Jazz and piano drifted through the open windows of wine bars and hotel restaurants. Laughter and singing. The clink of fine porcelain and crystal. All of it sounded hollow. As if the whole town was mocking me.

I found an empty bench and sat for a while, content to be alone in my stupor. The harbor looked especially beautiful at night, the twinkling lights adding an air of magic. At the top of the rock, the palace itself was a splendid sight, illuminated by floodlights. A hack I might be, but I could still see beauty where others wouldn't notice. Partly from habit, partly from obstinacy, I raised my camera and found some sort of solace in the silhouetted forms of the buildings and the blurred lights that came in and out of focus as I tried to steady my hands. I turned then to the water, focusing my lens on a lone fisherman casting his net in the dark, waiting patiently to see whether he would be lucky in his haul. In his tired, weathered face, I saw myself. Alone, adrift, casting my net, waiting for what might be revealed when I pulled it to the surface.

"Damn you, Sophie," I muttered and then louder, shouting to the stars. "I bloody loved you!"

I sat for a long time then, lost in the agony of what could have been, and what could never be, and what was never mine to have in the first place. I didn't care about the wedding to-morrow. I didn't care about any of this. The only thing—the only person—I cared about now was Emily.

What an idiot I'd been to ever imagine that I could make a home in this movie-set-perfect place of millionaires and princes. I didn't belong here. I belonged to miserable gray old London, with its dodgy boozers and unpredictable weather and a cat who treated me with the contempt I deserved. Mostly, I belonged with Emily. Wherever she was, so should I be. What the hell did it matter whose picture got the front page? I'd spent too long looking through my lens at other people's lives. It was time to start looking at my own.

I could already hear Emily's squeals of delight as she jumped into my arms, could feel the perfect weight of her as she wrapped her legs around me.

The fairy tale was over.

It was time to go home.

41

SOPHIE

The day of the cathedral wedding arrived with the first sunshine in a week, yet despite the bright morning and the joyous occasion, I couldn't find it in my heart to be happy. I felt numb and confused, part of me relieved and part of me despairing as I replayed the events of the evening over and over in my mind. I couldn't believe I'd given Lucien the ring back, but I didn't regret it for a moment. It wasn't like me to be so impulsive, so resolute, but whether she'd intended it or not, something Grace said to me had really hit home. *"I think that women can do anything they decide to do. Follow your heart, Sophie."* I would never forget the look of shock and anger in Lucien's eyes. It was a look, I now realized, I'd seen many times before when things didn't go his way. I was only sorry it had taken me so long to do the right thing, and that I had misled James in the process.

I'd searched for him for over an hour in the rain, looking everywhere I could think he might be, but he'd been swallowed up by the night. He wasn't at his hotel, either, so I did the only thing I could and left a note for him. I'd written it with shaking hands. "Please make sure he gets it," I'd urged the concierge, gripping his hand in mine. "It's very important. Please." He'd assured me he would deliver it personally, and arranged for a taxi to take me back to the apartment. "You're drenched, madame. You'll get sick if you don't get warm and dry soon."

In the moment, I'd hardly cared.

Only when I was back at the apartment in Cap-d'Ail and had pulled off my sodden dress, tearing a seam in my frustration, did I allow myself to fully give in to my emotions. I cried for the lost journal, for Papa, for the property I was forced to sell, for wasting my time with the wrong man. Mostly I cried for James, for the hurt I'd caused him, and for the hurt I'd brought upon myself.

My gaze settled on the journal he'd given me, the beautiful flowers embossed on the front. I opened it to the inscription inside. *To the future of Duval. And to us. —James*

I had one more chance to make things right, to salvage whatever future we might have.

He would be at the wedding—he had to be. His job depended upon it. I didn't care that Lucien would also be there. I didn't care about the inevitable whispers and gossip that would follow me to my seat. All I cared about was explaining myself to James. Apologizing for the mistakes I'd made.

I dressed in a dusky rose crepe jacket and skirt, wrapped a cape around my shoulders, and settled my pillbox hat over my chignon. In a nod to the princess's trademark style, I added my sunglasses before I left the apartment, glad to hide my swollen eyes behind them.

I took the early bus to Monaco, keen to leave the apartment before the time Lucien had previously arranged to pick me up. I presumed he wouldn't show, but I didn't want to be there if he did. Another argument was the last thing I needed. While the other passengers gossiped and tittered like a flock of starlings, so excited about the wedding, I sat quietly alone at the back of the bus, watching the blue waters of the Mediterranean shimmer in the sunlight and wondering what the day would bring.

From the Place de la Visitation in Monaco-Ville, I walked the short distance to the cathedral, past the rainbow-colored buildings that lined the narrow winding streets, Monegasque flags at every window, decorative flowerpots with blooms of red and white. The atmosphere was jubilant and the setting so beautiful I felt my mood lighten a little as I arrived at the cathedral, sunlight gleaming against the brilliant white facade. A red carpet and white silk canopy had been set up for the occasion. An honor guard of the Compagnie des Carabiniers du Prince, American sailors, and Boy Scouts stood watch, awaiting the royal party and esteemed guests. The formality and fanfare, though exuberant, was respectful and elegant. I marveled again at the fact that I'd been invited to such a glittering event, which would include European royalty, millionaires, diplomats, and movie stars.

I looked on as more guests arrived and sauntered up the red carpet in their finery, but my attention was focused on the press. I scanned every face beyond the area roped off for the wedding guests, studied every man with a camera, but I didn't see James anywhere. Surely even he wouldn't be late today. Where was he? Heart in my throat, I willed myself to be optimistic. He would be here. He had to be. Just as a fragrance needs time to mellow and settle against the skin, I knew I must wait patiently to see what traces of our relationship remained.

Despite my nerves and restlessness, I held my head high as I waited to be seated. When my turn eventually came, I followed the escort inside the cathedral, the red carpet soft beneath my satin shoes. I took my seat beside an ornate marble pillar near the back, placed my handbag neatly on my lap, and tugged the creases from my gloves. I was relieved to find the seat beside mine was empty. No sign of Lucien. I fidgeted and glanced at the guests who were already seated: a dazzling array of Hollywood stars, heads of state, notable Monegasques, and members of the extended Kelly family. MGM cameramen lined the walls on either side of the nave, a tangle of wires and cables snaking around their feet, their television cameras fixed firmly on the two gilded thrones at the altar. For a woman whose name had been made in front of the camera, it was ironic that the marriage that would take Grace Kelly away from her beloved movies would be the last picture she filmed.

The cathedral bells chimed the hour. Time moved on.

While the guests to my left were bathed in a burst of sunshine as they awaited their princess, I sat in shadow, waiting for my future.

42

JAMES

I woke to bright sunshine, an enormous hangover, and a relentless knocking on my hotel room door.

"All right. I'm coming. I'm coming," I called, my voice gravelly from too many cigarettes, all my good intentions having fallen away beneath the influence of too much whiskey. I stumbled out of bed fully clothed, squinting against the light streaming through the open curtains. "Did somebody die?" I asked as I opened the door. "Is the place on fire?"

The concierge was a little taken aback by my appearance. "Good morning, monsieur. This arrived for you late last night." He handed me an envelope. The perfume immediately gave away the sender. "The young lady who wrote it was very distressed, not to mention absolutely drenched."

I shoved the envelope into my pocket and laughed. "Good. Serves her right."

The concierge hovered at the door. The gray at his temples and the lines around his eyes lent him an air of gravitas. "She insisted I give it to you in person. It is, of course, none of my business whether you read it or not, but she looked terribly upset."

I felt as if I was being scolded by my father. "Yes. Thank you. I get it. Is there anything else?"

"No, sir. That was all." He turned to leave. "Will monsieur be attending the wedding today?"

"Yes, monsieur will be attending the wedding." I rubbed my forehead and willed the room to stop spinning. "If monsieur can recover from the worst hangover of his life."

"It is a very happy day in Monaco. A day for falling in love, *non*? Not a day for falling out."

I sighed. "I'll read the letter."

"*Bon*. Enjoy the festivities, monsieur."

I gave him a few francs for his trouble and unsolicited advice, and closed the door.

It was seven thirty. I was due at the cathedral by nine; guests had been told to take their seats by nine thirty at the latest.

I took the envelope from my pocket and put it on the desk. Part of me was intrigued to see what Sophie had to say for herself, but a stubborn part of me was determined to ignore her, get the wedding over with, and go home.

Most of the night was a blur, but there was one image I couldn't get out of my mind. The way he'd dipped her for a lingering kiss. The way she'd glanced over her shoulder, her eyes locked on mine as they'd rushed inside the opera house.

"Not so lucky after all, eh, Walsh," I muttered as I splashed water onto my face and pondered my reflection in the mirror. I looked as terrible as I felt.

After a strong pot of coffee, my head began to clear a little. I sat on the bed and did what I'd known I would do from the minute the concierge put the envelope in my hand. I opened it. I had to know what possible explanation there could be for what had happened. The sound of car horns tooting in celebration and of music drifting through the streets fell away into the background as I read Sophie's words.

My dear James,

I'm so sorry. I don't even know where to begin, but please believe me when I say I wasn't expecting Lucien's proposal, nor did I desire it. I was furious with him and returned the engagement ring immediately. He can toss it into the harbor for all I care. It means nothing to me, but it would mean everything if you could find some way to forgive me. I've looked everywhere for you. Where did you go?

My relationship with Lucien is—was—complicated. Please believe me when I say that it was over between us long before last night, long before you arrived in Monaco, but Lucien isn't used to being told no and he needed someone on his arm for the wedding events, for appearances' sake. I felt I owed him that much before we parted ways. There are other reasons I stayed with him, too. Lucien has business interests in Duval and I owe him money if I can ever be truly free of him. I let myself believe I needed his influence, but now I realize I need nothing from him at all. We all make mistakes, and Lucien Marceau was mine. I only wish I'd explained all this to you long before tonight. You deserved better, and now I have only myself to blame for making such a mess of everything.

I hope to see you at the cathedral, but if we miss each other, I will be at the casino clock tower at eight tonight. Meet me there? Even if you can't forgive me, please let me tell you in person how I feel about you.

My papa taught me that to be a parfumeur *is to be a keeper of memories. That every scent has the power to remind us of something, or someone. You are captured in all my memories of the past year. You are part of my story, James; the notes that linger the longest. I will never forget you.*

Sophie

I put the page down and lay back on the bed, staring at the ceiling. I thought about the journal I'd chosen for Sophie, and the rose-tinted sunset when I'd given it to her, the violet-scented paper blooming anew as she'd unwrapped it. *"Today will always be violets,"* she'd said, pressing the book to her nose. I'd known it would never replace the one she'd lost, but I'd hoped it would encourage her to carry on, to fight the big commercial developers threatening to buy her out. *Today will always be violets.*

Picking up the page, I breathed in its scent. "What will today be, then, Sophie? What memories will we hold on to?"

A few days ago, I'd believed she would be part of my future. But everything had changed so quickly. Now I had to decide if

I would meet her at the clock tower, if I still wanted my future to include her, or not.

But first, a wedding. I would make my decision later.

I'd almost finished shaving when another urgent knock at the door interrupted me.

"Hell's bells!" I mumbled. "What is it now? Can't a chap get any peace?" I grabbed a towel and dabbed at the shaving cream above my lip as I opened the door.

The hotel manager stood in the corridor, his face ashen.

I knew instantly that something was wrong.

"Monsieur, I am so sorry." He shook his head as he handed me a small piece of paper with the hotel crest on the top. "An urgent message from a hospital in Scotland. There has been an accident."

My mind reeling, I read the scribbled message. *St. Andrew's Hospital. Inverness. Three passengers injured in car crash. James Henderson is next of kin. Please contact him as a matter of extreme urgency.*

The towel fell from my hand as her name tumbled from my lips.

"Emily."

43

SOPHIE

As a hush settled over the congregation inside the cathedral, I took a last moment to absorb the setting. My perfumer's nose was drawn to the cascades of white flowers draped from chandeliers and hanging baskets overhead, a decadent fusion of lilies, snapdragons, and lilacs. Their scent mingled with that of dozens of pillar candles, their flames dancing in eager anticipation of the arrival of the bride. I placed my wrist to my nose and took a long breath in, savoring the scent of the perfume that had led me here, to this grand cathedral, on this grandest of occasions. "*Something new,*" she'd said. Any moment now, Grace Patricia Kelly would walk down the aisle in front of the world's gaze, and she would do it all wearing a Duval perfume. *My* perfume. *Coeur de Princesse.* I only wished Papa could be here to share the moment with me. I imagined him in the empty seat beside me, and smiled.

The somber organ music began, and the congregation rose to their feet. Flower girls and bridesmaids in their yellow satin and chiffon gowns began the procession, their steps timed by twos, their faces alight with excitement. Once they'd assumed their positions at the altar, the music changed and, finally, Grace made her entrance.

All eyes and cameras were fixed on her stunning gown as her father escorted her to the top of the aisle: an ivory taffeta bell skirt, a cummerbund accentuating her dainty waist, an intricate lacework collar and sleeves. Tiny pearls on her bodice gleamed beneath the candlelight, while her lace veil fell in elegant cascades from an elaborately beaded cap. She was utterly exquisite. She always had been, of course, but today she carried a different air about her. Something regal and refined. This was the day she would leave behind the life of a Hollywood starlet and make history as the first American princess. For a moment I forgot my troubles and smiled for my new friend. How exquisite she was, how exquisite it all was.

At the altar, John Kelly kissed his daughter's cheek and took his seat. Trumpets blared, announcing the arrival of Prince Rainier behind them. He was striking in a dark military coat, decorated with medals and the red-and-white sash of the Order of Saint Charles. As he knelt before God, country, priest, and the millions watching around the world, Rainier glanced nervously at his bride. I wondered what they were both thinking in that moment, the pinnacle of an unexpected romance of only a year, and a frenetic week of celebration here in Monaco.

I wondered if James was thinking about me in that moment, too.

The ceremony was elegant, serious, regal in every sense. When it concluded, Her Serene Highness Princess Grace of Monaco walked with her prince down the aisle and out onto the cathedral steps, where they stepped into a cream-and-black Rolls-Royce. I managed to catch the back of the vehicle as it turned a corner and headed off for a processional drive through Monaco's streets. The happy couple would greet their people and return to the palace gardens for a luncheon.

"Good luck, Grace," I whispered, although I doubted she would need it. A long and happy future stretched out ahead of her like the view of the vast Mediterranean she would wake to every day.

With the wedding party dispersed, I walked through the crowds, searching for the only face I longed to see. Most of the photographers and reporters had already moved on to the reception at the palace. There was still no sign of James. Doubt mixed with dread and I struggled to remain calm. At the very least, he would be at the casino later, wouldn't he? He had to be.

I smoothed my skirt and walked the short distance to the palace. Eight o'clock couldn't come soon enough.

44

JAMES

Monaco to Scotland

Everything became a blur as I called the hospital in Scotland and heard the devastating news. Marjorie and Humphrey were killed instantly in the accident, and Emily was in a very bad way. Details were sketchy, but the nurse informed me their car had left the road on a steep mountainside in a remote part of the Highlands. Though she spoke calmly, she urged me to hurry.

It was unbearable to be so far away. Somehow I packed my suitcase and made travel arrangements. Somehow I left a note for Sophie with the concierge. Whatever she'd planned to say to me at the clock tower, whatever future there might have been for us, was erased with each panicked line I scrawled on the page.

I left Monaco within the hour, the celebratory flags and royal crests that decorated the streets fluttering their farewell. This time it wasn't *au revoir*. This time it was goodbye. The next available flight out of Nice wasn't until the next day so I took the train north to Paris, from where I would fly to Edinburgh.

As I watched the French landscape pass by too slowly, I remembered the last time I'd traveled through France to England, dropping everything to be with Teddy. The helplessness and despair I'd felt then, I felt again, but tenfold. I pressed my cheek against the window, closed my eyes, and prayed. I promised to never leave Emily again, if only God would see her through this. Why couldn't the damned train go faster?

I slept in fits and starts, my dreams filled with nightmarish visions of a broken body thrown among the heather-strewn mountainside. My little girl. She was all I had in the world. And now that her mother was dead, I was all Emily had in the world, too.

THREE WEDDINGS, ONE PRINCESS

Monaco greets Her Serene Highness Princess Grace.
Angeline West reports for the *Herald*.

This morning at 10 A.M. a Philadelphia girl, Grace Kelly, married the man of her dreams, Rainier Louis Henri Maxence Bertrand Grimaldi of Monaco. The third in a series of ceremonies, today's event was held in the Saint Nicholas Cathedral of Monaco, the off-white church atop *Le Rocher*, the Rock as the locals affectionately call it, upon which both the palace and its place of worship were built centuries ago. The ceremony was a very formal affair with all the pomp and circumstance one would expect for royalty.

While the first two weddings (a civil ceremony that was performed twice) fulfilled legal contracts in Monaco and Kelly's studio contract with Metro-Goldwyn-Mayer, today's Roman Catholic ceremony was the grand occasion we'd all been waiting for, and was watched by an estimated thirty million television viewers around the world. MGM's exclusive rights to film the wedding were brokered as part of Miss Kelly's decision to end her seven-year contract with the studio.

Her Serene Highness has sailed through all three occasions with poise and stamina, but it was, perhaps, no surprise that the emotions finally got to her. The famous "ice queen" shed several visible tears as the seventy-minute ceremony was performed in Latin and French.

Princess Grace stunned onlookers in a *peau de soie* and lace masterpiece created by Helen Rose of MGM, which took three dozen seamstresses six weeks to make. Prince Rainier appeared regal in full Monegasque military dress. The ceremony was attended by six hundred guests, including stars from the screen such as Ava Gardner and Cary Grant, and shipping magnate Aristotle Onassis.

After the ceremony, the couple rode through Monaco in a Rolls-Royce to greet their public. One of the largest crowds appeared to be at the post office, where a special commemorative stamp of the royal couple was being sold.

The prince and princess returned to the palace grounds, where friends and family were served a light luncheon and drank champagne long into the afternoon. When it was time to cut the cake, Prince Rainier produced his sword, much to the delight of the guests. The six-tier cake featured a replica of the palace in spun sugar and scenes from Monegasque history. I can happily report that it tasted as lovely as it looked.

After the palace reception, the newlyweds will board the royal yacht *Deo Juvante II* for their Mediterranean honeymoon. It is understood they will be joined by Princess Grace's beloved poodle, Oliver.

We at the *Herald* send our hearty congratulations to the happy couple. May they have a very long and happy life together.

45

SOPHIE

Although it felt strange to be on my own at such an occasion, without Lucien at my side to steer me this way and that, it also felt right. I didn't need anyone to speak for me. I had my own voice, and I soon found myself engaged in conversation as I mingled with the other guests in the courtyard inside the palace walls.

The atmosphere was happy and relaxed after the stiff formality of the cathedral ceremony. The tables were covered with white linens and decorated with flowers and dinnerware, and waiters rushed to and fro, topping up glasses with champagne. When Grace and Rainier arrived, everyone clapped and cheered, and the orchestra began. The royal couple greeted their guests with radiant smiles. The hectic week of events was coming to a close, and they were madly in love, the rest of their lives ahead in which to discover each other. I could be nothing but happy for them.

When the grand buffet was announced, I filled my plate with smoked salmon, cold lobster, and caviar, but I picked at it idly, my appetite suppressed by worry. In a matter of hours, I'd gone from nervous to anxious, hopeful to despairing. Perhaps James felt that what we'd had between us couldn't be repaired, despite the honesty of my letter. His absence from the wedding spoke volumes.

I put my plate down, intending to leave the reception and head to James's hotel to try to find him one last time, but a woman dressed in cornflower-blue satin tapped me on the shoulder.

"Pardon me, but are you Sophie Duval?"

"I am." I smiled and shook her hand as she introduced herself.

"I'm Janice Carmichael, of Carmichael department stores, New York." She held out a business card. "A reporter, Angeline West, pointed you out. Your perfumes are ravishing, Miss Duval. Grace smells divine, exactly like the princess she was born to be. I wonder, are you accepting commissions? I'd like to try some of your samples, possibly carry a line of a unique fragrance in our stores for a trial run."

I perked up at the praise. "Thank you, you're very kind. It was an honor to develop the fragrance for Grace. As it happens, I'm in the process of developing a new line of fragrances, including a variation of *Coeur de Princesse*. I'd be delighted to send you samples."

Janice nodded. "Wonderful. I've recently taken over the

beauty department in our stores and we're going in a new direction. More *haute couture*, if you will, and I absolutely love the idea of hosting a boutique French perfumer."

We made plans to meet in Cannes in a few days' time, before Miss Carmichael left for New York.

My heart swelled with pride. I'd worked so long and so hard for Duval to be recognized, and it seemed the tides were turning at last. Another thing Lucien and Maman had been wrong about. Success had been just out of reach, but in my friendship with Grace I'd been given a second chance, and a little bit of magic.

I decided to stay for the duration of the reception.

As the party drew to a close, Grace slipped away to change into a light gray dress suit and a white hat, and the couple waved from the palace balcony as they prepared to depart for their honeymoon aboard the royal yacht. I found myself at the front of the crowd as they rushed past beneath a flurry of confetti. Grace didn't have time to stop, but as she looked at me with those blue eyes of hers, she placed her hand to her heart and mouthed, "Thank you. Be happy."

It was the perfect goodbye.

Beneath a setting sun, I made my way to the clock tower, hoping to find James already there, hardly daring to imagine he wouldn't show up.

After waiting an hour, I accepted that he wasn't coming. Unable to bear the thought of leaving Monaco without him, I decided to try his hotel one last time.

Thankfully, the concierge who had helped me last night was at the front desk.

"*Excusez-moi,* monsieur. I'm looking for a guest. James Henderson. I was here last night."

Concern filled his eyes as he stepped around the desk and took me to one side. "Yes, I remember you, madame." He cleared his throat. "I'm afraid Monsieur Henderson left in a hurry early this morning. I believe he was headed to the airport."

My heart plummeted to my feet. "To the airport?" I fought to control my despair, and I started for the door.

"Wait! Miss!" He rushed after me. "You are Sophie Duval?"

I nodded, numbly. "Yes."

He stepped back to the desk and returned with an envelope. "He left this for you."

My heart beat wildly as I took the envelope and stumbled through the hotel door. Hands shaking, I tore open the envelope and read the message.

Sophie,

> *There was a car crash in Scotland. Emily is badly injured. Her mother was killed. I'm sorry, but I must go.*

James

I couldn't take it in, couldn't believe what I'd read. My mind raced, my emotions flipping from anguish for James to a strange sense of relief at the realization that he hadn't left because of me. But however I tried to process it, there it was in black and white, one of life's greatest truths: the very happiest of days for some end in the greatest sadness for others. I said a silent prayer for James's little girl, and for him, as I imagined him racing across the countryside, heart sick with worry.

I traveled back to Cap-d'Ail as night draped gently over Monaco's hills, bringing a day of joy and love to a close. Even with all that had happened, I felt another truth fill me with assuredness and a measure of comfort. That whatever happened next, whatever the future held for me and for Duval, I would do it on my own.

Perhaps James was only meant to be in my life for a short time, a jolt to finally shake me out of my relationship with Lucien. I would always be grateful for that, and see my time with him as a gift.

"To be a parfumeur is to be a keeper of memories, Sophie. Every scent will remind you of something, or someone."

Perhaps I had already collected all the memories I would ever have of James, and if so, I must treasure them: his smile, his laughter, his belief in me. Even if he wasn't meant to be part of my future, he had shown me the way toward it, and for that, I would never forget him.

With the wedding over, and James returned to England under such terrible circumstances, I found solace in the place I'd always felt happiest. I returned to my workshop in Grasse. The familiar sight of the dear old buildings, the rugged hills dotted with greenery, and the blue spring sky helped to ease the pain. I sought distraction among the flower fields and busied myself with different formulas, working long hours to fill my days, often falling asleep at my desk.

And then the day arrived when I knew everything would be all right. I woke early. As I sipped my coffee, I ran my hand over the soft leather cover of the new journal, turned to the first blank page and wrote the date at the top. I'd worked hard to live up to Papa's expectations, to be all he wanted me to be. Now it was time to believe in my own talent, and take my first steps toward reinvention. Grace had given me so much, and now with interest from the Carmichael department stores in America there was hope on the horizon.

As my hand paused over the page, a flood of memories filled my mind: James's hands on my face, a sleepy morning sky erupting in a blaze of color as we looked out from the verdant hills, the scent of dew and the faint hint of minerals from the rocky cliffs around us, apricot jam on bread at his bedside one morning.

I scribbled frantically, capturing the first inklings of the head, heart, and base notes.

Lever du Soleil. Sunrise.

A new beginning.

PART THREE

BASE NOTES

*Notes that assert themselves when
the others have evaporated;
scents that diffuse slowly, with respect to
time. The notes that linger the longest.*

I avoid looking back. I prefer good memories to regrets.
—GRACE KELLY

46

SOPHIE

Grasse
September 1982

My papa often said that sad news conjures happy memories. Today has brought the very saddest news, and as I sit on the terrace of the old house and watch the sun slip away, I think about much of my life. Mostly, I think about the people I have known, the happy moments we shared together. Memories made.

Beside me, the wall where I used to lean my bicycle. I can still feel the juddering in my arms as I cycled over cobbles and the ruts in the lanes, can still hear the bright trill of the bell as I waved hello to someone or other, or shooed a lazy cat out of the way. I understand things about the past now, see things more clearly. Without much of a family to call my own, I made one for myself in Madame Clouet, Jacques, Monsieur Renault, dear Natalie, and everyone who worked so tirelessly with me here. Many of them are gone now, of course. The boulangerie is a shoe shop. The old picture house where I'd stared, awestruck, at the beautiful stars of the screen is a restaurant. The only stars I watch now are those in the skies above. They appear as if by magic, one by one, until they are unfathomable in their millions.

The air carries a trace of midnight jasmine and cool limestone and I breathe in deep, savoring the perfumes of the night, the natural scents of my beloved Provence. These are the moments when I long to have someone beside me to share such quiet pleasures with, moments when I wonder what sort of wife and mother I might have been, had life taken a different turn. I wonder, also, if I'd been a good daughter. I had certainly tried. I'd done the best I could, looking out for a mother who was so self-destructive, who nearly destroyed me and all that I loved. If she had only been different. If I'd had a daughter of my own, might I have understood her struggles more? Ifs. Buts. Maybes. Memories and regrets. They are all carried in the stars.

I pick up the *journal de fleurs* beside me and breathe in the scent of old paper. Dear Papa, captured on every page. I thumb to the back and smile as I read my first ideas for the formula of *Coeur de Princesse*. In the end, I'd found the journal shortly after the wedding celebrations. It was hidden behind a cushion in the house in Grasse, or rather, left there mistakenly by Maman. As was my habit, I'd kept the note I'd found tucked inside.

Madame Duval,

Here it is! It was easy enough to obtain in the end (a strong martini helped), but Sophie will search thoroughly for it the moment she notices it is missing. Dispose of it immediately, or hide it well. This will be difficult for her, but we both know she must let go of the past. We can then concentrate on building a new future for the Duval estate.

I look forward to visiting soon.

Lucien

In the evening's silence, it seems almost impossible that such anger and resentment could have ever troubled this quiet old house. Cruel words and accusations thrown around like pebbles tossed by the waves. My boyfriend and my mother thought they could prevent me from making new fragrances, that in my despair and without the crutch of Papa's notes, I would give up—forfeit everything, so they could both profit.

They'd underestimated me.

I smile, though I'd once felt so bitter about it all. Like a glass stopper in a bottle of parfum, the fragrances of the past are captured in time, and I cannot recall the memory as sharply as I once did. As with all old wounds, the pain of their betrayal has faded. Despite everything, I miss Maman in a way. I wish she could have seen my success.

And then my thoughts turn to James. I never stoppered my memories of him. His name brings another smile to my lips. There were so many things left unsaid. So many questions that still linger: What might have happened if he'd made it to the clock tower? Did he ever receive the letter I sent shortly after his daughter's accident? Did she recover? Was he happy? Did he ever think about me and wonder similar things? But now is not the time for seeking answers. It is a time for remembering.

I take a sip of wine and savor the rich flavors on my tongue. I am grateful that my palate and my famous nose are as keen as ever, that I can still enjoy the delights and the success they bring to me. Duval thrives, as do I. My only concern is who will love Duval when I am gone? A fitting question for a day that has brought such sadness to me, and all of Monaco.

Tears prick my eyes as I straighten the bundle of letters on my lap, a little museum of correspondence curated over the years, an intimate record of a princess whom only a privileged few of us ever knew as a friend. Her words carry such poignancy now.

My dearest Sophie . . .

She started every letter that way. From the very beginning she treated me as an equal, as the best of friends. It was how she treated everyone. Her crown and sash made her a princess, but in her heart she was always Grace Kelly, a devoted Irish American girl from Philadelphia who loved her family and knew what it meant to have good friends to turn to. I hope she knew what she meant to me, what a difference she made. I'd told her often enough in my replies, and on the many happy occasions when we met, sharing our hopes and our worries, our opinions on this outfit and that fragrance.

I read through some of the old newspaper cuttings, and wander in memories of happier times. Then I pick up the morning newspaper, and read the words again. I still can't comprehend the headline. I simply cannot believe that our dear Princess Grace is gone.

PRINCESS GRACE DIES

Prince, and all of Monaco, in mourning.
Angeline West, special report for *Le Figaro*.
September 15, 1982

Her Serene Highness Princess Grace of Monaco died in
the hospital last night, thirty-six hours after she
was badly injured in a horrific car crash in the hills
near her home. Her daughter, Princess Stephanie, age
seventeen, who was in the car at the time of the accident, was released from the hospital earlier today.

The fifty-two-year-old princess broke a thighbone,
collarbone, and three ribs in the crash when her Rover's
brakes reportedly failed and the car plunged 120 feet
down the hillside. A palace spokesman in Monte Carlo
announced that the beautiful former film star had died
of a cerebral hemorrhage at 3:30 P.M. "Unfortunately it
is true," he said. "The princess is dead."

Tributes to the princess have been pouring in from
around the world. In London, a Buckingham Palace
spokesman said, "I am sure the queen and other members
of the royal family will be shocked and saddened by
the news," and in Washington, President Ronald Reagan
said he and his wife, Nancy, offered their condolences.
"As an American, Princess Grace brought character and
elegance to the performing arts and always found time
to make important contributions to her craft." The
princess's many former co-stars were devastated by
the news of her death. In New York, a spokesman for

Frank Sinatra, who starred with her in *High Society*, said, "Along with the rest of the world we are stunned, shocked, and totally grief-stricken at the news. Grace was a gracious, wonderful woman who was a princess from the moment she was born. We still cannot believe it. Our hearts go out to her husband, her children, and her family here in the United States."

The sentiment is echoed by us all.

The princess will lie in state at the Ardent Chapel in the Grimaldi palace, and the funeral will be held on September 18 at the Saint Nicholas Cathedral of Monaco, where she married her prince on such a joyous occasion in April 1956. A marble slab laid in perpetuity with fresh flowers will mark her final resting place in the cathedral.

Rita Gam, one of Grace's bridesmaids and best friends, said the following about her friend's remarkable transition from a Hollywood movie star to Monaco's beloved princess: "The last time I saw Grace was, in my own imagination, when she was on the yacht chug-chug-chugging away into the Mediterranean after the wedding was over, and I realized there was no more Grace Kelly. Grace Kelly was a memory. Grace Kelly was history. There was only Princess Grace of Monaco."

Princess Grace herself once said, "I would like to be remembered as someone who did useful deeds, and who was a kind and loving person. I would like to leave the memory of a human being with a correct attitude and who did her best to help others."

She most certainly did that.

In a last gesture to the woman he loved with all his heart, Prince Rainier has requested that he be laid to rest beside the princess when the time comes. He is reported to be inconsolable with grief.

47

JAMES

Monaco
September 1982

Aboard the TGV from Paris, I lean my head against the window and study the photograph in my hand. My eyes settle on the familiar image: Grace Kelly in the grounds of the royal palace, her future as a princess waiting for her in the historic walls, her life as a Hollywood movie star already rolling away to the distant hills. I turn the image over. On the back, a scribbled note. *Grace and Rainier. First meeting. May 1955. Monte Carlo. JH.* I smile for a moment as I think of Sanders's face the day he saw those photographs, and then I remember why I'm in France, and the smile fades.

My gaze wanders then, beyond the window. I watch the

landscape as it changes from the verdant valleys and vineyards of the Loire to the rolling hills of Auvergne. When hectares of olive groves and rocky soil come into view, I know I'm close to Provence, and my heart flips in response. I've always wanted to visit at this time of year, the intense heat of summer having left with the tourists, the villages and towns returned to their quiet routines as the waterfront coves shimmer in aqua and cobalt. The pull I'd once felt toward the Côte d'Azur tugs at me again. I only wish I were visiting under better circumstances.

As the train rattles on, I close my eyes and think about everything I'd given up to remain in London. I'd muddled through, trying my best to fill the gap, to be mother and father to Emily. I baked a birthday cake every year, patched up grazed knees, and soothed a fevered brow. It wasn't always easy, but I never complained. I'd made a bargain that if Emily survived her injuries, I would never leave her again. And I didn't, not until she'd grown up and made a life and a family of her own. Even now, I find it hard to be away from her.

It was Emily who'd insisted I come. *"Go, Dad. Princess Grace was special to you. You used to tell me about her all the time, remember?"* Princess Grace had filled my stories over the years, but it was another woman who'd filled my heart.

I study the photograph again and think of that crazy week I spent in Monaco, how magical it all was, how magical *she* was.

Sophie Duval.

We thought we had all the time in the world.

What fools we were.

❊ ❊ ❊

Monaco has altered a lot in the years since I was last here, but it is the change in atmosphere that I notice the most. The cheering crowds, the fluttering red-and-white flags, the boom of celebratory cannon fire—all the things I remember from that week of weddings—are hushed now. Everyone is in mourning, speaking in respectful whispers, understanding one another's grief. Yet my tears are not only for a princess. They are for what, and whom, I left behind.

I walk along the narrow shuttered streets, through a square in Fontvieille where the scent of late-blooming roses, orange blossoms, and mimosas infuses the air. I think of how Sophie would coax the delicate perfume from their petals. *"We are alchemists, Miss Duval. Magicians!"* I recall the letters I'd written to her in the months during Emily's recovery. It helped to write it down, spill it out onto the page. I never sent them, of course. What was the point? Sophie was in France. I was in England. Circumstances had thrown us together beneath the brisk breezes of the Cannes waterfront and had torn us apart as violently as a winter storm. Life had moved on, and so must we.

I swallow hard as I approach the palace gates, a palpable sense of loss carried on the warm September breeze. I join the back of a long line of mourners, nodding my regards to those around me while we wait to say our goodbyes.

The cathedral bells toll their mournful sound.

A reminder of how easily life can be snatched away from us.

A reminder that we must grasp it while we can.

48

SOPHIE

Monaco

The air is fresh as I step from the car. The breeze that ripples the leaves on the palm trees, and sends the hem of my skirt dancing, is laced with memories: salt water and cannon fire, champagne and strawberries, *Coeur de Princesse*. It is all still here, as if the very walls of this famous pink palace remember a better, happier time. I straighten my gloves, adjust my hat, and crouch down to check my reflection in the side mirror. I add a slick of lipstick. I want to look my very best for her.

I pull my jacket around my shoulders and take my place in the long line that winds through the palace gates. Nobody speaks. We stand in respectful silence, alone with our grief and our thoughts.

It is a time for remembering, and my mind tumbles back to

another day when I stood here, waiting patiently, wondering if James would be there. The cathedral bells had pealed so cheerfully then to celebrate a princess. A slight smile touches my lips as I think of those blissful few days in a city alive with romance. I let out a long sigh, releasing some of the tension from my shoulders. It is difficult to be here. To remember.

An hour passes and we move forward a little.

I lift my hand to the lapel of my coat, twisting the brooch to set it the right way around. A posy of forget-me-nots, beautifully formed in a ceramic glaze. Grace's gift to me. *A memento,* she'd written in her note. *A reminder of how we met.* All her words have a special poignancy now. All the lines she delivered in her movies. All the wisdom she offered in the countless interviews she gave over the years. But the words I remember more than any others are those she whispered to me the day before her wedding. *"I think that women can do anything they decide to do."*

I've carried those words with me these past decades, choosing my own way, making my own decisions. It hasn't always been easy, and has often been lonely, but I have always looked forward, never back.

The cathedral bells ring once more.

The line moves forward.

I step inside.

I approach the coffin with reluctant steps. I want to see her, but I don't. Not like this.

She looks for all the world as if she's sleeping. Not a mark on her face, no visible signs of the violent car crash that took her life. Monaco's princess. Hollywood's darling. A wife. A mother. A woman whose circle of trusted friends and advisers I'd once been a part of.

No matter how much I look at the ebony wooden coffin, open to the waist to allow her subjects to pay their last respects, I can't believe it. No one can. None of it makes any sense. I dip my head and say a prayer as I file slowly past, unable to reconcile the haunting stillness with the vivacious woman I'd known. And yet she is in death as she was in life: beautiful, elegant, serene.

The scent of the orchids that line her coffin laces the air with their delicate perfume, classically floral with a trace of vanilla and lemon. I close my eyes and inhale, visualizing the page in my journal: *Orchids for love, beauty, and strength. Impossible to distill in sufficient volumes to capture the fragrance.* Love. Beauty. Strength. Everything Princess Grace embodied.

I stifle a sob as I open my eyes to look at her one last time. Her high-necked white lace dress conjures memories of the one she wore on her wedding day. There was never a bride more beautiful, and I was there to see it all. A smile tugs at my lips at the memory, despite the tears that thread in ribbons down my cheeks. What a gift life had delivered when Miss Kelly walked into my boutique in Cannes. How could either of us have known what significance that whirlwind week would hold in store for our futures. She, a princess-to-be. Me, a troubled young woman on the cusp of something remarkable. We came from such wildly different worlds, and yet when everything else was stripped away, it turned out we weren't so different after all.

I cross myself, whisper a silent prayer, and walk on.

The shuffle of mournful footsteps echoes around the lofty spaces inside the grand chapel, the silence interspersed with the occasional gasp of grief, the somber ache of our collective sorrow, and the haunting song of the bells from the thirteenth-century palace tower that chime to mark the country's mourning.

As I wait patiently to sign the book of condolence, I think about what I will write, how I can adequately express what I really want to say: that I knew her, that I admired and cared for her, that I understood her on a level few others did. But my thoughts are interrupted as I pick up the pen and read the messages from the mourners ahead of me. One, in particular, makes me pause.

Au revoir, sweet princess. James Henderson.

A shiver runs over my skin.

He is here?

I'd wondered if he would come. Wondered, but never allowed myself to believe it. So much time has passed, and yet . . .

Putting the pen down, I look up, scanning the room left and right, searching for him among a sea of faces. And there he is, leaning casually against a great marble column, his hat under the crook of his arm. He smiles hesitantly, tilting his head to one side as if he is framing me for one of his photographs.

My hand flies to my mouth as I walk toward him. "James?" My heart leaps to attention, even after all these years.

He says my name. One word. "Sophie."

"But . . . you came . . . you're here." My words hardly make sense. After all this time. After all the imagined moments when I would see him again. Here he is.

"I had to say goodbye," he replies. "I can't believe she's gone."

I shake my head. "None of us can. And did you? Say goodbye?"

"I wished her *au revoir*. I always hated goodbyes, Sophie. You know that better than most."

We stare at each other a moment. He is exactly as I remember him. A few lines around his eyes show the years that have passed, but the smile is the same, the crooked nose, those amber eyes, warm as brandy. And a familiar fragrance hangs in the air between us. Tobacco and leather. *Mémoire*.

"You look well," he adds. "Very well." He smiles at the delight that must have shone in my eyes.

"As do you, James. You haven't aged a bit."

"You also lie very well, but I'll gladly accept all forms of flattery. They are rather sparse these days."

He looks at me in a way that nobody else ever could, just as he had all those years ago. "Are you rushing off?"

I shake my head. "No. You?"

He smiles, thinly. This is not the time or the place for his usual broad grin. "Then would you have time for a coffee? Or a slice of cake? Both, even? I don't know about you, but I'd rather not be alone. I could do with some company to cheer me up."

I nod. "That would be lovely."

Outside, in the palace grounds that had once seen such joyous celebration, the bright sunlight chases away some of the chill from the chapel and I feel my bones relax as this charming, adorable man I have loved for half my life stands beside me once again. I notice how his eyes stray to my ring finger, how he smiles when he sees that it bears no ring. I am pleased to see he doesn't wear one either.

"Of course, I haven't a clue where we might find coffee and cake," he adds.

"Neither have I. Let's just follow our noses."

He holds out the crook of his elbow. "Shall we, madame? *Enchanté.*"

I laugh lightly. His French is as terrible as ever.

My arm looped through his, the years become yesterday and we leave the palace together in respectful silence, happy to meander along Monaco's winding streets, content to see where they might lead us as we find each other again.

RIVIERA WEDDING FOR COUPLE WHO
MET THROUGH A PRINCESS

Long-lost lovers tie the knot.
Angeline West reports for *Le Figaro*.
October 1982

Earlier today, a renowned French perfumer, Sophie Duval, and an award-winning photographer, James Henderson, were married in a small, private church service in Grasse, France. A few close friends from the area and Mr. Henderson's daughter, along with her husband and four children, were also in attendance.

The couple dedicated their service to the memory of Her Serene Highness Princess Grace of Monaco, who, they say, first brought them together in a serendipitous series of events that coincided with the romance between the young Grace Kelly and Prince Rainier III, and culminated in their "wedding of the century" in Monaco in April 1956. Princess Grace commissioned the then relatively unknown perfumer to create a bespoke fragrance for the occasion. Sophie Duval has often credited Princess Grace with saving her family business from financial ruin.

The happy couple will reside at the Duval family home in Grasse, where they plan to grow older together, disgracefully.

ACKNOWLEDGMENTS

We're so grateful for our wonderful, wise agent, Michelle Brower, without whom we would never have met. Her creative input and guidance are everything. To our editor at William Morrow, Lucia Macro, whose support and faith in us inspires us to tackle exciting but challenging book projects—we have a wonderful time working with you. To the entire team at William Morrow, thank you for weaving your magic and turning our words into a book for readers to hold in their hands. Special thanks to Diahann Sturge and Mumtaz Mustafa for the stunning design, inside and out.

No book is complete without many hours of editing and integrating feedback from our brilliant critique partners and colleagues. We send a special thank-you, a fierce hug, and an Aperol spritz to Kris Waldherr, and to Hazel's sister, Helen. We also have so much gratitude for all the book bloggers, reader discussion groups, librarians, booksellers, and our author tribe, who cheer us on at every turn and share the book love so selflessly. Special thanks to the Tall Poppy writers and the readers of Bloom; to Andrea Katz of Great Thoughts, Great Readers;

Amy Bruno of Passages to the Past; Barbara Khan of Baer Books; Sharlene Moore and Bobbi Dumas of the Romance of Reading; Susan Peterson of Sue's Booking Agency; Kristy Barrett and Tonni Callan of A Novel Bee; Cathy Lamb, Laura Drake, and Barbara Claypool White of Reader's Coffeehouse; Mairéad Hearne of Swirl and Thread; Margaret Madden of Bleach House; Barbara Bos at Women Writers, Women's Books; the Women's Fiction Writers Association of America; Jenny Collins Belk, Nita Haddad, Davida Chazan, and many, many more. Our cup runneth over!

To our family and friends, whose unwavering support has buoyed us when waters were rough, and who cook the dinner, and help the kids with their homework, and take us out for emergency wine and gin: thank you. We love you and couldn't do any of it without you.

Finally, to you, dear reader. You are the reason we do what we do. Thank you, from the bottom of our hearts. Let's do it again soon. H & H.

About the authors

About the book

Insights,
Interviews
& More . . .

Meet Hazel Gaynor

Deasy Photographic

HAZEL GAYNOR is the *New York Times* and *USA Today* bestselling author of *A Memory of Violets* and *The Girl Who Came Home*, for which she received the 2015 Romantic Novelists' Association Historical Romantic Novel of the Year award. Her third novel, *The Girl from The Savoy*, was an *Irish Times* and *Globe and Mail* bestseller, and was shortlisted for the Irish Book Awards Popular Fiction Book of the Year. In 2017, she published *The Cottingley Secret* and *Last Christmas in Paris* (cowritten with Heather Webb). Both novels hit bestseller lists, and *Last Christmas in Paris* won the 2018 Women's Fiction Writers Association Star Award. Hazel's most recent novel, *The Lighthouse Keeper's Daughter,* hit the *Irish Times* bestseller list for five consecutive weeks. Hazel was selected by *Library Journal* as one of Ten Big Breakout Authors for 2015. Her work has been translated into ten languages and is published in seventeen countries to date. Hazel lives in Ireland with her husband and two children. ᔰ

Meet Heather Webb

HEATHER WEBB is the internationally bestselling, award-winning author of *Rodin's Lover, Becoming Josephine,* and *Last Christmas in Paris* (cowritten with Hazel Gaynor), which won the 2018 Women's Fiction Writers Association Star Award. Her most recent novel, *The Phantom's Apprentice,* reimagines the story of the Phantom of the Opera. She is also one of six authors behind the French Revolution collaboration *Ribbons of Scarlet.* Her novels have been translated into over a dozen languages worldwide. Heather is also a freelance editor, public speaker, and blogger at award-winning writing site WriterUnboxed.com. She lives in New England with her family and one feisty bunny.

The Story Behind
Meet Me in Monaco

Tragedy often brings out our real affection for someone, and perhaps this has never been more evident than in the shocking accident that took the life of Princess Grace of Monaco so cruelly in September 1982. In a similar way to the reaction that reverberated around the world after the sudden death of Diana, Princess of Wales, Princess Grace's death was also felt as a global tragedy, an event so shocking we still talk about it today.

When Grace Kelly won an Oscar at the age of twenty-six, and went on to marry Prince Rainier of Monaco shortly afterward, her private life played out in the most public way. Perhaps, as we did with Diana, we felt we knew Grace in some way, and therefore grieved for her, though most of us had never met her. But what influence might a woman like Grace Kelly have had on those who did come into contact with her, however briefly? This was the question we wanted to explore in writing *Meet Me in Monaco*. We wanted to understand the very ordinary people caught up in a most extraordinary love affair between an American actress and a little-known prince. We wanted to highlight the people who surrounded Grace in the months, weeks, and days leading up to her wedding, and who were among the most deeply affected by the untimely death of one of the most loved stars of Hollywood's Golden Age. We hoped to illustrate how Grace's kindness, influence, and courage touched the lives of those around her.

There is—unsurprisingly—a lot written about Grace Kelly, and our research led us to many fascinating books and accounts of her life. Some were intimate family portraits, while others offered a more scandalous, tabloid-style portrayal of Kelly's life, especially her love life. Newspapers and magazines at the time were full of speculation about the circumstances surrounding the wedding: talk of a two-million-dollar dowry being paid by Jack Kelly, Grace's father; rumors about tests being carried out to confirm Miss Kelly's virginity; allegations that Grace had recently been engaged to Oleg Cassini, and was possibly pregnant; a belief that Grace only agreed to the marriage to seek her father's approval.

One book in particular, written by one of Grace's closest friends and bridesmaids, offered a fascinating insight into the emotions of a young woman sailing on the S.S. *Constitution* from New York toward a new life in Monaco, giving up everything she'd known for love. How interesting that in 2018 we saw such striking similarities in the short romance and wedding of Prince Harry and Meghan Markle, an actress leaving her career and American home to take up a royal role as Duchess of Sussex. The second American princess—history repeating itself, as it so often does.

Research is everything for a historical novelist, and between books and articles, old newsreels and newspaper reports, we discovered a tantalizing detail about Miss Kelly's now-iconic wedding dress being packed for its journey from New York to Monaco amid rolls of tissue paper scented with a perfume that had been especially made for her wedding day. Again, our novelists' minds saw an intriguing angle to the story. Who was the perfumer who made that scent? And who were the harried photographers chasing the perfect shot of the most famous woman in the world, and caused near riots in Monaco in the days leading up to the wedding? Our fictional characters—Sophie Duval, a passionate perfumer, struggling to secure her father's legacy, and James Henderson, a press photographer searching for far more than Hollywood glamour through his lens—were inspired by real people and roles that were connected to Grace and the royal wedding in surprising ways. Our novelists' gaze also wandered behind the scenes of those famous images of Princess Grace on her wedding day. Who was the woman behind the Hollywood smile? What were her private thoughts behind the many public appearances?

Our research also took us on an incredible trip to Monaco to follow in Grace's footsteps, as well as to the beautiful flower fields ▶

of Grasse on the Côte d'Azur. Grasse is famous for its perfumes, and is where our character, Sophie, has her fictional perfumery, Duval. To step inside France's famous perfume houses, whose history goes back centuries, and make our own perfumes there, brought goose bumps and plenty of fresh inspiration. Sophie, and all her struggles and passions, became very real! We also read about the many couture and perfume houses who vied for Miss Kelly's attention at the time of her wedding, and how she met with female representatives of those businesses. Many women, celebrities especially, have a trademark fragrance, and we wondered: What if an ambitious young *parfumeur* caught Grace's attention? In reality, Grace was a fan of Krigler perfumes, attributing her good luck to the fragrance *Chateau Krigler 12* when asked by a journalist during a red carpet appearance. On her wedding day she wore *Fleurissimo* by Creed.

We were also intrigued by the idea of fates being intertwined and how a chance meeting with someone can set our lives on a very different course, as was the case with Grace Kelly's impromptu meeting with Prince Rainier while she was at the Cannes Film Festival in 1955. This chance meeting with a prince changed everything for Grace, just as Sophie's and James's lives change after a chance encounter with Miss Kelly, and each other. The what-ifs are often the pivotal moments in life, after all.

In writing *Meet Me in Monaco*, we discovered that Grace Kelly was far more than an icon of the silver screen, or the princess she later became. She was also a dear friend, devoted daughter, loving wife, and doting mother. To many, she will always be epitomized by Howell Conant's stunning photographs of her wedding day, and Helen Rose's exquisite *peau de soie* and lace dress—one of the most copied gowns in history—but it is in the less formal images, casual snapshots taken by family and friends, where we really see the true spirit of a woman who loved life and had so much more to live for. Through the lens of Sophie and James and their proximity to Grace Kelly during her transition from Hollywood star to Princess Grace of Monaco, we hope to honor her memory and bring her story to a new generation of fans, as well as show a different side of her to those who, like us, have long admired her. ⟿

What Happened Next

On September 13, 1982, it is believed that Princess Grace suffered a stroke while driving herself and her daughter Stephanie to the palace after a retreat at their country home in Roc Agel. Along one of Monaco's famed corniche roads, she lost control of her Rover, plowed through the stone retaining wall, and drove off the ledge, plunging down a mountainside over a hundred feet high. The car somersaulted as it plummeted, causing both passengers—who weren't wearing seat belts—to be tossed around inside it. Stephanie suffered minor injuries. Princess Grace, after a fatal blow to the head, died from her injuries the day after the accident.

Four hundred mourners attended the funeral, and nearly one hundred million people watched her funeral on television. Prince Rainier was so grief-stricken, it was rumored he might abdicate in favor of his son. He never recovered from Grace's death, and never remarried.

Grace and Rainier were one of the first celebrity couples to gain the sort of media attention we see so often today. Rumors of an unhappy marriage surrounded them, yet those closest to the couple maintain that they truly loved each other, and that Grace embraced her life as a loving wife, mother, and princess. As with any relationship, only those involved can ever know the real truth. Princess Grace and Prince Rainier lie in rest beside each other in the Cathédrale de Notre-Dame-Immaculée (more commonly known as Monaco Cathedral, or Saint Nicholas Cathedral) in Monaco-Ville, where they were married on such a memorable occasion twenty-six years earlier.

A genuine philanthropist, Grace founded charitable foundations, hosted galas to raise funds for orphanages and hospitals, established Monaco's first day care to aid mothers in their career paths, and was named president of the Monaco Red Cross—the most active of the international chapters of the Red Cross. But her heart lay with the arts. In 1964, she founded Les Boutiques du Rocher (a series of stores to support local artisans), and in 1968, she founded the international Monte Carlo Ballet Festival, now known as the Spring Arts Festival. In fact, Grace was so committed to helping artists realize their dreams during her life that, upon her death, Prince Rainier created the Princess Grace Foundation–USA. For over three decades, this still-flourishing organization has donated four million dollars to institutions as well as more than four hundred artists worldwide. ▶

What Happened Next *(continued)*

Princess Grace always felt a strong attachment to her family's Irish heritage. To honor this, Prince Rainier established the Princess Grace Irish Library in Monaco in 1984. The library operates today as a vibrant cultural venue, with lectures, historic collections, and residencies for Irish artists. During their state visit to Ireland in 1961, the prince and princess visited the cottage in Mayo where Grace's grandfather had been born during the Great Famine in 1857.

Today, the royal family in Monaco continue to preserve the legacy of their beloved princess. ∽

Publicity shot of Grace Kelly during her time at MGM.

Further Reading

If you would like to read more about Grace Kelly and her life before and after becoming a princess, we found the following books incredibly helpful—and also stunning to look at!

The Bridesmaids: Grace Kelly, Princess of Monaco, and Six Intimate Friends by Judith Balaban Quine

Committed: Men Tell Stories of Love, Commitment, and Marriage edited by Chris Knutsen and David Kuhn

Grace: Her Lives—Her Loves: The Startling Royal Exposé by Robert Lacey

Grace Kelly: Hollywood Dream Girl by Jay Jorgensen and Manoah Bowman

Grace Kelly: Icon of Style to Royal Bride by H. Kristina Haugland

Grace Kelly of Monaco: The Inspiring Story of How an American Film Star Became a Princess by Jennifer Warner

High Society: Grace Kelly and Hollywood by Donald Spoto

Once Upon a Time: The Story of Princess Grace, Prince Rainier and Their Family by J. Randy Taraborrelli

Remembering Grace, LIFE Great Photographers Series, photographs by Howell Conant

True Grace: The Life and Times of an American Princess by Wendy Leigh

Reading Group Guide

1. There's something about iconic women who are surrounded by tragedy. What is it about them that captivates us? What other women whose lives were shrouded in tragic circumstances have fascinated you over the years?

2. Do you believe Grace Kelly gave up too much to marry Prince Rainier? Would you have followed your heart and done the same, or would you have chosen a different path?

3. Scent is closely associated with memory. Can you think of a time you smelled a fragrance that whisked you away to a moment in your past? What scents transport you, typically?

4. The paparazzi was just becoming rampant in the 1950s. Would you say their coverage has changed in the last seventy years? How so? What would you consider appropriate versus inappropriate news to report? Have you been a consumer of paparazzi photos and articles?

5. *Meet Me in Monaco* focuses on Grace Kelly's life from first meeting Prince Rainier to her tragic death in 1982. Which aspects of her story especially surprised you, or resonated with you?

6. Grace and Rainier were said to be charmed by each other during their first meeting and got to know each other through the letters they wrote in the following months. Do you believe in love at first sight?

7. Many relationships come with a sacrifice, and James and Sophie's relationship is far from straightforward. How did you respond to their blossoming romance?

8. Both James's and Sophie's lives change dramatically after their interactions with Grace. Have you ever met a celebrity, or do you know anyone who has? If so, what happened? ▶

Reading Group Guide *(continued)*

9. Grace Kelly's wedding is still remembered as one of the most iconic events in modern times. Her wedding dress also regularly tops the list of most beautiful wedding gowns. Have you watched any modern royal weddings, such as those of Kate Middleton and Prince William, or Meghan Markle and Prince Harry? Why do you think we are so fascinated with royalty and celebrity?

10. The Golden Age of Hollywood left us with an incredible legacy of women whose style, elegance, and newsworthy lifestyles have captured our imaginations for decades. Which Hollywood stars—living or dead—would you invite to a dinner party, and why? ∾

Eulogy for a Princess

Excerpt from a speech given by Jimmy Stewart at a memorial held for Princess Grace in Los Angeles, September 29, 1982:

> "You know, I just loved Grace Kelly. Not because she was a princess. Not because she was an actress. Not because she was my friend. But because she was just about the nicest lady I ever met. Grace brought into my life, as she brought into yours, a soft, warm light every time I saw her. And every time I saw her was a holiday of its own. No question. I'll miss her. We'll all miss her. God bless you, princess." ⌒

Publicity shot of Grace Kelly during her time at MGM.

Discover great authors, exclusive offers, and more at hc.com.